SterlingHouse
PUBLISHER INC.

ISBN:1-56315-154-5

Paperback Fiction

First Printing --1999
Library of Congress #98-87013

Request for information should be addressed to:

SterlingHouse Publisher, Inc.
The Sterling Building
440 Friday Road
Department T-101
Pittsburgh, PA 15209

Cover Art: Michelle Vennare-SterlingHouse Publisher
Typesetting: Pam Muzoleski

Printed in Canada

CHAPTER ONE

After one in the morning, Ellie walked through the dark alley toward the parking lot, a short-cut toward her car. The rain had stopped, lucky for her she thought, remembering lightning and a downpour smearing the large windows of the bar. Ellie hadn't brought a coat to work with her, and she had expected to get soaking wet.

Ellie stepped around the puddles in the dirt lane. Their slick surface reflected the neon lights hanging above the store fronts down on the corner.

She could hear a cat howl loudly, almost a snarl, then she saw it bolt from under a wooden staircase, followed by a tomcat. The cats disappeared into the numerous shadows formed by the zigzag brick walls.

The business district was a jumble of adjacent old buildings, she noticed. Ellie glanced toward the gables as she walked toward the alley's exit, her eyes attracted by the movement of pigeons along the roof.

Ellie stopped in her tracks and gasped. In the splitsecond her attention was diverted, someone had stepped out of the shadows between the brick buildings and blocked her way. She'd almost run into his chest.

Ellie backed up a step.

"Don't run away." Under his black stetson, his eyes turned into slits. His large hands formed a firm grip on her forearms.

Immediately, Ellie recognized him as one of the customers at the Bedford bar she'd served only minutes before. Ellie laughed shortly as she tried to pull her arms free. "Let me go. You scared the daylights out of me."

"Where are you off to now?" The tall stranger smiled rudely, showing his teeth.

"Home." She was upset he ignored her request to let her go. Ellie writhed a bit more, but he pinched her arms so tightly she almost cried out.

"Oh, I thought you might be looking for something more interesting. Want to come to a party?"

Ellie had no intentions of being nice. She shrieked loudly, "Not really. It's just too late."

His eyes moved in their slits. "Where's home?"

"We're saving up to buy a house in the country."

"Well, good for you!" he laughed. Somehow her working in a bar and being able to buy something was funny. He laughed again.

Still, Ellie just wanted to get home, and she wondered why she wasn't getting this point across to him. She checked him over carefully. To her, he was a big guy with a mean, stubborn expression on his face.

"If you're smart, you'll want to party the next time I ask you," he said. Letting her go, he took a pack of cigarettes out of his pocket and lit one.

At the same moment Ellie heard people talking, inadvertently passing the alley's exit at this late hour. Ellie sighed with relief as she stepped around him. "Good night!" She tried to make her voice sound bright to cover up how scared she was.

"I can wait!" He glared at her. The threatening way he spoke made Ellie cringe.

Ellie ran to her car, her shoes clipping the sidewalk. She turned the key in the ignition. The motor went click, click. Darn, Ellie thought, when she couldn't get her car started.

Frantic, Ellie kept turning the key and pumping the gas pedal, but nothing happened. Glancing over her shoulder, she saw the stranger was leaning against a dark store front. The bright end of his cigarette made a semicircle.

Ellie saw a cop car pull in front of him. All Ellie could see was his stetson hat. Then, both heads turned in her direction, and the man in the stetson pointed and gesticulated. Ellie could hear loud tones, but she couldn't understand what they were saying.

An instant later, Ellie felt numb, as the cop walked over and knocked on her car window. "What's going on here?"

Ellie rolled down her window. "No problem. I just want to get my car started and get home."

"That man over there said you offered yourself to him for money."

"What?" Ellie was flabbergasted. She didn't know what to say. Maybe she did look suspicious. It was late, she was alone, and she was sort-of dressed up, but she had a reason to be there. "Look, officer!" she said.

The cop repeated the accusation more loudly, saying she was desperate for money.

"That's not true!" Ellie gasped, outraged at being accused. "He's lying."

"Get out of your car and show me your driver's license."

Insulted, Ellie thought if she could get her car going she would drive over his foot. Over the cop's shoulder, she could see the stranger's white shirt, a bright, harsh echo of light in the dimness. Ellie wondered why he was still hanging around. She thought, "I'll have to watch this bastard, as he's obviously two-faced." If he caused her trouble once, he'd surely try it again.

"You should watch who you hang around with," the cop said.

With his flashlight, the cop searched her car. "Come down to the station and discuss your relationship with this man."

Ellie said, "I can't get my car going."

"You said that before. Try not to confuse the issue."

Biting her lip to hold back angry tears, Ellie decided to be brave. "Lay a charge or forget it," she said loudly.

"I can do that right here on the street," the cop said testily, getting out his notebook.

As the cop took notes, the stranger came over and leaned against Ellie's car. She didn't like the appraising way he stared at her from under his stetson, as if he figured he could already take things that belonged to her.

"Get off my car," Ellie snapped.

Seeing the nonchalant way he moved away from her car, Ellie thought he didn't give a damn. He was trying to cause trouble for her. If he persisted, he could turn her life upside down.

The cop asked him, "How did you meet her?"

"She works in the bar." The stranger smirked. "It's what people say about her. When a woman looks like she does, there's sure to be trouble. There's others who'll agree with me."

The cop stepped toward the stranger, and they talked in a low voice for awhile.

Ellie began to think she couldn't straighten the cop out. Their conversation implied the stranger was more believable than she was, meaning she had got herself into a bad situation.

"He was the one accosted me rather than the other way around," Ellie blurted, trying to interrupt them.

The cop turned to Ellie and took the handcuffs off his belt. "It would be better for you to come willingly."

The cop reached for Ellie's wrist and snapped the handcuff around it. Then he grabbed her other arm and secured her hands behind her back.

"What's going on here? What are you doing to that little girl?" Ellie heard a bright voice, and she gladly turned to see who had come along. She saw a smiling, masculine shape more than six feet tall. "Pick on somebody your own size. Baker, you jerk, go arrest somebody else. Wayne, you son-of-a-bitch, bugger off. I can't take my eyes off you for two minutes."

"You don't understand about this, Quantz. She's the problem." Wayne pointed at Ellie.

For a moment, Quantz's eyes appreciatively followed her outline. Ellie thought maybe he liked her, and she was glad to see somebody who would take her side.

"Wayne, you numbskull. Don't you know who she is? She's Vern Menzies' old lady. He'll be on top of you."

Ellie wondered how Quantz would know Vern, but he probably worked with him. Almost everybody in town worked at the same factory.

Then, the cop tried to explain to Quantz what happened.

"You never get anything right, Baker," Quantz said.

"All right. You have to make a statement, too." The cop reluctantly reached behind Ellie and unlocked the cuffs.

Ellie sighed with relief.

"I just did and it better not be in writing," Quantz said.

The cop shook his head as he put his notebook away. "All of you get home before I change my mind." The cop thumbed at Ellie. "I'll let you off with a warning. Next time will be different." The cop drove away.

Wayne said to Quantz, laughing. "He'll be on your ass now, helping something like that out." Ellie noticed Wayne couldn't meet her gaze now. She was scared, as she had made an enemy of Wayne. It bothered her what he might be saying about her whenever he got the chance. He could ruin her reputation. Ellie wondered in a panic what she could do to stifle his mouth.

"He knows when he makes a mistake, doesn't he?" Quantz winked at Ellie, making her feel better. Ellie was amazed at how lightly Quantz referred to her problem, now that he'd solved it.

"I hope so," Ellie said, glaring at Wayne.

"Where have you been anyway?" Quantz said to Wayne.

"I've been away. I don't know why I come back to this place. God made it and then God forgot about it," Wayne said, sounding disgusted. "I got a bum deal as soon as I got back. Come on, I'll tell you about it."

Quantz started to follow Wayne with an easygoing saunter Ellie liked. How easily he'd got her out of this predicament!

"Wait! Don't go yet!" Ellie called out before she realized he might think she was being too friendly. "I can't get my car started."

Immediately, Quantz came back to Ellie. Wayne cleared his throat loudly and slunk away.

Ellie thought she'd seen Quantz before. He had light brown hair, blue eyes and a constant smile on his face. He probably worked with her husband Vern, if he wasn't exactly a friend. Immediately, she wanted to make a good impression. Quantz was the kind who took life easy, appearing not to worry which was amazing to Ellie. To her, he was a calming influence when she was threatened. Also, he was good-looking, Ellie thought approvingly, looking at his generous shape under his blue check shirt and loose-fitting tan slacks.

"Here, I'll help you get your car started." He got out his battery cables, attached them to both vehicles, and in a short moment her car was going.

"Thanks," Ellie said. "For a minute, I didn't think I'd get home tonight. I was beginning to freak out."

"You'll be fine." Quantz smiled at Ellie, and Ellie smiled back. "Good things come in small packages," Quantz said, in a friendly way, Ellie thought.

Ellie took the remark to mean he liked her, and his amiable smile made her feel good. Ellie decided she liked him back, especially the approving, suggestive way his eyes followed her outline.

"Wayne lied about me," Ellie said firmly. She wondered what she going to do about what Wayne told everybody.

"He's a blabbermouth and a troublemaker." Quantz patted her on the arm. "Try not to take it personal. That guy's been drinking. And when he's been drinking, he's a different person."

Ellie wondered if she should try to explain how she felt. "I hope so," she said ruefully. "That experience was awful."

"I'll talk to him," Quantz said, sounding friendly. "I'm around if you need somebody to talk to. Maybe we can get together some time." Maybe he was feeling sorry for her, Ellie thought, but then she realized Quantz was asking for a date in a roundabout way.

"Maybe some time." Ellie gave Quantz a kiss on the cheek.

"It's getting late." Quantz squeezed her hand and got in his car.

Ellie was happy to be driving home, and she was glad Quantz had come along to help her. The whole menacing experience was nothing, Ellie tried to tell herself, but she was shaking like a leaf. The next day she figured she'd be able to go back to work, and the whole thing would blow over. She had been accosted and almost arrested. How would she keep this quiet?

The dreadful person, Wayne, and his accusations threw her ordinary, placid life into a shambles of speculation she didn't like. Ellie wondered if maybe she'd done something wrong. Maybe he stopped her because she was so simple-minded.

Relieved to see her home on Willow Street, Ellie pulled into the lane. The duplex was a dark grey shadow against the navy sky, with thunderclouds still bunched and threatening overhead. The outside light was still on. Ellie hurried up the steps, unlocked the door and once inside she switched off the light. She felt glad to be home after her rather unreal night.

No sooner inside, she heard another crack of thunder and the downpour started again. She made herself a drink to calm her nerves.

Upstairs, Ellie was surprised to see Vern still sound asleep, not the least bit worried about her. Then Ellie checked her small kids, Robert and Susan. They were sound asleep too.

Ellie peeled off her clothes and slid into bed. Ellie put her arms around Vern, but he rolled over away from her with hardly a murmur. She squeezed him and rubbed his arms. Vern growled at her, "Leave me alone."

Ellie felt left out and unimportant. She sat up and finished her drink, trying not to be too upset by Vern ignoring her in bed beside him. He'd been working overtime a lot lately, and once asleep he never liked to be disturbed.

All Ellie wanted Vern to do was roll over and love her and everything would be fine, but his sleeping hulk was turned the other way. She slid her arms around him again, but his sleep continued undisturbed. She had thought love would solve everything right now. Why was she still awake and fretting, and Vern still asleep? She didn't intend to tell him what happened. She just wanted to know if he still loved her right this minute.

Ellie thought about what had happened. She was impressed by Quantz's concern. Quantz was there to help, and Ellie had accepted. She thought his friendly smile was something she hadn't seen too much of lately.

Ellie couldn't believe her new job for the summer would cause her this much hassle. All she wanted was to save up for a house in the country, as it was something they were both looking forward to, Vern maybe more than her. Who would think there would be so much trouble?

* * *

CHAPTER TWO

At quarter to five the next afternoon, Ellie's shift at the Bedford was almost over. Ellie had been run off her feet, because on Friday, customers had converged on the bar from all over the town, in their Chevrolet Camaros, Ford Mustangs, and dune buggies. They had quite a thirst on. When it was hot, people drank more. The summer, already hotter than usual, had just started. Ellie Menzies hoped the vacation season would be long, because the summer was the only time the lakeside town of Goderich, population 7200, came alive. She figured she could make money this weekend coming up.

Everywhere, men in bright shirts, paisley, floral or patchwork print and long sideburns expected their drinks. Secretaries and their bosses had stopped in. The orders were piling up. Ellie spilled foam down the sides of the glasses and on the counter as she filled the trays. Even the change was wet.

Ellie wore a navy sleeveless t-shirt and a white skirt, but she had worked up a sweat. There was air-conditioning in the Bedford, but maybe it had quit.

"Beri's dragging her ass getting into work today," Ellie muttered under her breath. "Where is she?"

The beer cooler was almost empty of certain brands, but when Ellie stopped working to fill it, customers barked at her for orders.

"If my wife phones, tell her I'm on my way," Quantz said to Ellie. He was standing around watching her, with his elbows on the bar.

"Sure thing." Ellie set four drinks on her tray.

"You're not paying attention."

"Yes, I am." Ellie wondered why he would be wanting her to stop for him. His timing was real bad, she thought.

Quantz, Moose, and Vern, Ellie's husband, were at the bar with beers sitting in front of them. All the regulars were hanging around, too. Some had been there since lunchtime. They drank the same thing every time. It got so Ellie could set up their drink without them asking.

"If my wife phones, tell her I've gone to see George," Quantz called to her. Ellie thought he was trying to get her attention, but he should stop bugging her.

"For Pete's sakes, can't you see she's busy?" Moose asked. Moose was smaller than the other two, but he was a lot louder. Moose had told Ellie he'd got his name from the hunting expeditions he went on up north.

"Drinking up your paycheck again?" Vern asked Quantz.

"I'll drink her while she lasts." Quantz flashed his perfect teeth. "Then when the money runs out, I'll have to be sober. Thank God the weekend's here."

"You can say that again," Ellie smiled at Quantz as she picked up her tray.

"Finally, she takes time to talk to me. I thought she wasn't speaking to anybody after last night."

"What happened last night?" Vern said to Quantz, then he studied Ellie, as if he expected an explanation in two quick words.

"Nothing really. I don't have time now, Vern. Later." Ellie's heart sank. How could she explain what had happened without making Vern angry? Quantz, Vern, and Moose worked together at Champion Road Machinery Company Limited, in different sections. For sure they'd tell each other everything, Ellie thought.

Ellie glanced quickly at Quantz. He watched Ellie run back and forth, and open and shut the beer cooler. The way Quantz stared back at her, as if his eyes were attached to her ass with a string, made her uncomfortable.

Finally, at five to five, Beri showed up. Steve, the boss, came in after her.

"You're busy! Why didn't you call sooner?" Steve asked.

Why didn't she call sooner? Good question. "I didn't think of it, I was so busy!" Ellie flushed.

Steve turned up the stereo. The country song, "Crystal Chandelier" filled the room.

"What can I do?" Beri asked.

"Take a look around you!" Ellie gestured toward the people wanting drinks. "The two tables in the corner."

Beri flipped her shoulder-length bleached blonde hair. "Who are those people?"

"I don't know," Ellie said, impatiently. Beri didn't wear underwear, so there wouldn't be creases on her smooth-fitting clothes. Ellie thought Beri was more sophisticated than she was, as she'd never go without underwear. Beri smoothed her tight skirt down before she put on her apron.

Beri went out on the floor and took orders while Ellie set up the drinks and ran the till. Steve washed the glasses. "I don't like to get behind," he explained to Ellie as he lifted them from sink to sink. They were washed, rinsed, and put in the disinfectant solution for a few seconds. Then, Steve sat down at the bar and had a beer.

Quantz, Moose, and Vern wanted another beer, too. Ellie reached for the fresh goblets on the rack.

Ellie noticed the stranger from the night before had joined the four men sitting at the bar in the shadowy heat. Today, he wore a heavy dark worsted suit despite the summer weather. He ordered a draft and Ellie set it up.

This afternoon, Wayne looked straight through Ellie, as if he was on the prowl. The expression on his face was odd, as if he figured he was going to be able to one-up her. Ellie thought he didn't need to be looking at her like that.

Ellie stared at the sink, trying to avoid his gaze. Then she went to the other end of the counter and cleaned ashtrays. If she hadn't had to work overtime to help Beri catch up, she wouldn't have to talk to him.

"You guys still okay?" Ellie's voice squeaked as she looked up at Vern's glass still half-full.

"Ellie will be thirty soon." Vern let out a sharp bark of a laugh. Vern liked to tease her. "Give her another few weeks." Ellie wished he hadn't brought that up. It made the conversation seem so personal.

"She doesn't look it," Moose said. "I didn't think she was any older than I am. I'm twenty-four."

"I guess that's a compliment," Ellie said to Moose. She wondered how he would know how old he seemed. As far as she was concerned, he was still wet behind the ears.

"But it bothers her, though," Vern said.

"How could it?" Quantz asked. "She's exactly the same age as me."

"I thought you were older," Vern remarked. He peered pointedly at Quantz's receding hairline and ran his hand though his own thick head of hair.

"Ellie looks good though," Quantz said. "Her outfit really suits her figure."

"He probably just likes to watch the way she bends over," Moose said. "Ooh! Bite my tongue!"

Hearing them discuss her, Ellie wished she could fall through the floor.

"I thought her behind was rather pear-shaped," Quantz said.

The dark-haired stranger at the end of the bar spoke up. "I like women like you with small breasts and full thighs. What's you opinion of garter belts?"

His remark made Ellie cringe, as she thought the comments about her appearance were getting out of hand. Ellie had already given him drinks or she wouldn't have served him. Steve had told her she didn't have to serve people if they weren't nice. Ellie thought if she didn't need the money she would quit right now. She threw her towel on the sink.

"I should smack you. That's my wife!" Vern pointed at Ellie.

Ellie thought if Vern knew the half of what had been said last night, he would be so sore he would do something he'd regret, and she didn't want that. She didn't want to let these guys treat her like a puppet on the string with their remarks.

"If Vern doesn't pop you in the mouth, I will," Quantz said. "That's Wayne over there," Quantz said to Vern.

"Give us your phone number too, so we can do something about you," Ellie told Wayne who had a foolish grin on his face.

"Ellie's getting to look well-used, eh Vern? You should know." Moose swivelled his head back and forth to get their reaction.

Ellie glanced at her husband as she gave him his beer. Vern glared at Moose. Ellie knew he hated the guys to joke about her appearance.

"You're a dickhead," Quantz said to Moose. "Look at Vern, there. Smoke's coming out his ears. You'll get fired."

"I would too, if I didn't need you," Vern added. "So knock off this shit before I forget how bad I need you."

"This is after work, so it doesn't count," Moose said.

Vern drummed the table with his fingers. Then he tapped his glass.

"It doesn't hurt to give Ellie a compliment now and again," Steve said, laughing. "How old will she be? Thirty? I didn't think she was that old. Did I tell you about the report the liquor board made out on you today?"

"No, what did it say?" Ellie was curious.

"They thought you were about twenty-three. I'll talk to you about it later. Okay?" Ellie thought it odd the way he focused in on the estimate of her age.

"In trouble already," Moose laughed at her.

There wasn't a great deal Ellie could do about the camaraderie, other than wait for them to find something else to talk about. Vern would pick a fight when they got home. Ellie didn't see how picking a fight with her helped matters any.

"Ellie's mad at us," Quantz said.

"No, she's not," Moose replied as if she wasn't even there. "She's cool." He tried to be noncommittal now, after causing such a commotion. Ellie could hardly keep smiling, since she felt like an insect on a pin being scrutinized the way she was.

"Yes, she is. Look at her face," Quantz said.

Ellie cleaned the ashtrays, then restocked the cooler.

At the end of the bar, the lanky, black-haired man in the worsted suit and stetson nursed his beer.

"What do you do for a living?" Ellie asked Wayne, trying to be polite.

"I'm a disbarred lawyer."

Ellie was surprised. "What are you doing here?"

"I'm in Goderich for a drink," he continued, "and to collect unemployment insurance. I have the greatest respect for the lawyers in this town."

"Why were you disbarred?"

"When did you lose your virginity?"

Ellie laughed out loud immediately. Wayne was incredibly hostile, and she thought she could make things better by being polite!

"I've got drunk in better hotels than this," Wayne said bitterly. He tipped the beer bottle up and put it back on the counter.

Ellie walked away from him and wiped the bar carefully. Then she washed the remaining glasses. When she turned, she noticed the men had taken their drinks to the end of the room and Wayne had left. She was glad he was gone.

Ellie felt she was in for a mess of trouble. Vern was glaring at her from the far table. What was he so sore about?

Moose's wife, Cathy Chapman, came in and prissily settled herself on a stool. "Hi, Beri." She waved at Moose's table. Then, turning to Ellie, she said, "I'll have Wink, straight up."

Ellie thought Cathy and Beri seemed to know each other well. Cathy was younger.

"Here's your soda pop." Ellie had added a cherry to Cathy's drink.

"I'm pregnant again, and we already have three children," Cathy explained to Ellie, her round face framed with long red hair. "I've been a mother since age sixteen."

"Get a load of that!" Beri laughed. Ellie knew Beri had no children yet and she wasn't married either.

"Do you have children?" Cathy asked Ellie as she sipped through her straw. The stiff way Cathy sat on the stool was comical, but Ellie tried not to laugh. Ellie was no one to talk about drinking since a couple of drinks made her talk funny.

"I have two," Ellie confided. "A boy and a girl."

"That's nice," Cathy sighed deeply. "Two! Only two!"

Beri rolled her eyes and Ellie laughed at her.

George Toogood came in. He had wild hair, a long beard, and one earring, but Beri was trying to clean him up. Beri talked a lot about marrying him, but she went out with other guys, including married ones.

George stared at Ellie as if he didn't know who she was, but he'd been in before. He waved a huge arm at the men sitting at the end of the room, then he stood beside Beri and Cathy towering over them, staring at Ellie so long she felt uncomfortable.

Finally, Beri said, "Have you met George?"

"No," Ellie said.

"You have now," George chuckled. Then he put his arm around Beri and held her close.

Beri laughed in her throaty voice. "This is Elaine, but everybody calls her Ellie. She's our bartender."

"You guys look happy," Ellie said.

"I have a buzz on, not a rip," Beri confided. "It was those drinks I had this afternoon besides the pills. I try not to take too many when I come into work." Her pupils were dilated. "Want some?"

"Not this time around," Ellie said. "Maybe later."

"She's only been here two days," Beri explained.

George grinned at Ellie. His eyes were hard. Ellie felt like he was giving her an appraisal.

Leaning closer over Beri, he asked her a question in such a low voice Ellie couldn't hear. Then he disappeared.

Beri said, "He's working on our cottage when he isn't fixing other people's houses. It's going to be nice," Beri confided.

"I'd like to see it some time," Ellie said, grabbing her purse. The bar had cleared from the late afternoon's bustle. Vern was sitting alone at the table finishing a drink.

"I hope it's not always going to be like this," Vern said grumpily as she approached.

"It's a desert in the winter. You won't be here by then. Let's go." Ellie stifled a yawn. She wondered why she felt tired so early in the evening.

Vern got up from the table, and they left together.

* * *

CHAPTER THREE

After they left the Bedford Bar, Vern and Ellie picked up their children at the babysitter's house. Ellie saw disapproval on Mrs. Stewart's face and she quickly check her watch. "Am I late?" she asked.

"Don't make a habit of it," she said sourly.

"Sorry," Ellie said. "There was nothing I could do."

Then they packed some clothes and food and drove their Ford Explorer to their camp.

The trailer camp at Black's Point was three miles south of Goderich. It was on a bluff overlooking a sandbar and rocks surrounded by shallow water.

"We're only two seasons, winter and summer," Ellie told her kids excitedly as she saw the beach. "I can put away my fur coat and don my shorts."

"Aren't you missing two seasons?" Vern said. "Don't tell them stuff like that."

At Black's Point, their trailer was hidden in the birches and cedars on the top of the bluff. Vern missed the driveway in the dusk and had to back up.

By the way he slammed the trailer door, Ellie could tell he was still sore, but when he built a roaring fire she thought he was over his temper.

"It was nice of your parents to let us use the trailer before the summer rush," Vern said. "But I'd rather we waited until it was warmer at night." He rubbed his hands over the flames and added more wood.

"Are you going to keep the fire going all night?" Ellie shivered in her sweater. She touched Vern on the shoulder. He turned away from her and went for more wood. He returned with an armful.

"We might as well. It's so cold," Vern said gruffly.

"Why don't we go to bed?" Ellie suggested, since she had put their kids to bed while he got more wood.

"What's the point in going to bed? You would just pick a fight over the competition you say you've been getting lately."

"Well, it's up to you." Ellie thought Vern was acting like a jerk, but she still loved him.

"Up to me? It's never up to me. You do what you like."

"What do you mean?" Ellie asked defensively.

"Get a better job," Vern said angrily.

"I would if I could."

"Huh! You don't try very hard." Vern glared at her across the fire.

"That's not true. I've applied for all kinds of jobs," Ellie said defiantly.

"See it your way."

"I can't believe you'd be mad about it."

"You're stupid."

"Oh! You aren't even listening! You never listen." Ellie was so angry she was almost in tears. When Vern hurt Ellie's feelings, it was like he was trying to take a strip off her, as if he was peeling an onion.

"You cause your own problems," Vern accused Ellie.

"You were ignorant, too, at work today," Ellie said. "It looks good on you to be jealous." Ellie felt ignored, unloved, a second fiddle.

"I don't want my wife working."

"Too bad. I've got plans." Ellie thought she should remind him of their planned house in the country, and about the courses she'd signed up for and still had to pay for.

"Harumph!" Vern grunted. Then, he turned his back on her.

Ellie stared at him across the flames. Folding his arms across his chest, with his back to her, Vern sat like a stone. He could be uncommunicative for weeks. Ellie didn't want fights like that to happen.

Ellie remained silent. She didn't think it was fair to get picked on at work, and then be blamed for it at home. Sometimes, Ellie thought being married was like being pulled by a ball and chain on one end and hung up by a rope on the other.

Ellie threw some more wood on the fire, making it splutter because it was wet green wood. She wanted his arms around her in spite of his temper. "We could sleep out here with our feet to the fire. What do you think, Vern?"

Vern turned around to face the warmth. His grey eyes had a mocking expression in them. The firelight caught the thick stubble on the jowls he was getting.

"About what? I'm the one who never gets listened to," Vern said, sounding obstinate.

Ellie said, "I think I'll go to bed. Stay out here if you like." Ellie got up stiffly.

"You're getting to move like an old woman," he said, as she walked around the fire. "The way you walk and the way you act."

Ellie laughed out loud. Vern hated it when she laughed at him. Laughing at him was one of the few things she could do to get back at him. She stood close in front of him with her crotch at his eye level and laughed and laughed. Then she went to the trailer and opened the door.

"Stay in there, then," Vern said angrily.

"Shut up, or you'll wake the children."

Inside the metal camper, Robert and Susan were fast asleep. She bumped around in the dark, but she didn't awaken them. After she used the washroom, she crawled up to the wide bed at the end of the trailer. She could hear the fire crackling. She saw Vern's dark shape in the firelight. He would sit out there until he was nearly frozen before he would come to bed. Ellie was so upset, there were tears in her eyes. Ellie called to Vern again, but he wouldn't come to bed.

When Ellie woke up in the morning, Vern was in bed reading the paper. The radio was blaring.

"Isn't that kind of loud? Turn it down," Ellie demanded.

"Didn't you sleep last night?" Vern was wearing only his t-shirt, and it was obvious he was waiting for sex. Ellie wanted to punish him for the way he treated her last night, so she ignored his hard-on.

"Like a baby," she said.

"That's one of the things I don't like about you, Ellie. You never think about it."

"Think about what?"

"Sex. Es-Ee-Ex. Got it?"

"Sounds like you have a list of things you don't like," Ellie said belligerently.

"I'll write it out for you to study. In fact, I'll do it right now."

"What's number one?"

"Like I said. Sex. Lack of it."

Ellie laughed. "That again. Whose fault's that?"

He put his paper down and grabbed her by the ears and gave her a long, mushy kiss. The stubble on his jowls scraped across Ellie's chin. His tongue was sticky, soft, and hot. "I have to get up," she said, squirming away.

"Do it later," Vern said. "You'll wake the kids up."

"Wait," Ellie said. He put his arm across her and pulled her nightshirt up. Vern ignored her request to wait. He rolled on top of her, pinning her with his legs. He stuck his penis in her crotch, with difficulty, as she was tight. His eyes were shut, and he was breathing heavily in her ear.

She tried to roll out from under him.

"You wouldn't be trying to discourage me, would you?"

"What a thing to say! It's only nature calling."

He had his hands on her bum, squeezing it. He had his tongue in her mouth.

Ellie grabbed his balls to increase his ardor. Soon, Vern groaned, extra loud and deep.

He kissed her nose and held onto her hair. "Did you get past it?" Vern rolled to the side, pinching her arm with his weight. The radio was blaring away. A gardening show, how to eradicate crabgrass.

"What do you mean by that?"

"Did I put the fire out?"

"I didn't know it was that urgent."

"I didn't know either until I got going. I can't hold back forever." Vern pulled the sheets over himself.

Ellie watched him use the sheets to wipe off. She hated it when he did that. "Quit that."

Vern's eyes were wide open now. "What are you waiting for? You were in such a hurry before to go to the washroom. Do you want me to do it again?"

"Not right now."

"Story of my life."

As Ellie crawled over Vern to get out of bed, he laughed and whacked her on the bum.Ellie bumped her head on the trailer roof. She let the door of the small washroom slam shut behind her. She used the toilet, showered, and washed her light brown hair. As she combed out her hair, she studied her face in the mirror. It was smooth and bland. She looked perfectly calm, but she didn't feel that way.

Ellie was really upset with Vern because he was dumping on her like everybody else. As she stared at herself, tears welled from her blue eyes. Ellie sniffed back the tears. She didn't want Vern to think he had upset her. She had to contain her feelings or admit defeat. She wiped her face and put on some makeup.

Ellie thought their sex life was disastrous. She wasn't in the right mood, and Vern didn't seem to care. It was like a game that neither of them wanted to play, or, if they played, they did it half-heartedly. Ellie put on some perfume and combed her bangs. She found two white hairs just over her right eye. She wondered why she hadn't noticed them before. When she looked, she couldn't find any more white hairs.

"What woke you guys up?" Vern's voice echoed strangely in the small camper.

"Mom flushing the toilet," Susan said, lisping brightly. "I have to pee."

"Mom banging the door," Robert sounded disgusted. "Too loud."

When Ellie came out of the washroom, she saw her kids staring at her over the edge of the table.

"How come you were so long, Mom?"

The expression on Robert's face was just like his father's. At four, he resembled his father, physically and temperamentally.

Ellie shifted her gaze to Susan, who was two and a half. She smiled in her winning way. "I'm hungry," Susan said. "Can I do the cooking?" She had an extremely soggy diaper sliding off her bum. It didn't seem to be bothering her at all.

"Sure," Ellie said.

Vern groaned and covered his eyes. "Not again."

"Oh no," Robert said, and put his hand to his head like his father did.

Susan stepped out of her diaper, left the soggy pile behind and climbed on a chair. Ellie laughed and handed her the cereal box.

After breakfast, Vern drove several miles inland to a farm which had a mixed variety of fruits: cherries, pears, peaches, and apples. The early summer day was perfect, not too hot or humid.

They picked sweet cherries, Bing and English, and then they started on the sour Montmorency cherries.

Ellie pulled the cherries off by the bunch. To pick more quickly, she squeezed them so that the stems and pits were left on the branch. The juice dribbled down her upraised arm and into her armpit. When she licked the juice off, it wasn't as sour as she had expected.

"I think I'll check out the rest of the orchard," Vern said as he left Ellie up the ladder picking. Ellie thought it was typical of Vern to leave the work for her. The dirty look Vern gave her over his shoulder made her feel bad, like he made her feel so often lately.

Robert picked a few cherries, ate a few, then sat down and pushed his truck around. Already he knew what he liked to do and what he didn't like to do.

Susan sat under the tree. She sucked on cherries, getting juice all over her cheeks and chubby little legs. Her blonde hair stuck to her face. She rubbed her eyes with her fists.

Ellie had filled all but one container. She climbed back up the ladder with the basket to get the biggest cherries. Robert had climbed up into the tree.

"Look, Mom." He hung from a branch swinging back and forth.

"Stop that. You'll fall."

Where was Vern? As Ellie craned her neck and twisted around, the ladder slipped and slid down the trunk. Scrambling for balance, Ellie missed a rung. Her leg scraped the wood. She grabbed a branch, holding the ladder in an awkward, suspended position with her other arm.

Ellie used her body to swing the ladder back into place and gingerly climbed off. She grabbed one small basket of cherries to carry, but three were left behind.

Vern was chatting amiably with the saleslady. They didn't interrupt their conversation to look at Ellie when she approached carrying Susan. Robert followed them.

Ellie felt stiff. Her leg had been wrenched in the fall, and her arm was scraped. She put Susan down, removed the branch wrapped around her neck and pinched the leaves from her hair.

"Where's the rest of the cherries?" Vern asked. "Did you pick any at all? Or did you eat them?" Then he grinned at the lady, and she laughed merrily. Ellie thought he said so much because he had an audience. Vern was just being silly because the saleslady was smiling at him.

Ellie pointed back over her shoulder. "You'll have to pick the baskets up. Pay for them first. And hurry it up, will you, so I can take these two to the lake?"

"Why should I have to pick the grass and the leaves and wash the dirt out of the cherries?" Vern asked angrily.

"Because I fell and some leaves fell with me," Ellie said, showing Vern her scraped shin.

"Ugh!" Vern said.

"Gee, I hope the tree wasn't damaged," the lady said.

"It's not," Ellie said. "I'm the one who's hurt."

Vern grumbled all the way to get the cherries, stashed them in the back of the car and then he started the car. "I can't understand why you needed so many anyway."

"I could buy some jam easier than this," Ellie said.

"You're the one who wanted to come here," Vern accused.

"It was fun before." Ellie wondered how such a pleasant experience could turn out so badly.

"Fun's always what you make of it," Vern said piously.

Ellie was convinced her marriage was on the rocks, since Vern made an issue of simple things like picking berries.

"Sarcasm doesn't become you," Ellie said.

"The mood you're in, nothing I do would suit you," he said in a smug voice.

She thought the day was past salvage. By the time they got back to the trailer, Ellie had a headache to go with her other aches and pains. Vern stayed in the car while Ellie got the kids out of the back seat, then he took off again.

Ellie took the kids to the beach again. When he returned, six hours later, she didn't ask where he'd been.

By nightfall, it was raining heavily. Ellie lay awake most of the night. Towards morning, the rain leaked into the trailer just above her head. Drip, drip, drip, right on her face.

* * *

CHAPTER FOUR

Sunday morning, after a sleepless night, Ellie's head was throbbing. There were cherries everywhere. The tiny fridge in the trailer was full of cherries. Ellie took them out to find the milk and orange juice. They had cherries on their cornflakes for breakfast.

Ellie, Robert, and Susan went down to the lake. The water was cold after last night's rain. Gloomy clouds hung heavily over the lake. The wind sent choppy waves across the water. Ellie plunged into the water. It was so cold it made her forget her headache. She stayed in the water, shivering, after her kids ran back out. She thought maybe she should stay there forever.

When Ellie saw them watching her with sullen, purple faces, and wrapped in their towels. She came out of the water.

When they reached the trailer at the top of the bluffs, Vern was slouched in a lawn chair outside. A basball cap rested on his mirror sunglasses.

"Too chicken for the water?" Ellie asked. She was so cold she couldn't stop shaking.

"I was down earlier and stuck a toe in. It was too cold for me, so I'm surprised you went in."

"It's refreshing."

"Oh. It makes your bruises stand out."

Ellie wrapped her towel closer around her.

"We're having a few friends over this afternoon," Vern said.

"Who?" Ellie tried to sound pleased.

"I ran into Quantz and Moose in town yesterday. You'll be happy they're coming over."

Ellie groaned. "What's that supposed to mean?"

"Whatever you want it to mean," Vern said.

Ellie thought the guys must be trying to suck up to Vern. Vern was susceptible to that.

"Why didn't you tell me so I could get some food?"

"I forgot." Vern slumped down in his chair and pulled his cap down over his nose.

"Do we have enough beer?"

"Probably not."

"Well, don't sit there. Go get some."

"You don't need to be ordering me around."

"Forget it, then."

"It doesn't matter what it is, you pick a fight about it." Vern got up from his lawn chair, banged it shut, and threw it against the trailer. The clanging of the metal made Ellie shiver. "Be careful! That's my parent's trailer." Ellie thought Vern was just trying to make her mad.

While Vern went for beer, Ellie cooked some potatoes for salad. When Vern returned, he didn't speak to her. Ellie had to bite her lip to keep tears from rolling down her cheeks. She didn't want to let Vern know how much he'd upset her.

As Ellie put the salad in the trailer fridge, a royal blue jeep with a vinyl roof drove drove up to their trailer and splashed to a stop in a puddle.

Ellie walked toward the jeep.

Moose jumped out. "Hi, how are you!" Then he realized he had landed in a puddle and shook his foot. "Wait till I back up before you get out," he told Cathy. Cathy was already behind the wheel. "She's one step ahead of me."

"She sure is," Ellie said.

"Quantz and Norma are coming later," Cathy said, as she helped three red-headed kids, who looked just like her, to slide down from the jeep.

"I'll have to dry my sandal in the sun and wipe between my toes. Even the grass is wet out here," Moose said.

"You weren't watching where you were going," Cathy said, lifting her heavy red hair off her neck.

"Nice day, ain't it?" Moose twisted the end of his handlebar moustache. The ends of it were waxed.

"Better than last night," Ellie said, shrugging.

"Sure." Moose glanced at Ellie then away, as if he was about to ask her something. Ellie wondered what Vern had said to him. Moose sat in a lawn chair.

"Is it too cold to take the kids down to the water?" Cathy asked.

"No, it's not too cold," Robert said. "We were already there."

"It's too cold," Vern said. "Have a beer instead. Wait for the lake to warm up."

Vern opened one for Moose and handed it to Cathy. There was a lot of beer. Vern had a case of Labatt Blue, and Moose brought a case of O'Keefe's Old Vienna.

Cathy dropped the beer, and it spilled on the grass, foaming out of the bottle. "You'll have to open another one, Vern. I'm sorry. My hand shook." Cathy took the new beer to Moose and sat beside him. Her kids joined Robert and Susan in the sandbox.

"That's okay."

"That's why we party outside," Moose said, laughing. "You can't see the mess."

"But it brings out the bugs," Vern said. "I like camping except for the sand and the bugs."

"Shoot 'em," Moose said.

Vern laughed.

"He doesn't like the cold and the wet either," Ellie said.

"She's always criticizing me," Vern said, sighing.

"I see Ellie drivin' around. She always smiles and waves, but she never stops. She just keeps goin'. Why dontcha stop and say hello?" Moose drawled. "Are you too busy to talk to me?"

"I'm like everybody else in this town, going nowhere," Ellie said, feeling discouraged.

"She's never too busy," Vern said. "Ellie never does anything." Ellie was shocked to hear this new dig of Vern's in front of company.

"Well, I thought with her new job she might be," Moose said.

"It's the only job I could get for the summer and Vern doesn't like it."

"You can say that again," Vern said.

"Nothin' much happens in this town. It never gets any bigger. Almost everybody's gone to the city so they can get a job," Moose said. "It's a town with its collar up, shuttin' out the world."

Ellie laughed at Moose's joke. "I don't want to live in the city, though. We want to buy a house in the country," she said. Ellie could listen to Moose all day. He was funny. He was carefree and friendly. His speech was lazy, with slurs and dropped endings. Ellie talked the same way, she thought. She didn't know if it was an accent or just laziness.

"I'll be right back." Ellie went to the trailer. She had made a cherry pie, which she had just taken out of the oven.

"She looks busy to me," Moose said. He came over to the picnic table where Ellie had set the pie. "What are you drinking? Straight coke?"

"Rum and coke."

"No ice? Warm?" Moose stood closer to Ellie. Now, Moose was friendly, like he had been on Friday afternoon.

What did he want? That was cynical, Ellie thought. "Why do you ask? Is there a choice?"

"No, not if you're gravel-running, out on the road far from town, and don't have a cooler." Moose smiled. "I'm planning a tour. Let's do it some time," Moose said in her ear.

Ellie was incredulous. "You're in a mood today." What was the matter with this guy? He was too young for her, even if she wasn't married.

"You're funny," Ellie said.

"Funny ha ha, or funny queer?"

"You're just making jokes. I'm the one dang near ready for the ashbin."

"Do you have one foot in the grave?"

"No, but sometimes I think things are over for me."

"No, you don't, because that's me. It's a serious possibility," Moose said, suddenly down. Ellie was surprised at how suddenly his mood switched.

"You're too nice to be gloomy," Ellie said, patting him on the shoulder. Maybe he was trying to make her feel sorry for him and it worked.

"Why is that drink taking so long?" Vern interrupted.

"Yeah, what are you guys doing?" Cathy asked, sounding suspicious.

"Melting the ice," Moose said, joking.

"He's breathing on it," Vern said.

"I'll have a rum, too, instead of another beer, but I need the ice." Moose reached into the covered container.

"Mine's fine. I just hadn't put the ice in." Ellie picked up her drink. It tasted strong and warm. The bubbles fizzed wildly, unadulterated by ice cubes.

Moose gave Ellie a quick kiss on the cheek.

"What are you doing?" Vern came over to get his third beer. "If I wait for service, I'll die of thirst. Are you pretending or something?" Vern eyed Ellie's warm drink.

"As if pretending was illegal," Ellie blurted.

"No, but gravel-running, driving around with a mickie of booze in the glove compartment, is."

"Are we doing it?" Ellie asked, exasperated.

"No, but you were talking about it," Vern pointed out.

Moose, Cathy, Vern, and Ellie sat around with their drinks and looked at each other.

"Happy birthday, Ellie." Vern raised his glass.

"The same, for a special person." Moose clinked Vern's glass, then Ellie's.

"I can't believe you knew that and never said anything," Cathy accused Moose.

"She'd rather nobody knew," Vern said. "She's sensitive about it."

"It's still a few weeks away," Ellie said, "but I appreciate the thought."

"Over the hill, but she doesn't look it, does she?" Moose said, winking at her.

Cathy said to Ellie, "I'm sorry I didn't bring a present. I would have if I'd known. I guess this was something the guys cooked up. You don't have any wrinkles. I hope I look like that when I'm thirty," Cathy said.

"It's because she's so chubby. It'll soon start to show." Vern laughed but Ellie knew he was serious. Ellie glanced away so Vern couldn't see the tears starting in her eyes.

"If you said that to me, Vern, I would tell you to move on. I'd say, hit the road," Cathy said, giving him an amazed look.

Vern sniggered.

"Don't laugh. I would, too," Cathy insisted.

"In a few weeks, I'll be leavin' my youth behind, forever. This is Vern's surprise for me. A commemorating party. What do you think of that?" Ellie's voice was higher than normal, because of the strong drink she'd downed. She went to get herself another one.

"Well, it's a big moment!" Vern rolled his eyes.

Moose agreed.

"I think she's drunk," Cathy said in a low voice to Moose.

Moose told Cathy in a low voice, "She's not. Don't be so loud." Ellie felt the conversation now was polite but icy.

Ellie could see Cathy viewed her extra strong drink with obvious displeasure. Cathy was pregnant again. She didn't show yet, and if she hadn't told Ellie the other day, she wouldn't have known.

As soon as her children tired of the sandbox, Ellie lit the barbecue and cooked the hamburgers and hotdogs.

The smoke from the barbecue was like a magnet. Soon, five small children were staring at Ellie. They all had dirty faces.

"Why are you cooking now for?" Vern asked. "It's not even dinner time, and Quantz isn't here yet."

"You can eat later, if you want," Ellie said.

"We might as well all eat," Cathy said. "It will be less work for Ellie." When Cathy came over to help Ellie, Vern and Moose came too.

As soon as the food was cooked, Ellie put the platter on the table and covered it so it would stay warm.

"That's all we do around here," Vern said. "Eat."

When they were eating the cherry pie, Quantz drove up.

"Here's the turkey now," Vern said.

"Don't call him that," Moose said.

"He's no better than anybody else," Vern said.

"No, but don't call him that," Moose insisted.

"We're always waiting for him, even at work," Vern said.

"Well," Moose said.

Ellie felt better than she had all weekend when she saw Quantz get out of his Camaro. Was she feeling the rum?

"Where are Norma and the kids?" Cathy asked, her head sticking past Moose.

"The in-laws are over, but I thought I'd stop to say hello." Quantz shuffled his feet and put his hands in his pockets.

"Set down over here. We've been talking about you all afternoon," Moose said.

"Unless it's interesting I don't want to hear about it." Quantz sat down between Vern and Ellie.

"The food's cold, though," Vern said, "or maybe you've eaten already."

"Oh!" Ellie said. "I can cook some more. Or you can have some dessert."

"Do ya want to know what we said?" Moose said. "You're lookin' spectacular. You're wearin' new clothes instead of the same thing every day."

"You've been around here too long," Quantz said to Moose. "How are you going to be able to sell graders abroad talking like that?"

"I'll use my winning smile."

"You sound just like her." Quantz pointed at Ellie. "You have to be sophisticated if you want to negotiate."

"What's that supposed to mean? What's the matter with the way I am? What's so good about you?"' Ellie's voice rose.

Ellie was shocked to think that Quantz might think she wasn't good enough for him.

"Nothing. You're just local, that's all," Quantz said smugly.

"Oh!" Ellie yelled. "So are you. A local dude." She didn't think there was anything wrong with being local.

"Quantz is a salesperson. Moose is going to be one, and travel," Cathy explained to Ellie as if she didn't understand.

"Maybe, if I can talk right," Moose said. "Not like Ellie."

"Well, I'm sorry, I didn't mean to be critical. It just came out that way," Quantz said, leaning toward Ellie. He moved his chair closer.

Ellie stared at him critically. He had light brown hair with a faintly receding hairline. He had blue eyes, and when he smiled they smiled too. He was an altogether ordinary-looking sort, but he was the friendliest, most exciting thing she'd seen so far. Good, she thought, except Quantz put on airs.

Quantz asked, "Have you gone back to school?"

"Why would you be interested?" Ellie had just finished high school and decided to start college courses.

"Why wouldn't I want to know?"

When Ellie told him, Quantz leaned closer to her and stared into her eyes. During their conversation, Ellie found herself trying to copy the way he said things. Quantz laughed at her.

"Why are you laughing at me?" Ellie asked.

"It's the way you talk."

"Gee, it doesn't take much for you to find a joke, does it?" Ellie said, offended.

"You notice things about people. You're observant," Quantz said. Then he laughed.

They were all laughing. Moose made Ellie laugh. Ellie made Quantz laugh. Vern laughed at Ellie, even when she didn't want him to. What a mess things were in.

"If you weren't bigger than me, I would poke you in the nose," Ellie said, jokingly.

Quantz patted her on the shoulder. Then they got up at the same time and bumped into each other. Her nose reached the second button on his shirt. Ellie laughed. "It's a good thing we don't have to dance together."

"See what I mean. Only you would think of such a thing," Quantz said, giving Ellie a squeeze. Ellie thought Quantz was a little too friendly, but Vern was in serious discussion with Moose, so he didn't notice.

Then, Ellie noticed Cathy watching them disapprovingly. Cathy was such a snoot-face. Ellie figured Cathy had no right to judge her.

Ellie considered whether she should have the drink Quantz got for her because she had already had one more than her usual. Ellie tipped it out when Quantz walked over to sit with Vern.

When Ellie looked up, Cathy was staring at her.

"It was really sweet of Vern to have a party for you," Cathy said. "You must find it a nice surprise."

"Vern never does anything without a reason," Ellie said. Ellie wanted more attention from Vern, and she'd been upset all weekend about why she wasn't getting it. Even the surprise party he'd planned for her was a source of disagreement, whether or not to serve the birthday cake Vern had bought from a bake shop with Ellie's cherry pie. Ellie was almost in tears. He probably didn't mean any of his sarcastic remarks. She was the one at fault, and she was too sensitive.

"Still, it must be nice to be thought of," Cathy said. "We'd better go. It's getting late."

Moose and Cathy loaded their small children to the jeep, and bounced down the rutted road.

Vern and Quantz went down to the beach. When they came back, Quantz left.

As Ellie cleaned up dinner, she felt the evening getting chilly. Then she packed the Explorer to go home. She had a sunburn on her arms, her face, and on her nose particularly, but she was still white around her eyes. She looked funny. If she wasn't so sore from her fall, she would laugh at herself.

* * *

CHAPTER FIVE

About nine Sunday night as soon as Ellie and Vern Menzies reached home, their phone rang. He grabbed it off the wall, mid-way into the second ring. "It's Tiny," Vern told Ellie. "They're going to walk out. Any more double-talk from management and they going to do it."

Ellie had heard there was trouble at work, trouble they never expected because Champion was one of the largest businesses in Canada. It manufactured graders.

Ellie knew the plant had never had a strike, but there was one pending. Seventy-two of the six hundred men had been laid off already in June. More layoffs were expected.

"There's no orders coming in!" Ellie could hear Vern almost yelling. "What's even worse, existing orders are being cancelled because of financing problems in Brazil. We've no work!"

Ellie had never expected this to happen because Vern had worked at Champion for sixteen years, since graduating from high school. Vern was now a foreman, but he had worked on the line operating all the machines so when things went wrong, he knew what to do.

Since Vern was a union steward, he was usually on the phone as soon as he was inside the door, but a phone call Sunday night was something different. To Ellie, it meant something drastic had happened over the weekend.

"We've been without a contract for a year. That won't help our situation any. Inflation is a major issue, so the guys want a cost-of-living clause written into their contract when we do get one."

Ellie heard Tiny arguing on the other end of the phone about what the contract should say.

Vern had told Ellie there was talk of a strike, but they'd be crazy to do it. He didn't think Champion would close down permanently, but they might if there was a strike. There was a problem with the motors in some of the graders in Bolivia. Because of engineering and production problems, management was talking about wage cuts, if they didn't go ahead with more layoffs. The men wanted more pay, and management wanted to give them less.

After he hung up the phone, Vern went to the washroom. Ellie could hear him being sick. "Christ," he swore. He was barfing up black, so she knew his ulcer was bothering him.

Ellie thought Vern being between the men and management was a no-win situation. Sometimes she felt sorry for him, but mostly there was nothing she could do to help. When his inability to solve the problems bothered him and he took it out on her, Ellie resentfully thought it served him right. Vern was crazy to be complaining about her getting a job when he might lose his. He didn't think he would be laid off. He had seniority.

Vern worried and fretted almost all night long, so that the next morning Vern slept in and was late for work at Champion.

When he went out the door, not stopping to kiss Ellie goodbye, Ellie said, "Wait, I need the truck."

Vern swore, but he waited, leaning against the doorjamb. "Why do you leave it so late to tell me?"

"I forgot."

"Hurry up then."

Ellie grabbed her raincoat to cover her pajamas.

"Can't you walk to work?" Vern rubbed his head.

"Gee, thanks," Ellie said facetiously. She wanted to go back out to the trailer and have it in spotless order for her parent's next inspection.

"I thought that's what we came back to Goderich for. Christ!"

"It won't take long and it's easier for me." Vern, Ellie and two kids eating toast drove the four minutes across town.

"I don't know why you can't be more organized. You must have shit for brains to expect me to rush and be late like this," Vern said. Most mornings he didn't speak, and most of the time Ellie thought it was a good thing.

Ellie thought Vern's temper was caused by the present problems at Champion.

He took his job seriously. Listening to complaints bothered him. Being a foreman was hard, but the pay was higher than just working on the line.

In a moment, Ellie could see the parking lot at Champion was almost full.

As Vern's green Ford Explorer pulled up at the gate, a grader completed and primed, but needing a finished coat, went by. It was a bitter lemon color, but soon it would be painted a bright orange or yellow.

Vern leapt out of the truck with his lunch pail, and went through the gate, past the security station.

Ellie continued around behind the factory. She drove the truck between the railway tracks along the river and the sprawling group of buildings on the right. The grader, on a test-run, zoomed suddenly around a corner.

Ellie jumped, startled. The truck swerved and narrowly missed the chain-link fence. The suddenly accelerating roar of the grader motor was like a shot of adrenalin. Her heart beat faster. The hugeness and the sound made her shudder.

When Ellie glanced up, she saw George Toogood laughing behind the wheel. Idiot. Why wasn't George filling potholes with gravel and continuing his test-run in a regular fashion, instead of playing games?

Ellie drove past huge stacks of iron piled neatly behind the chain-link fence. The yard also contained stocks of railway ties, black V-shaped blades, and several graders waiting for paint.

Then, Ellie drove home. As she got out of the truck, she noticed the day lilies were just opening. The orange lilies multiplied and bloomed for several weeks every year. At seven in the morning, they were drooping, but later they were wide open. Ellie marvelled at their orange openness.

Robert went right to the grader in his sandbox. He scraped and levelled the sand, creating mounds and culling or scooping ravines.

"Robert, have you had enough breakfast?" Ellie asked.

Robert gazed at his mother. "I'm too busy for food."

"Come on, Robert, and finish your breakfast." Ellie took Susan and Robert by the hand. Robert's chin fell as he left his grader behind.

For breakfast, Ellie cooked them some scrambled eggs. After eating, Robert went back out to the sandbox. Susan stayed inside with Ellie.

Ellie cleaned up the house and got ready for work. Since Ellie had found grey hair yesterday, she combed her long brown hair this way and that way. So far she hadn't found any more grey. Ellie saw dark circles under her eyes which bothered her. The person Ellie saw in the mirror consisted of hair, eyes, and a body which changed all the time. She was too heavy, too thin, or just right. She had lost weight or gained weight. She thought her real self existed somewhere else or was different than the image she saw in the mirror. She put makeup on her eyes to hide the dark circles and combed her hair the other way to hide the two grey hairs.

"I look so awful," Ellie said, exasperated with what she saw in the mirror. "Old as the hills!"

"No, you're not. They're making new hills every day," Robert said. He stood at the washroom door, waving his grader covered with grit. He dropped it, leaving a pile of sand on the floor.

"That doesn't mean I'm new," Ellie said, pointing to her hairline. "Two gray hairs. I'll just get more until I die."

Robert sat down on the pile of grit from his grader and watched her put her lipstick on. He finally said, "No, you won't. Wash it out."

Ellie laughed. "I'll just get more."

"Like Grandma and Grandpa?"

"Yes."

"Will Grandma and Grandpa die?" he asked.

"Yes," Ellie said, "when they get old and grey."

"Will Susan die?"

"Yes, when she gets old and grey."

"Will you die, Mom?"

"Yes, when I get old and gray. Everyone dies."

Robert thought for a minute. "I'm never going to go grey."

"You're silly, but I love you anyway." Ellie realized Beri, Moose and Quantz thought the same way Robert did, concerned with the now, convinced they wouldn't die. The idea of their own mortality must be foreign to them, she thought, by the way they acted.

Robert hugged and kissed Ellie. He put the powder on her nose and got it in her eyes, too.

When it was their turn to get cleaned up, both Robert and Susan resisted.

"Why do I have to wash my hair? I like to be dirty," Robert said. Susan cried over the shampoo in her eyes.

"You have to clean up anyway. What will Mrs. Stewart say?"

When they dawdled over picking out their clothes, Ellie told them to hurry up.

After Ellie drove to the Bedford, she worked from 11:30 am until 5 pm. Mondays were slow so that was when she cleaned the bar, polished the mirror, and rewashed all the glasses.

At about twenty to four, when Ellie was on the phone putting in her beer order, Vern stuck his head in the door.

"I'm helping George with a roof. I'll be home later." Vern didn't wait for Ellie to answer. He went out the side door.

After Ellie put the phone down, George ambled in and slid onto a stool.

"Did I scare you this morning?" he asked.

"Why would you think that?" Ellie said coldly.

"Don't be angry, darlin,'" George said. "I'm just doin' my job." He pushed the hair out of his eyes. With his beard, long hair and earring, Ellie thought he looked wild and scary. "I have time for a quick one. Was Vern talking to you?"

"He just came in this door and went out that door." Ellie pointed.

"Didn't he stop for a drink? What's his rush? Maybe he's gone somewhere else for a drink."

"Why would I care?" Ellie asked, thinking George was picking fault in her relationship with Vern.

"Don't get hostile. Just kidding. He's gone to get nails."

"He'll be starting without you."

George shrugged. He drank up and left.

As Ellie left work, she wondered what George and Vern were up to besides fixing the roof. What she knew of George already was that you didn't mess with him. She sighed as she drove to Black's Point taking Robert and Susan with her.

It was dark by the time Ellie drove home. Robert and Susan were asleep in the back seat. After she put the kids to bed, Ellie stayed up to watch the news. Then she phoned to see if Vern was done with the roof yet, and a drowsy-sounding Beri told her they couldn't finish because they'd hit a snag. Ellie went to bed.

After about an hour's sleep, Ellie rolled over onto Vern's side of the bed. Suddenly, she was wide awake. Vern wasn't home yet. She had been dreaming she was in somebody else's warm arms. Tossing this way and that, she couldn't get back to sleep.

Ellie felt something was drastically wrong between Vern and her. They had been fighting a lot lately. Worse, she thought, they never seemed to make up after their fights any more.

Pulling the sheet over her shoulders, Ellie started to think about the past weekend. The temptation of another man's arms around her yesterday had been inviting. She was starting to wonder what it would be like to be with another man.

Vern was becoming a stranger. He was jealous when he had no reason to be. Always finding fault with her, he couldn't see his own shortcomings. He wouldn't accommodate her no matter what. Ellie remembered asking him for something which he completely forgot about.

She'd been awake for an hour, Ellie thought. The longer she stayed awake, the angrier she got. Where was Vern? If he was out drinking late, it normally would be a minor problem. This time, it seemed to pile up with the events of the weekend. She didn't know if she wanted Vern to come home or not. Vern used to be her passion. When did she start thinking of Vern as a used-to-be? Ellie thought she would cry if she wasn't so angry. My marriage will just get worse, she thought. I'll lose interest, then the way we get along won't matter any more.

Headlights flashed past continuously outside her window. Then, finally, a set of lights paused.

Ellie heard the rumble of George's flat-bed truck in the drive. Vern and George had stopped for drinks after their job was done, so many drinks Vern was loaded. Ellie could tell that from his loud voice. Through the open window, Ellie could hear them talking in the driveway, as if they had all the time in the world. The truck door slammed. She hoped the neighbors didn't hear them.

Vern came in the back door. Ellie could hear the back door slam. He thumped up the steps, stumbling on the last step.

"God damn," Vern cursed, switching on the hall light.

Ellie turned her face to the wall and pretended to be asleep.

Vern came into the room. Ellie could hear the rustling of clothes and feel the bed move. As he pulled the sheet over his legs, he leaned over Ellie.

Ellie was glad to see him in spite of her anger. Just as he put his arm over her, Ellie turned her head. Her face met bushy wet underarm hair. The smell of his armpits was overpowering, like a skunk.

"Pugh," she said, and she flicked on the light.

Vern shielded his eyes with his hand. "What did you do that for? Turn the blasted light off."

"No, your voice isn't loud enough," Ellie said stubbornly.

"You know what I've been doing and where I've been. So what's the problem? Turn the dang light off."

Ellie wasn't impressed with Vern's response. She was mad to start with, and she had had two hours to think.

Ellie sat up in bed and glowered at Vern busily scratching his arms. His face was swollen, and the flesh around his reddened eyes was puffy.

Vern got a stupid look on his face. "You're sitting up with your arms around your knees. Tee-hee. It's the middle of the night. Tee-hee. Lie down."

Ellie didn't turn the light off or lie down. She should have gone to sleep, or kept pretending she was asleep.

"What are you waiting for? I hope you weren't waiting for me to come home," Vern said.

"What's that supposed to mean?" Ellie was alarmed. She depended on Vern.

"I probably would have wakened you anyway."

"Really?" Ellie was close to tears.

Vern pulled Ellie over to his side of the bed. He kissed her, then he reached over her. As he turned the light off, he wet her down with his armpit.

"It's hot up here," he apologized.

"No kidding."

When they were finished, Vern whispered something loving, yet distinctly foreign in Ellie's ear.

"What did you call me?" Ellie said incredulously.

"I don't remember. What did I say?"

"You called me Beri!" Ellie accused loudly.

"Is that all? I've been looking at her all night, that's why," Vern said, chuckling. "She's kind of a punchboard, anyway, she's had so many boyfriends. Why would you be worrying about her?" Vern threw up his hands. "Look Ellie, I'm sorry. It was just a slip," Vern said sleepily.

"It's funny how you men know all the dirt about somebody." Ellie threw a pillow at him.

"Hey, take it easy." Vern held up his hand.

"Well, <u>I'm</u> not drunk. I don't see how you can say it's just a mistake, laugh it off, and think things will be all right."

Vern groaned, "So there'll be trouble in the morning?"

"Have you been sleeping with her?"

"Would I do that to you?" he asked. Ellie didn't think he was taking her seriously. She thought answering a question with a question was no answer, but a hostile signal that the conversation wasn't to be continued.

"You don't respect me," Ellie said.

"Gawd." Vern rolled away from her. He was asleep and snoring in a moment.

Ellie was mortified. Vern didn't care if her feelings were hurt or not. He just said whatever he could get away with, whatever he thought would wash.

* * *

CHAPTER SIX

At home, Ellie felt so bland and numb all day after their fight, she actually was glad to go to work Tuesday night.

About ten-thirty p.m. Beri came in just to visit, Ellie thought, but she wasn't glad to see her. She was such a liar. Ellie thought Beri was trouble on two legs, cruising for a showdown, and if she kept after Vern she might get it smack between the eyes.

What Beri thought of Ellie was impossible to tell. Beri kept her head down. She played with her rye, stirring the ice and sticking the straw in her mouth.

"Is this a social call or what?" Ellie asked brusquely. If Beri wanted something, she wasn't going to get it.

Beri was so surprised she took the straw out of her mouth and held it in the air. "What went on last night, anyway?" Beri asked, innocent as hell, Ellie thought.

"Why ask me?" Ellie said shortly.

"I meant, after Vern went home. I don't know what Vern told you, but I showed him my new bedroom furniture." Beri was almost simpering.

"The bird's-eye maple stuff?"

"Yes, my new antiques." Beri was pleased.

As far as Ellie was concerned, the furniture was old, ugly, and squeezed into one small room. Beri couldn't walk around her bed. Did her remark throw light on the situation or didn't it? How odd Vern found a reason to be in Beri's bedroom.

"Vern was late for work this morning," Ellie said.

"So I heard," Beri said, touching Ellie on the shoulder. What's this? Ellie thought. She wants to be friends again?

"How did the roof go?"

"Well," Beri said slowly, as if the roof wasn't the issue and it wasn't.

"Didn't they finish it?"

"They had to stop. Sheathing has to be replaced before they can continue. Whenever that happens." Beri shrugged. "I don't worry about it."

"You don't seem to worry about anything."

"That's not true. I'm not what I appear to be." Beri surprised Ellie by trying to confide in her.

"What do you mean by that?"

Beri sighed, "Did you ever wonder about my name?"

"No. It hasn't been top priority," Ellie smirked.

Ellie noticed Beri was staring at her ready to tell her life story.

"What about your name?" Ellie asked.

"B-e-r-i." Beri spelled it, opened her purse and took out a cigarette. "It's after a street in Montreal. When I was there, I had a real good time. I figured, with a good name, I win. When I was Gertrude, I was a loser. Ever been to Montreal?"

"Yes." Ellie remembered the good time she had with friends in the cosmopolitan city, a mixture of skyscrapers, ancient houses, and brick streets.

"I was there last year for my thirtieth birthday, and ever since my life has changed for the better."

"Why's that?"

"I had a lot of affairs, one right after the other which made me feel better, like I wasn't missing so much in life. Now I've got George. Maybe we'll get married."

Beri was a pot-head when she mixed drugs and alcohol. "So Montreal changed your life."

"What did you do in Montreal?" Beri asked. "Meet anybody?"

"They didn't like us Ontario girls much."

"What happened?"

"They got over it." Ellie smirked.

Beri's mouth dropped open. Then, she told Ellie details about her sex life Ellie didn't want to hear. "I guess I don't want to get married, or I would be by now," Beri said. Beri was so mixed up she couldn't make up her mind, Ellie decided.

"You're nuts," Ellie said. "Out to lunch."

Beri's expression was hostile. "By the way, Steve said his wife complained about the way you cleaned the mirror yesterday. You left too many streaks."

Ellie turned toward the mirror. It sparkled.

"She did it over," Beri said, triumphantly.

Ellie was silent. She didn't know what to say. She was flabbergasted at the backstabbing expression on Beri's face.

As Beri smugly lit another cigarette, Ellie rearranged the stack of glasses.

Ellie saw Moose came in. The ends of his moustache were waxed and curled. He had a beer and bought Beri another rye.

"Like my new shirt?" Moose asked Beri, sticking out his chest and leaning closer to her. As Moose chatted Beri up, he glanced at Ellie. "Everybody visits Ellie," he said. Maybe Moose took it for granted Ellie liked him because she was listening intently.

"How's it going, Ellie? Vern paying enough attention?"

"Why did you ask Ellie that?" Beri's voice was shrill.

"No reason. I'm just being friendly."

Moose shrugged when Beri gave him a hard stare. "Don't you think Ellie should change her name? It's so ordinary," Beri said. "And lighten her hair."

"What's wrong with ordinary?" Ellie asked, alarmed.

Moose made a face at Ellie. "I think she's cute the way she is. Blonde is so brazen."

"The way you said it sounds so demeaning. What's the matter with my blonde hair?" Beri yelled.

"Nothing. Nothing. What did I say wrong?"

Beri glared at Moose, but he put his arm around her and whispered in her ear. She didn't move away. Soon she was laughing.

Ellie had the impression Beri was friendly with everybody just to feel good. Ellie tried not to make a remark on the way Beri was acting.

At eleven-forty, Quantz came into the bar. He gazed at Ellie. "I'm in need of a friend. What about you?"

Ellie flushed. She was glad to see him. She felt a rush of pleasant sensations when Quantz stared at her. When Quantz's eyes were on her, Ellie was so nervous she dropped a glass and broke it.

Toward midnight, Steve came in to help close up.

Quantz stared at Ellie so much Steve said, "What's going on between you two here?" He pointed at them both.

"Having a drink after work," Quantz said, "is all."

Steve couldn't keep the smirk off his face as he finished his drink. Then he left.

"I see no one begged him to stay for another drink," Moose said. "I thought he was going to buy us one."

Beri laughed so much she almost choked on her drink.

"He's funny, but not that funny," Quantz said.

Tiny Grosste came in. "This stool's hot. Who was sitting here?" He was almost eager.

"The boss."

"Oh." Tiny's eyes imitated his mouth, Ellie thought.

"You sound disappointed," Moose said.

"I wouldn't want to take anybody's place. I'll have my beer, Ellie." Tiny timidly peeked at Ellie.

Ellie set up a beer.

"So you made it through the work order, did you?" Moose glared past Quantz at Tiny. "You're always behind."

"Behind or not, I'm here, safe and sound."

"Anything happen since I left?" Moose rolled his eyes at Ellie. "Do they want to strike?"

"There's never been a strike at Champion," Tiny said.

"Tell us something we don't know," Quantz said, calmly stubbing his cigarette in an ash tray.

"Where else can they get a job in this town? It's practically the only place for a man to get a job, other than the salt mine and it's hard to get in there," Tiny whined.

"So what else do you know? Tiny, you old stinker. Bring yer ugly face over here and tell me what happened at work tonight," Moose said.

Tiny didn't move.

"Well?" Moose asked, after a minute of silence.

"An older guy had a heart attack in the heat tonight," Tiny said confidentially.

"Who was it?"

"I don't know."

"God, for stupid." Ellie was surprised at how vehement Moose was.

"Don't call me stupid. It was like a smelter in there. I didn't feel too good, myself," Tiny said, whining.

"The men could go on strike over the fans not working," Quantz said thoughtfully.

"Well, he had a heart attack because he had to lift heavy cast out of a box. He asked for help from a crane but he didn't get it," Tiny explained.

"Is he going to be okay?"

"I don't know," Tiny said.

"Boy, are you ever stupid," Moose said. Ellie was shocked at the way Moose was talking. He must be crazy to mouth off at a big guy like Tiny.

Nothing happened. Tiny's eyes got narrow, black and aimless. He gulped his beer and left.

"I guess he doesn't like our company," Beri snickered.

Ellie thought Tiny was the kind of person nobody liked, unless of course they could use him for some reason.

"Want another drink?" Moose asked Beri. "It's ten to one, last call."

"Okay," Beri said. "One more. It's not often I get to visit."

"Okay," Moose said. "Me too. A quick one. Then I gotta go."

After Moose and Beri left, Quantz lit a cigarette. The smoke from the cigarette wafted across the bar.

Quantz's cigarette was fresh smoke added to the heavy stale aroma of the bar, which Ellie thought hinted of boredom.

Still, the smoke threaded thinly across the bar. Its clinging smell lazily moved past Ellie's nose.

Ellie washed the glasses and put them away, wiped the tables, and put the ashtrays to soak. While she waited for customers at the end of the lounge to drink up and leave, Ellie leaned against the sink.

Motionless, Quantz held his cigarette in his right hand. Tonight he was like a smiling statue.

Ellie waited for him to say something. She figured he might ask her out. She'd been hoping he might.

Quantz blinked. He smiled at Ellie and stared at her. Except for the smoke from the cigarette, he could be made of solid wax. What was taking him so long?

All of a sudden, Ellie felt tired. She stifled a yawn.

"Maybe you're bored," Quantz said, laughing weakly. Ellie thought maybe he was as nervous as she was.

"It's been a long night," Ellie said. She was beat.

"Go home to bed," Quantz said, reaching across the bar and gently touching Ellie's cheek, forehead, and neck. "I'll finish up." Quantz got off his barstool.

"You moved!" Ellie laughed, turning to ring the last drinks into the till. "We have to go soon anyway."

"Come out with me for awhile. So far, you've been ignoring me."

"Don't say that!" Ellie said. She thought Quantz knew she liked him. "Are you asking me for a date?" There was a moment of silence as she thought of what else to say. Her heart skipped a beat as she realized he was asking her to go with him later and she'd just said yes.

Quantz gawked at Ellie. His hand supported his chin. "You don't sound too keen. Did I say something wrong?"

"No, you didn't," Ellie said, after a moment. "I'm interested. We can go out after for a few minutes." Ellie wished for a miracle to happen so that Quantz would lighten up, and be back to his normal self.

"You're making me feel I should stick around." Quantz was coming on to her, but Ellie was used to good-looking men.

Staring at her forlornly as if he was expecting something, he was making Ellie nervous. Ellie was surprised she wanted to be with him at much as she did. He'd asked her before so it seemed natural. Maybe her resistance was down.

"All right, then, we can go out later tonight if you want." Ellie thought she would turn inside out while she closed the bar. Ellie wasn't tired any more. She was happy Quantz was waiting for her, so happy she could have sung out loud.

Finally, when the customers at the end of the lounge left, Ellie ran to lock the door.

Quantz dragged the garbage can out. Ellie almost dropped the till trying to get through the door so she had to pick up the change scattered on the floor.

"You must be in a hurry," Quantz said.

"No, are you?" Ellie flushed, not wanting more delay.

"No," Quantz smiled.

In the other lounge, Ellie handed Steve her till.

Steve smiled. "All done?" When he saw Quantz following her, he frowned.

"He has a crush on you," Quantz whispered at the back of her neck.

Ellie laughed. She was afraid, too, if Steve took a dislike to her that she might lose her job. Already she thought the boss was too friendly, too interested in what she was doing. Quantz was warning her, maybe.

"Let's have a drink while Steve counts the till," Quantz said.

"We'll both have a drink," Ellie said loudly. "Make mine a rye."

When they both sat down, Ellie thought Quantz was quite a bit larger than she was. His leather jacket squeaked as he moved. He smelled like warm skin, leather and beer. Ellie wanted to put her face in his shirt.

Quantz's foot touched Ellie, so she glanced at him. His face was serious. Ellie felt this was a monumentally important decision she was making on the spur of the moment, as if it was devil-may-care.

Ellie worried that Quantz would change his mind. Why would she worry? He was planted in his chair. Five minutes ago, she didn't care if he stayed or not, but now she looked forward to making love with Quantz. Ellie thought he was concerned about her, and she needed it.

"Drink up quick," Quantz said. "Let's go. We'll hear about this tomorrow as it is."

Steve glowered, but Ellie ignored him. She thought what she did after work was none of his concern.

Ellie pulled her mohair sweater on and rose from her chair. Quantz followed her out the door.

At almost two in the morning, there was no one on the streets. Quantz opened his car door for her. The night was so cool there was frost on the windshield.

Quantz drove his brown Camaro down to the end of a No Exit street and parked. The branches cascaded over the car, like dark fronds or arms rubbing the hood.

"If somebody comes, put your head down." Quantz turned the motor off.

"Sure," Ellie said.

"Lock your door."

"Are we having company?" Ellie had the jitters.

"Heh, heh, that's what I like about you, your off-the-wall sense of humor. Everything serious is almost a joke."

"It's no joke." Over her shoulder Ellie saw the street was shadowy, dark, and lonely, and she wondered if headlights would come up behind them. Her sense of unease soon disappeared as Quantz leaned toward her, putting his arms around her and turning her face up toward his.

Ellie was thinking how amazing and wonderful it was to be doing something so simple, such as hugging and kissing Quantz, who up to this point was a relative stranger. He felt so different than the husband she was used to. With the increasing intensity of his squeeze, she thought, gee, I really like this guy. I like the way he feels, smells, and kisses, and the things he says, the way he waits for me to kiss back. I like him for no other reason than for hugs and kisses, and by the looks and feels of things he likes me too.

Except for a darkened house a vacant lot away, everything around her was secluded. His firm arms blotted out the streetlight. His warm neck was a place to kiss. His chin rubbed and pressed against hers, his mouth searching for hers.

Quantz kissed Ellie, lips wide open, his tongue filling up her whole space, and in response, her tremulous tongue darting to find grooves under it, over it, then beside it. Quantz's kiss was deep and long, lasting and lasting.

Ellie thought she liked getting Frenched with Quantz better than anybody else. His deep open-mouth kiss made her want to climb on him, her emotions responding to the invitation he made with his tongue. Her urge to complete the love-making grew more insistent. She thought she would die if he didn't want to make love any more than this once. She was sure they could only be together once.

Ellie was breathless. She pulled away to take a breath, afraid to let it out, as if it would spoil things.

Quantz slid his arms underneath her shirt and in one movement undid her brassiere hook.

She pulled her nylons and panties off. She left her shirt and sweater on even though no one could see through the frosted windows even if they wanted. They were a warm huddle in chilly surroundings. "Ooh." She jumped as the seats were cold on her bare skin.

Quantz lifted her onto him. He stuck his cock into her. Ellie felt penetrated, thinking sex was the most important thing in the world to do, a line of spasms running through her from one entrance to the other.

Quantz felt so hot that Ellie didn't want it to end. Ellie thought she could get addicted to the way Quantz felt in her, as he made her feel the best she had ever felt.

Quantz put his arms around Ellie's backside and held her close until she had an orgasm.

Ellie hung on his neck. Forgetting she was in a limited space, Ellie jerked her elbow back to get in a better position, but she honked the horn. She checked to see if the entire neighborhood was standing out in the cold in their pajamas, and Quantz checked too.

Quantz pulled Ellie closer. "Take it easy. Let's get out of sight." They slid down on the seat.

Eight minutes later, they both climaxed. Her legs wrapped around his body, as if she wouldn't let him get away. She grasped him firmly each time he groaned at the results of his thrusts.

Ellie was amazed that an ordinary thing such as sex could be so wonderful.

Then a sharp sound startled her. The CB radio in his car cackled with static, and an impatient male voice came on asking for location, using a code name Ellie didn't recognize.

Immediately, Quantz reached over and turned in off.

"Why are they calling so late?" Ellie said. "Call back and find out."

"Later. It can't be anything important." His short tone of voice made Ellie feel closed out.

She was suddenly scared, realizing she liked Quantz too much, wondering what could happen if someone found out about them. When she thought of the questions Vern would ask her, she immediately felt guilty. When she caught herself automatically comparing Quantz with Vern she felt guilty. What would she tell Vern?

"It's getting really late." Ellie shivered as she did up her shirt. She wanted to get home as soon as possible and undo what she'd done. Maybe she'd say she'd worked late, got a pizza after.

"Is this just for sex?" Quantz asked as she pulled on her pantihose. "We can get together once in awhile."

"Looks like it." Already Ellie lied about her feelings, because she didn't want Quantz to know that already she liked him more than Vern.

"Good! All I think about is sex, if I don't get enough." Quantz touched her nose.

"Aren't you going to ask me why I need the sex?" Ellie asked.

"Next Wednesday night?" Quantz laughed.

"Sure." As soon as she said it, Ellie wished she maybe hadn't agreed to see him again. She started to worry about the things that could go wrong, about Vern finding out. How would he treat her? He might leave her.

Did Quantz like her enough to leave his wife and be with her all the time? Probably not. She thought if Quantz liked her, he'd keep after her, and she'd have to decide what to do. Why had she made love with him without thinking carefully? Their lovemaking was supposed to be one of those spur-of-the-moment things, a one-night stand, that's all, but Quantz made Ellie feel good holding her and kissing her. Quantz made Ellie happy. She was too happy to be scared. Ellie thought Quantz was like a fresh face without grudges or a past. She felt full of anticipation like she was when she was a teenager without too many disappointments, when she went out on a date.

Quantz drove Ellie back to her car and she went home. Her house was in darkness, but the outside light was still on. So far so good, but she'd started on a course of action that could lead to disruption of her family life. Half an hour ago, it didn't matter, but now she wished she hadn't made love to Quantz because she knew when he asked her again, she wouldn't refuse. Then what? Ellie was pulled in two directions. She felt guilty and happy all rolled into one.

She got out of her car and went into the house. As soon as she saw her children sleeping in their beds, she felt scared. What if Vern left her and took them with him?

Vern was a sleeping hulk rolled up in his blanket. Ellie put her arms around him. She thought drowsily about what Vern would do if he found out? He had such a temper.

How could she risk blowing away her marriage in one night, not even one night, more like an hour or so? How could she be so stupid? Ellie decided she couldn't meet Quantz for their next date. She fell asleep thinking it was going to be hard as she found him irresistible. So irresistible.

* * *

CHAPTER SEVEN

For the next few days after Ellie was with Quantz, she thought things were fine. She thought about him all the time, but Vern was the same busy annoyed person and her kids were busy. So far, so good, she thought.

Then, Ellie went to pick her kids up at Mrs. Stewart's as planned after her day shift, and her kids weren't there.

Ellie, instantly panic-stricken, couldn't believe her ears as Mrs. Stewart explained:

"Robert had a bruise on his leg today, so I called the Children's Aid. I called them last week, and they said if I noticed anything to give them a call."

How had Robert got his bruise? Searching her mind, Ellie couldn't think of anything he'd done while she was around.

"How could you do this? I want my kids."

"You'll just have to wait. They're under observation," Mrs. Stewart said smugly. Ellie could see the dislike on Mrs. Stewart's face and she wondered what she had done to make such an enemy out of her.

"Well, they can't take kids just like that without warning." Ellie nervously adjusted her top.

"Well, they can and they did." Mrs. Stewart shoved a card at Ellie with a name and a number on it for her to call.

Ellie, frantic with rage and fright, could see that she wasn't getting anywhere with Mrs. Stewart who had a gloating expression on her face. She almost jumped up and down.

"How could you," she shrieked at Mrs. Stewart. "How dare you rat on people?"

"You're your own worst enemy," the gray-haired woman said with a sneer on her face.

Ellie got back in her car and drove out the lane, careening around the corner. She went home. What else could she do when she was in a state like this?

As soon as she got home, she phoned about her kids and the society asked for extra clothes. When she took the clothes over to the address on the card, she wasn't allowed to see them. "This is like torture," she told them. "You don't have any reason to stall."

But they did stall, until Vern phoned several times and three days when by and Ellie got her children back along with the statement that there was nothing wrong with them.

"Whose idea was this?" Ellie asked in a fit of pique, but she didn't get an answer. Vern told it was all her fault because she was working where she was. Ellie couldn't see how it was her fault, and they had an argument over it. Ellie felt that Vern was dumping on her unfairly, although she was happy he'd got her children back for her when she couldn't seem to do it.

After three days with the Children's Aid, Robert and Susan appeared the same but Susan's skin was dry because she didn't have skin cream. Ellie spent quite a bit of time touching them and buying clothes and toys for them.

Ellie was so upset she cancelled her date with Quantz, and she thought she would never see him again. The following week, he called her at home. When she heard his deep voice on the phone, it was such a surprise, she felt faint. "I haven't seen you in a while," he said. "Want to go out?"

"Yes, er I mean, okay," she said. A commitment like this was a mistake, so she felt like a fool, but she wanted it all the same.

Quantz laughed. "That's good. Tomorrow then."

The next day, Ellie hurried as she was eager to see him. She drove her truck down a side road, almost out of sight of the highway because of a cornfield, and she was glad to see Quantz's Camaro. But his face was quizzical.

"Something wrong?" she asked as she got in beside him.

"A motel is better than a back road. What do you think?"

"Sure. Shutting everybody else out is incredibly romantic." Since the motel was only two miles away, they were quickly walking in the door. Ellie was breathless.

"We have all summer," Quantz said, "We are going to do it in different places all summer. And in different ways."

Quantz's smile was full of confidence.

"Great. It's just great." Ellie's chest heaved with anticipation. It was fine with Ellie to go to this motel which wasn't very busy this early on a week night. For her second meeting with Quantz, Ellie had told Vern she was going to a Tupperware party.

"Wait till I bolt the door."

"We have nothing to do but be together." Ellie pulled down the covers on the bed and sat down. Watching Quantz walk, she told herself she wanted him no matter what. She thought about the consequences, that she shouldn't be here, but her guilty reluctant feeling lasted about the length of time it took him to cross the floor.

Quantz was wonderful. Taking the cigarette out of his mouth, he wedged the chair under the doorknob. He checked the curtains for closure, and then he took the keys out of his pocket and put them on the table. "Let's see. We have four hours. What'll we do first?" He flung himself on the bed, flat on his back. Reaching for Ellie, he said, "We can get in bed and not get out of it until it's time to go home."

"I have to be home by midnight." Ellie was nervous so that she was fiddling with her clothes. "Even earlier."

"Do you have to? I can stay out all night."

This made Ellie think. She hesitated. This was going to be a problem, the differences in their lifestyles. Maybe the next time he asked she would refuse. "I shouldn't be here." She got off the bed and walked up and down. "Somebody'll see us. For sure."

"Don't worry," Quantz said, not budging off the bed, holding his arms out for her. "My car looks the same as everybody else's from the road."

"You're not worried? You wedged the door."

"Well, it's just a precaution."

"For what?" Ellie had the jitters.

"Let's have a beer." They drank some of the beer and Quantz put his cigarette on the bedside table. They started necking.

"You're a sweetheart," Quantz said. "Take it off, and get under the covers. Hurry up."

"You take yours off first."

"All right." Quantz stripped, then he got into bed and waited. While Ellie took off her clothes, he watched. "Everything," he said.

Once they were both under the sheets, Quantz kissed Ellie again. A real deep long one, like before, the kind that takes a person up in a hot air balloon.

"I like the way your skin smells," Ellie said.

Quantz laughed. Then he got on top.

"Put your arms around my neck." Then he touched her legs so she would put them around his. There was a great deal of Quantz to hang onto so he felt great to Ellie. At this moment, Ellie felt that their love was going to solve everything that had gone bad in her life.

"I really like this," she said in his ear.

"We could stay this way for a week or a month if we didn't have to go home," Quantz said.

After he came, he stayed on top. Ellie moved. "I have to go to the washroom."

"Don't get up."

"It's kind of difficult not to, isn't it? With all that beer?" When Ellie got up nude and walked to the washroom, Quantz had another hard-on.

When she came out of the washroom, Quantz covered his eyes with his hand. "Wear my shirt," he whispered.

"Why?"

"It's too adventurous. What if somebody saw you?"

"They won't. What if they did?"

Ellie went over and looked out the window. "There isn't anybody out there."

"Get back in bed. I just like to get in bed and stay there."

Ellie got back in bed and covered herself with the sheets and Quantz lifted the sheets.

"I like your breasts."

"Why?" Ellie found this hard to believe as she had small breasts and a large pear-shaped rear end. Hadn't he already said so?

"Because I just do. They're shaped to fit my hand with nothing hanging over."

"Vern thinks they're too small."

"I like your bum too."

"There's enough there to hold you up."

They made love a couple more times, then they had some more beer.

"If they had a stopwatch on us, we couldn't do it any faster," Ellie said, out of breath.

"I think you're trying to kill me," Quantz sighed. He was sitting up in bed. He was leaning against the headboard with an indulgent smile on his face, the snowy sheets pulled to his waist, the image of hedonism, pleasant, perfect, happy. Since he looked good enough to eat, Ellie nuzzled his shoulder. Then, she quickly pulled the sheets up over her body. Quantz sighed, "I probably won't be able to keep up this pace. We're the same kind of person," Quantz said. "We are entwined as one."

Ellie felt fabulous. "You're romantic. You're old-fashioned." She thought maybe he liked her quite a bit.

"Yes, I am." He sounded surprised at the thought. "You're more astute than I thought." He sounded pleased.

When he leaned back again on the bed, Ellie said, "I should go." She dressed. Then she picked the beer empties up.

"You don't think I worry about a little thing like that, do you?" Quantz said, in a sarcastic tone of voice.

"No, of course not," Ellie said, but she felt she had had her fingers rapped and she wondered why. When she followed him out, she left the empties behind.

As she got in Quantz's brown Chevrolet Camaro, she saw two men staring at them leaning against their rig. She didn't like the inquisitive, hostile expression on their faces as they waited. Ellie wished they were a married couple going out for a late-night pizza rather than a pair of cheaters sneaking home. She dreaded what Vern might say to her.

Quantz lit a cigarette, taking his time, and then he started his car and let it idle, as if it didn't bother him at all that the truckers were watching with intent curiosity. "Is this your first affair?"

"Why would you ask me such a thing?"

"I've had a couple of other affairs, in the past, of course. I had a girl once who was the most beautiful thing I ever saw. Then I saw her at a dance with somebody new. It darn near broke my heart." Quantz took the cigarette out of his mouth and checked the end of it. As he stubbed it out and started another, Ellie noticed he had stains on his fingers and bits of tobacco on his lip. "You can be my woman for awhile. I'll take you places. I'll buy you a gold necklace. You don't have one, do you?" Ellie caught her breath as he said these promises. Things were going too fast for her. Quantz was asking for a commitment.

"No," she said hesitantly.

"Good."

Then Quantz put his Camaro in gear and away they went.

"Keep your head down now, as we're almost in town."

Ellie thought if anyone saw her doing this, bobbing up and down, like a jack-in-the-box, they would think she was the silliest thing in the world, when she had a perfectly good husband and children at home, to be out with a man who was nothing at all but a lover. Ellie felt so silly with her head under the dash, that she started to laugh.

"What's so funny?"

"Nothing." But it struck her as humorous how important the sex was to her.

"Want to quit?"

"No." Ellie was willing and reluctant, addicted and superficial. She felt like an idiot.

"Don't bump your head." Quantz touched her on the head. "What about next week?"

"Next week is fine." Immediately, she began to think of ways of getting out of it, because of the excuses she had to find, and the guilty feeling she would have afterward. She was about to tell him her problems of the past few weeks, about her kids, but he seemed preoccupied or in a hurry. He didn't seem to have personal problems to tell. Maybe he just kept his negative side to himself. When he reached Ellie's truck, he kissed her.

When Ellie got home, she slid into bed beside Vern. She thought he was asleep, as he didn't respond to her touch. When he went to work in the morning, he didn't awaken Ellie so she slept in. Ellie was pissed off with Vern. It was mean of him to leave her, because she had to rush to get her house-work done and her kids ready and be on time for work at eleven-thirty in the morning. It's ridiculous to be late like this, she thought.

"Another hard night?" Steve said. He was behind the bar.

"Sorry, but I slept in," Ellie said.

"It's almost noon," Steve laughed at her. Ellie thought she was five minutes late.

At noon, Mr. Blue came in for his morning beer. He was the Bedford's best customer. "I lost so much money last night." He had bags under his eyes and a sour demeanour as he gloomily sat at the bar, hanging his head over his beer.

Steve had his morning beer with Mr. Blue. "Who won?"

"Not me. I lost."

"I heard you. Who did win the pot?"

"Quantz. He made me mad, coming in late, staying until morning and winning."

"He did!" Steve sounded surprised. At the mention of Quantz's name, Ellie could feel her back stiffen. She could almost feel Steve's next question. "That's kind of a surprise, isn't it? I wonder what he'll do with all his money?"

"Eh, what?"

"He wins most of the time, doesn't he?"

"No," Mr. Blue said, slowly. "Eh?"

Ellie thought Mr. Blue had the wits of a crocodile, since he sounded so slow in his speech. But then, he played cards all night and worked all day. Ellie didn't want him looking at her, even if he could see through those bleary eyes. Then when he asked her if she was a prostitute, and how much she charged, she thought she was hearing things. She didn't make an issue of the remark; she just ignored it. There wasn't a lot she could do about it. After lunch, Mr. Blue went back to his shop.

All afternoon, Ellie tended the customers who came into the bar.

At five o'clock, Vern came in with Beri. They perched on the stools side by side with a particular air of satisfaction about them.

As they ordered their drinks, Ellie realized Vern was watching her with narrowed eyes, the slits gleaming. "Where were you last night?"

"Out, I told you. At a Tupperware party. Then we had food and drinks after."

"You didn't buy anything?"

"I ordered it."

"Did you order my stuff, too?" Beri asked Ellie.

Ellie had put her order in ahead, so she could say yes she had.

"I didn't see the truck there," Vern said. "Somebody told me they saw you somewhere else."

"You were checking on me? I don't like that." Ellie said unhappily, trying to stifle the tears.

Vern shrugged. When Beri finished her rye, Vern said to her, "Let's go. We've got to pick up that plywood for George."

Ellie was shocked. "Why are you doing that now?" But she didn't get an answer.

After they left, Steve said, "I don't know what kind of an arrangement you have. It must be an open marriage, one of those magnaminous kind of relationships. Sounds like you have your cake and eat it too. Or do you? What about Vern?"

This wasn't the first time Steve had made a sarcastic remark about her personal life, and Ellie wondered what he was leading up to.

"Vern and I have our ups and downs, but mostly we stick together," Ellie said, hoping she sounded calm. Maybe Steve thought he was doing her a favor, but his interest bothered her. She wished he would mind his own business.

Ellie was glad to leave Steve behind, collect her kids from her new babysitter, and return home for the dinner hour.

Tonight, Vern was late, maybe deliberately, making Ellie feel even worse. The dinner was ready, and soon it would be ruined. Ellie wondered where she had gone wrong. Vern was late all the time, and she was liking somebody too much, somebody she shouldn't be with.

Ellie wondered what had happened to her, because in her mind and actions, her husband was no longer her main man. The way Vern was acting with Beri, Ellie thought it was just as well, and she was just lucky Quantz had come along. Ellie realized the way she was thinking could lead to disaster, thinking two wrongs made a right. What if Vern took up with Beri for good? Ellie thought he probably wouldn't.

Maybe they could sell their half of the duplex, because it wasn't a happy home now, Ellie decided, and buy something they liked better, such as a house in the country. Maybe it was because Vern worked shift work, rotating days then afternoons, so that they were seldom home together now that Ellie was working too.

After seven o'clock, Vern arrived for supper. He couldn't look at her. Ellie thought he had guilt written all over his face. She bit her tongue. "We should sell the house. Maybe it would help."

"Not now, for God's sake. I have a meeting tonight," Vern barked.

"Excuse me!" Ellie said.

"I don't need your bitching. Just serve it up."

When Ellie put the food on the table, Vern ate hurriedly. He asked for seconds of the steak and mashed potatoes.

Ellie watched him. "Can't the meeting wait? I don't like being a pit stop."

"Why, what's your problem?"

"You've hardly had two words to say to me lately."

"I've been busy. I've had a lot on my mind and you seem to be doing what you like anyway, no problem at all." Vern rolled his eyes and threw up his hands.

"You're too tired after your date with Beri?"

"So that's it?" Vern started to laugh. "Jealous? Looks good on you."

"It looks bad. Everybody is talking," Ellie confessed.

"Let them talk. Words are cheap. Hot air."

"Just the same, I don't like it."

"You're the one who wanted to work there."

"Not that again. You're just using it as an excuse not to get along." Vern's face was a mixture of disbelief and interest. Ellie continued, "The kids have gone to bed early or haven't you noticed? We could go to bed, too."

"Well, I guess I could miss the meeting."

"You make me feel like I have to beg."

Vern didn't seem too eager, maybe since he'd been with Beri. Ellie knew Vern wouldn't tell her what he'd been doing, so she didn't ask. Ellie just wanted to put Vern in a position where she could tell him to perform. She wondered what made her so hard-hearted all of a sudden. Maybe she wanted to compare.

Ellie took her clothes off.

"Look at the tan lines on your skin," Vern laughed.

Ellie walked over to the window and pulled the living room drapes shut. Vern laughed again.

"What's so funny?"

"Your ass is like two white pigs in a sack when you walk."

Vern had a tummy and bony legs, but it didn't seem to bother him. Vern never got a tan, not even a burn. His flesh was white and soft and covered with little black hairs.

"We're going to bed and the sun isn't even down?" Vern asked.

"Yeah, and on the couch, too."

Tires crunched gravel in the drive next door, and Vern leapt up from the couch and went to the kitchen window to see who it was. He was completely naked.

"Who is it?" Ellie asked Vern.

"The people next door."

"What are you so nervous about?"

"Nothing."

"Come back here. Someone will see you," Ellie pleaded.

"The windows are high." Vern scratched at his crotch.

When Vern came back to the couch, he had a hard-on. Ellie giggled when she saw it. Vern was amorous now, grabbing her arm and wrenching her around. Vern flipped her over, using the couch as a prop and went at her backwards. In a few moments, he got off like an explosion.

"Not too romantic," Ellie said, massaging the twinge in her back. Maybe she was expecting too much, because she had to ask, and Vern was reluctant or in a hurry. She wanted to see if Vern still liked her, if they still had something special they used to have going for them.

"Don't you feel like a woman?"

"No."

"You don't respond properly. You wouldn't know your ass from a hole in the ground."

"You're so sarcastic."

Ellie felt bad, and she thought there was no reason for it, as Beri was no prize and no one to be jealous over. What was she supposed to do? Wait until he thought of having sex?

Right away, Vern reached for his socks. "I don't have all night to spend with you, that's all."

"I always thought what a person said was really important. What's with you anyway? Did you enjoy yourself, Vern? It doesn't seem like it."

"I'm busy and I can't wait for you."

"I'll remember that for next time."

"You're so gloomy. You see the negative side of things. You have a dripping bag over your head. Give it a rest," Vern said.

Ellie wondered what made them want to hurt each other so much. The meanness and pettiness that invaded their lives threatened to take over.

Vern finished dressing quickly.

"Don't you want to put clean clothes on?"

"Gee. Why would I need clean clothes? I said it was a meeting. You can think of more reasons to hold me up."

Upset, Ellie started to snivel in spite of herself. She felt her needs had become very unimportant.

"Oh, for God's sake! What's the matter now?"

"Not a thing!"

"You got what you wanted, didn't you? So what's the matter now?"

"Nothing!"

"It doesn't look like it, but I don't have time to get it figured out, now, if ever." Vern grabbed his jacket, almost tripped over Ellie's leg as she sprawled naked on the couch. He threw his jacket at her. Then, he ran out the door.

The way Vern was made Ellie upset. He had a great opinion of himself, which meant that she never got anywhere discussing things with him. Trying to have a conversation or be intimate just made things worse. Fighting to the bitter end, he was obtuse enough about human nature that Ellie couldn't insult him in the same way he insulted her. Ellie thought Vern hated her. He had loved her once, but she couldn't remember when.

As Ellie cleaned up the dishes, tears ran down her face and onto the dirty dinner plates.

Then she had a shower, and the tears and sobs mixed in with the soap and water. She didn't know what she was crying for, as she had no intention of looking back, at anything.

* * *

CHAPTER EIGHT

When Vern came home from the meeting later that night, he told Ellie bad news, that Moose had tried to commit suicide, so when Moose came in to say hello the next day, Ellie was surprised to see his innocent eyes, bouncing step, and carefree smile. She noticed that his right wrist wrapped in a thick bandage was mostly covered by a long-sleeved shirt.

She thought he had every reason to be happy, so why would he want to put an end to his own life?

"Hi, what have you been doing since I saw you last? I'll have a beer even though I don't need it." Moose patted his little belly. He grabbed his beer and slurped it.

"What happened?" Ellie asked, because she wanted to hear his side of the story.

"I stood up my date with death," Moose said, in a jocular tone.

"What!" His reply wasn't what Ellie was expecting. She was expecting a cover-up.

"I sliced it on broken glass. I had an accident, I said." Moose sounded testy. "Why do people have accidents?"

"I believe you." Ellie tried to be sympathetic.

"No, you don't. You don't sound like you believe me at all." Moose looked petulant.

"Yes, I do," Ellie repeated. Ellie knew Moose had sliced his wrist with a shard of glass sticking out of the window frame trying to get in his front door.

"They said I cut it because I was suicidal. But I talked them out of that idea. Otherwise I would be spending time on the Psych Ward. I locked myself out and cut my arm reaching the lock. Ain't that a catastrophe?"

"I guess so." Ellie didn't believe he would do a desperate, stupid thing like put his fist through a window, like they were saying he did. He could have severed a vein on the sharp shards and bled to death. Maybe he was mental, but he looked and acted normal.

"My problem is I have one thing and I want something else," Moose said to Ellie in an irritable voice.

Ellie had wondered why he came to check on her almost every day, but she asked, "So what's bothering you? Is it what's going on at work?"

"I'm going to be promoted at work. They're trying to groom me, make me presentable. I have everything that a person could possibly want," Moose said. "But it's not making me feel good. I'm miserable." Moose looked disconsolate and lonely.

"We have that in common." Ellie thought she was miserable too, but she just hadn't done anything about it.

"Why, is the old man hard on you?"

"Right now, we're fighting all the time."

"Why?"

Ellie shrugged, trying not to meet Moose's eyes.

Moose studied her for a minute. "I have a mind, you know, but you'd never know it to hear me talk. I have to go to English classes and get my grammar up."

"Maybe you're being too hard on yourself. Everybody takes English."

"Didn't I hear you say you were taking courses and Vern's mad about it."

"He thinks stuff like that is a waste of time and money. I wrote a poem once that somebody set to music but I didn't keep a copy. I could write another. It would be better than trying to remember, wouldn't it?"

"I don't know."

"Once it's gone, it's gone." At high school, Ellie's teachers encouraged her to be a writer, but she hadn't followed it up. She was too busy getting married and working.

"I spend time thinking, but it doesn't get me anywhere." Moose's lashes were thick and fair. A girl would envy such looks. As Moose played with his beer glass, Ellie waited for him to say something revealing.

"I'll have another beer," Moose said. "Going back to school is like starting over again. I'm scared. What if I fail? Will I lose my job?" He was almost wild-eyed with fear, so that Ellie felt like putting her arms around him.

"You're real smart, Moose. You can do it."

"I've got big dreams too, such as owning my own factory some day," Moose said.

"You're real smart," she repeated. Ellie thought there was nothing wrong with a dream because it was something to look forward to.

"I wish you could be different, more outgoing," Moose said. "We could get it on together."

"Oh, ah." Ellie felt was stupid to be so surprised and so tongue-tied. "You must like older women."

"I'd rather have a broad than a chick. They don't put on such an act, such a prim and proper act. You're a broad."

"Moose!" Ellie was shocked.

"I didn't mean anything by it. I meant you're experienced and sophisticated."

"Maybe in a month or so when things cool off."

"Why, you in some kind of trouble with your old man?"

"No, but he's upset about what's happening at work right now." Ellie thought they had got closer because they both had troubles and both needed a confidant.

"So am I. I might not get promoted. I'll still be doing overtime," Moose said.

Ellie saw Beri came in at five to nine. She looked perfect, freshly made up. She wasn't a pretty woman, but when she walked about the room, everybody would look at her springy gait. She squinted at Moose. "You've been avoiding me."

"And hello to you, too," Moose said, giving her a hug.

"Why don't your friends call you John? Why don't you have a name like any normal person would?"

"I hunt wildlife. That's why the guys call me Moose." Moose eyed her figure. "You sure look good tonight."

"Don't flatter me like that. It's disgusting," Beri said. "You hunt a lot but you don't catch much, do you?"

"Ooh," Moose kissed her. "Sorry."

Beri gave Moose a supercilious look. "Don't patronize me!"

Ellie thought Beri probably considered Moose inconstant, as he sure appeared to be. When Beri went to the washroom, Moose said, "It'll take all my skills to get back in her good graces."

"She'll phone your wife," Ellie pointed out reasonably, "to get back at you."

Moose ignored Ellie. "I hear you and Beri went shopping."

"What's it to you?"

"Now you're both mad at me," Moose said. Ellie thought to be the recipient of anger must be his normal state.

"Are you going to leave your wife for her?"

"Not unless I have to. I may have to. Cathy is hot these days. Ooh, hoo, hoo, is she mad at me." Moose sucked air between his teeth. "I stayed out all night playing cards with the boys. I might get kicked out for awhile. Can I come and live with you?"

"No." Ellie could imagine problems.

"You're a hard-hearted woman."

"That's a laugh. I thought I was a pushover."

"You're a hard worker. Cathy never does anything around the house, but she reads all day. I guess I better get on home while the getting's good." Ellie thought Moose was just as sober when he left as when he came in. He only had two beers. He never had any more than two that Ellie saw.

Moose had just gone out the side door, when Beri came back from the washroom. She had paid extra attention to her makeup, but she didn't seem to notice the empty stool.

"He said he had to get home," Ellie explained.

"Kind of early for him, isn't it?" Her expression was stony, cold and dazed. She was high, maybe. She wasn't supposed to smoke them in the bar, and most of the time she respected that rule. She skated around in her heels replacing the ashtrays.

Tiny came into the bar looking for Moose, groaned, and left again. "You girls aren't much help," he said over his shoulder.

"How about that! Wanting to borrow money from Moose," Beri told Ellie. "What a jerk!" she told Tiny's disappearing back. To put in time, Ellie wiped the counters and filled the cocktail containers.

At about nine-fifteen, Ruth Jimson came into the bar, followed by Steve. She sat at one end of the bar, and Steve sat at the other, observing Ruth drink a rye.

Mr. Blue came in and bought Ruth a drink. She had two rye in front of her, and Steve's expression verged on belligerent. Mr. Blue was in such a good mood that he tipped Ellie a dime instead of a nickel.

"Quite the romance!" Steve said to Ellie.

Ruth Jimson wore extremely tight short skirts, and Steve would have put her out right away, but he didn't want to offend one of his best customers. Finally, Steve asked Mr. Blue, "What do you see in her?"

"She has nice legs," Mr. Blue laughed. "She has long slim legs. Don't you, Ruth?"

"You're a flatterer today," Ruth said, her face like a fish.

"Have another drink and then we can go somewhere," Mr. Blue said. Ruth was an amazingly fast drinker.

"I should be at home," Ruth said. "I have things I should be doing at home."

"Like what for example?"

"Like washing my hair."

Mr. Blue grimaced with pain. "You could come out and feed the chickens. Then it won't matter."

"Chickens? I thought you were a businessman!" Steve laughed loudly. Mr. Blue blushed beet-red.

"Shush up, now. You'll spoil things." Mr. Blue bought a round of drinks for everybody at the bar, including Ruth, just so it wouldn't look like he was coming onto her, and he counted out the cost of the round nickel by nickel, wincing with every nickel. He didn't leave a tip for Ellie.

Ellie noticed Ruth had come near, so she turned around to see what she wanted. "Am I a baddie?" Ruth asked Ellie in a low voice. Ruth had long curly black hair, very red lipstick and puffy eyes behind her glasses. She was forty-six. "Should I go?"

"I don't know. It's up to you."

"Maybe Mr. Blue wants a wife," Beri interrupted. "Here's your chance."

"He's so suffocating. He's so obsessed," Ruth said.

"Men get like that," Beri said.

"Do they?" Ruth said, her voice like a honk. "What would I knooow?"

Ellie thought Ruth was getting tanked, finally. She was not a cheap drunk.

Ruth gave Ellie a small cardboard box. "Here's something for your birthday." Ellie found a small necklace with a pendant on it.

"You really shouldn't have." The gift made Ellie feel uncomfortable, so she handed it back to Ruth. Ruth gave Ellie a dirty look. "I wanted you to have that so badly," Ruth chided Ellie. "It means we could be friends."

After Ruth tucked the box back in her purse, she went to the washroom, swinging her behind and Mr. Blue watched her every move.

"She has great legs, but she sure drinks a lot, doesn't she?" Mr. Blue told Steve.

"You're famous for your affairs, aren't you?" Steve said.

Mr. Blue put his head back to laugh, and Ellie could see the gaps in his teeth when his mouth was wide open like that.

Ruth came back from the washroom. She sat beside Mr. Blue. Wayne came with her, dressed in black shirt, black slacks, and black stetson, just the person Ellie didn't want to see. She thought his expression was as black and rude as his outfit.

Wayne sat down beside Steve and ordered a beer. "Still working here," Wayne glowered at Ellie. "You're tougher than I thought. You must need the money."

Ellie noticed he was unpleasant, but Steve was glad to see him. "What business brings you back to town?" Steve asked Wayne. For a few moments, they discussed their upcoming deals, the cost of a new restaurant.

"You can buy this hotel for less than the cost of a franchise," Steve said.

Beri laughed behind her hand at Ruth settling herself beside Mr. Blue. Then Beri got called to the back of the room for orders. There was a lake freighter in port.

Steve watched Ruth staring at the sailors.

"You can always go with them if you don't want to go with Mr. Blue. If you're that hard up," he said to her.

Ruth yelled, "My money is as good as anybody else's. Even yours, Steve. You must have a lot of money stashed away somewhere."

Steve's mouth dropped open.

"You're out for all you can get, aren't you?" Steve asked Ruth. "You're a gold digger, no shame to you at all!"

"What do you mean by that?" Ruth shrieked. She was outraged. She must be vastly drunker than usual, Ellie thought.

"C'mon, Ruth, let's go!" Mr. Blue grabbed her arm.

Ruth gazed meaningfully at Ellie as Mr. Blue pulled her by. Maybe she was down on her luck, Ellie thought.

"He won't speak to her after," Beri said. "He's a nice man and Ruth is, well, not much."

"I think he'll be heartbroken if she turns him down," Ellie surmised.

"You're an innocent," Beri said.

"You watch yourself," Wayne said very quietly as Ellie set up his second beer. "I'll see your children disappear for good."

"You wouldn't!" Ellie gasped at his threat. She noticed he laughed at her reaction. Ellie disliked him intensely.

Ellie thought there sure were different ways of looking at people. Mr. Blue was a respected businessman but a slob, and Ruth Jimson was a hooker but she was like a lucky baby found on the street in a garbage bag, having avoided suffocation, starvation, and exposure. Compared to Wayne who Ellie thought was the worst, lowest worm of a person she'd ever met, they were wonderful people. She could have thrown daggers in his back as he left the bar, but they'd be more like paring knives.

At eleven-forty, Ellie saw Quantz came in after the evening shift. Why hadn't he bought her a necklace yet?

"What's up?" His face was happy and expectant.

"I should ask you that," Ellie said, suspicious.

"What's going on between you two?" Beri scrutinized Ellie as she set up the drinks for Beri's order.

Quantz said to Beri, "I heard what went on here last night. This place has a terrible reputation."

"I wasn't working." Beri's voice was shrill. Beri sounded as if she was going to freak out.

When Beri left with her tray, Quantz asked Ellie, "What is the matter with her? Usually she is cool."

"She can leave you alone," Ellie said, tensely.

"You would be jealous." Quantz reached over the counter, but Ellie ducked his arm.

Beri came up beside Quantz. He said, "I was just reaching for an ashtray."

"Why would I care what you people do?" Beri said.

"Man, you're uptight. What's the trouble? You can tell me." He whispered in her ear.

"It's nothing." Beri left the room.

"You make a good shoulder to cry on," Ellie said.

"You're jealous." He had a smirk on his face.

"I'm not in the least." Ellie's tone was frosty and a bit possessive.

"Doesn't sound like it." Ellie noticed Quantz was carefully watching her face.

"Are you still here?" Beri demanded of Quantz as she came back into the room.

"If you keep going to the washroom, you'll get fired," Quantz said.

"Keep it up and you'll get cut off." Beri looked down her nose at Ellie as she collected her order. She dropped the money onto the floor.

Ellie had to pick it up to ring in the order, and give Beri the change. They glowered at each other. Ellie thought Beri was mad she that liked Quantz.

"You girls should lighten up. Enjoy life. I'm free and easy. I do what I like," he said. "The world is a vast opportunity for insecurity."

"We don't want to be like you, got it?" Beri was hostile. "You blabbermouth!"

"Be cool. It's the only way to be," he said. "The only way is to go with the flow."

Ellie laughed, because those were her sentiments right now. She leaned on the counter in a friendly way to talk to Quantz.

When Beri came back from delivering her order, Quantz and Ellie had their heads together.

Beri took Ellie around the corner.

"What's the matter with you? Why do you like him? He has a wife and children!" she said, hissing. "Not to mention you have a husband and children."

Ellie shrugged. "Beri, you're jumping to conclusions."

"Good!" Beri went to clear the glasses off the tables.

Quantz refused a refill.

"I can only have one drink. I have a card game tonight," Quantz said. In a way, Ellie thought he was kind of exciting. "I shouldn't even go. I'm into heavy stuff way over my head."

"Why?"

"I got a knife in the side after a poker game in Toronto," Quantz said, quietly. "It could happen again."

"You didn't tell me that!"

"I won a lot of money. I'm good, I'm lucky, and I'm crazy. I guess they thought they could take me." His grin was even and confident, his voice calm. Quantz could really bluff, Ellie thought. He could play-act anything and be believed.

"You're lucky they didn't kill you."

"You're right. They could have," Quantz said. His grin was getting unnatural. "I went into a restaurant and bandaged it up in the washroom. Don't look at me like that. It's healed up." Quantz lifted his shirt to show Ellie. The scar was like a pink salmon slash on his ribcage. "I've had a good life, so I guess I won't worry about what could happen tonight." He sounded as if he was trying to explain something, since he was laying it on so thick.

Ellie didn't want an explanation. She wasn't married to him. Lucky her. "What did you tell your wife?"

"I told Norma I fell down the steps." He searched his pockets for his cigarettes. Then, he rummaged for his lighter. "Seen Moose?"

"He left just before you came in."

Quantz turned to see what Beri was doing, and then he glanced at Ellie to see if she was watching. She was.

Quantz put his cigarette lighter back in his pocket and stood up. Ellie noticed he constantly checked on things. Ellie thought he worked both ends against the center. When he went out the door, Beri smirked. "I think you're nuts to like a guy like that. You can't trust guys like that."

Ellie thought if he messed around she'd kill him, but probably someone else would beat her to it. She felt in a compartmentalized way that ignored reality that their spouses weren't involved in this secret relationship where Ellie and Quantz considered each other first and foremost.

Beri worked hard so they would be through on time.

Then, they had a drink with the band members. The dim light made Beri's face tougher and her expression exaggerated. "How come you didn't tell me about

Moose?" Beri's shrill voice was like a siren.

"I thought you knew," Ellie said. "Everybody did."

"All you can think about is your lover. Your standards in men aren't too high," Beri said. "I know you two are sweet on each other. I can see it in your face. What are you going to do about it?"

"I don't know." Ellie sighed. She felt so discouraged she had another drink instead of going straight home.

* * *

CHAPTER NINE

At the Bedford on Friday, the fifteenth of July, watching the eight-sided square from the bar's window, Ellie thought everything important in town happened here, socializing in the park, or shopping. She thought it was a symbol of frustration to be faced with a continuous reflection, like a treadmill, rather than looking out and beyond.

Ellie saw Beri driving around the square in a brown corvette, her bleached hair swinging behind her, and her snappy car travelling many revolutions.

Then, Ellie saw Moose following her on his motorcycle. His helmet covered his face, but Ellie noticed the thick bandage on his wrist. A young girl held on behind him.

Beri looked far from cool. With a dazed expression on her face, she drove recklessly around until the cops pulled her over for speeding.

Beri snatched the ticket out of the cop's hand, stormed into the Bedford and threw her keys across the bar's counter. Moose followed her in.

"I thought you were going to drive over the cop's foot," Moose said, chortling.

"Don't get funny," Beri snapped. "You laugh at fucking everything."

Ellie thought it was a good thing the bar was almost empty the performance they were putting on.

Moose continued to laugh at Beri. "You'll be walking now, won't you? You'll have too many points off your license."

"You just wait till it happens to you," Beri said.

"It'll never happen to me," Moose chuckled.

George Toogood came into the bar. When George heard the news, he laughed too. "She'll be calling me all the time for rides. How will she get to work?"

"Okay, laugh!" Beri said. "Wait till it happens to you."

"I doubt it will." George grinned, showing his teeth. Ellie saw that George's brown hair was tousled, and his long beard dishevelled. His delicate rhinestone stud earring was an odd contrast in his tough exterior.

Ellie thought he glowered at her so it rattled her.

Every time Ellie opened her mouth, she thought the situation got worse and worse. His emotionless stare was unnerving. Ellie thought that he had more to him than he appeared.

"You look cool," Ellie shuddered as she set up his beer.

"Beri's never seen the real me. She's too busy getting into scrapes." George never lost his wide grin.

"What's that supposed to mean?" Beri squealed.

She smoked pot and drank all the time, trying not to be bored, Ellie thought. Maybe George could make her life more interesting.

George put his arm around Beri to console her and calm her down. "I'm a tiger in disguise," he said, his arm flopped over her shoulder.

Beri rubbed her nose against George's shirt.

Moose said to Ellie, "I wish I could have a relationship like that. I didn't know she liked George that much." Moose's face showed worry lines.

"Don't you like Cathy?"

"You're right. What would I do if I wasn't married?" Ellie thought Moose was well loved, but he couldn't always remember it. Moose said, "It's nice to be married. Don't you like to be married?"

"Well, sometimes I do and sometimes I don't," Ellie said.

"If it wasn't for my kids, I'd be gone."

When Ellie looked up in surprise, Moose shrugged. Ellie wondered why he confided in her. What was he after? Then she figured she was the captive audience. Beri was angry, and Cathy was busy.

Ellie thought Moose liked to be romantic. What he didn't get from one woman, he got from another.

"I don't think I'll ever be in love. Women take advantage of men," Moose said sadly.

"What happened to make you feel that way?" Ellie wanted to be considerate of Moose's fragile feelings.

"I had a bad experience."

"So what else is new?" Ellie thought of her disappointing experiences.

Moose laughed. "You're hardhearted."

Moose had got dumped by a young woman, or got found out. Ellie couldn't remember the details. He made promises and didn't keep them. He played one person off against the other. Ellie didn't want to get tied up with such a man.

"You have so much going for you that I find it hard to believe you could get so blue," Ellie said, commiserating.

"Do you think I'm blue? I guess I am." Moose's wavering eyes reflected his moods, a precarious elan or intermittent gloom. "I'm afraid of growing older. Look at me." He pointed to his little potbelly, and the faint creases on his forehead.

"Most of us are married," Ellie said. "It's no big deal. It's like wearing shoes instead of going barefoot."

Moose groaned. "How unromantic."

"It's not unromantic. It's just realistic."

"You're shy and a bit uptight. I'll give you something to help you relax. I've been drinking all day and taking these too." Moose pulled a bean out of his pocket. He pressed it into the palm of Ellie's hand. "That will help you forget. You'll get a buzz on."

Ellie fingered the bean reluctantly. "Why would you give that to me?"

"Take it and then tell me what you thought of it." He seemed so eager and so serious over something like a pill, like a kid over a candy. Ellie put the bean in her purse.

"You'll like it. I'm into states of mind and going with your emotions. It's like dreams."

Ellie smiled. "I think love is everything." Ellie thought sex and love wrapped up together were the most important thing, but she wouldn't dare tell Moose that. She would seem to be encouraging him. "Love is wonderful when you have it."

"That will help," Moose said.

"What will help?" Beri asked, all ears now.

"What are you two doing?" George asked.

"Talking, weren't you listening?" Moose asked.

"No," George said. His forehead knotted. "I have this feeling I missed something."

"Too bad. You can't have everything."

Steve came in with Quantz and Vern. Ellie thought immediately Vern was watching her more closely.

"Isn't this a cosy foursome?" Steve asked. "What are you talking about?"

"Marriage," Ellie said.

"A good subject," George said.

"Be single," Steve said. "Forget about marriage."

"I've never been single," Moose said. "I've been married for a hundred years."

"And it never gets any better," Steve said.

"No," Quantz agreed.

"You guys," Beri said. "Aren't they awful?"

"I'm staying out of it," Ellie said, aware Vern was watching her.

"What's the matter with your marriage, Quantz?" Beri asked.

"I don't discuss my private life at this bar," Quantz said.

"Why not? Everyone else does," Vern said.

"No kidding," Moose said, in disbelief.

"I'm not like some people who can't keep their mouth shut," Quantz said. "Or keep their stories straight."

"I'm in trouble now. You jealous or something?" Moose said to Quantz. "Everybody is on my case. Especially Cathy."

"Cathy phoned Norma last night to check what went on the other night, to see if you had gone to the card party after all," Quantz said. "And Norma told her you didn't show."

"Oh, shit. She never said anything to me," Moose said.

"Not yet, you mean," Quantz said.

"She's gathering in the evidence. She'll kick me out again. Thanks for warning me."

"What's a friend for? But Jesus, I wish you'd be more careful," Quantz said. Ellie could see Vern just shaking his head.

Ellie noticed Steve was listening intently with his mouth hanging open, trying to hear as much as possible.

But the bar was getting noisy, full of customers on the Friday night, so Steve ran the till, and Ellie went on the floor to help Beri.

Ellie didn't notice the young girl sitting beside Moose at the back of the room until Cathy came into the bar. Moose got right up from the table and walked over to Cathy. The girl put down her drink and disappeared.

"Doesn't Sally want to say hello to me?" Cathy asked.

"She's babysitting," Moose said. "She had to go."

"That's odd. I called her and she said she was going out. I had to ask my mother. Again," Cathy said.

"Let's have a drink, you and I," Moose said. Moose squeezed Cathy on the shoulder and glanced at Ellie. "Don't mind us, we're just friends. Bring us a couple will you? I'd be lonely without her." He squeezed Cathy again. Cathy smiled, her thin lips pressed together. They sat down at the same table.

When Ellie took their drinks over, she cleared away the glasses. The girl's pop was half-full.

"We just got started," Moose said.

"Save my place, will you," Cathy said, patting the seat of her chair. "I've got to go to the washroom."

Moose laughed.

Ellie went back up to the bar.

"What are they saying?" Steve asked.

"He never learns," Vern said drily, "to leave the drinks alone and to have one woman at a time."

"You guys," Beri said. "What do you think of this bunch, Ellie?"

"Yeah, really. There's the main action and then there's the one's who watch," Ellie said. She was unimpressed.

"Moose has good luck with women," Steve said wistfully.

Quantz, Vern and George laughed at Steve.

Cathy came back in and sat down. She had a vacant, far-away expression on her face. Cathy and Moose talked in a huddle, with their two red heads together. Cathy looked very unhappy. Then, Moose put his arm around her, and together they walked out of the bar.

"I don't think he can keep it together," Vern said, as they left.

"His bad luck just piles up," Quantz said. "He's wet behind the ears, green and inexperienced."

"Oh, I don't know," Steve said. "I envy him."

"Keep cool," George said. "I think I'll be on my way."

Ellie watched George and Vern go out the side door. She wondered what they were up to. Steve went upstairs.

Quantz had another beer. Ellie washed up. "I think we should be careful," he said to her. "We're lucky we weren't caught. I had blood on my underwear but I got them washed before Norma found them." Ellie thought she must have started her period, and didn't realize it until she had sex.

"That's good." Ellie thought this mistake was bad luck.

"Moose is nosing around," Quantz said. "He's asking questions."

"Well, he can mind his own business." Ellie raised her chin.

"He won't. It just isn't in him."

"Moose likes to have power over his friends. He knows a lot of people." Ellie thought Moose was trying to initiate a new relationship with her.

"What do you mean?" Quantz sat straight up, instantly curious.

"Like you, for example. He gets you to cover for him until things return to normal with his wife."

"Cathy and Moose have knockdown, dragout fights. Even if Cathy is covered with bruises, Moose doesn't win."

"Maybe you don't help enough." Ellie put her hands on her hips. She thought these men stood back and watched. They thought the women's feelings were umimportant.

Quantz shrugged. He was so nonchalant. That's what Ellie didn't like about these men. They didn't really give a damn. One way or the other, they just kept trying the stories until one washed. If things got hot with one woman, they just shrugged and went to the next.

"Maybe she's just sick of it," Ellie pressed her point.

Quantz shrugged again in a careless way that was so irritating.

Ellie saw Moose came back into the bar later on that night. He was in a bad mood, his face a black scowl. He told Ellie he and Cathy had just had another terrible fight.

Tiny came in and sat beside Moose. Vern came in too, and Ellie was surprised to see him for the second time in one night.

"What's happening?" Ellie asked Vern.

"Meetings. Trouble," Vern sighed. He looked weary.

Moose tipped his beer up. Ellie thought maybe he was trying to drink himself into oblivion.

Tiny was trying to negotiate something with Moose.

"Don't come on to to me," Moose said softly. He didn't say it nicely. His voice made the hair on Ellie's neck stand up. Ellie saw him glaring at Tiny.

Tiny sidled closer to Moose, crouching his head over the bar, his hair almost dangling in Moose's beer.

"All I want to do is borrow some bread for a few days," Tiny whined to Moose. "You owe me one."

Moose lifted Tiny's hair away from his beer. "I told you never to mention that again," he said, in a threatening voice.

Ellie wondered why Moose would owe Tiny money, if it would be over a card game or a favor, but that couldn't be true as it was always Tiny who was borrowing, wasn't it?

"Some people can't take a hint," Moose continued.

"Too bad," Tiny sneered. "This is never going to be over."

"I've decided I'm not going to back down. You can threaten all you like and I'm not going to cave." The half-scared, half-angry expression on Moose's face made Ellie recall an earlier threat Tiny had made. Ellie wondered what it was all about.

Ellie glanced at Vern to see what he thought of this conversation, but he was talking to Quantz.

"What makes you think I won't stick a gun in your face," Moose continued, "if it gets in my way too often?"

"You won't do that!" Tiny muttered, almost a whisper. "I'm not the one you have to worry about. All I'm trying to do is help."

Ellie was shocked at their conversation.

"I warned you not to push it!" Moose leaped off his stool, knocking it to the floor with a crash. He pummelled Tiny's face. He picked up a stool, swiping the bar clear. In one motion, he broke glasses and banged Tiny's forehead.

For a moment, Tiny cowered on the floor, stunned by the blow to his face. Then he grabbed the edge of the bar to get up. Tiny was a big guy, and he towered over Moose as he stood against the bar, clenching and unclenching his fist.

Moose poked the end of the stool toward Tiny, as if he was goading him.

"Here, cut that out." Vern, Quantz and a couple other customers pushed Tiny aside and briskly escorted Moose out into the back alley.

Ellie handed Tiny a rag and he mopped at the blood oozing from the cut over his eye. "Why would you help me? Nobody else does," he asked Ellie as he disappeared through the side door.

"Don't drip on the rug," Ellie said, pissed off.

Steve came downstairs, though the bar and out, as Ellie pointed toward the rear exit.

Ellie followed Steve outside. She was startled at the commotion in the alley, the wrestling and shouting. She was jumpy with nerves.

Ellie was afraid what was going to happen to Moose, when he was being threatened like that. Suddenly, as she saw him trying to protect himself against the guys who were supposed to be his friends, she thought he was acting desperately, as if he was going to be killed and what could she do to prevent it? She couldn't decide who his enemy was, and maybe he couldn't either so he was fighting with everybody. She had never seen anyone move so fast and so viciously, as Moose did, writhing from their grasp.

Moose was kicking and fighting like a crazy thing. He had broken a bottle and he was brandishing it. Everybody had backed off.

"Get back into the bar!" Steve said, but Ellie stood paralyzed behind Steve.

Moose had his back to the brick wall and he edged back and forth holding the broken bottle under his friend's noses.

"Just try me. Anybody want to try me?"

"Calm down," Quantz said in a friendly manner. He reached for Moose and Moose kicked at him.

"Keep your hands off me!" Moose breathed heavily as the others stood back.

"You're crazy," Quantz said.

"I'll take you on, I'll take you all on." Moose jerked and waved the bottle in a semicircle. Moose moved away from the wall and quickly Vern got behind him and lifted Moose off the ground pinning his arms back.

Immediately, Steve belted Moose across the mouth.

Vern threw the broken bottle into the garbage bin.

Steve was fuming. "Consider yourself lucky if I don't lay a charge. Go home before I call the cops, and don't bother coming back here."

After Moose roared off in his car, Steve, Vern and Quantz followed Ellie back in for a drink. "He's cut off for the rest of his life. Moose was always a troublemaker," Steve said. "Maybe someday, he'll grow up."

Ellie watched them drink their beer, amazed they were laughing and cool, and she was shaking like a leaf. She thought Moose was headed for serious trouble and he didn't seem to want to do anything about it.

"Cut them off before they get like that," Steve said sternly to Ellie.

"It's past one o'clock," Ellie reminded Steve. Her mouth felt terribly dry as she watched Steve get another beer for Vern and Quantz.

"Is it? Gee, this night has passed quickly. I didn't get done what I was going to do when I went upstairs," Steve said.

"You're quite a guy. What would we do without this hotel?" Quantz asked.

"It's not you. It's that friend of yours," Steve said to Quantz. "Whew!"

* * *

CHAPTER TEN

After the fight, Vern took Ellie home.

"It was nice of you to wait for me," Ellie said. "A pleasant surprise."

"I don't want to make a habit of it. You have to behave yourself, or I'm going to take drastic action." Vern's expression was glum.

Ellie thought Vern had heard what Wayne had had to say to the cops a few weeks ago. She felt bad because she thought she was innocent. "You're jumping to conclusions, Vern."

"I'm warning you. Don't you forget it." Vern went to bed and left her on the couch. Ellie figured by his response that he didn't believe her, so she spent a sleepless night. She couldn't get relaxed and comfortable.

At 11:28 in the morning, Ellie reached the bar. The stale cigarettes and booze didn't cover up something reminiscent of a butcher shop, fresh, oozing and raw - Tiny's bloody nose and Moose's cut hand. Ellie almost turned around and went home, but she collected her till, switched on the lights.

Steve followed her into the lounge. "If you don't feel like working I'll do it. I mean it."

"No, I'm fine. I feel fine." Ellie figured she must look tired.

Mr. Blue was the first one in the door.

"Did you hear about the uproar we had in here last night?" Steve asked Mr. Blue.

"Was it on the news?" Mr. Blue said slowly and stupidly.

"No," Steve said.

Mr. Blue ordered a bottle of sparkling wine.

"The way you're dressed you could date the queen," Steve said.

"I'm going to a wedding." Mr. Blue wore a navy suit and so much aftershave that Ellie sneezed.

"I think I'll go upstairs. You'll be all right, won't you?" Steve asked Ellie.

"Sure."

"Talk to you later," Mr. Blue said to Steve. Steve waved goodbye.

"Ah-ooh," Mr. Blue said softly. "What's new with you? "

Ellie ignored his remark. Mr. Blue finished his bottle of sparkling wine and asked for another one. He waved a wad of cash in front of Ellie's nose. "Want to earn some of this money?"

"What do you mean?" Ellie thought he didn't need to be after her for a twosome. Blue put his money away. She had to admit she found his money appealing but him repulsive.

Beri flopped her wide-brimmed hat on a stool beside her and her large shopping bag on the floor. "Whew, it's hot out there. You're lucky you're in the air-conditioning." It was easy to see what kind of frumpy mood Beri was in. "Everything exciting happens in this bar, isn't that right?"

"Not since I've been here," Mr. Blue said slowly, grunting and scratching. "Maybe you'll be more amiable."

Beri stared at Mr. Blue. Then she whispered to Ellie, "He's got a whole bottle by himself? Don't give him another. If you have to cut him off, he'll threaten to get his gun and shoot you."

"What?" Ellie said.

"That's what happened to the other girl when she cut him off."

"What?" Ellie asked again, put-off and angry. "I'm in the wrong business. Maybe it's the people I'm associated with." Ellie was disgusted.

"I didn't mean to upset you," Beri said.

"No problem," Ellie said, sighing. "I'm target practice."

"They're aiming." Beri laughed.

Ellie didn't like the fact Beri found her discomfort funny. But that's the kind of person Beri was, Ellie thought. Nasty.

Mr. Blue finished his bottle without an Ah-ooh or a groan and away he went.

"What are you doing in town today?" Ellie said.

"Shopping."

"What are you looking for?"

"Just looking." Beri shrugged. To Ellie, that meant she was putting in time, waiting for something to happen.

"For trouble?" Ellie said with her razor-sharp tongue.

Beri blinked. "I just had an accident, put a big ding in my car, but I can't put it through insurance because I'm not supposed to be driving. George will kill me."

"Why, what happened?"

"I'm not sure. A blue jeep with a vinyl top drove smack into me. But she didn't stop. I just drove away and parked behind Woolworth's, out of sight. What am I going to do?"

"You're not hurt, are you?"

"No, thank goodness."

"Was it Cathy? Sounds like her car!" Ellie said.

"I don't know for sure. She wore a big sunhat," Beri said vaguely. Then she brightened, "How's Vern doing?"

"The same as yesterday when you asked." Ellie was irritated Beri changed the subject.

"Isn't he working a lot?"

"All the time. Isn't George?"

"Yeah, isn't that unusual? Just before a layoff, the men get lots of overtime. I can't figure it out."

"Vern doesn't get off 'til three-thirty."

"Neither does George," Beri said. "And anyway, I don't want to tell him because he'll kill me because of the insurance. Do you think Vern would help?"

"Probably."

Ellie noticed Beri made no move to phone a garage or anything. She waited in the Bedford lounge for half the afternoon. Usually, Beri wouldn't hang around for no reason. Maybe she was waiting for Vern. Vern was running her down like you wouldn't believe, but he was nice to her when she was around.

"Moose and Tiny can't come in here any more," Ellie said. Then she added, "There's no point in waiting."

"Oh, Steve'll let them come back. He always does. He likes the smell of money," Beri said impatiently. Ellie thought he sure does, getting up partners for people coming into town.

"Fights aren't good for business," Ellie said soberly.

Beri looked at her watch. "Listen, I have to run. See you later."

It was three o'clock and Beri practically ran out of the bar, probably to see Vern, since Ellie worked till five o'clock. The pair of them thought she was so simple-minded. It was a situation which nobody would win. Normally, she would try to discourage Beri by being around her all the time, but right now Ellie was mad at Vern. Ellie worried that her marriage was breaking up and neither fighting nor ignoring the issue was helping.

Ellie thought Beri and Moose were people who attracted trouble like a cloud of dust and somehow she had got caught in the middle. So Cathy drove into her, Ellie mused. Beri sure tried to cover that up in a hurry.

Ellie took a tray of beers to a flood of eight guys from the Saturday overtime shift at Champion. They wore t-shirts, jeans, and peaked caps, rumpled as if they wore the same things all the time, even slept in them, but that can't have been true. They probably changed once in a while.

Ellie heard them discuss losing their jobs at Champion in the near future as she set down the tray.

"Bring another round in a few minutes." A guy circled the two tables with his arm. "Then I gotta go."

Soon, Ellie felt hot and sticky. Maybe the air-conditioner wasn't working very well.

Quantz turned up just before Ellie got off work.

"Don't they have anything better to do?" Quantz thumbed over his shoulder at guys drinking. "Don't you?" Ellie teased. "Rather than bug me?"

"What the hell--I work, cut grass, play cards. We can take the rest of the afternoon off. When are you through?"

Ellie thought he should know by now what time she worked until. He had to be reminded of things that happened every day. If Vern had asked because he was in a hurry, she would be annoyed, but since it was Quantz reaffirming his conscious state, so he knew what time of day and where he was, his questions were fine.

"I should be going home, though." Ellie thought she should be trying to save her marriage.

"Let's do something."

"Somebody will see." Ellie worried about being discreet. If Wayne could get something on her to tell Vern, he would use it like a crowbar. She didn't want to give Wayne a crowbar.

"Let them." Quantz smiled. Ellie grabbed her purse and followed Quantz.

They went down to the marina behind an abandoned warehouse. Sex like an on-off button, and that was it. He zipped up, ready to go.

Ellie was disappointed. Instead of a boatride, she got to bonk. She felt an emptiness, a vast chasm between them. She had thought love would solve everything. How could she reconcile her hopes of a love affair with Quantz, if Vern dumped her and Quantz wouldn't take her on?

"A ten-minute fix. I think I'll have it over again," Ellie said to Quantz.

"You would, too."

"Can't you wait until Tuesday or what?" Ellie was angry.

"Don't be mad. Taking the boat out would mean a couple of hours."

"And we would be seen, right?" All of a sudden she wanted to keep him longer.

"I'd be in trouble for sure." Quantz nodded. His arm was hanging out the window, impatiently rapping the door. He was staring at the masts of the sailboats looming over the rows of trees. Then he glanced over his shoulder at the warehouse.

Ellie thought Quantz wasn't taking her seriously. All he wanted was a few minutes of skin, muscle, and tissue rubbing together. The memory lasted longer. Ellie wanted more. She liked everything about him, the way he smelled, tasted, and felt.

Ellie figured her hopes of love weren't going to materialize. The casual way Quantz treated her made her feel insecure. Up until this point, she'd been accepting what he offered.

"Give me a call maybe if you can find the time." Ellie pulled on her clothes. "I have to go now." She'd hoped he begun to like her more than this.

"You're in a hurry, now. Was it something I said?"

"No," Ellie said. She tried hard to be civil. She could see that Quantz was hesitating as if all of a sudden he had some time and it irritated her. "Do you want to stay longer? Have you changed your mind?"

"I have to go, too, you know." Quantz leaned back and studied the masts which showed above the trees. "What are you doing tomorrow?"

"We have a picnic or something."

"I'm going to church, and then I'm playing bingo with my folks," Quantz said.

"Oh," Ellie said, noting he had everything planned, and he tried to fit her in, as if she was a missing piece in his puzzle.

"Tuesday, then?" Quantz asked and Ellie agreed. Quantz smiled, gently squeezed her hand, and started his car. If Quantz was disappointed because she was cranky, he didn't show it. He knew what he wanted and came right out and said it. Ellie wished she could be the same.

When Ellie went home, she thought about Quantz. She was convinced it was only natural she would fall in love with another man, when she wasn't getting enough affection from Vern. When Ellie thought about divorce, she realized she probably wouldn't ask for one, because Quantz didn't seem commited and she wasn't ready to leave Vern, maybe not even if things got really bad, and go out on her own without her kids. When Ellie had an affair with Quantz, it was pleasant. He made her feel good, like seeing a rainbow did.

The next day, Vern, Ellie, Robert and Susan had a regular family picnic. They went down to the beach. Many sailboats with white sails like flags dotted the blue horizon. Cirrus clouds like gossamer puffs hung above them. It was a fairweather scene.

Ellie wanted this picnic to be a good one. Under the pavilion there was shade and breeze even though it was a hot day.

Robert picked out a table and he could hardly wait for lunch. Ellie had purchased some Kentucky Fried Chicken to have with salads so it wouldn't be so much trouble for her. Vern paid for it, after arguing about it, and in spite of herself, she couldn't help wondering if he felt guilty.

"Can't we eat now?" Robert said. "The smell is driving me famished."

"Don't whine."

"Well, you can't expect him to wait forever," Vern said, picking up a piece of chicken and eating it.

"How do you expect me to teach him anything when you do something like that?"

Vern shrugged and sat down.

"You could wait until I put it on the plates," Ellie said, "before grabbing it."

"Why? It's just going into my stomach," Susan said.

They ate everything except the coleslaw.

After lunch, Ellie took Robert by the hand, and Vern carried Susan. They went for a walk on the boardwalk. There were family picnickers and people sunbathing and kids with bare bums running around.

As they walked along the harbor, Ellie saw Quantz and Moose roar past in Quantz's motorboat. They waved. They had big toothy grins under their sunglasses.

Vern laughed and waved back.

"What's the matter with you? Can't you wave?" Vern asked Ellie. "You look a bit peaked. Aren't you enjoying yourself?"

"I'm fine. It's nothing," Ellie said.

"It doesn't look like it."

"I have a headache." Her head might explode.

"A face-ache, too." Vern was complaining about her appearance again, she thought.

"So? Is it causing a problem?"

"Whatever you say," Vern laughed softly. "You might as well enjoy yourself while you can. That could be you." He nodded at someone in a wheelchair. Now, Vern was threatening her, too! Ellie supposed it was an attempt to keep her in line.

"He's got problems I don't have, that's for sure." Vern was making Ellie mad. He was so superior and critical. "Why don't we ever go sailing, Vern?" Ellie realized she was always wishing she was somewhere else. What was she going to do about it?

Vern shrugged, as if he didn't care. He was a landlubber and Ellie knew it.

Towards evening, George and Beri just happened to be down at the beach. "Isn't the sunset lovely?" Beri simpered.

The low sun reflected on George's teeth. "Sure is," he said.

While George and Vern discussed the roof they were working on, Beri and Ellie looked at each other. "Well, what's new?" Beri said. Ellie thought it was funny how their paths crossed all the time. The only way Vern could see Beri more was if he lived with her, Ellie noticed angrily.

When Ellie and Vern got home, they had a big fight about how much time Vern was spending with Beri. Ellie worried that she was making things between them worse instead of better.

By Tuesday afternoon, Ellie had thought better of not coming, because she and Quantz took equal risks, such as risking their marriages and losing their families. Ellie kept her dates with him, even if she thought something might happen, and so did Quantz. She was convinced they loved each other equally, which was good, because she thought if you loved someone more than they loved you, they're always making excuses and have little time for you. Quantz always had time for her. Ellie was glad she wasn't married to him because then she would have to face reality rather than hoping things were going to improve. She thought her love life was important, the beginning, the middle and the end of her current existence.

Tuesday night at the motel, Ellie said, "I wasn't even going to show up at all. What do you think of that?"

"You'd come," Quantz, sounding unimpressed.

"What makes you so sure of yourself?" Ellie prodded.

"You asked for it twice Saturday, didn't you? Trying to kill me?"

"I was just trying to get you going."

"No, you wanted it."

"I won't argue."

"You could take your clothes off, instead of complaining about the past," Quantz teased Ellie.

Ellie peeled and they went to bed. Quantz just seemed to <u>know</u> when she was ready. His cock seemed to curve up into her, touching her everywhere important so that she was wild for him. Ellie liked the way he felt stuck up in her.

"Do you think we're getting too close?" Quantz lay back in bed, scratching his head.

"It's not bothering me," Ellie said. All Ellie could think of was the present moment of pleasure.

"Me either."

He was a liar, Ellie was sure. Because she was lying, covering up her feelings, she figured he was doing the same.

Quantz put his pants on to go out to the car and get more beer, and then he returned and took his pants off.

Ellie watched Quantz avidly, gripping the sheets tight below her eyes.

He tugged at the sheet and poked at her flesh.

"Why are you shy, when you weren't before?"

"I'm play-acting." Ellie was playing games. Maybe he'd be interested enough so she could tell him things.

"Hard to get. A little late now!" Quantz showed his teeth. Ellie thought he had a proud smile of gold-capped dominance. Maybe she'd made a mistake.

"Are you trying to take advantage of me?" she asked. "I think you are."

"No, I'm just careful. I work hard, I play hard, but I'm careful when I'm in someone else's territory. I'm used to being beat up by jealous lovers. I've had quite a few adventures." He glanced at Ellie as if he was going to tell her all the details.

Ellie listened politely to his dark side, tangles from which he's had to extricate himself. The words echoed in her head. If he was trying to get her to confide, it didn't work. She thought her private life was just that, private. "You're quite a bit more experienced than I am," Ellie said.

"This is all in the past now that I have you," Quantz said. "Sometimes I don't get away without a hassle. I've got quite a reputation."

Ellie thought she was the one getting the hassle. She slid her arms around him and kissed his shoulder, and then rested her chin on it.

"I wouldn't like to be confronted with your extra girlfriends," Ellie said curtly, wanting to be the only one.

Quantz was a good-time man. That was all. There was nothing else, just lovemaking once in a while, and that was it. Maybe he was trying to find out if she would be jealous or not.

"It's all in the past." Quantz stroked his chin.

From what she knew of him, Quantz solved situations. Ellie thought there were two kinds of people in her life, people who caused situations, and people who solved them. Quantz was the kind who solved them. She wasn't going to spoil it by questioning where he's been and what he's been doing and turn the love-solution into a mess.

It was on the tip of Ellie's tongue to ask Quantz about Wayne, what kind of a connection there was, when Quantz commented, "You don't say much, so you are hard to read."

"I have a lot on my mind, a lot of problems I keep to myself."

"Oh." There was an impressive silence.

As far as Ellie was concerned, they were both thinking hard. Ellie reflected that he wasn't what he appeared to be because of his hidden connections. Quantz was thoughtfully eyeing her up.

"I wonder if you're seeing me because of how you're getting along with your husband," Quantz said.

"That's true," Ellie said, snuggling into his arms, "but I also like you for you."

"Be careful," he said, "as Beri is asking, too, about how you're getting along with Vern."

* * *

CHAPTER ELEVEN

Just as Ellie pondered that none of her friends or even the people she just met were what they appeared to be, Moose invited her and Vern over to his house the following Saturday night.

Besides, Moose had told Ellie, it would give Cathy a chance to know them, and it would give her a reason to clean up the house. He explained his friends at the bar made Cathy feel out of it so everybody was to visit and be nice.

By the time Ellie, Vern, Beri, and George got to Moose's house, he was high.

Ellie could tell by the way he flew out of his bungalow to open her car door and how high-pitched his voice was.

"What do you think of our place?" Moose's small white house had a carport, a patio, and a pool.

"I like it," Ellie said, looking around appreciatively, wishing she had her house in the country.

"Got the front door fixed?" Vern asked.

"Like new. As soon as this comes off, I'll be entirely new." He showed Vern a smaller, flesh-colored bandage on his wrist.

They all went into the house, and Ellie and Beri found Cathy in the kitchen. Her straight red hair was so shiny, smooth and perfect it looked synthetic. Her tummy stuck way out, more noticeable than before.

She had three small boys already. Pictures of her family hung in frames on the wall, or were set on the bureau, and on the television.

"My wedding pictures," Cathy said proudly. "I was eight months pregnant at the time. Can you tell?"

"No, they're very nice," Ellie said.

Beri snorted. "You've always been a little bit too chunky." Ellie thought Beri didn't need to be so rude.

Cathy's smile wavered unsteadily. "I'm not always pregnant. It just seems that way."

Moose, George and Vern came into the kitchen after Moose showed them everything. Moose put his arms around Cathy, clinging to her passionately. He was so pathetic, acting like he was glad she was there, but he would say otherwise when she wasn't around. Moose told Ellie that Cathy had the brains of a bowl of vegetables. Ellie wished that she didn't remember these remarks when she was visiting Cathy, because they made her feel sad.

"This is my number one girl," Moose said.

"When is it due?" Vern asked.

"The end of September," Cathy said.

"Do you want another boy?"

"No, I'm hoping for a girl."

"How is the old man treating you?" Moose said, giving Beri a tight squeeze right in front of George, but George for once didn't seem to mind.

"You're drunk," Beri said to Moose. George rolled his eyes at Ellie.

"Not yet," Moose said.

"He's on something to lift his mood, so he can't drink," Cathy said. "You can get everybody a drink, John."

Beri laughed. "Every time she calls him that, I wonder who she's talking about."

"She's the only one who doesn't call me Moose," Moose said to George. George's good eye was straight and the other pointed straight up.

"I never have. He wasn't Moose when we were first married, so why would I call him that now?" Cathy said.

"She thinks names like Killer, Hellcat, and Big Bear are unacceptable," Moose explained to George.

"They're a letdown when you see the real thing," George said.

Moose chuckled, "Maybe so."

"We had a whole album of wedding pictures made up," Cathy said shyly. "They cost seven hundred dollars."

"I can see they're special," Beri said in a sarcastic voice. "It's hard to believe it was only seven years ago when the pictures were taken. You've changed so much," Beri continued. Ellie thought it was mean of Beri to be so critical of Cathy because she was still mad about the car accident. Also Cathy has what Beri wants or thinks she wants, Ellie thought.

Moose, George, and Vern leaned against the cupboards, watching as Cathy turned the pages of the album. Her face was getting pink and shiny. "Are you sure you want to see these?" She asked nervously. Ellie thought Cathy's photos were far nicer than Ellie's snaps were.

On her wedding day, Ellie had high hopes for the future, too. She expected that she would be happy eventually being married to Vern, if not at first, or all the time.

Cathy's eyes were shiny and almost tearful as she pointed to many photos of their house when it was new. "We've almost got it paid for, and now it looks like John will get laid off."

"It's awfully hot in this kitchen," Moose said. "Come out to the patio." George and Vern followed him out.

Cathy made herself a soda with lemon. "Add some more to yours."

"Okay, thanks," Ellie said.

"What do you really think of them?"

"They're nice."

"My eyes are too wide apart and my cheeks are too fat. The pictures are really good except for that." With her long, red hair and blue-green eyes, most people would say Cathy was pretty.

"She knows nothing except being married," Beri pointed to the photos.

"You'll have to give her a chance!" Ellie said. She thought that was a limiting thing to say about somebody.

When Beri used the washroom, Cathy said to Ellie, "Boy, her ass is sure getting big. George must be rubbing it all the time. Do you think they will ever get married?"

"I hope so," Ellie said. "She's impossible now."

"Beri is a bad one," Cathy said. "She's trying to cause trouble. I would watch my back, if I were you, Ellie. There are some things you ought to know. It's only fair."

"What do you mean?" Ellie asked.

"You almost have to feel sorry for somebody like that."

"She likes to get her own way," Ellie said.

Cathy made a sound of exasperation.

"You don't know what she can be like. John said she's trying to make time with Vern," Cathy hissed. "You should watch out. She could hurt you."

Moose came up behind them, putting his arms around both. "I wouldn't want to hurt Ellie either. She's too nice."

"Do you know who we're talking about?" Cathy asked.

"I guess so," Moose said. "She's a hose-bag, anyway, available to whoever wants it."

Ellie and Cathy laughed, and when Beri came back from the washroom, she wondered what they were laughing at.

"It's about nothing," Cathy pointedly said to Beri.

There was a great, awkward silence as Beri's face grew long.

"It's about me being a pickle-head," Moose said.

Ellie thought how inconsistent Beri was when she laughed and let Moose squeeze her. Last week, Beri wished he was dead and buried when she heard he tried to do himself in, she told Ellie, but she was trying to move on and forget him.

Beri wrapped her arms around him. It was all lovey-dovey now. Moose extricated himself and got another drink, but with liquor this time. Then he went out onto the patio to join Vern and George without saying another word.

Ellie thought he was getting oiled up so that he could face the next situation, when Cathy told him who drove into her and why. That blowup could happen right away. Maybe that's why he left the room.

"He acts like a spoiled child," Beri said.

"Have some of your own, then you'll know," Cathy said.

"I should," Beri said. "The birth control pills are bothering me. My legs swell and I'm tired all the time."

"Maybe you're already pregnant."

Since Beri was taller, Beri looked down her nose at Ellie and Cathy. "Maybe I'm not," she said smugly.

Cathy's eyes flickered with amusement at the joke on Beri. She said, "This will probably be the last time for a dance. If the plant closes down, we'll have to stay at home all the time," Cathy said.

"Oh, don't you think we're good for him?" Beri's remark made Cathy's face fall.

"They'll play cards day and night," Cathy said.

Moose had come back to get Vern and George their drinks.

"We'll have our card games somewhere else, then, if it's bothering you like that," Moose said. His voice was brittle and his eyes were glittering. He sounded like he wanted to pick a fight.

"I said day <u>and</u> night," Cathy said. "Don't you listen?"

"You disapprove of everything I do, so what's the point?"

"The point is there's more in life than playing cards."

"It's as least as valuable as the time you spend reading the trash you read."

"Oh, is it? You just use cards as an excuse to get away from me."

"You're probably right. Anybody would want to stay away from you."

"We've been married for seven years and this is how you treat me!" Cathy yelled. Once she was riled she was formidable.

"Seven years of hell!" Moose roared back in Cathy's face.

"You haven't seen anything yet!"

George and Vern came into the kitchen. Vern watched them argue, amazed, as he got his own drink.

"How do they stay married?" George asked Ellie. "Living like that must make him nervous."

When Cathy and Moose stopped yelling to see everybody grouped about them, Ellie could see that Cathy and Moose were surprised their fight was taken seriously.

"Is it like this all the time or is it just because you have an audience?" George asked.

"This is nothing," Moose said. "She throws things."

"Worse than that, she drives into people," Beri said.

"Never mind that stuff," George said, dragging Cathy and Ellie out of the kitchen. They went out to the patio and stood together watching the sunset.

"We've always lived near the lake, never inland. It wouldn't feel right," Cathy said to Ellie. "The lake can change color with the weather."

This evening, Ellie could see the water was like satin, as if someone smoothed it with a spoon. A sailboat was out. The silhouette was against the sky. It had dropped anchor, or it was waiting for a breeze. The sky was almost apricot making the clouds and the water look royal blue.

"When I was younger," George said. "I used to go out with the fishermen. It was boring all day long. Lifting the nets, not finding much, and moving again. We could stay out there a week before we got a load."

"You scared the fish away," Moose interrupted the little huddle.

"Is that what you do in your motorboat?"

Following him, Beri said, "HA, HA, HA," in a distinctly unfriendly voice.

"You look better than you sound," Moose said. "Thank goodness. I especially like those dangly earrings."

Beri's earrings rested on her collarbones and they rattled as she swung her head. "These are my Bayfield earrings. I'm glad you like them."

"Oh," Ellie said, standing beside Beri holding her drink. "Are those the ones we got when we went shopping in Bayfield?"

"Yes, don't you remember?"

"They look bigger. And brighter."

"I need something to wear with them, instead of these old clothes." Beri held out her pale blue skirt and touched her blouse.

"Beri's closet is full, but she has nothing to wear," George said. "I don't know what she does with all the clothes she buys."

"What did you buy this time?" Vern came over to Beri. "Nice." He fingered the earrings.

"You would complain if I wore anything like that," Ellie said.

"Ellie never buys anything nice for herself. I always have to tell her to do it," Vern said nastily, Ellie thought.

"You just never notice," Ellie said.

"She wears the same thing all the time," Vern said. "Look at what you've got on today. That skirt and blouse combination looks like you're going to work."

"I don't wear this to work!" Ellie said, shocked to hear Vern say something negative about her white satin shirt and black skirt, which she thought looked nice with her small, neat silver jewelry. She didn't like to be gaudy or conspicuous.

"I didn't say that. It's just the sameness," Vern said.

"At least, you're not falling out of them," Moose said.

The men sat down in the lawn chairs. Beri and Ellie stood beside them. Cathy was putting ice and sliced fruit into the punchbowl. Cathy's outfit hugged her sizable bulge, making her look bigger than she was, since it was tucked under her belly and over her rear like that.

"It would take a tent to cover her up," Moose said.

Vern leaned over to hear what Moose had to say.

"She's always too heavy. Clothes don't cover that up."

"You're awfully hard on her," George said.

"Yeah, you're right. She has a lot of good qualities.Generous and loving. But she never does anything around the house," Moose said.

Ellie walked over, set her drink down and helped cut up the fruit and cheese for the tray.

"Your place looks really good anyway, Cathy. You must have just done the windows," Beri said, coming over. Her face was a sneer but her voice was polite.

"We've been busy so it's a wonder I got anything done," Cathy said. She sat down.

"Why's that?" Ellie passed the tray around.

"We were at the bike rally in Wingham this week, but it was raining, and we couldn't have any of the events. We tried to make the best of it so we didn't have to cancel and go home. The men were running and sliding in the mud. Two of them were naked, trying to see how muddy they could get."

"Imagine, Beri, what you missed!" Moose said.

"Were you one of them, Moose?"

"No. It was too cold."

"Pity."

"Some of those men are crazy," Cathy said. "After the mud fight, they raced their bikes to the top of the hill and ran smack into a pile of lumber. One biker says, Gee, I should have checked to see what was on top of the hill."

"Imagine him trying to pull the slivers out of his naked ass," Beri said, laughing merrily. "Ouch."

The women laughed and laughed and laughed.

Moose's face was very red. "They were lucky they weren't hurt."

"They didn't even need a shower, as it started to rain so hard," Cathy said. "I just handed them a bar of soap."

Beri chortled louder than anybody. "We'll never say anything about what you're wearing as long as it's something, anything, rather than mud and slivers."

"Don't look at me," Moose said. "I wasn't doing it."

Cathy cleared her throat, loud and long. Beri laughed and Ellie laughed. The women were finally enjoying themselves, whether it was the drinks or what.

"Where are you working now?" Beri asked Cathy.

"I was at the A&P." Cathy shrugged.

"She quit after a few weeks," Moose said.

"Well, I'm not quitting my job," Beri said.

"I guess not," Cathy said loudly. "You're on your own. Maybe you'll never get married."

Abruptly, George came over and leaned over Cathy's chair.

"What am I? A nothing?" he asked quietly.

Cathy's mouth hung open. She must have wondered why George was leaning over her.

George was smiling quietly, but the general impression he gave was anything but friendly. "I said, who do you think I am?" George was so laid back it was hard at first to know what he meant. "Am I just the doormat? I thought I was the same as a husband."

"Is it a problem we're not married?" Beri said.

"If you want to know about married, ask Cathy. She knows enough about that to complain," Moose said to Beri.

"If you want to know about Beri, I'll tell you, John. She hired a private eye to spy on you. I'm surprised you didn't know," Cathy shouted.

"I think Cathy needs to get relaxed," Vern said.

"That's powerful punch," George said. "It would relax a dinosaur. Whoops, I didn't mean to make a remark about your size."

"I can't have any," Cathy said. "Beri should have some more, then she'd level with you." Cathy grabbed a piece of orange and cherry out of the punch bowl and plunked them into Beri's glass. The punch splashed on Beri's clothes.

Ellie watched Moose take Cathy's arm and steer her beyond the pool to the river bed. They were dark moving shadows.

Ellie was surprised Cathy knew as much as she did about Beri and Moose. Beri hired a local private detective, to scout around and see what Moose was up to, but she didn't want to pay her bill, and she left it until Filbert submitted it at Small Claims Court. It was common knowledge, except Cathy wasn't supposed to know.

"The way you guys are!" Disgusted, Ellie reached for the door. Inside, George was watching TV by himself.

Soon Cathy, Moose, Beri and Vern came back in. They piled into the car and went down to the town outskirts to the Union Hall for the dance.

The cool fresh evening air was invigorating. By the time Ellie reached the hall, she was almost excited, as if her man enjoyed taking her out for once. Vern was in a good mood and actually asked her to dance.

Partway through the evening, Ellie went to the washroom and checked out her make-up. Beri sat on the counter smoking a cigarette, swinging her leg back and forth. "I told George that I quit smoking. I also told him I gave up pot."

"How come he doesn't smell it when he had his nose in your shirt?"

Beri was silent for a minute. "He doesn't say anything."

Ellie powdered her nose and patted a bit of powder on the circles under her eyes. Beri stared at Ellie powdering her face.

"I'm starting to count the wrinkles around my eyes. I don't see any on you," Beri said.

"I have circles." Ellie patted some more on, and put her compact back in her purse. She reached for the door.

"Wait, I'll come with you." Beri's heels clunked against the counter as she slid off. She threw her cigarette in the toilet.

Coming out of the washroom, Ellie found Vern and George waiting for them. Vern grabbed Ellie. "Let's dance this slow dance."

In the dim light, with the country band and Vern's arms around her, Ellie wished they got along better. If Vern was always like this, Quantz wouldn't be so important to her. Ellie thought there must be something the matter with her not being able to make Vern like her all the time.

* * *

CHAPTER TWELVE

About ten in the morning, Ellie was out in the yard with her kids when she saw smoke smudges over the east part of town. She heard sirens, and two fire trucks roared by at the end of the street where she lived. In another moment, another wave of sirens went past, followed by many cars and trucks, hurrying towards the fire. To Ellie, it looked as if the entire eastern sky was filled with smoke.

Ellie grabbed Robert and Susan and got in the truck. Ellie knew without being told that the plant was probably on fire. In a few moments, they drove up to Champion. They got out of the truck and stood with the crowd.

Champion was a complex of buildings. Smoke billowed out of one of the sixty by one hundred-foot steel buildings. Two firetrucks with flashing lights were in the parking lot. Firemen in yellow coats and boots leaned ladders against the smoking building. Hoses were strewn across the pavement.

The onlookers were people Ellie didn't know. She searched for familiar faces, men who might have been still working when the fire broke out. She estimated there were about 250 men standing around who might possibly have been working this morning. She heard one of the men saying with kind of a laugh that the fire broke out at coffee break time, and luckily none of the men were in the area where it started or people would have been hurt.

Most of the crowd stood behind the wire fence or behind the roped-off area. When Ellie looked for a reaction in their faces, she noted how calmly curious and intently interested they seemed in the fire. Then she saw Vern and George standing near the security station.

Ellie and her kids moved closer to Vern, just behind the fence. Ellie held Susan, and Robert wrapped his arms around her legs.

The smoke had got much heavier since Ellie had arrived, and it didn't look as if the firemen were going to get the fire out any time soon.

Ellie thought, what tough luck to have something like this fire happen the week before layoff. It shed a bad light on the men, she thought, and it was going to make it harder for them to keep their jobs.

Suddenly a voice at Ellie's shoulder said softly, "I think we'll see this plant blow sky high." Ellie turned to see Tiny grinning down at her. "It's more than a fire," he continued. Is that a promise or a threat Ellie felt like asking, but she knew better than to taunt him.

He told her dynamite had been planted in the paint depot where paint, turpentine and cleaning chemicals were kept. "If the fire gets there, the plant will blow up."

"How do you know this?" Ellie asked, shocked.

"Trust me," Tiny said. Then he said the fire had been started in two places so they wouldn't miss their objective, with clothes soaked in kerosene and stashed in barrels, papers lit in kerosene puddles and paths leading to the paint depot.

"The fires were lit on either side of the offices, the wooden area, in which a fire would burn readily," Tiny said.

"How did you get in?" Ellie asked Tiny.

"Not me, the others," Tiny reminded her. He told her they had got in through the roof vents over the weekend and set up the hot spots to set alight this morning.

Ellie was shocked at his information, and she didn't know whether to believe him or not. She thought if he wasn't guilty, he would enjoy bragging about it. She thought he wasn't smart enough to do it. But she wondered how he would know.

Firetrucks arrived from other communities. Ambulances had their sirens going as they screamed to a stop and opened their doors. Somebody must have got hurt, Ellie thought.

While Ellie listened to Tiny, Vern and George had come over. "They're discussing right now whether it's arson or not," Vern said to Ellie. "I see everybody in town is here."

They discussed with Tiny how the arsonists might have got in to place the kerosene and the dynamite. "Only the guy with the keys to the paint depot would know that," Tiny said to Vern.

Vern listened politely to Tiny but it was obvious from the expression on his face he didn't believe Tiny.

Ellie knew Tiny was bitter about the way he was treated, and he might have started the fire. Or someone else might have. She'd heard Vern say the relationship between the men and the foremen was at an alltime low.

"They're checking the lunchpails now," Vern said to Tiny. "I just thought I'd tell you."

"Don't take it personal," Tiny said. "It isn't just you who rides me."

"It's because morale is low," Vern explained.

"It doesn't help to be stopped at the guardhouse and your lunchbox opened and checked. It makes a man stop and think. It makes him wonder why he's being treated like a criminal."

"What are you trying to say to me? Don't say anything you'll regret. Be careful!" Vern shook his head in an argumentative and touchy way. Vern had told Ellie he felt he was between a rock and a hard place, between management demands and men with their backs up. Ellie thought maybe he was trying to pick a fight with Tiny. She thought Tiny was just mad, and that he really wouldn't do anything illegal.

"I'll burn the place down, if anybody accuses me of being a thief. Just watch," Tiny said.

"Why, did you get stopped at security this morning?"

"I wasn't the only one," Tiny said.

"Did you have something?"

"What do you think?"

"Be cool and wait. Don't talk about a strike now. It just makes management exasperated," Vern said to Tiny.

"You're a bit of a prick," Tiny said, annoyed.

Ellie saw Vern's face fall. When Vern tried to be a good guy, he got upset if others didn't like what he said.

"If we line up more than five minutes before the punch-out time, we get told off by a prick like you," Tiny continued. "If we are away from our machines to use the washroom, or if we read dirty books on our break, we are in trouble with a prick foreman like you."

"Don't call me that again. It's hard to be a boss when you're goofy the way you are. Most of the time, when management complains, I don't say anything," Vern said.

Ellie knew the other foremen would tell the superintendent about Vern's men standing around, and the super would be down Vern's neck.

"The way you talk you'd think the whole situation was Vern's fault," Ellie said to Tiny.

More firetrucks arrived. The word was out the fire hadn't been contained, and the offices were burning.

"It's unlikely anyone is still in the offices," George said.

"I heard today the topdog is on the verge of a nervous breakdown," Vern said.

Vern and George looked around for Turnbull.

"He's not likely here," Vern said.

"Why, is he firing people again?" George asked.

Vern nodded. "I don't think he's hurting. Turnbull has a home in Arizona, a private plane, and a yacht. I could tell Champion was in trouble a while back because the super started riding us about production."

"Then I would get shit all the time, and I would get the dirty jobs," Tiny said.

Ellie heard an enormous explosion, or more than one, which seemed to come from the center of the plant. Then there were more explosions and it had to be in the paint depot. A windstorm swept dirt into Ellie's eyes, and her kids stuck to her tighter than ever.

In front of them, the fire took right off, with windows exploding out of the offices.

Two people on stretchers were loaded into the ambulances.

"Who got hurt?" Tiny asked.

"There's some people overcome with smoke inhalation," George said. "The fire's really taken off with this wind."

"I'm glad I did what I did then," Tiny said. His cap flew off, and his hair was blowing around.

"What did you do?"

"I'm losing my job anyway."

"So's everybody else," Vern said. "He's going broke. He's used pension money to pay bills and now the union wants their pension money back. You could say Turnbull has his back to the wall." Vern said that with the fire it looked as if their jobs were coming to an end.

"You'll vouch that I was here talking to you, won't you?" Tiny said, jiggling on his feet.

Vern's face got glum. "You've started the fires, haven't you?" Another wave of fire sirens whistled as trucks came in from other communities.

"Why do you ask me that?" Tiny insisted. "Ask others."

"It must be some fire to have all the trucks out," George said.

"They're afraid it'll go sky high," Vern said.

"It will too, I know it," Tiny said.

"You'll go to jail for this," Vern threatened.

"No, I won't," Tiny said, lifting his chin. He had a weird light in his eyes. "Prove it. It's not what a person says, it's what a person does." Ellie's mouth dropped open to hear this conversation. She almost said, "I'm a witness," but she wasn't. It was only talk.

"You've been threatening for weeks," Vern pointed out.

"So? There isn't a thing you can do about it. You'll be sorry you were so mean to me."

When Tiny looked at Ellie, he snickered. "Do you think I can be in two places at once?"

"Probably not," Ellie said.

Tiny snickered again, his shoulders shook.

As the ambulances scurried away, Ellie took her kids home.

When Vern got home way after midnight, Ellie was in bed. Vern smelled of smoke and liquor. Ellie sat up.

"I can't believe Tiny would be so stupid," she said. "Who else has as big a grudge as Tiny?"

"Almost everybody, just right now. They're sure somebody deliberately set the fires, when the plant was still in operation. It's arson for sure," Vern said. He rolled over and went to sleep.

After a meeting the next day, Vern had bad news. Management was so mad about the arson Vern was afraid Champion would close down entirely and move out of the country. "If that happens, maybe we'll go out west," Vern said.

"We could easily do that. Let's sell our house," Ellie said. "Let's check the paper. We can get the Calgary Herald."

Vern glowered at Ellie. "You're so eager."

"Why shouldn't I be?"

"I don't know what kind of a job I'd get out there," Vern said. He was negative, Ellie thought, when he thought of the reasons why he couldn't do something.

"If it was up to me, I'd be gone like a shot. I don't particularly like it here." Ellie hugged herself as she thought of the awful problems she had to deal with, and a solution so easy.

"It'd be like starting over again from scratch."

"That means we're not going, doesn't it?" Ellie said, shortly. "I'd like to go. What about me for a change?"

"Don't get all wound up about it. I said I'd think about it, okay?" Vern sounded angry, probably from a hangover. "I think I'll go lie down while you get supper ready."

"Sure," Ellie said shortly. "I'll get right at it."

Vern laughed. "Better wait until we get some information before you get your bags packed." Vern liked Ellie when she bitched at him, so she had to go lie down, too.

"You don't have to take all your clothes off," he said. "Just your bottom half."

"You in a rush to get somewhere?"

"Out west."

"You're making fun of me." Ellie felt disappointed.

"It's my privilege."

After their quick one, Ellie dressed and got dinner ready. Vern complained about the spaghetti.

"This is the same thing we had the other night," Vern said. "I like a bit of variety."

"You don't have to eat it if you don't want to. You can throw it over your shoulder."

"Don't get hostile." Vern ate the pasta hurriedly, talking between mouthfuls, not leaving anything on his plate and then he took a piece of bread and wiped up the sauce.

After dinner, Vern went to a union meeting and when he got home he sounded upset. "From the sounds of things, the Goderich plant will close down for sure. The men are so angry they're going to do something about their status before it's too late."

Vern was in a hurry with her like he was before. Ellie wondered if her marriage was turning into a blow-through kind of relationship, or she was turning into a roll-on, roll-off kind of facility. Vern staying out late most nights irritated Ellie. There was plenty for them to fight about.

There was no more work for Vern now, the fire forcing the layoff into effect early. But business was booming at the bar, so Ellie still went into work.

Ellie looked up the next day and saw Moose and Tiny side by side with their elbows on the counter expecting their beer. They'd had a talk with Steve and their lifetime cutoff had lasted a week.

"What's this?" Ellie asked.

"He likes me," Moose told Ellie. "Don't look at me like that. We're just going to have a couple and then we're going to take off."

"Sure thing."

"I thought we had got it all figured out. I thought we had got life by the tail," Tiny said, whining to Ellie.

"Your wife will have to get another job."

"You're in this too," Tiny said.

"I can always drive taxi," Moose said.

"How many taxis does a town of 7200 need?"

"I'll trap muskrat then," Moose said.

"Dreamer." Vern came up behind them. "The dreamer and the arsonist, what a pair!"

"You can't call me that. I've denied everything," Tiny said belligerently to Vern. Ellie was sure he'd been telling the truth in a bragging sort of way.

"What will you do? Buy a farm?" Moose cackled.

Vern's face reddened at Moose's sarcasm.

"We'll grow mushrooms in our basement," Ellie said.

Moose and Tiny laughed. "A worm farm." Ellie smirked to see Vern's discomfort. He liked to have a perfect image.

"Don't let your face hang down like that, Ellie. It makes you look ugly," Vern accused.

"That's my problem. It's my face," Ellie said. She had always got hell over her supposedly sulky face.

"She's the hardest working woman I've ever known," Moose said softly.

If it wasn't for Moose, Ellie thought she might have started to cry. Vern was like a garbage dumpster ready to unload on her. Ellie was a spot of grease on the pavement.

"We have enough problems without picking on the women," Moose said.

"You're right," Vern said, after a moment.

"You agree with everything," Moose said.

"I have to," Vern said. "I'm always catching hell."

"You can't win an argument with Vern," Ellie said, "because the first thing you know, he'll have switched sides. If you ask him a question, he won't answer it. He'll only tell you what he wants you to know."

"Ooh, does she know you!" Moose said.

"She notices things about people," Tiny said.

"Dry up, Tiny. You wouldn't know if it was dark or morning," Vern said. "Maybe that's why you started the fires."

Tiny ignored Vern's bait. "I have tickets for a glass turkey, a forty-ouncer of whiskey, for charity," Tiny said.

"Is that how you're going to earn your living?" Vern asked. "It's illegal as it's advertising."

"Are you going to buy a ticket or not? They're three for a dollar and I only have ten left. It's for a worthy cause, spinal bifida."

"Tell us another one."

"I guess no one wants a ticket," Tiny said.

"Not right now," Moose said.

Tiny put his book of tickets away and got up and left.

"Let's you and me go out for awhile," Vern said to Moose in a low, oily voice, putting a hand on his shoulder. "I'll fill you in on what's been happening."

His voice dropped so Ellie couldn't hear what he was saying. Vern sounded as if he had something in mind he didn't want Ellie to know about. She was sure of it when Moose glanced at her to see what her response was.

Ellie picked up a rag and went to wipe the counter at the end of the bar, as far away as possible.

Up they got and hardly said goodbye. Maybe Vern hadn't noticed that about himself, that he was always in a rush and his mind was always elsewhere. But Ellie sure noticed it.

After she finished her shift, Ellie felt kind of down. She felt Vern's temper was on edge, as was everybody else's, and she was in the middle of something happening. She felt as if she was standing on the edge of a volcano about to erupt, or if didn't erupt, somebody might push her in anyway.

* * *

CHAPTER THIRTEEN

For two days, Ellie had been cleaning up her house.

The plant had closed down. Ellie had heard Vern saying the fire would have forced a closure anyway. The guys were without work, and they wanted to play cards all the time.

Ellie didn't know what to think when Moose asked her if she would have the next card party. She wanted to make sure her house with its brown shag rugs, oak panneling and tiffany lamps was as nice as possible for the guys.

Moose had said to Ellie, "We could have it at our house again, but Cathy might not like it."

"Well, Vern wants to and I don't see any reason why not," Ellie said. "It'll be fun for a change." She looked forward to the party as she ran the vacuum cleaner around.

At eight o'clock Wednesday evening, July 27, Quantz, Moose, George, Vern, Mr. Blue, and Mr. Dick sat around Ellie's antique kitchen table.

Ellie checked to see who wanted drinks.

Mr. Dick, a pawnbroker, was at all the card games for higher stakes. Mr. Dick had brought a case of beer.

Mr. Blue was working on a bottle of wine. He threw a hundred dollars in the center of the table.

"A little high to start, isn't it? Take it back and put a ten out," Mr. Dick said. "You do this every time."

"It's just to soften you up," Mr. Blue said.

"We've all got the point," Mr. Dick said.

"I've been drinking beer all afternoon. It'll probably kill me if I start on the hard liquor," Quantz said, as Ellie had the rye bottle out.

George and Vern each had a rye.

The experienced card players took advantage of the innocents right away. Vern and Mr. Blue were relieved of their cash. Ellie was starting to think this way of earning a living wasn't such a good idea.

"We don't take checks here," Quantz said to Mr. Blue.

"I hope you'll take an I.O.U. on my car," George said.

Vern had to get more cash to stay in the game. Ellie gave him some of her tip money against her better judgment.

They had finished a couple rounds when Turnbull and Wayne arrived. Like everybody else, the top dog at Champion was looking for a job, Ellie figured. But she wondered what Wayne's problem was as he glared at her. Unlike the others, they didn't bring their own drinks.

Quantz's smile got wider as Turnbull lost the next round. Ellie thought Turnbull's personality showed on his face, which was florid. He was about fifty, in the heart attack zone, with bad nerves and a temper, she'd heard. Ellie didn't know why Turnbull came to play cards with Vern and the guys, but maybe somebody had invited him.

Ellie watched the card game, amazed.

"Figured you'd clean up quick, didn't you?" Quantz said.

"Higher stakes than I'm used to," Turnbull said.

Mr. Dick threw a wad of cash on the table and called their hands. Mr. Dick wore a suit with a yellowed shirt that needed cuff links, something that was in style twenty years ago. Mr. Dick fumbled with the cuff links on his shirt. It was his turn to show a card, but he hesitated. Ellie thought she saw him trying to push a card up his sleeve. But then the card he needed dropped from his hand onto the table and he scooped it up.

Turnbull glanced across the table to see what was holding things up. Ellie saw that most of the men didn't watch Dick too closely.

"What the hell are you doing?" Turnbull asked Mr. Dick.

Dick didn't answer. He grinned and showed his card. It was another Queen making two pair and taking the pot.

"You can't cheat me!" Turnbull yelled. Ellie saw Turnbull leap up from his chair and move around the table faster than she thought possible for a man of his bulky size. In a split second, Turnbull had his sizable hands wrapped around Dick's neck. Dick's face was turning purple, and he was protesting wordlessly, as he tried to pry Turnbull's massive hands loose.

Quantz got up from his chair, his cigarette dropping out of his mouth.

"Let go, you son of a bitch, you'll kill the bastard," Quantz said. Ellie watched, startled.

"I don't care if I do," Turnbull said. He dragged Dick into the washroom, shoved Dick's head into the toilet and held it there until Dick spluttered.

"I'll hold your head there till you drown. I'll kill you for sure, if you ever do that again."

Ellie wondered if this is a display of the boss's famous temper, and if so, what she was supposed to do about it. Not in my house, she almost said, you're making a mess. Instead she went for the mop.

Turnbull flung Dick backwards and knocked Vern off his chair onto the floor. The two squirming men landed on top of Vern. Vern pushed against them with his legs. Vern groaned. "Get off."

"Get out of my way, Vern. I'm going to kill the bastard," Turnbull said.

"What's happening? I didn't hear that, did you?" asked Quantz.

"No, I didn't hear anything," Mr. Blue said. He was bleary-eyed. "We ought to kick yous both outa the game, interruptin' a serious effort like this." Mr. Blue watched with his jaw hanging slack, but he didn't budge from his chair.

"Please go home," Ellie said, ineffectively swinging the mop.

"We're working on it," Quantz said. Quantz tried to pry Turnbull's hands off Dick's throat before he strangled him to death. Moose wrapped his arms and legs around Turnbull's back trying to pull him off, but he was a bigger, determined man.

"Should I hit him or not?" Moose asked Quantz. It wasn't just everyday the top dog got a chop in the neck, Ellie thought.

"How are we going to explain this if you kill him?" asked Quantz. Ellie thought that's all she needed, how to explain a dead body, or maybe two dead bodies, in her kitchen. She could hit them with the mop.

Wayne remained sitting at the table. He lifted his drink out of the way. "You maybe shouldn't kill him as he writes out your paycheck."

"Very funny." Vern kicked at them.

"I'll give the bugger cement shoes and drop him overboard in the lake," Turnbull said.

"Yeah right. Why else would you have a yacht?"

Turnbull laughed at Quantz's joke. A deep raucous laugh. "Haw, haw, haw. I should use it oftener." He let Dick go. Ellie saw Dick crumpled on the floor. Dick was puking and coughing as he rubbed his neck. "I oughta press charges," he said, in a croaking voice.

"What do you take me for? A fool?" Turnbull spluttered. "You're lucky you're alive. You can't cheat me! It would be the first time!" Then, he lifted Dick by the shirt and threw him against the wall. Dick wasn't a small man, but he bounced against the wall and collapsed like a piece of newspaper on the floor.

Ellie watched with her mouth hanging open. She thought Turnbull was way out of line. What could she say to these guys when she was outsized and outnumbered? Vern looked flabbergasted, as if he couldn't remember where he was.

"Better go on home," Mr. Blue said to Mr. Dick. "Better quit while you're ahead."

"What would you know? You just sat there and watched this guy try to kill me." Dick rubbed his neck.

"Get the hell out," Vern said weakly, as Ellie leaned on the mop.

But Dick waited. He gagged and choked.

"Get moving!" Turnbull was slamming his fists together. "Get out before I throw you out." His face had turned an alarming shade of red.

Dick finally went out holding his throat.

"What happened there? I missed it," Moose said, sitting back down and grabbing his cards to check them over.

"It's not like you to miss the action," Quantz said, He got himself another drink. George got up too. Ellie noticed George didn't make a move until the fight was over.

"No, I usually cause it," Moose said. "Hell, this game's ruined."

"What's with everybody?" Mr. Blue said. "I haven't won a hand yet."

Vern straightened up his chair, gathered up the glasses and gave Ellie a look meaning get us some more drinks, quickly. To Ellie, who was disgusted with them, it seemed like kind of an anticlimax to have a drink when somebody had almost been murdered.

"Want a stiff one?" Vern asked Turnbull.

"Well, why the hell not? I'm not that religious."

Obviously, Turnbull wasn't ready to go home either, so Ellie was disgruntled to see everyone sit back down.

After a few more deadly serious hands, Ellie heard a knock at the door.

When Ellie opened it, a cop, Baker, was standing there.

"What happened here tonight?" the cop asked.

"What do you mean?"

"We've had a complaint. There was a disagreement here earlier, and I'm checking it out."

"You can see there's only a group of friends here," Vern said, coming to the door. "What can I do to help you?"

"Can I have a look around?"

"No, I'm sorry. This is private. You must be mistaken."

The cop leaned around Vern to look at the now quiet group at the kitchen table. But the cop didn't push Vern aside, he left again without asking any more questions.

"The dirty bugger," Turnbull said. "Tell him to find his own fun." After quite a few drinks, he called for a ride home. He wouldn't let anybody drive him, even Wayne. Ellie hoped this didn't mean Wayne left his car in front of her house. In five minutes, headlights showed in the door and out he and Wayne went.

"He's probably cleaned out of money, but he wouldn't admit it. I don't think he won a hand," Moose said.

"I thought Turnbull was going to have a heart attack right then and there," Quantz said. "He was shaking and swearing. He was so angry I don't think he cared two figs if he killed Dick right at that moment. All I could think about was how to get rid of the body. It's funny how your mind works in a situation like that."

"All I would worry about is the money," Mr. Blue said. Mr. Blue was still sitting at the table.

"I noticed you scooped it off the table when we heard the knock at the door. Do we have to check your sleeves too?" Moose asked.

"No," Mr. Blue said. "You have to take my word for it."

"I don't like that, though, the cops coming around. I thought maybe it was your neighbors complaining of the noise, Vern," Quantz said.

"They've done it before, when we've had a party," Vern laughed weakly.

"That guy Dick, though, has some nerve."

"He sure does."

"We'd better lay low for this week. Next week though, we'll have a game, but don't tell Dick," Quantz said.

"I've gotta go," Mr. Blue said. "See yuh." He grabbed his hat and disappeared.

"If anybody is asking about what happened at this game, or who was involved, say you don't know anything about it," Vern said. Ellie wondered how she was going to get that know-nothing story to wash.

"They won't believe us," Ellie told Vern.

"No, but they'll just want to hear the gossip."

"Let them hear the gossip, then. Who cares?" Ellie threw up her hands.

"You don't mean that." Vern put his arm around her.

"Nobody likes Dick, though. He's lucky to be alive because he's tried that stunt before. Maybe he thought he could get away with it this time," Quantz pointed out.

"Get a load of Turnbull though. Wasn't that a shocker?" Moose said.

"I told you he was crazy, or damn near crazy. Didn't believe me, eh?" Vern asked Moose.

"You know him better than I do," Quantz said.

"I like him better than I like that son of his," Vern said. "I found that son of his sleeping one day on a pile of boxes. Out partying the night before, I guess. I told him to get down off there and get to work and he asked me if I didn't know who he was. I said I sure do, all the more reason to get your ass in gear. He said he'd tell his old man, and I said you do that and see where it gets you. He swore at me and called me a mother-fucker."

"I know who you mean," Quantz said.

"What do you think will happen when he takes over from his father?" Vern said.

"You're an awfully serious person, Vern. Why would you worry about that?" Moose said. "After all that's happened this week?"

Ellie thought she didn't care if she ever saw the silly old guy again, but he had used some of his personal money to keep the plant afloat in hard times because the business had been in the family a long time.

"You think he'll go broke?" George asked.

"I do." Vern listed the reasons they thought so: red figures, imperfections in the parts costing thousands, graders being sent back as unsuitable, problems with working conditions.

"I think it's just talk," Moose said. "Let's have one more hand."

Quantz won the last pot from this rather nefarious game. Moose was dead broke, with empty pockets. George had to hand over to Quantz the I.O.U. for his car.

After they left, Vern asked Ellie what she thought of their poker games.

"I guess they're the equivalent of women's Tupperware parties, aren't they?" Ellie said, cranky she had so much cleaning to do.

"You don't have to be so bitchy."

"I'm not," Ellie said loudly.

At work the next day, Beri asked Ellie what happened at the game. "It's the talk of the town." Beri couldn't keep the smirk off her face.

Ellie figured George had told her, but hadn't given her enough details. Ellie's feelings were hurt as she figured the game did nothing but hurt her reputation and cost her a saved-up stash of money. That's what she got for listening to the hot-shot men, she figured.

Ellie almost said to Beri, why don't you ask Vern yourself? Instead, she said, as innocently as possible, "Why, what did Vern tell you?"

"You mean George, don't you?" Beri held her cigarette in the air.

"Yes, I guess I do," Ellie said.

"Not a thing," Beri said, emphasizing each word. What a good way to have things, Ellie thought.

* * *

CHAPTER FOURTEEN

After the card game at her house, Ellie felt she had to fend off too many questions. The next week, her life settled down to a dull roar, or more nearly normal, she thought, and she looked forward to seeing Quantz again.

Late in the afternoon, Quantz stopped his car at the edge of the meadow, surrounded by cedars, dogwood, and thorn trees. They got out of the car. The earth felt warm and moist where Ellie and Quantz were sprawled on a blanket.

Quantz lay back, his arm holding his head up off the ground. He was relaxed, smoking a cigarette, casually and slowly. Ellie thought he was doing what Vern would never do, waiting calmly and happily for the urge for sex to surface in him, acting as if he had all the time in the world, and Ellie was short of it, as usual. She had to be home from shopping in a few minutes.

Ellie ran her fingers up and down his chest. She unbuttoned his shirt. His body had a softness to it, so she squeezed and patted him. She thought he was gorgeous.

He stubbed his cigarette in the dirt. Then he rolled over towards Ellie, stroking her arms and legs, making her back thrill. His touch was hardly a touch at all.

She stuck her nose in his chest. He smelled of cologne and sweat. She wondered if he liked her as much as she liked him. She could come right out and ask, or pick the petals on a daisy like a kid would. Quantz made her feel like a kid. She figured she was a child of insecurity wanting to be loved.

"Let's do it," he said suddenly.

"Why? You think I'm just for sex," Ellie teased.

Quantz looked confused. "Right. You're made for sex."

"I'm glad you think so." Ellie felt itchy, maybe it was the sun, or the meadow's atmosphere. Her relaxed frame of mind made her feel forward. So she climbed on him, with her clothes still on and thumped her pelvis against him. She thought it was a case of mind versus twat. He laughed.

"You could lift your skirt," he suggested.

Quantz held up her head with his elbows on the ground. She thought it might fall off and roll away, she was so close to her climax. Then he stopped and looked at her.

"What happened to your underwear?" he asked.

"Does that bother you?" Ellie had wanted to save time. She thought she was being bold and wanton.

Interested, his drive was insistent and steady. He held back, but Ellie drew him in. His hardness was a pivot Ellie had to lift and lift for, and finally she could hold back no longer. It was ecstasy. She was crazy for him.

Ellie put her arms around his neck, not letting him pull away. They kissed. She was clinging on him, because she wanted him to get into her as far as possible. He gave her the deepest kiss she'd ever imagined.

When he lay on her, Ellie held onto his backside. She wrapped her legs around him until he groaned, the sounds bass and harsh. She moved a bit under him, just to get more comfortable.

"I could do this all night," Ellie said.

"Oh, you," he said. He rolled to the side and Ellie reached around his middle and held him. "Better give it rest for awhile."

"Yeah. For a week or two."

Quantz searched in his pocket, lit another cigarette, and passed it to Ellie.

She puffed the cigarette, holding it between two fingers, but she choked.

"Take it easy," he laughed.

"What are we going to do if we get found out? Are we going to get married?" Ellie asked. She had been thinking all week of asking for a guarantee, or a commitment, if they were to continue to see each other.

Quantz was silent for a long moment. A look of intense consternation crossed his face. Ellie grabbed her beer which had become very warm from the sun. There was a bug in the beer that she fished out.

"How can you drink that? Here, let me get you a cold one."

"No, don't bother. It's drowned."

He pulled on his pants, went to his car and got two cold beers. He handed her one and she took it and set it aside.

"You're all I think about. We're in a dangerous situation, don't you think?" He put his hands in his pockets, wriggling them, as if he was nervous.

Up until this point, she hadn't thought he was serious. Now she realized it was mutual. "What are we going to do?" she repeated.

"Maybe we should give up the drinks. Try it sober."

"I mean what are we going to do tomorrow, or the next day, or next week."

Somewhere in the afternoon haze, Ellie remembered the afternoon had passed too quickly. She had finished the warm beer and the cold one, too. Maybe she didn't feel love at all but the effects of booze, relaxed and altered senses.

"I only take one day at a time. Next time, it'll be me asking what to do, probably," Quantz said, as if the matter was solved and dropped, just like that.

Ellie was kind of disappointed to hear him say that.

"I only had two beers," Ellie said.

"I've been drinking all day. Next time, I won't. I am starting to think about us at work, looking forward to us being together. I've never done that before." Quantz sounded serious.

Ellie frowned. Maybe it would be easier not to want to hear about the future or mistakes being made, or the fact they were getting serious. All she wanted to do was live for the moment, too. She was stealing a few hours from the day. No one had to know. They were soft in the head, unwary lovers, marked for life. There was danger involved. If Vern found out he could shoot them, and he would almost be within his rights, as Ellie and Quantz were doing what they weren't supposed to be doing.

Ellie started to feel she should get a move on. She got dressed and handed Quantz his shirt.

"Don't you believe me?" Quantz fiddled in his pockets. "Let's do it over again."

"I'm late, or I would," Ellie smoothed down her hair with a comb.

"I'm just kidding. Next week? Don't worry if you can't come."

"I'll try," Ellie said. She thought, he didn't seem to want to make a decision, and if he gave her an out, she might take it. She'd be crazy not to. Since lives change and can't be repaired, she should have kept away, instead of venturing into the dangerous world of make-believe. Ellie thought about him in the middle of the night, or she woke up in the morning thinking about him. The real world wasn't important, only he was important. If she couldn't be with him, then thinking about him was second best.

When Ellie went home, she was in a daze. A few hours in his arms felt like it should last forever. In between dragged on mercilessly. She felt discouraged.

When Ellie went home, she had a shower and made herself a cold drink. She was sitting at the kitchen table in her housecoat with a towel wrapped around her head, and Robert and Susan were eating milk and cookies beside her when Vern walked in the door.

"What's the matter with you?" Vern sniffed her drink. "It's gin!"

"So? You can drink and I can't. Is that it?" Ellie got up to pull the supper out of the fridge.

"You're getting emotional again," Vern said, red-faced from rage or his day working outside with George, Ellie thought. "Why do you walk around with a drink in your hand? Where have you been anyway?" Vern continued.

Ellie pointed at the bags of groceries still sitting on the counter.

"You just got here, didn't you? Why have you had a shower? Who have you been seeing?" Vern said suspiciously.

"I'm just getting ready. Diane's coming."

"Diane's coming? You're lying, you stupid bitch," Vern yelled. "I know you've been sneaking around, and I'm pretty sure who it is."

Ellie glanced at Vern's angry face. She wondered if Beri had said something to him. Beri would if she could cause trouble.

"You can't listen to gossip," Ellie said, trying to think of something to say to calm Vern down. "You can't trust people, what they say."

"I can't trust you, you mean!" Vern said. "I heard Quantz is spending a lot of time in that bar and he's probably up to no good. The both of you are no good."

Ellie didn't like to be accused. She vowed she wasn't going to admit her affair, because of what might happen and because this afternoon she thought she wasn't ready to leave Vern for Quantz, and Quantz wasn't ready to leave his wife for her. She was going to try awhile longer to save her marriage. "You don't mean that," she said, going to put her arms around Vern, but he pushed her away. "You're just mad over nothing," she said.

"Don't bother about supper, I don't have time to wait," Vern said shortly. "And I won't be able to talk to your sister. I have another meeting to go to tonight. I'll probably be late." Vern laced his boots back up and went out the door.

Ellie bit her lip. She wondered how she could have caused so much trouble by just sitting at the table and leaving the groceries out. She thought this was their most bitter fight yet. She put Vern's supper back into the fridge.

Her kids went to watch TV as Ellie put a few of the groceries away and set some hotdogs on to cook.

Ellie had just reached for her t-shirt and jeans when Diane stuck her head in the door wearing a huge red afro hair-do and a pink shirt. Diane and her husband were at the trailer and Diane had stopped over for a visit while her husband was at a baseball game.

"Did I just miss Vern? What's his rush? What's eating him?" Diane asked Ellie.

Ellie blurted, "I don't know what's happening to us. Everytime we're together, we fight. I'm sure he's seeing somebody."

"Do you have somebody?" Diane's face was serious.

Ellie thought for a moment, before she reluctantly admitted, "Yes, I do, and our fights are getting worse and worse."

"What would mother say if she knew?" Diane asked, her forehead wrinkling into ridges.

"She doesn't know, so why worry?" Ellie said, shrugging.

"That's not like you. You never used to be so blase, so unconcerned about what others think. You speak your mind more than you used to. And aren't you drinking a lot?"

"You sound just like Vern," Ellie sighed.

"I didn't mean to."

"I had a couple of drinks. It doesn't take much with me." Ellie reached over to wipe the milk off Susan's face.

"You don't have to explain."

"He drinks a lot, too, especially with the layoff, but if I do it, it's an issue. I'm not sleeping well, either. A few drinks helps."

"If mother knew you had a boyfriend she would rail at you. You know how proper she is."

"She drives me up the wall."

"Why? She's just concerned." Diane could be obtuse at times about how Ellie disliked being bossed around.

"That's fine for you to say. You hardly ever see her. She's always bothering me about things I don't think are important."

"You'll feel better later. You're under a lot of pressure right now. Maybe you should stop seeing him."

"I'd die if I had to do that," Ellie said.

Diane peered closely at Ellie. "You probably just came from there."

Ellie thought she must look a bit bedraggled. She pushed her hair back off her forehead. "It's not quite that urgent." It wasn't just bonk and run, but it was true, wasn't it, she did things like that.

"In the long run, it won't work," Diane pronounced. "What about your children?"

Robert and Susan, their mouth full of hotdogs, suddenly looked guilty to be eating.

Ellie sighed. "Do you want a drink with your hotdog?" She wanted Diane to be a better listener. Right now, Ellie wasn't getting what she needed from Vern. "You're not going to tell her, are you?" Ellie pleaded, as she handed Diane the mustard. Her parents had taken a cottage in Muskoka for the summer instead of coming to the trailer every weekend.

Diane's eyes were distrustful. "What does Vern think?"

"I think Vern has his mind on other things."

"Oh, I see. I wondered if Vern had somebody else. I don't know how you're going to keep all this together," she said knowingly then she laughed, but it wasn't a hilarious kind of laugh. It was one of extremes.

Ellie was scared the first thing Diane would do when she left would be to tell Mother. She couldn't avoid it. They got along because their personalities were alike, and Diane would tell something on Ellie that was supposed to be a secret. She always had. Then Ellie would get it in the neck. Ellie had always wanted Diane to be a confidante, but she never had. Ellie would tell something important and Diane would use it on her, like the time she wanted to go to the prom and she couldn't because Diane had told on her. Diane didn't care then about Ellie's feelings, and it looked as if she didn't now.

"Don't you remember what she was like when we were young?" Ellie asked, and remembering made her angry. "She was uptight about sex. She'd take our questions so personal. She'd say, 'Don't be so stupid. If you don't know that, I'm not going to tell you.' Didn't she say that to you?"

"Well, Ellie, you know she's hard to talk to. You have to lighten up. Don't let your teenage years bother you." All of a sudden, Diane had got older and not prepared to listen. She yawned, in a bored way. She lifted her feet onto the coffee table as if they were too heavy. Clunk. Clunk.

The dour expression on Diane's face made Ellie think she was her mother all over again.

Her mother had no sense of humor about sex. She was the Royal Arse that way. She'd cover the toilet seat in public washrooms with paper towels before she'd sit, taking so long Ellie thought she'd disappeared down the hole.

Ellie thought her mother's attitude was real funny now. Ellie joked about the gin she kept under her bed and which smelled like stale perfume. Ellie thought her prudery must have been an act, because when Ellie was young, her mother would sail out of the house in the middle of the afternoon, and the bathroom would reek because she had just washed herself. Then she'd sun herself in the semi-nude, right in front of everybody. Ellie angily remembered her sweaty body odor and her inconsistent habits, especially when her mother had punished her all the time. Ellie thought angrily if they wanted to punish her by spoiling the prom, they should have done it before she had bought her dress.

"If you do say something, I'll never speak to you again," Ellie said, pouting childishly.

"Don't have a temper tantrum." Diane started to laugh.

"I think you're very bossy," Ellie said, picking fault in Diane's personality. "You like to tell people what to do." Now that Diane was married she was bossier than ever.

"Oh no! I've been trying to avoid that happening to me!" Diane roared.

"No, I'm just kidding," Ellie wanted to placate Diane so she wouldn't tell.

"No, you're right. I do go on about things," Diane said. She had a rueful expression on her face, the exact opposite of her outgoing hair style which she had colored a flaming red. It used to be dark brown or streaked-blonde.

Ellie laughed. "I've never seen your hair black."

"How come your hair is brown?" Diane demanded. "You don't have to let yourself go, just because you are married. I liked it better lighter. When I was single I envied you being married."

"I can hardly believe you would think that," Ellie said, marvelling, trying to remember being happily married, and Diane wanting to be the same.

"Don't let a momentary aberration get you down. You're reacting to what Vern's doing. I'm sure Vern loves you, even if he doesn't seem to at this moment. All you have to do is wait."

"What am I going to do in the meantime?" Ellie exploded, getting angry with Diane's lack of understanding of the urgency of the situation. "It's not that trite."

"A family is too important for it to be just for sex," Diane said, firmly. "Isn't it?" she repeated, demanding Ellie agree.

Ellie felt she'd become a disruption to everyone's life, a regular nuisance. If the reason for her love affair wasn't solved, and her relationship with Vern didn't improve, what was going to happen to her then? It looked as if there might be a big blowup with her family, if she couldn't convince Diane to keep quiet.

Ellie reached for the gin bottle and slopped a bit over Diane's glass and then filled her own halfway. Susan wiped her nose on Ellie's leg and then reached for Ellie's drink.

"Stop!" Ellie pushed her drink away and wiped her daughter's face with a towel. Why would she think things would get better because she'd explained and Diane listened and maybe sort-of understood even if she didn't approve?

Together they finished the gin bottle and when Diane left, Ellie went to bed.

Vern wasn't home yet.

In an hour or so, Ellie awoke terrified, not knowing for a moment where she was, suffocating, gasping for breath, thinking she was face down in water, and her mother was standing over her watching. She'd had this dream, before, more than once, Ellie thought, remembering it in terror whenever she awoke suddenly.

What woke her up? Was it noise on the stairs? Ellie looked around uneasily but could see no one. Vern wasn't home yet.

* * * * *

PART TWO

* * * * *

CHAPTER FIFTEEN

Over the weekend, Vern and Ellie had spent time at the trailer with Diane and her husband before coming back to Goderich.

Ellie figured she must be one of the only ones still working as Champion had been closed down more than a week.

Ellie thought it was kind of stupid of Moose to be hanging around the bar. Moose had got another chance by sucking up to the boss, but Steve might change his mind if he saw him too often.

"What's new?" Ellie asked Moose. She still had a headache from the gins she'd had over the weekend, and she hoped her pain didn't show on her face.

Moose shrugged and slurped his second beer. He appeared to be lost in thought, his eyes pale and blinking behind his fair eyelashes. "You tell me."

Ellie laughed because Moose was playing games with her. He was the one with the shiner and the fat lip, and he hadn't told her yet what happened.

When Quantz came in, Moose's face reddened. Moose's eyes flashed with interest.

"When the hell did you get out of jail?" Moose demanded.

"Don't rub my nose in it." Quantz sat down on the stool.

Moose hit his buddy on the arm. "Never learn, do you?"

"You were in jail?" Ellie's voice cracked. She was so shocked she almost fell against the counter.

"Didn't you hear what happened?" Moose asked Ellie, then he turned to Quantz. "I can't believe you didn't tell her. You're in here all the time."

Quantz shrugged. "There's nothing much to tell. It was the usual questions such as why I'm living beyond my means, and the earnings I have at cards."

"Christ, I'm the one who was in the fight. And you were the one watching," Moose said.

"It wasn't over that," Quantz said.

There was quite a bit of silence.

"What happened?" Ellie asked as she figured he wasn't going to say.

"Who put up your bail? I heard it was Wayne." When Quantz didn't answer, Moose said, "I can't believe the reason was that you're living beyond your means. You've got rust holes in your Camaro. What kind of lifestyle is that?"

"They just kept asking the same questions and they never liked the answers," Quantz said.

"Looks like quite a fight you had." Ellie stared at Moose's face which was marked by cuts, bruises and swellings.

"He was straightening people out. Again," Quantz told Ellie.

"Women." Moose grinned from ear to ear. "Two of them, Cathy's babysitter, Sally, and Tiny's daughter."

"It's your fault, anyway. You've had them in here," Quantz said

Moose ducked his head into his shirt collar. "I'm always catching it about her."

Ellie realized the girl was the one Moose took around town on his motorcycle and who had been in the Bedford before.

Both girls were underage and they slid past Steve's bouncer to listen to the band. Tiny's daughter was big, and the bouncer couldn't tell she was so young because they had false I.D. Sally was smaller.

"What happened?" Quantz asked Moose.

"The girls got in a fight with another woman and they were swearing and rolling on the floor. Talk about drawing attention to themselves."

"I heard Tiny tried to separate them," Quantz said.

"The other woman kicked him in the nuts. Some girl with heavy cowboy boots," Moose said. "Then I got in on the action."

"You were fighting with everybody. Even the cops." Quantz stroked his chin.

"I guess I was drunk. It's not like me to stand by and see young women get into trouble even if they're fighting dirty." Moose rubbed the long lapels on his brown leather jacket, squirming back and forth on his stool. "The cops would have hauled us all off to jail."

"Not everybody," Quantz said. "Tiny didn't get charged."

"Why not?" Ellie asked.

"When the cops came, he knew enough to disappear. When the cops asked him about the fight, he told them the guys he was sitting with were underage. As if they weren't doing their job, so he didn't get charged."

"Tiny's smarter than he looks," Ellie said. He could get himself out of scrapes whereas Moose couldn't. Moose hung around, Ellie thought, when he should get lost.

"I gave the cop hell but he didn't think it was funny. Baker said, `Look, your tongue is your worst enemy. You'll end up on skid row if you don't curtail your drinking.'"

"You should take it easy," Quantz said.

"I love to fight. I'm good at it." Moose's face got shiny with excitement.

Ellie thought Moose was always trying to get attention, and wanting to enlarge on it.

"You won't be so popular here any more," Ellie said, "if you keep it up." Which wasn't the truth, as Moose got away with almost everything.

Moose grinned at Ellie, then he turned to Quantz. "How was the food in jail?"

"You're making fun of me. I didn't stay for the entree."

"Naw, don't take it so hard."

"Why aren't you at home?" Ellie said. "This isn't a good place for you to be after everything that's happened."

Moose hung his head like he lost his best friend. "Can I stay at your house?" He reached across the bar and touched Ellie on the shoulder.

"I told you 'no' before," she reminded him.

"Just for a while, as Cathy told me to get the hell out and not come back. She called me all sorts of names. She was mad as a starving she-witch about the girls fighting. I told her I got falling down drunk. She didn't believe me. She said, 'You've been drunk too often.'"

"You're a scrapper when you've been drinking. You have a complete change of personality," Quantz said.

Steve came into the bar. "You're back."

"Yes sir," Moose said. "You can't keep a good man down."

Steve laughed. "Your face is pretty bad, but you should see Tiny's face. His left eye is swollen and his lip, if you could find it, would have a bandage on it."

"He's an ignorant bastard. I should have killed him."

"I should cut you off, for being so rude," Steve said.

"But you won't, because I'm so entertaining. Right?"

"Don't make me regret this," Steve barked. "This is the last night you can drink here." Then, he guffawed when he saw Moose's shocked face. "By yourself. Set mine up."

Quantz laughed, in that queer, dry way of his, with a tickle at the end.

Ellie laughed too, because they were all so stupid.

"Moose is looking for a place to stay," Quantz said.

"You could stay with Mr. Blue," Steve said. "Did you hear what happened to him? He gave his car and some money to Ruth while he played cards with the boys and she buggered off with some guy. He's heartbroken."

"He's always heartbroken," Moose said. "Let me stay with you."

Quantz shrugged.

"Yes or no? I'm desperate," Moose said. "This is what the world is trying to do to me!" Moose showed his bruised wrist. It was the same wrist Moose had slashed in the broken window. The wound had healed but the scar was still vivid in a purple bruise the size of a grapefruit.

"Okay, you can stay, but just for a few days," Quantz said.

"You're a good buddy." Moose patted Quantz's back.

"What happened to your wrist?" Steve asked.

"Fucking cop almost broke it while he was trying to handcuff me."

July 26, 1999
17 Village Green Crt.,
Point Edward, Ontario
N7V 4J4
(519) 336-8535

Book Editor,
South Bend Tribune
W, Colfax Ave.,
South Bend, IN 46626
tel: 219-235-6161

Dear Editor:

I've also enclosed a copy of my new novel. In "ILLUSIONS," Ellie is searching for something more than fighting with her husband Vern when she fell in love with Quantz, but she forgot about the heart-wrenching consequences. The story provokes revealing questions about what is

If you decide to do a review, please keep this copy. As well, I've enclosed SAE for your reply.

If you prefer, we could discuss the story over the phone or you could recommend someone who might be interested in doing a review.

I'm looking forward to hearing from you.

Yours sincerely,

Sandra Orr

Sandra Orr

"You're an idiot. You were trying to get away," Quantz said.

"He could have an assault charge as well as a drunk and disorderly." Steve swivelled his head from Moose to Quantz.

"It might be worse. The cops came around and asked me what went on just because I was standing there," Quantz said.

"Are you in over your head?" Moose accused Quantz.

"No. At least I don't think so. But, I don't think I should have been questioned or put in jail," Quantz said.

"It's your reputation for operating in the shadier circles, the cash in the middle of the table. Norma's the only thing that reminds him of the straight and narrow," Moose told Ellie. Ellie thought they were talking in riddles, not wanting to lie and not wanting to tell the truth either.

"The cops think I'm in on everything," Quantz said. "They asked about the fire, about Dick and the money, about the fights."

"Well, there's not too much that goes on that you're not a part of," Moose said.

"They also asked who was doing well and who wasn't, and if the rumours about a Sheriff's sale at your place were true," Quantz continued.

That made Moose choke. "Just because I lost the other night at cards and you won?"

"I'm joking. They asked about the attempted murder at our weekly game."

"Dick must have told."

"Maybe. It's depressing to be thought of as shady. Every time they want to know something, they come and see me."

Ellie thought it would be creepy to be questioned all the time. Cops in a small town were always out on the road, watching everyone and talking to everyone, developing certain opinions of people. Ellie wondered what they thought of her, watching her hang out with Quantz.

"It would be better to sleep out in the rain than be in jail." Moose sounded sorry for Quantz. "Getting questioned is no better than a kick in the pants. That's what they say about being in jail."

"I'll talk Cathy into taking you back. I'll put Norma on it," Quantz said suddenly.

"Yeah," Ellie said. "It would be better for you to patch up. It's not too late for you to have a turnaround in your fortunes. You just have to quit drinking so much. You just have to wait for Cathy's temper to cool."

Moose paused. "You make it sound easy but it's hard."

Quantz laughed. "You never learn. That's your problem."

"I'm stupid. Is that what you're trying to say?"

"Just naive. You should go back to Cathy and lie low," Quantz said curtly. Ellie thought he didn't want Moose hanging around his house too long.

"You perfect people make it sound easy," Moose sounded discouraged.

Quantz shrugged. "I have my own problems. I don't like inquiries about my personal life."

"Do you think Tiny is up to his old tricks?" Moose asked Quantz.

"If he is, they'll keep it a secret, if they can."

"He's a disgusting person."

"Nobody could prove he screwed his kid. Ever."

"No." Moose lowered his voice. "But, it's no secret what Tiny's problem is. Last time he was in court, nobody heard a word about the outcome of the trial."

"Why not? Cases of incestuous sex make headlines."

"Those headlines get squashed here. You wouldn't believe what goes on here. They are obsessed with sex," Moose confided to Ellie. "And the papers won't print anything damaging. That cop asked me if I was screwing one of the girls, so I smacked him." Ellie figured she heard about almost everything that goes on, good or bad, mostly bad.

"You're fucking crazy," Quantz expostulated.

"I might have to go to jail, for resisting arrest and for whacking that cop on the mouth. He deserved it, though. I'd do it over again," Moose said.

"This is your first offence."

Moose nodded. "The cops said I would need a good lawyer." He complained about his curfew. "I can't stay late at the Bedford, and I have to do volunteer work."

"Cathy will appreciate your limited freedom," Quantz said. "Maybe you can present your case that way. The curfew will help your marriage."

"It's cramping my style," Moose said.

"You never learn, do you?" Quantz asked. "It's what your problem is."

Moose smirked. "My problem is, I just knock around with a bunch of rough stuff, like you, messing up my life."

"You're likely to get yourself killed, the way you carry on," Quantz said. Ellie wondered why there was a lot of talk about getting killed. She thought for sure such strong jokes weren't meaningless.

"Well," Moose replied. "It's nice to see you care. Actually I'm just teasing you. I only asked you if I could live with you to see what you would say. If I was around Norma, I wouldn't be able to control myself."

"That's what I'm afraid of."

Ellie saw Quantz looking at her out of the corner of his eye, as if he was assessing her reaction to the whole conversation. Then he reached across the bar and put his hand over her mouth. He drained his beer. "Gotta go," he said and away he went.

Moose was watching Ellie, all eyes, silent for once, as if he was surprised there was something he didn't know about.

"What was that all about?" Moose asked Ellie, the minute Quantz was out the door.

"Nothing," Ellie said. "He's always being fresh."

"Are you getting it on with him?"

"No, I don't like him much."

"You can't trust him. He doesn't commit to anyone for any length of time, not even Norma."

"How do you know that?" Ellie was dismayed.

"If I stayed with Quantz, he'd be jealous. There'd just be trouble and then we wouldn't be friends any more."

"Really?" Ellie's voice had a testy edge. She thought his explanation unreliable because they couldn't trust each other about their love lives.

Then Moose told Ellie he had a new girlfriend. "She's thirty-four." His voice dropped to a whisper as if what he said was the most wicked thing ever. "Don't you believe me?"

"No." Ellie thought there was a large gap in their ages.

"You're not as old." The expression on Moose's face was thoughtful--blatantly and unabashedly as he made his mental sexual comparisons. It was intent concentration, as if Ellie was in a fishbowl and he was a predatory cat.

"I guess not," Ellie said lamely. Ellie felt very uncomfortable, vulnerable, and edgy. "Don't you have something to do?"

"What a question!" Moose complained.

Ellie was very unhappy about what he told her about Quantz being unfaithful all the time. Moose was just trying to manipulate her. He just wanted a quick one, or a place to stay for a few days so he didn't have to listen to the heat at home. Moose wasn't even a confidant, as she wouldn't dare tell him things because of what he might do, or who he might tell.

Ellie figured Moose didn't like her much and it was because of the way Vern treated her. She thought because Vern didn't like her much, then nobody else did either. She thought she would have to be tougher as as result of being used all the time.

* * *

CHAPTER SIXTEEN

Since Saturday was Ellie's day off, she took Robert and Susan to the mall. While she compared the toy merchandise, the manager called her into his office. He treated her as if she was trying to pull a fast one, asking if she had items on her she hadn't paid for. She said that was impossible as she hadn't picked anything out yet. After some stalling, he had to apologize.

Ellie felt bad. All she had wanted to do was buy some beach balls and water wings, but Ellie was so angry she left without buying anything at that store. She figured the manager was watching her because her husband was laid off and she worked in a bar.

Late Saturday afternoon, Ellie took her children down to the beach after she went home and cut the grass. Robert had been asking all day so he jumped up in surprise when Ellie told him to go and put his suit on.

They drove down to the lake and parked on the top of the hill. There were private cottages along the lakebank. A wooden sign saying 'The Dalrymple's' hung in front of the cottage on the right side.

Ellie could hear a woman was singing in that cottage. She warbled with her stereo creating an eerie sound through the hemlock and pine.

The wind was strong, but Ellie could hear her singing. Through the rustling trees, Ellie could tell that she was quite a bit better than someone who sang in church. She was a prima donna with a powerful voice.

The stereo was playing in conjunction with the wind and Ellie could see that Mrs. Dalrymple was alone in her screened porch. Quite often, the cottager's grandchildren would be down at the beach when Ellie took her kids there.

Ellie had never personally met Mrs. Dalrymple, but she knew all about her. Everybody talked about her early singing career. She had been somebody, with a real sense of personality, even if it was in the past.

Ellie pondered what her own personality or sense of identity was. Maybe that was why she was having an affair with Quantz, as if that made her into somebody special.

Wanting as much love as she did from Quantz, she thought it was love until the problems started to happen, then she wondered if she was doing the right thing. She thought it was love, but maybe it was just sex, physical lust covered up with reasons and hopes. Maybe she was considering what spending the rest of her life with Quantz would be like. He had high hopes to measure up to, like the one he had of being a good lover. He was so concerned what Ellie thought of the sex, and her opinion was so crucial to his self-respect, because for him, being without love was like freezing to death.

On the path to the beach, the sharp stones hurt Ellie's feet so she wished she had worn shoes. "Watch the steps and don't run or you'll fall head over teakettle."

"You'll fall head over teakettle, Susan." Robert's voice sang out.

Mrs. Dalrymple's dogs dashed toward them, snarling and barking. Susan and Robert jumped.

"Get away," Ellie snapped angrily at the boldest mutt. At her sharp voice, both dogs dropped their tails and returned to the cottage to lie at the front door.

As they proceeded down the path, suddenly Ellie realized she heard only the wind's shrill sound through the cedars. The woman had stopped singing. Maybe she had heard Ellie yell at her vicious mutts. Ellie didn't really care as she thought her singing sounded off-key with the wind.

Susan stopped to pick up a snail. Ellie saw many snail shells, yellow and brown striped, along the path down to the beach under the hemlocks and cedars.

"Don't put that in your mouth, Susan," Ellie said. Just as she said it, Susan fell and scraped her knee on a stake jutting out of the dirt beside a step. She started to howl so Ellie picked her up and carried her down the path.

As Ellie brushed the branches out of the way of the path, she glimpsed the lone figure staring at her through the hemlocks. The woman was swaying a bit, making a dark shadow in the bright sun. At the beach, the wind from the west was so strong that Ellie could hear no sound from land.

Ellie saw the waves had whitecaps. At the shoreline, the water was tumultuous.

The undertow could be dangerous when the water was rough like this, but Ellie noticed the shore here was shallow and straight, and Robert could take on the waves pounding the beach. He waded out and turned to splash in on the crests time and again. Ellie stayed at the water's edge with Susan as she played her endless game of dipping the shovel and emptying the pail.

The wind buffed the sand against their skin and stung their eyes. Then Robert tried to skip rocks, but he made them plop. Ellie chose a rock so flat it looked like dough rolled out. She showed him how to flick his wrist. The rocks skipped three or four times on the water.

Robert kept aiming for the breakers.

"You should wait until the water is calm, Robert."

"I don't want to wait."

Ellie saw several motorboats cutting into the whitecaps, passing near the shore.

Quantz pulled a water-skier with his motor-boat. He was showing off, coming in too close to shore and turning his head to see if Ellie and her kids were looking. When Quantz slowed down to pass the beach, Moose lost momentum and fell over into the water. Ellie waved and Quantz waved back, but he had to stop and help Moose out of the water.

Some sails, one-person small sailboats, and larger sailboats were out. The stiff breeze made it a good day for sailing.

Quantz turned the boat out into the lake in the direction of the breakwall and came back, making a large circle, going at top speed. Then he slowed the motorboat and drove it into the shallows and up on the beach.

Ellie and her kids ran down the beach to watch. They helped pull the bow into the sand. Quantz pulled and Moose lifted the motor up.

"It's windy out there. I had water up my nose all the time," Moose said. Water dripped over his bulging tummy, down his legs, and into his running shoes which he wore because of the stones in the shallows.

"By the end of the summer, you'll be good at it," Quantz said.

"As long as you don't forget you've got somebody on behind."

"You should have been able to stay up."

"Bull," Moose said.

Quantz pulled on a t-shirt while everybody watched. "I'm bashful."

Moose snorted. "You lift weights so that you can impress the women."

"That is just to keep my heart in good condition," Quantz said, "so I can live longer."

Moose snorted and pulled his shirt on. "What is the point in living forever, if you can't do anything? There is no point in making plans any more. I might just as well put an end to things right here and now." Moose went down to the water's edge and angrily threw rocks.

"Moose is real low," Quantz said.

"Why does he get like this?"

"I don't know. There is no reason to get upset, as far as I can see," Quantz said. "You do your time and you takes your licks. When the going gets rough, you ride with the tide."

"Moose always wants more than he has. He makes an issue out of everything," Ellie said.

"He has big ideas," Quantz said. "He is like a spoiled kid. I had many siblings so I had to fight for my share."

Moose came back from the water and glared angrily at Ellie and Quantz. "What have you two been saying about me?" he asked.

"Nothing," Ellie said, surprised at his temper and sullen face.

"Some friends I got," he complained.

"We just care about you," Ellie said.

"Doesn't look like it," he said. "I could see it from the water."

Quantz avoided eye contact with Moose. "You're imagining things."

"I ask a normal question and it turns into a hassle."

"You guys."

"So I'm crazy, what's your excuse?"

Moose was wet and shivering in the cold wind. So Ellie wrapped her towel around him.

"You're all oily. It's awfully cold today for a suntan, isn't it? Yuck." Moose tried to get away from Ellie, but she grabbed him. She figured he was trying to treat her like she was his mother.

"Did I touch you?" she asked, wiping her greasy arms on his chest. She thought his reaction was funny and uptight.

Moose put the towel around Ellie's neck, pulling it tight on both ends.

"Quit. Don't. Stop!" Ellie croaked.

"Don't stop. I love it," Moose said. "You can't decide." Moose released Ellie and flicked his towel at her, missing.

"Ouch," Ellie said anyway, as she jumped away. Ellie didn't like the side of Moose which always prompted him to be provoking people. "Don't hit me or you might not like the reaction."

Quantz's t-shirt stuck to him as he hadn't bothered to dry off before he put it on. It was like a second skin. So were his shorts. Quantz had a bulge in his bathing shorts which showed what he had, Ellie noticed as he put his arm around her.

Ellie was so cold that her skin stood up in little bumps all over. Her skin was pale in contrast to her wet blue bathing suit. Her long brown hair was plastered to her head.

During the past week, Quantz and Ellie had gone to the beach. People way down the beach with heads moving like periscopes had watched Ellie and Quantz. Since they were together a long time in the water, Ellie got so cold she ached. She wasn't relaxed enough to get off, but he did. He seemed to be able to do it anywhere, in any position, and she thought they were getting too bold. Ellie had to put her suit back on and come out of the cold water in front of this attentive audience, which bothered her.

Quantz still had his arm around Ellie, the only warm spot on her. She shivered.

There was an awkward silence, as Ellie realized that Moose was watching them with a smirk on his face, her towel over his shoulders. "Look at the lovebirds," he said.

Ellie stupidly chewed on her fingers. Her mouth must have been hanging open. She thought Moose had a different attitude when she was rubbing him with the towel. Who would he tell?

Automatically, Ellie moved away from Quantz and he dropped his arm. She was convinced they were either idiots, or they were emoting and letting everybody knew how they felt about each other.

"I must think about it a hundred times a day." Moose chortled at Ellie. "Look how her bathing suit makes the most of her sexy shape."

Quantz laughed, too. "At least we're thinking along the same wavelength."

"Thinking about sex is sometimes better than the real thing," Ellie said. Ellie had a lot going for her: looks, smarts, work, kids, a husband, so it was too bad she wasn't happy in her love life.

"You would say that," Moose accused. "Before I was married I thought I was going to get sex all the time. Now I hardly ever get it."

"Are you still hopeful, though?"

"It used to be a thrill to have a kiss or a feel. Now a kiss doesn't work because we're liable to have a fight before we get any further."

"If it's shoot and go, real quick sex, you won't have time for a fight," Quantz said.

"I might as well give up. I don't know why I even go home," Moose said disconsolately.

"What are you so discouraged about? You're like you were a few minutes ago!" Quantz and Moose sounded jaded, joking about something they could hardly remember.

"I can't even talk about it things are so bad."

"Like what?" Ellie reflected Moose had gone back home, but things couldn't be working out like they should be.

Moose shrugged. He turned away from Ellie and walked toward the shore.

"He's not taking the curfew well," Quantz said. "Trouble again last night. I don't know what's going to happen."

Maybe Moose heard Quantz, even with the continuous crashing of the waves and wind in the background. He was scuffing the sand with his toe. Ellie thought that Moose didn't enjoy what was happening to him, or took it for granted. He was fragile, which meant things bothered him that didn't bother most others.

"Everybody gets despondent but you have to keep in control," Quantz said.

"I'll remember you're such a wiseacre with all the advice you have to give," Moose snarled, "when something terrible happens." He gave Ellie her towel and stood beside Quantz, glaring at him.

Ellie thought Moose was perturbed because he thought Ellie and Quantz were picking on him.

"We just want you to look after yourself," Ellie said.

"You two just think I might do something disastrous, like put a plastic bag over my head or something like that. Then how would you explain it?" Moose said bitterly.

"It's not that at all," Ellie said, but maybe it was. Moose was so sensitive. She shook the sand of out her towel and wrapped it around her shoulders again.

"Then what is it? You two are acting like lovebirds all of a sudden," Moose complained. Ellie wondered why Moose was so critical of them. Maybe Moose lost the girlfriend he was talking about. Maybe he and Cathy were fighting again. Ellie couldn't understand why he would get such a low mood but she knew that these things happened.

"I don't want to have to explain it, so look out for yourself," Quantz said. His squinting eyes were everywhere but on Ellie. He was uncomfortable with the wind blowing sand in his eyes. Vern walked toward them. Ellie had forgotten he was coming to the beach for his late afternoon swim. He had just got off working at George's place. He wore cut-off jeans for his bathing suit. "It's cool here compared to that roof."

"Are you through?"

"No, we quit before six because we couldn't get it finished tonight."

"It's Saturday night," Moose said. "You guys work all the time."

"Not all the time," Vern said. "Just most of the time."

"If you think it's cool here, wait till you go in," Ellie said. "It's freezing."

Vern's eyes were like ice as he looked at Ellie. He pulled off his shirt and threw it onto the sand.

"You look like a drowned rat," Vern said. "Cover yourself up."

Ellie was covered with goosebumps and when she wondered what the reason for his negative remark was, she looked down and noticed that her nipples stuck out with the cold. What was the big deal? He either acted as if she didn't exist, or he was mad at her. Sometimes Ellie thought just looking at her made him mad, as he would find points to criticize in her appearance.

"Why didn't you give me your shirt, then?" Ellie demanded.

Vern threw it at her. Then, Vern strode toward the edge of the lake.

Robert came out of the water to say hello to his father. His lips turned blue with cold.

Vern let out a yell and rushed past him into the breakers.

Robert turned to follow him back in.

"Stay out! Look at you!" Ellie yelled.

Robert paid no attention to Ellie so she grabbed him and bodily kept him from going back into the water.

"When are you going to take me out in your boat, Quantz?" Robert's teeth were chattering.

"Only if your mother comes too," Quantz said.

"Oh, she is scared of boats," Robert said.

"I hope not," Moose said.

"You drive too fast," Robert said.

"Oh-oh," Moose said.

Vern's head was disappearing under the water more than usual. Ellie thought she should keep an eye on him in case he hit his head on a rock and didn't come up again. Usually he just stood out there up to his neck until he was cool enough to come out, but with the waves, the water was either waist-high or over his head, and he was trying to jump the waves.

When Vern came out of the water, the hair on his chest was a wet black mat and his ears stuck out of his hair. He appeared pale and cold.

"Why don't you come for a ride in the motorboat, Vern? Maybe you could try the skis," Moose said.

Vern shook his head. "I can't stay up."

"That's probably because you weren't going fast enough."

"I'll watch you from the boat," Vern said. "You get on the skis."

"Okay, let's go out now," Moose said.

Ellie opened her mouth to ask Vern how long he was going to be, for supper and stuff like that, but she didn't want to interrupt when he was having a good time. It was getting to be a habit of his, missing supper and coming home late at night.

Vern's face was inscrutable as he glanced at Moose. They gave each other knowing looks the way people do who share a secret and don't want it known. Ellie wondered what that secret could be. Squinting could mean one thing and staring another. She was never too sure about Vern. Or Moose, either. He was so moody.

Vern and Moose and Robert walked toward the boat.

"Aren't you coming, Quantz?" Moose asked.

"Be right there," Quantz said. He watched Ellie out of the corner of his eye.

She wondered what Quantz was thinking about. When she didn't respond immediately, he said abruptly, "See you later."

Ellie had felt very uncomfortable with Quantz staring at her because maybe he thought she was inconstant and would dislike her for it, so she was relieved when he shoved off in the boat with Vern and Moose. Robert sat in the boat watching.

At the beach, the wind was so strong that they were getting chilly. Ellie carried Susan up through the cedars. At the top of the steps, Ellie let Susan walk.

Ellie could see Mrs Dalrymple still standing in her screened porch, her back to the lake, impatiently tapping the bottom of her glass. Maybe she was waiting for them to walk past. Ellie thought the lonely woman didn't like what she surveyed, the endless, wave-capped lake, the rows of cottages, and her own empty spotless kitchen. Ellie hoped she wouldn't be the same way, alone all the time when she grew older.

* * *

CHAPTER SEVENTEEN

When Ellie told Vern she'd been accused of stealing, he said unsympathetically, "What do you expect? They're probably watching everybody. It's the way you're acting." His caustic remarks made Ellie wish she hadn't told him. It had got so she couldn't even tell Vern something that bothered her and expect a humane response.

Once the first week of August arrived, the summer was half over and Ellie was relieved to see a definite end to her bar job. After her shift, Ellie sat down with Moose and Quantz in one of the empty captain's chairs around their table and had a rye. On the stereo, the song "Please Release Me" was playing. Ellie thought it was one of the saddest songs she'd ever heard.

"I hope you don't expect me to keep up with you." Ellie said to Moose.

"If you slide under the table, I'll drive you home," Moose said. His moustache twitched. "Have another."

"It does feel good." Since Ellie hadn't eaten since her breakfast toast, two ryes made her feel woozy.

"You're being decent," Quantz said, "but what would be wrong with me driving her home?"

"What are you going to do for gas? I thought you were broke," Moose laughed. "We cleaned Turnbull out again!"

"I'm down several thousand dollars." Quantz's confident smile was made of even, perfect white teeth.

Ellie thought even people Quantz had bested before would believe those direct blue eyes. For a guy without a job, it was a lot of money to lose, so he had nowhere to go but down.

"If you didn't win, who did? You're not celebrating losing, are you?" Ellie asked.

"Turnbull acted stunned when he lost," Quantz said.

"It was like taking milk from a baby."

"His face got real red," Quantz said, "but he paid up, with a check."

"I lost all my drinking money. I had to drop out when I sure I was on a roll," Moose complained.

"Who won?" Ellie repeated. Maybe they only discussed losing and kept winning a secret.

"It was more like an exhibition game. Don't take it seriously," Quantz said.

"It sure sounds serious to me," Ellie said.

Moose stared at Ellie as if he was somewhere else, under a bare lightbulb in a garage trying to think, for instance. "Tiny lost his entire paycheck, so that his family will have nothing to buy groceries with for the next two weeks."

"George is stupid or he would have dropped before he lost his car," Quantz said.

"Here's Beri now," Moose chortled. His head turned as she walked to the bar counter. She wore a bell-shaped beige skirt gathered about the waist which made her look bigger.

Beri came to their table, her full skirts swishing. "Do you want another round? Rye, Tequila Sunrise and a beer?"

"What will you do without your car, Beri?"

"What car?"

"George lost it in the game last night." As Beri's mouth dropped open, Moose started to laugh.

"I'll kill him," Beri said.

"Don't do that before he pays me the money he owes me," Moose said.

Now that Beri lost her license and wrecked her car and George lost his car in the poker game, they had nothing to drive, Ellie smirked to herself.

Beri glanced down at Ellie. "Look at the company you're keeping. Are you sure you want another?"

Ellie pulled her straight skirt a little close to her knees.

"Sure, I'm sure." Ellie's voice felt thick. If she had another drink, she was going to feel even more stupid than she felt right now.

The door opened and Tiny's wife Lou waddled in. She was an obese woman who wore her shirt hanging outside her slacks.

"Seen Tiny?" Lou asked Beri.

Beri shrugged. "Been at bingo?"

"I'll wait." Lou walked to the bar and sat down.

Ellie knew Lou played bingo almost every day, but she didn't want Tiny to know about it, so she told him she went shopping. Tiny joked about it behind Lou's back.

Lou had a drink, her bulky form spilling over the stool.

"Are you sure you haven't seen Tiny?" Her voice broke in disbelief. It was uncomfortable all way round.

"Listen, if I knew where he was, I'd tell you," Beri said loudly.

Moose confided to Ellie in a low voice. "He probably didn't go home last night, because he doesn't want to tell her he lost all his money. Everybody lost except Mr. Blue. He won big."

Quantz shook his head. "Maybe you should take Lou home."

"You take her home," Moose said. "Then you could tell her what happened." Quantz started to laugh.

Disgusted with the guys, Ellie went up to the bar and stood beside Lou.

"What's wrong?" Ellie asked Lou. Lou blew her nose.

"She's only trying to get me to give her a few free drinks," Beri said. "Crying won't do it."

While Ellie stood at the bar, Wayne came through the door and stood behind her shoulder. He squeezed her arm so tightly she almost cried out. He wouldn't quit bothering her.

"I've lost patience with you," he said in her ear. "You didn't go and be nice to that client when I asked you. You're to go back there tomorrow night." He frowned sternly.

"I couldn't get a babysitter." Ellie wasn't that afraid of him, because she'd already decided what she'd do to him, if he carried out his threats. Wayne probably wouldn't act as Vern was at home a lot with the kids right now anyway.

But since Wayne was almost squeezing Ellie's arm off its socket, she agreed and he let go of her. As far as she was concerned, there the matter would end, until he tried something else. She knew where he lived. She'd found that much out from Quantz, when she'd asked him about Wayne. She just hadn't mentioned what he'd asked her to do.

"What are you up to, Wayne?" Beri said loudly. "Go sit down." Ellie grinned at Beri in relief, happy she was friends with Beri, and Beri could keep Wayne under control.

"Will you guys never learn to quit wasting your money?" Beri demanded as she followed Ellie back to Quantz and Moose's table. "Losing looks good on you." She spoke to Moose in a strident, patronizing way, as if she was more intelligent, way up here and he was way down there.

Moose almost choked on his Tequila Sunrise. His red moustache was covered with foam and his eyelasses fluttered. "You'd think we were married," he said playfully, "and I only just met you."

Beri's face fell.

Ellie felt as if her head was made of air and her voice was coming from somewhere else. "Don't let him get to you," she said.

Moose ordered Ellie another drink and himself another Tequila Sunrise.

Beri's face was bored as she impatiently tapped her order pad with her pencil. "What's the matter with you? You know you can't handle it. Why are you letting him buy you drinks?"

"Why not? I'm a good listener and besides, I'm off work."

"He's always drinking," Beri said. "It's no excuse."

"Bitch," Moose said, after she walked away, her backside swaying. "What did I ever see in her?"

If Beri heard him, she didn't turn around. Ellie could see her give Wayne a beer, set up their drinks and then she returned.

"What did I ever do to you?" Beri set the tray down on their table with a bang, her voice squeaking.

"You exist," Moose sneered.

"Stop that," Quantz said.

"Maybe you guys should drink up and go. Don't you have anything better to do? You guys are turning into drunks." Beri collected the empties and smacked them down on her tray.

"That'll be four-twenty, you drunks."

Ellie could tell from their faces they were ready to punch her in the mouth. Ellie knew better than to call them drunks, and she hadn't been around that long. Even though it was probably true, and from the way they were acting, might soon become the only thing that was true about them.

Beri gave Moose a dirty look as he shoved her a handful of small bills. Moose tried to be nice to Beri. He gave her back the change, a large tip. "I didn't mean what I just said. Let's make up," Moose said.

She gave the bills back to him. Her voice was acid. "It's not too smart, to spend all your available money, when you don't have a job, is it?" Beri turned away from him.

"Come back here," he said.

"What you do is none of my business," she said over her shoulder. Her hips were wobbly as she balanced on her high heels.

"Just as long as you leave it that way," Moose called to Beri's back in a joking fashion. Then, Moose said to Ellie in a low voice, "Jesus. She might phone my wife. I'm already in the doghouse."

Ellie couldn't help laughing at Moose's predicament and the way he described it. She was too drunk to worry.

"What am I going to do?" Moose's round eyes were extremely disconsolate.

"I'll be darned if I know," Ellie said.

Moose knocked the chair over as he got up from the table. Quantz caught it and straightened it up. Moose put on his jacket and left.

"His marriage is causing big problems for Moose," Quantz said as he watched Moose go out the door. "He should be minding what is his instead of throwing it away. Cathy might kick him out again."

"Cathy seldom carries out what she says she's going to do," Ellie said. "She often changes her mind."

"True, she always takes him back, so he's sure of her. He's too confident. It's the same when he plays cards. He wins a few hands early in the game. He has a few drinks, and pretty soon he gets careless and loses more money than he should. He'll have to play again next week to make up what he lost. Anyway, why do you care?"

"I don't."

"Doesn't sound like it," Quantz said, annoyed. Wayne got up from his stool, glared significantly at Ellie and left. "I noticed you talking to Wayne, too. What did he want?"

Quantz was jealously glaring at Ellie. She loved every minute of it. He had been the great silent one, and now he was showing how insecure he felt.

"I didn't realize you watched me so closely, who I talk to and who I don't," Ellie said happily.

Quantz said angrily, "You had better start looking after yourself and stop worrying about everyone else."

"I hadn't realized I was doing that."

"You're too trusting," Quantz said.

"Thanks for warning me." Ellie wondered how he could possibly know what the likes of Wayne was up to. From now on, she wouldn't spend another minute worrying about that guy.

"Who's going to look after you when you are old?" he said. "Think about it."

Ellie was pretty sure Quantz wasn't going to be liking her when she was old. It was just for now. She figured he wouldn't remember who she was when she got older.

"If I live to be old, I'll consider myself lucky," Ellie said. She was so drunk she didn't know whether to laugh or cry, and she didn't know whether to believe the half-promise he made or not. He sounded real enough to Ellie, but that was their problem: tentative, sort-of sincere plans to possibly be together, but so far they hadn't made the break.

Ellie didn't finish her drinks so Quantz drove her home. Vern checked his watch as she walked in the door. She wasn't too late, so he didn't say much. Ellie told Vern Quantz decided to return the favor, and she should known better than to have drinks on an empty stomach.

At three the next afternoon, Ellie, Vern, Robert, and Susan drove to Champion so Vern could get his pay. Vern had been unusually quiet all day, so Ellie wondered what he was thinking. "Nothing," Vern replied. "Nothing important."

The lot was crowded with the cars of men who had come to pick up their last check at the makeshift office in the middle of the lot.

Ellie saw Tiny and George. They appeared to be having a serious discussion. George Toogood was angrily thumbing Tiny's shirt. Tiny had a stupid expression on his face.

"What's going on?" Ellie asked Vern.

"Tiny won the paycheck pot last week." Vern got out of the truck and leaned on the open door. "George is mad about something. All the guys at work except Tiny know better than to mess with George."

Ellie knew the guys had to be careful what they said to George as he had a reputation for being ruthless.

"Stay in the truck," Vern said, but Ellie said she needed some fresh air.

George ran the paycheck poker game at work. Men who thought they had a good set of numbers got George to compare their stub. Since this was their last pay, they were extra emotional over this poker game.

Vern sauntered across the lot. Ellie saw the men comparing their pay stubs, then put the receipts in their pockets. If the serial numbers on a guy's paycheck that week made the best poker hand, he would win the kitty. This kitty was larger than usual as they had contributed ten dollars of last week's pay toward this week's pot.

Vern waved to George and Tiny, then he went into the makeshift portable building.

Ellie watched George and Tiny in the huddle. It was obvious Tiny had bad nerves from the worried look on his face. Vern said he needed to have the nonsense knocked out of him and settle down. Vern thought Tiny was worth saving, because he was a good worker.

When Vern came out of the portable, he stopped to talk to George and Tiny. Ellie knew why George was waiting for the men, but there wasn't a lot Vern could do about it. Paycheck poker was illegal at Champion. Everybody knew it, but nobody wanted to quit playing because the odds were so good. They thought paycheck poker was an easy way to make an extra bit of money. The fact they might not get called back to work lent an urgency to the situation.

"It has to be a straight flush or pairs," George told Vern, "to beat my hand. Let's see your numbers." Everybody was disappointed that Tiny had won the pot last week, but there wasn't anything they could do about it. Tiny sidled up to Vern as he pulled his stub out.

Vern handed George his stub. George's voice was really loud. He was usually careful to keep the game out of Vern's sight, but he was annoyed about something.

Ellie saw George's lazy eye move around in a disconcerting way. The wayward eye gave him an exotic appearance. "The women like it," he had told Ellie when she tried not to watch him. If Beri wasn't working, he would get in Ellie's car without asking. He didn't take no for an answer. Ellie didn't like to be surprised.

Ellie walked toward the men as George checked Vern's stub, then Tiny's.

George poked his finger at Tiny. He said loudly, "Now, I remember what was funny about the check stub you showed me last week. You showed me the same check stub before. Grosste, you're ripping us off, presenting a check that was a week old in place of last week's check. You changed the dates and photocopied the stub, but I remember those numbers almost won the week before."

"I don't want to know anything about this," Vern said.

"I haven't done any such thing," Tiny said vehemently. "Prove it."

Moose came out of the portable office.

Tiny complained to Moose about the way he was treated over last week's win, in spite of the dirty looks from the foremen standing in the door of the makeshift building.

When Moose told Tiny to keep quiet, Tiny stopped other men and told them.

"We could ask to see the check stub again," Moose decided after a discussion with George. "And see if it's fake. We should have thought of this happening and wrote down the numbers."

"I had, but I couldn't find the list. If it's true, all hell will break loose. Let's keep it quiet," George said. "Wait until most of the men have got their pay and have gone home before you say too much about doing anything."

But Moose didn't listen to George. He went up behind Tiny and said in a menacing voice that made Tiny jump, "I want to see that check stub."

Tiny turned around. "Why? What for?"

"We just want to see it, that's all," Moose said.

"I'm just waiting to see who wins this week. Isn't that all right?" Tiny almost whined.

"Just show it to us," Moose repeated, "and we'll leave you alone."

Ellie saw Moose, George and Vern confronting Tiny and there was a line of sullen, angry faces behind them. Tiny cleared his throat. "Well, come over to the car. It's in there."

"Why would it be in your car?" George demanded.

Ellie saw George Toogood approach Tiny. George was six-feet, five-inches tall and weighed two-hundred and sixty-five pounds. He worked day and night. Not much got past him and no one argued. Tiny Grosste was almost as big, but Tiny was lazy and mean. Ellie could see he might be desperate and afraid, because maybe George had him cornered.

Moose pulled at Tiny Grosste's sleeve and asked him again in a low, civil manner about the check stub.

Tiny acted as if he couldn't understand why Moose was so riled up. "What gives?" he asked. "Do you want the money back? I thought I won it fair and square so I spent the money. If you didn't want me to have it, you should have asked for the money back, right away, when I still had it."

George grabbed his coat. "If you're lying to me, I'll shake the shit out of you."

"I..I'm n..not lying," Tiny stuttered.

"Prove it, then!" George almost spit in his face.

Tiny invited George around to the house to see the check stub. George agreed. Tiny went to get his car. George followed. He opened his truck door and hung on it, waiting.

"I smell a rat," Moose said. "Things are getting phonier all the time. He'll probably buy him off with a bottle of booze."

"George is no fool," Vern said.

Everybody knew about the phony check stub now.

The men hadn't driven away after picking up their checks as they usually did. They waited in their cars with angry, contorted faces. Only Tiny was gunning his motor. The others watched. They were immobile.

"Don't let him get away," Moose cried.

At that moment, several cars zoomed toward the gate.

Tiny Grosste drove his car toward the gate, but several of the guys had already blocked the exit with their cars. Tiny tried to back his car up and head for the other exit. Cars circled his and tires squealed in the dirt. He couldn't get anywhere even if he bashed his car into their cars.

Men swarmed Tiny's car. Since Tiny had his doors locked, they started to rock the vehicle. Moose picked up an iron bar and smashed the rear windshield and crunched one fender. Then, he went around the car and smashed the driver's window open and unlocked the door. He pulled Tiny out, but Tiny slammed the door open against Moose, and ran.

"Don't let him get away. Search the car. Find the stub," Moose said.

After a tussle with six men, Tiny fell to the ground.

Moose stood over him shaking a crowbar. "Talk, or I'll knock your brains out."

Tiny covered his head. "You don't mean that. Haven't you done enough damage? Why are you being so mean to me?" Then, Tiny whined about his kid's glasses. With disdain on their faces, some of them went over and kicked the wheels of Tiny's car and pounded their fists on the dented hood.

George grabbed Moose's arm. "What's the matter with you? Why are you doing this?"

"Break this up. Get on home. Now, the supers will know about it. I won't be able to do anything. You guys are finished," Vern said loudly.

"Let's get out of here," George said.

George drove off the lot and down the side street. Most of the men followed him. Ellie was amazed at their stolid expressions. They'd just threatened to kill somebody but you'd never know it from their faces.

Tiny was slumped beside his wrecked car.

"Are you all right?" Vern asked Tiny.

Tiny mumbled. Vern helped him up. To Ellie, Tiny appeared dazed and so scared he was probably shaking in his boots.

"Go on home before you piss yourself," Vern said.

"Thanks, man. I thought they were going to kill me."

Tiny got into his smashed car and pulled the door shut. To Ellie's amazement, the wreck started. He drove it off the lot.

Ellie watched him leave. Then, she went with Vern towards the truck. Moose walked beside them.

"He accused me of being a stoolie, for telling you what was going on over the check stubs," Moose said to Vern.

"It wasn't the first time I heard it," Vern said. "You watch out. You were the one using the crowbar."

"Tiny looked at me as if he could kill me," Moose confided. Then he laughed as if it was funny. "Everybody will just hate him for spoiling a good thing."

"I think Moose is losing his cool," Vern told Ellie after Moose left in his jeep. "God knows what will happen next."

"We're all losing our cool," Ellie said as she held the truck door open for Robert and Susan. The parking lot was almost empty of cars, but she was shaking. "When I saw the men go crazy, I didn't know what to do, run back to the truck or stay."

Vern started the motor on the Explorer. "You probably did the right thing to stay in one place. You might have got driven over."

The thoughts of what might have happened to her kids made Ellie feel faint. "Whew, that sure was scary," Ellie said as she touched Vern on the shoulder.

"It sure was," Vern agreed, gripping the wheel so hard his knuckles were white. "If I'd known they were going to be like that, I wouldn't have come over."

* * *

CHAPTER EIGHTEEN

When Ellie mentioned to Vern how skilful he was at breaking up the mob at the plant yesterday, he only grunted. She figured she'd complimented him and he hadn't noticed.

At work, Moose didn't want to talk to Ellie about the problem he caused either.

"I bought a new shirt." Moose patted his rotund belly covered by his new black shirt. "My closet is full of shirts. Every time I'm down, I buy a new shirt. Do you like it?"

"It's black," Ellie said. "Does it match your mood?"

"It goes with my moustache. It makes me look older. The women don't think I'm such a baby face." When Ellie laughed, he said, "I don't think I have a future anyway."

"It goes with your hair, too." Ellie went to the end of the bar to clean the ashtrays.

"You aren't listening to me. Our friendship could be over." Moose stalked past where Ellie stood and went out of the bar.

In a moment, he was back, all contrite. "I want to talk," he said to her.

"Beri's been crying her eyes out and I think you might know what it's about."

He groaned. "Not that again. Let's not talk about her. I can't imagine what I saw in her in the first place. George thinks Beri is a basket case and needs someone stable in her life. He said she is touched."

"Well, I know she's not perfect. I think she should take her anti-depressants again."

Moose shrugged. "There's nothing I can do."

"I don't want to get involved either. It's too wearing."

"Let's get to know each other better. Let's go away for a weekend."

"It would be hard to arrange," Ellie said. Moose ended one relationship and started another, letting them heat up and cool off like the seasons of the year.

"Maybe just an overnight would be easier."

"I'll think about it." Ellie thought she must be nuts to consider being Moose's mother for a weekend, but she was feeling ignored since Vern was unpleasant, and Quantz was unavailable right now. She thought she must have a hard time waiting for people to pay attention to her.

"You can read people. You understand people. Tell me what happens when people don't get along," Moose said, as if he was wanting to tell her his life story.

"You're not getting along with Cathy?"

Moose shook his head. "I'm really disappointed in the women I know. One guy I know is divorced twice. He's drinking himself stupid because his girlfriend has someone else. He thinks he can't win. Three times and out."

Ellie figured she must be a sympathetic listener. She sighed. "I guess nobody can win. This summer's been awful. Vern's been really difficult."

"Norma and Quantz aren't getting along either. Somebody said hello to Quantz at a party, and he's been sleeping on the couch for a week."

"He didn't tell me that!" Ellie cried without thinking. The person who spoke to Quantz wasn't Ellie. It was somebody else.

"He wouldn't. He's pretty careful about what he says."

Ellie was too stunned to say anything for a moment. Then, thinking Quantz was unfaithful to her, she took a deep breath. "We could go away for a bit. We'd have a good time," she said quickly to Moose.

"Next weekend? An overnight?" Moose said.

"Great." Ellie thought she would have to think of an excuse, such as shopping or visiting.

"I think I'm falling in love with you. You seem to know what I want."

"We'll go away and get it over with." Ellie almost wished she hadn't said anything. Moose loved to make an impression, but he went to extremes. Sometimes she found him entertaining, but she was sure she was just another possibility to him. He was a very smooth operator when it came to women, the way he could flatter. Ellie thought him more a friend than a lover.

What Moose said about Quantz hurt Ellie. Even though it was really none of her business what Quantz and his wife did, Ellie couldn't help feeling she was stabbed in the back.

Ellie noticed Moose's eyes were angry, the pupils a sharp point. "What's the matter, now?" she asked.

"I'm going to commit suicide tonight," he said. "I'll swim out into the lake. I'll disappear into the blue."

Moose was full of wild propositions. Ellie thought she couldn't handle this all the time. She thought if Moose wasn't causing someone else a problem, he was causing himself one.

"Don't do it on the rug."

Moose glared.

"It was supposed to be a joke. Are you a magician?" Ellie asked.

He didn't laugh.

"If you do that we can't go away. We can go next week or the week after," Ellie said wondering if the date made things any better. It didn't.

Quantz came into the bar looking for Moose. Ellie couldn't him look him in the eye. He was such a liar.

"Let's not sit here in the bar drinking all day. Let's go out for awhile," Quantz said happily.

Moose said, "I think I'll finish my drink and maybe have another." Moose hadn't touched his drink.

"You're getting to be a barfly," Quantz said.

"Let's go fishing for the afternoon, then," Moose said. "I know a good spot."

"Sure," Quantz said. "I'll get my hip waders."

But Quantz didn't leave. He sat down at the bar to wait for Moose. Then, Quantz told Ellie about last year's fishing trip up north and the big fish they came back with. "We do better every year. This year the trout were real big."

"Where did you buy those?" Ellie asked bluntly, figuring they bought the fish to prove they spent time fishing.

"What's with her?" Quantz whispered to Moose.

Moose shrugged. Quantz started to grin in a silly way. Ellie ignored him and got busy at the sink.

Moose wiped the perspiration off his forehead. "Did I tell you about the sturgeon I caught last spring? It was so lively it flipped off the hook back into the river and I had to run after it."

Ellie had heard this story before, but she couldn't remember the exact details.

"It was about three feet long, wasn't it," Quantz said.

"Yeah," Moose said, "like a mermaid." Moose flexed his arms to the shape of his prize fish. It would be hanging on my wall if my wall was big enough." His eyes glinted underneath his baby-fine eyelashes as he looked at Ellie maybe a bit too long.

"You could always build a bigger house," Ellie suggested, "if your fishing luck continues."

"He can't keep up the one he has," Quantz said.

"I can do the building at night," Moose said. "I'm not sleeping nights. Hammering's better than pacing, right? At least it's productive. But the problem is, I don't want a new house, I don't even want the one I have."

"See, I told you," Quantz said.

"You're just joking!" Ellie smiled fondly at Moose who shrugged nonchalantly.

Moose headed for the door. "I'll get my stuff out of the garage and I'll see you down at the river."

"He'll go until he drops." Quantz pensively leaned his elbows on the bar. "Then, I'll have to drive him home. I'll give him a cursing and Cathy'll feel sorry for the poor guy."

"Is he getting desperate again?" Ellie removed Moose's almost-full beer glass and put the change on her tray.

"What do you mean?" Quantz's eyes flickered uneasily.

Ellie enjoyed Quantz thinking she was showing interest in Moose. What would his eyes do when he reached a conclusion? Look guilty? Ellie thought they were both liars and that he was the best example of it.

Ellie had noticed that her laughing at Moose's jokes made Quantz suspicious. She said, "He's doing things he's not supposed to again, like not working, like telling things on people. It makes him edgy."

"He's asking about us," Quantz accused in a jealous manner.

"Why?" Ellie asked, suspicious.

Quantz shrugged. "He notices things, he's around a lot."

Ellie wondered about the jealousy issue Moose was causing. If Moose found out things he'd tell and then she'd have to do something. Quantz would have to do something. Ellie thought most of their life was covering up what they were doing and doing penance if they were found out. She thought this couldn't possibly be the whole truth about them but it seemed to be.

"Really?" Ellie was testy. "He mentioned you and Norma aren't getting along."

"I've got that all straightened up." Quantz turned his head away so she couldn't see the expression on his face.

"It's none of my business how you and your wife get along." Should she mention what Moose told her?

"Before you here it from someone else, I said hello to someone at a party and I've been sleeping on the couch since. Norma has a short fuse," Quantz apologized.

"Like the rest of us," Ellie said. She thought about the consequences of this, everyone was jealous of everyone else, a suspicious truce that couldn't last.

"Everyone is asking about us, even Steve. But I always change the subject. I say you love your husband and we're just friends and the matter's dropped."

His remark made Ellie think they would stop their affair, but so far it was never more than a thought.

"It's because you hang about the bar too much," Ellie said shortly. "You should be on your way."

"You're not saying much. What are you doing after work, Ellie?" Quantz asked, not moving.

Ellie didn't answer right away. She was pissed off and she thought he knew why and was lying about it. Ellie thought Quantz was using the issue of their affair to cover up the fact he was seeing someone else and had got into trouble over it. She felt hurt and bewildered.

"Maybe we can have a drink," he continued. "I want to talk."

Ellie said, "I thought you were going fishing."

"Tuesday, then."

"Okay."

Quantz touched her cheek as he left, but Ellie pulled away from him. He wasn't supposed to touch her in public.

For the next few days, Ellie tried to sort out her dilemma. Ellie thought she should tell Quantz their affair was over, and she surprised at how upset she was at the thought of it. She was beginning to depend on Quantz. It bothered her to think she was expecting things from him. She was expecting things, like love, like fidelity, like what are we going to be doing tomorrow or next week. Their relationship couldn't materialize for any period of time.

Ellie felt her life was falling apart. It was obvious Quantz wasn't going to commit to her, since he couldn't commit to anything. If she asked him to commit, he would say he was thinking of her best interests, and he was, too, if she was going to stay with Vern. But what if Vern found out and ditched her? Ellie wondered what would become of her if her relationship with Vern disintegrated even further.

Ellie was perfectly aware that since Quantz wasn't going to do something to end their affair she had to, and she decided on Tuesday she would tell Quantz maybe they shouldn't see each other any more.

On Tuesday, they drove down a side road to the lake. Quantz's first words made her think he was trying to be wonderful and considerate for her welfare.

"Is Vern bothering you about it?"

"I just say everybody else hangs around, and they do."

"Are you going out with other people?"

"I'm not going to do that," Ellie said.

"Are you seeing Moose?"

"No, he just likes someone to listen to him. Why do you keep asking me that?" Ellie realized she was lying, just like he did. Maybe they deserved each other.

"Like you said, he's around a lot. He asks about things that aren't any of his business."

"How come Moose is taking over this conversation?"

"Because he's asking. He's never been any different." Quantz was gazing out the window, and Ellie was sitting with her arms folded staring straight ahead.

"My, you're quiet," Quantz said eventually. "I don't really have time if this is going to take forever."

"It doesn't have to happen at all." Ellie just thought Quantz was in a hurry and giving her a snow job. Was this where love had brought her, to an impasse of jealousy?

"It's really none of my business how you and your wife get along," Ellie said shortly. It was hard for her to cover her jealous feelings. She had stronger feelings than she first anticipated, than she first bargained for.

"You really are sore, aren't you?

"Let's say I don't like being given the run-around."

"We don't always have to make love, do we? I like seeing you just for seeing you." Quantz tapped the steering wheel with his hands. "I haven't taken anyone else out for ten weeks," he confided, which was the length of time Ellie had been seeing him.

"Maybe it's some kind of record for you," Ellie said. If she was this jealous, maybe she was ready to say either me or nobody, and up to this point she hadn't thought she was.

"Sure it is. You can't say the same."

"I'm not seeing anyone else," Ellie said determinedly.

"Forget it," he said.

Ellie thought Quantz and her were so jealous of each other, they were passionate.

"It's crazy to be carping at each other when we have so little time. Christ, this is getting like a second marriage."

"You said it, I didn't."

"I'm just kidding." Quantz put his arm around Ellie.

The remark made Ellie think. Maybe he was complaining about seeing her so often, but she liked his sex, the touching and necking. She counted on it. Ellie wanted to deliver an ultimatum and it had to be the right one, but the only thing she could think of at this point in time was to follow her feelings and leave things be.

Quantz's gaze was fixated on her lap. It was hard to miss his intent.

"Let's get out of here." Quantz opened his car door.

They went down the path and under the pine trees. Finding a thick layer of pine needles, they lay down.

Ellie rolled toward him. She thought fleetingly and guiltily he was probably sore she had questioned him, but he put his arms around her.

They made love and Ellie forgot everything. Her mouth was open with pleasure, her reaction to losing control.

Finally, he lifted her up and let out an immense reluctant groan. Ellie scraped her shoulders on a low-lying branch, giving her a welt she could feel as soon as he ran his hands over her back. His eyes had closed and he hadn't noticed how close they were to the sharp branches.

She could feel his muscles contracting and releasing as he reached a climax.

"You're dog-piss," he said, reaching for the tissue in his pocket, glancing at her.

"You're a cowpoke, then. You're a brute." Ellie realized she hadn't picked a good time to say the things she was going to say.

"Don't say such things," he said.

"It's the truth."

"Not for us, it's not." He gave Ellie an extremely dirty stare. "Where'd you get that idea?"

Ellie shrugged. With this perfect self-image he had, she thought he never liked to be expected to do things on demand or be caught at a disadvantage.

"Is this sex act some kind of a miracle for you?" Quantz asked rudely.

"Is it for you?"

"Well, it's because you need it." Quantz sat back and did up his clothes.

Ellie felt exposed and defenseless when it was obvious it was much better for her than it was for him. He must be starting to think he was God's gift, and she was in fantasy-land for agreeing with him.

"What's the reason for us being together tonight?" she asked, irritated. "Is it just the usual or is it something else? Like your having to sleep on the couch? We could forget it!"

"Didn't you get off?" he asked, so casual and insulting.

"What's it to you?" Ellie was angry it didn't bother him to take chances like it bothered her. Up until this point, she didn't seem to mind skirting the fine line of risk and discovery, but now it seemed to Ellie like she might have made one huge mistake.

"We're here because I like you," he said. "But I shouldn't be here."

"Neither should I, so drive me back to my car." Ellie was disappointed that he criticized her, and she didn't try to keep the disappointment out of her voice. She wanted to pick a fight so she could tell him where to go.

As far as she was concerned, Ellie was turning into a quick rip, for relief only. She thought their sex needs were like magnets, in which she felt at a disadvantage.

On the way back to the car, Quantz mentioned to Ellie, "Why are you sulking? Why would you be doing that?"

"Nope," Ellie said emphatically. "I'm not."

Ellie didn't like the smirk on Quantz's face. She was upset, thinking covering up feelings was easier for him, but it couldn't possibly be true.

For the first time, Quantz didn't mention when he could see her again. She got out of his car and unlocked her own.

Quantz followed her. "Most people take life easy." He stuck his head into the window of her car. "But you, I'm not sure what you want out of life or what you want from me."

"Maybe I don't want anything from you," Ellie said. What he said was a letdown, a comparison of his needs against her needs. Ellie felt like a loser.

Quantz had returned to his Camaro, started it up, and was driving away.

Ellie yelled after him. "I don't need your face in my life anyway. You're messing me up." She thought angrily he wasn't that important to her, and she was going to try and put him out of her mind.

* * *

CHAPTER NINETEEN

After Ellie broke up with Quantz, she felt quite mixed up. She thought Quantz was faithless and couldn't make a lasting decision. Ellie needed a friend and Moose did, too.

The next weekend, Ellie and Moose escaped in the car to Toronto. Ellie was determined this was going to be a romantic adventure, and she thought Toronto, a city on Lake Ontario, was a good place to pretend you're something you're not.

To Ellie, the sprawling metropolis was so different from where she lived she might as well have been going to another country.

Gilded and blackened windows of banks and offices towered above them. The windows were faceless, mirrored, and huge and Ellie wondered what was going on inside.

At five o'clock, the streets filled with businessmen in black suits, office girls, and maintenance staff. They were hurriedly striding past, and Ellie was no wiser what they did.

The smoky aroma of the sausage vendors claimed every corner, making Ellie hungry, but they were going to wait to eat later. Men with collars turned up ducked into doorways and down the stairwells into strip clubs. If Ellie was with Moose they justed looked, but if she was alone, they sidled over and called her sweetheart.

Moose put his arm over her shoulders. They made a strange couple, Ellie thought. Ellie wore a silver dress and silver shoes and Moose wore a brown suit.

Once the lights came on, Ellie noticed there were more than a few neon lights.

They went up the CN tower, a ringed spike of concrete disappearing in the night sky. From the top, Ellie saw the city was ribbons of lights. On the narrow walkway from the lookout to the elevators, the streets were far away. To look down left a hole in Ellie's stomach. Vehicles were toys and people were moving dots.

"If you fell from the tower, you would be nothing," Moose said.

"If I fell, I would be raspberry jam," Ellie said.

Ellie was aware that, in an instant, they could be nothing, if they decided to jump from this point in the sky. She thought Moose was a shadow under her elbow and she was a moth searching for light. They floated around the tower, as two silly tourists from somewhere north of the 401, that vast hinterland Torontonians only read about or saw on the way to their summer cottages. People in Toronto sometimes thought country folk were out of it, slow-moving and sleepy and didn't notice much.

Ellie had a standing joke about Toronto people. It was because of her city acquaintances. Sometimes when they left Toronto, they couldn't find their way back. One couple came to Goderich to visit Ellie and got lost going home. They didn't realize until they saw the sign, "Bridge to the USA," at Sarnia, that they had gone in the wrong direction. When they arrived home in Toronto, hours later, they were very angry. They cited bad verbal directions. "Did you see a lake on the way up there?" she asked. "Why are you blaming me?"

Ellie and Moose went into a bar. One lone man was staring vacuously while they drank beer and ate chicken wings, smoking a cigarette. He had watery, pale eyes as if there was a hollow person behind his skull, a dome thinly covered with a crewcut which showed the scars on his head. At least forty, he was old and scary. At another table, there were two young girls with round innocent faces and wild blonde hair with dark roots. They seemed to be waiting. Moose looked them over as the old man stared at Ellie.

In the washroom downstairs, there was a machine into which Ellie put change and got perfume. Ellie put some on; it was called "Charlie."

Then they went down into the subway. Ellie stood close to Moose and mentioned something about being cold. He mentioned something about throwing her under the wheels of the subway train. Ellie wondered if he was deliberately threatening her or not. Even so, she leaned against him. He gingerly put his arm around her to keep her warm.

Later, the same scary man from the bar was deliberately staring at her out of the window of the subway train as they walked past. It didn't seem to bother Moose, but Ellie was ready to freak out.

Ellie was wishing for Quantz. It was silly for her to be with one man and wishing for another. This happened quite a bit. She enjoyed Moose's company, but she still pretended that he was someone else. When they were walking down the street holding hands, Ellie was having a good time but she should have been somewhere else.

They stopped at a bookstore.

"When are you ever going to do anything with your writing?" he prodded Ellie. "Aren't you a writer?"

"Yes."

"Nobody will read it. Why do you do it?"

"I notice you reading the newspapers and magazines."

"It's not the same."

"It is the same."

"I don't read that romance crap. So why do you do it?"

"Because I can't sing."

"Can't sing?" Moose laughed. "That's really stupid."

"I have squeaky voice. The nameless sound that comes out is like it comes from a pond at night."

"You're a frog?" Moose asked.

Moose questioned her as if she had said the most ludicrous thing ever. Already, she had told him things she would never tell Quantz. She worried about Quantz's opinion of her, so she'd only tell him positive things.

"I'd like to be able to sing like some people in my family can sing," Ellie said.

"Let's hear you sing," Moose said.

"You would pay me to keep quiet."

"No," he said.

"Do you know any singers, like good singers, who are also writers?"

"No, but I know a lot of people who talk about writing," said Moose. "They don't seem to get a lot done."

"For a matter of fact, neither do I." She thought it was something she could always put off.

Ellie had goosebumps. For a summer night, it was cold. She was so cold she slid her hands under Moose's shirt sleeves, feeling his warm skin. He laughed but he took her hands away.

They looked at the store, but they didn't go in. There was a $1.99 section in the bookstore window, reduced to clear.

"That's where your book will be when it doesn't sell," Moose said.

"It has to actually be finished to be able to sell."

Moose took Ellie's hand, and they continued walking down the street. Later, they went to the motel, Maple Leaf Motel. Ellie thought it belonged to the Toronto underworld with all the fighting and yelling that went on.

Neither of them took their clothes off for awhile. Moose seemed to be nervous. Ellie touched him and he jumped. His jumpiness was like he just had sex but Ellie knew he hadn't. She wondered what to do. Perhaps he needed to get drunk.

Moose had quite a few glasses of wine. Then he started to crow about the young beautiful girls who smiled at him.

Ellie had quite a bit of wine too since they had bought a large bottle. She was starting to enjoy herself.

Moose had a very precarious erection, so that some assistance was necessary. Ellie sucked him so much that her mouth was sore. She could fall asleep waiting for him. Quantz would never let her go down on him but Vern would. In fact, Vern was addicted to it. He felt it was his due.

"Is it like this for everybody or is it just me?" Ellie asked. It took quite a bit of wine to get up the nerve to ask.

"You think too much," Moose said. "It doesn't happen too often."

Ellie thought if she got another mouthful she was going to give him some of the cum. After he came, she waited a minute holding the salty, strong mucous in her mouth. Then, she let on she was going to give him a kiss. She gave him a deposit instead.

He gulped it, complaining. "Whew," he said. "You wouldn't want to hold that in your mouth too long."

"I just thought you should have half." Ellie thought that was a very reasonable response but Moose turned his face away when she tried to kiss him again. She laughed. "Don't you like the way it smells?"

"No," he said, shuddering.

Ellie wondered why she was here. She must be nuts. He was interested in her and he wasn't interested in her. She couldn't decide.

"What do you think?" Moose pointed to his equipment.

"What do you mean?" Ellie asked.

Moose worried about the size of his penis and its performance. "Once I went to a prostitute and she said, 'teasles, kneasles, smallcox,' when she looked me over. I was so mortified I never went back."

"I like it," Ellie said.

Finally they did it doggie-style, and Moose acted vastly relieved. Maybe he was trying to prove himself.

After they were in bed trying to screw, they went out walking on the pier. There were boats tied up to be loaded.

"I will go out into the lake," he said, bemused, "and drown myself."

"I'm not a good swimmer," Ellie said, "so don't jump in the lake off the pier. If it is deep, I won't be coming in after you. Besides it's dark."

"I am guilty," he said. "You are innocent."

"What does that mean?" she asked. "Do you kill people?"

"No," he said, with a half-laugh.

"Do you rob banks?"

"No," he said, chuckling.

Ellie wished he wouldn't take himself so seriously. She half-surmised it was about sex, and his attitude about sex, that he was so guilty about. Maybe because he liked older women, he had a guilt complex. He was needy, he said, in the love letters he wrote her on the motel stationery. Quantz would never do that. Moose was a sweet guy. But, he made her jaw sore.

At the motel late at night, the walls were so thin that Ellie could hear everything. The windows were open, too. A woman's voice in the middle of the night went, "Eh, eh, eh." Ellie could tell the three sounds of climax were involuntary.

Moose was sleeping. He never heard it or if he did he never said anything about it. Neither did Ellie. The motel was noisy except between three and five in the morning.

Their long night wasn't the best. But neither Moose nor Ellie would have been satisfied with just talk. Ellie pondered maybe they were a threat to the social fabric of the universe or something stupid like that. There must be an ulterior purpose to the screwing around that they kept so carefully hidden.

Moose said it made him feel like such an animal to be screwing when the sun came up. "Maybe we should quit and try something else."

"That's fine with me." Ellie had a raw mouth. She'd heard toothless old women did this, so it didn't do a lot for her self-image.

Downtown the next day, they wandered around like two lost souls. They went to a Mexican restaurant with colored drawings of large toucans and small rooms filled with huge green plants.

Moose yelled the orders at the waiter. He wanted strips of beef, peppers, and onions in a red-hot pan. It was sizzling and smoky, too hot to touch. Ellie got the hot sauce for the nachos and he got the mild. He immediately switched them. He choked on the hot sauce and had to order a pitcher of water. Ellie thought he must be taking his pills again.

At the end of the meal, they received a chocolate mint candy. Moose ate his candy and pronounced it stale.

"Do you like your candy?" he asked. From his horrified expression, Ellie thought it was the most important question on the face of the earth.

"Yes," Ellie said, to please him.

Then, the waiter asked if they needed anything else. He reached to remove Ellie's water glass.

Moose said loudly, "Leave it there. She likes my cum juice better than she likes this lousy candy. She needs the water." The waiter jumped and removed his hand from the glass as if Moose had slapped it. He quickly left.

Ellie giggled at the ridiculous things Moose was saying. She kicked him with her foot.

"Stop that," Moose hissed. He grabbed her off the chair and pushed her along. She was laughing.

Two waitresses turned their backs and covered their faces when they walked out of the restaurant. Ellie could tell that they were thoroughly disgusted, but Ellie didn't care. She'd never see them again.

Then, they drove right home, even if it did take three hours, even if it was late. Ellie didn't want to stay another night. Not another word was said about them being together. Ellie felt the wide-eyed wishfulness she had in starting her affair with Quantz, the hope she had of love solving everything had turned into a bad joke.

Ellie thought it was great to get back home to normal old Vern, who just complained about getting too many baked potatoes when he was out in a restaurant.

* * *

CHAPTER TWENTY

On Sunday, Ellie and Vern Menzies went into town to watch the annual Kinsmen's parade. The Kinsmen, a volunteer organization for the union members, raised money for the community. The streets were crowded with people, and their cars and their lawn chairs.

At noon the sun was directly overhead. Ellie spread a blanket on the grass for Robert and Susan, and Vern sat in the truck with the door open.

In mid-August, Ellie saw that the grass was browning and the heat was becoming oppressive. It was almost as warm in the shade because the breeze hardly stirred the leaves. Haze arose from the hoods of the vehicles and the onlookers might collapse if it weren't for their rigid chairs.

The wait was so long Vern fell asleep with his head slumped on the seat.

Then, Ellie heard the ding of chimes on the next street. Vern awoke with a snort, his hair pressed up from the car seat. "What's that? It's that goddamn Normandy chime." The clock had a loud presence, with a ding-dong on the hour and four-note phrase on the quarter hour.

"No, it's the band. You've forgotten we're waiting for the parade."

Vern groaned. "What time is it?"

Ellie craned her neck to see if the bells would materialize into a band followed by a parade. The first band of kilts and bagpipes came around the corner, followed by a mix of sounds in the distance promising many more bands.

Ellie saw many fabulous floats that people had spent weeks decorating, sporting children in small cardboard buildings, decked with crepe paper flowers and skirts, one after another. As long as it didn't rain, the castles were awe-inspiring and the huts appealing.

Ellie noted the parade was two or three times as long as the yearly parade, because of the floats from the town's 150th birthday celebration being used over again.

Ellie was eager to see the float Vern had worked on. They guys from Champion had put wheels on an iron bed. Last night when Ellie was away, they had tried it out in the supermarket parking lot.

Soon, Ellie saw several of the guys from Champion walking by wearing pajamas and extended shoes. The clowns were followed by a mummy, a skeleton, and a guy with a large bandage on his head and a cast on his leg. He was supposed to be riding in the bed, but he had his crutches over his shoulder.

"What happened to the float?" Vern yelled.

"It fell apart," the mime said. "The front wheel fell off and we had to stash it."

"I waited all afternoon for this!" Vern was disappointed.

"It should have had four wheels instead of three. Then maybe we could have got around the course." He gave Vern the finger sign.

"The makeup covers up your bruised lip pretty good, doesn't it?"

"Vern!" Ellie said. "What was that all about?"

"We had a fight over the bed. He called me a liar so I smacked his face in."

Ellie's mouth hung open as she listened.

It was Vern's three-wheeled design that they used, and so it was his fault that it had fallen apart.

"We could go across town and watch it over again," Vern said. "We waited so long and this is all there is!"

"I thought you had a headache."

"I just said that."

Vern and Ellie, Robert and Susan got into the truck when the parade was over, but they were sitting in a traffic jam.

"Let's go somewhere private soon."

"Why?"

"It's getting away from me." Vern pointed to his penis which was like a drainpipe in his jeans.

"Vern, we're in public." She covered him with a newspaper.

"So? We can go park somewhere or don't you do that?"

Ellie gasped. She wondered what Vern was referring to, but he didn't seem to be angry, just impatient.

"Well?" Vern poked at her with his index finger.

"If you didn't enjoy the parade," Ellie said, "you don't need to take it out on me."

"It was a fiasco. You don't need to be so stuffy."

"Nobody will know about the bed."

"Everybody will know. Put your hand there. We're not going anywhere."

Ellie felt up his crotch. What was a drainpipe was now more like a culvert.

"I'm hornier than a two-peckered dog," Vern said.

"You're gross."

"You've turned into a tight-ass all of a sudden."

"You don't have to be so crabby about it. What do you expect me to do?"

"You could be more interested, is what you could do."

Then, they had a ridiculous extended argument over the length of the parade, why they parked where they did, and the size of the traffic jam.

When they got home from the parade, Vern was keen. Robert and Susan had fallen asleep, so Ellie took them upstairs.

Vern came upstairs, too. After all, an argument was a prelude to sex. Ellie thought maybe she could slide out of it.

"It's like a jackhammer, you had better do something."

Vern liked her to go down on him a great deal. He lay back on the bed and made it move around. Ellie put her mouth around it. Vern called this performing fellatio.

He found it relaxing.

"If you don't stop, I will come in your face."

"No, don't do that." Unless she was starving, it wasn't a treat and when was she ever starving?

So they did it regular. His kisses were searching and his body demanding. Ellie was a lot more willing than she would admit, so it wasn't long before she had a climax.

After she came, she had to turn over and they did it doggie-style. She got up on her knees with her ass in the air and her head down on the bed, just the position she wouldn't want to be caught in if someone walked in the door. Vern liked it this way better than the other ways. He used to tell her when he was ready, but now Ellie was supposed to know.

When she felt Vern get harder and all tense, she pushed against him. She chewed on his thumb to punish him, which he liked. His muscles throbbed until he made involuntary gasps that lasted and lasted like he was going to croak at any minute. Ellie was glad there was nobody listening. He bit the back of her neck and thrust at her with his pelvis.

"That was earthshattering," Vern said. He lay to the side, holding his head and cupping his balls.

"No, it wasn't."

"Yes, it was."

"I thought it had further to come, from your heels when it usually comes from your tailbone."

Vern laughed for once. "Where's supper?"

"You can get dinner ready."

"I have to wash the truck." Vern spent more time on his Ford Explorer than he did on anything else.

Ellie was in a hurry so she boiled the potatoes dry, and singed them black on the bottom.

Vern's face showed evidence of strain as he looked at his dinner. "Did I do something wrong? Are you mad or something?"

"No, why would I be?"

"This is a lousy dinner."

"You don't have to eat it," Ellie said unreasonably.

"What's the matter now?"

"I guess I just think it's better to do things at the proper time, at bedtime."

"It took too long, too," Vern said.

Ellie thought it was silly to argue how long the sex act should take. Most of the time it didn't take as long as anything else, even brushing your teeth.

"You had something else more important to do?" Ellie asked. Ellie wanted less hassle and to be satisfied more.

"Not at that moment in time."

His reply made Ellie feel disappointed. Sex was another dispute. Ellie thought it just added to the tension.

That night, Ellie counted the hot heavy days, thinking they couldn't possibly have had this many days, forty-two, without rain. It was so hot upstairs that she couldn't sleep. She sweated, tossed, and turned as the fans roared.

Ellie had never seen the grass and crops so parched at this time of year. Midsummer was normally dry, but never this dry. The grass was brown for miles, the corn in twisted spikes, and the grain short and sparse.

The next night, after her shift at the Bedford, there was fighting in the streets. There was swearing in the alley that led away from the bar, groaning and yelling that she didn't investigate, and that would disappear inside when the cold came. Broken beer bottles, fermented liquid running down the brick, blood splattered on the sidewalk. Another fight. As Ellie walked past, someone swore at his wife or some other female. Women wailed, doors slammed. When the children slept, the adults participated in a charade of violence. Ellie thought if it wasn't play-acting, there would be a lot of dead bodies around.

When Ellie got home from work at about two-thirty in the morning, Vern was in bed but he was still awake. He worried constantly over his job prospects, his energy taken up with anxiety. Ellie expected another fight tonight. Nights were usually bad. They railed at each other.

"I need a drink," Vern said.

"Sure. Wouldn't you rather have something to eat?" Ellie suggested.

"It's too damn hot."

Ellie got Vern a rye and herself one too. The ice cubes clinked against the glass.

"What kept you tonight?"

"Fighting in the street."

"Stay out of it," he said brusquely.

"I don't get involved. Heard about your job yet?"

Vern said, "I can't do anything right. I could just go out and shoot somebody. Life is hell."

"Well, what was it like before?" Ellie was impatient.

"The same," he said, after a moment.

Vern sat on the edge of the bed. The cubes were almost melted in his rye. He spoke in a droning sort of voice making it seem he was thinking out loud. "There seems to be no way out. I can't figure out what to do."

Vern knocked his drink back. He got up off the bed.

"Get me another drink too," Ellie asked.

"I'm going to get the gun." Vern's voice sounded low and deliberate.

Ellie was alarmed at his remark, as Vern had a rifle, a shotgun, and a hunting license, for deer in season. He could use them, but she never thought of him as a violent man. She lay back on the bed in her underwear patiently waiting for Vern to get her another drink.

There was a light breeze through the upstairs window. Maybe it meant welcome relief, a change in the weather. She heard the shed door bang so she thought Vern had gone outside to check. Ellie thought she should put a t-shirt on or pull the sheet over her, but instead she rolled over and fell asleep.

In an instant, she jerked awake. How much time had really passed, Ellie wondered then she saw Vern had the rifle out.

In the split second that Ellie woke up and became aware, she discerned that she was staring into the muzzle of a rifle topped with rifle-sights. The hair on the back of her neck stood on end. Ellie saw that Vern was staring out the window, not aiming. She saw the glint on the barrel as he went closer to the window to check the street.

"What's going on?" Her voice was a croak. She must have been crazy to stare at him paralyzed like that, not reacting or trying to run away. As Ellie watched him, he sat down wearily. The dark bags under his eyes matched his grey-tinged hair. He put the rifle across his knee, aiming the barrel at Ellie.

"Why do you have the gun out? What's happening out there?" Ellie was so scared her voice wavered. "Is it loaded?"

"Why are you so down on me all the time?" His voice quaked in a despondent way. "Why is everything I do not good enough?"

"I don't mean to be critical," Ellie said.

"It's obvious how you feel about me." Vern studied Ellie. "There's nothing out there. I'd heard a car stopping, footsteps."

"What's with the gun, then?" Ellie demanded.

"I have to keep you under control."

"That doesn't make sense." Ellie was confused about why she was getting blamed for his joblessness.

"You're the one that's crazy."

Ellie wondered what to do. In the morning, she'd hide the gun and she'd hide the ammunition.

"I'm not tired. I'll go downstairs and watch the movie," Vern said uncertainly.

"Why don't you put that away and come to bed?"

"Something might happen," Vern said.

"You'll get called back and things will go on as if nothing has happened," Ellie said.

"Do you really believe that?" Vern sounded discouraged. "Our lives have changed so much," he said. "Look how you've changed. I used to be able to count on you."

"I'll get us another drink," Ellie slithered out of bed.

"Is that your solution?" Vern asked harshly. "It's disgusting, how obsessed you are with booze. All it does is make you stupid. It makes you faithless."

Ellie started to realize she was in danger. She could no longer say she was innocent, knowing she had a life that didn't concern Vern, and maybe that was what he was mad about. Her lies and cover-ups were so overwhelming.

"I don't know why you have to take it out on me. But then you always do." Ellie stood beside the bed.

"Why don't you shit or get off the pot?" Vern said angrily.

"Why, are you asking me to make up my mind?" Ellie was surprised.

"Oh, for Chrissake," he replied, in a slurred voice. "You're such a stupid bitch."

Ellie felt a warm trickle running down the inside of her leg and down her foot. She was afraid to listen to him, afraid there would be no going back if she said what was on her mind, so she bit her tongue, hard, without meaning to. Ellie felt a dribble, then a flood. She was so afraid she pissed herself.

"If you want to shoot me, then go ahead, do it," she said, sucking her bleeding tongue. "What am I going to do now?" Ellie wasn't too sure what Vern wanted, not too sure of their marriage. In bed, they expressed their resentment. They had conflict, not love. Ellie went to the washroom for a towel to soak up the pee.

Towards four in the morning, when they were too weary to argue any more, a clap of thunder and lightning woke Ellie from her doze. Vern had fallen asleep in his chair. All of a sudden, a gusting wind swept into the house.

Ellie sat up. The rain was so heavy, coming down in sheets she couldn't see the street. In the morning, she learned how severe and destructive the thunderstorm was. Limbs were ripped off trees. One had crashed into the neighbor's roof across the street.

* * *

CHAPTER TWENTY ONE

In the morning, after Ellie swept up the glass from the broken window and mopped up her bedroom floor, she went to work. After work, she bumped into Beri.

"Let's have a coffee," Beri said.

"Sure," Ellie said. Beri trotted along beside Ellie to the coffee shop.

In spite of herself, Ellie was glad to see her. All day Ellie had felt under stress deciding what to do about her eroded relationship with Vern. Maybe Beri would listen.

"Vern and I had a big fight. I thought things were over for us but he was all right this morning. Maybe he was just drunk last night." Then Ellie took a deep breath to continue. She sure needed a friend right now.

"When do you think you might have time to go shopping with me?" Beri interrupted.

"Beri--" Ellie said, wanting her to shut up.

"George and I aren't getting along either, so I'm out looking for a male friend." Beri opened the door of the cafe. Ellie followed her to a table. "Don't bring us the dregs," Beri said to the waitress.

While they waited for a fresh pot of coffee, Beri went on and on about why she and George didn't get along, and why she didn't feel comfortable with him. She had difficulties with intimacy, but it didn't apply to her ability to talk, which was rather open-ended and lengthy. "We can't have sex at all right now because I have this vaginal infection that won't go away. Medication doesn't seem to clear it up."

"George keeps reinfecting you." Guys like George Toogood seemed to have women here and there, or so Ellie thought. The last thing she wanted to hear about was Beri's ass problems. Ellie was waiting to tell Beri how she was disappointed in her as a friend.

"Maybe. He doesn't like it much with all that goop. So we've quit but it doesn't make sense. The doctor said to do whatever it takes to get relief from the sex act. He thinks it might have something to do with chemistry, and that I don't climax enough." Beri's face was sheepish. This wasn't the first time Ellie had heard about Beri's sex problem.

"It's important to be satisfied." Ellie tried not to sound bored. "It might have something to do with your age."

The waitress set two steaming cups of fresh coffee in front of them. "Cream?"

"Sure. What's that got to do with anything?" Beri asked.

"Will there be anything else?"

Ellie shrugged. "Quite a bit, usually."

"No thanks. We're fine." Then, Beri watched the waitress leave and continued in a hushed voice, "There is this bar in Stratford where we can go. The men come right up. All I have to do is sit there. Do you want to come?"

Ellie thought she had to be kidding. A conversation with Beri was so one-sided. "No, I want you to get Wayne off my back. You do know him, don't you?" Since the last time she'd seen Beri, Wayne had tried a number on her again, impressing on her the importance of his clients and friends.

Beri laughed self-consciously. "I go there whenever George and I have a big fight." She stroked her chin as if she might suddenly confess something revealing about her personality, or more of what she said before.

"I'm talking about Wayne and his bad habits," Ellie repeated. If she went, she would just be bait or a confidant or maybe it was just a gloomy way of looking at things considering how depressed she felt right now. "I figured you'd know what I'm talking about."

"I do." Beri smiled happily as she waited for Ellie to decide. "I think Wayne just likes you."

"Maybe those Stratford dinks keep reinfecting you," Ellie said. Then she picked up her cup and sipped her coffee.

"I keep getting the impression Wayne has jobs for me to do. Is that the impression you have of him?"

"You're mad at me, aren't you?" Beri blinked at Ellie. "Why are you mad at me?"

Finally, recognition, Ellie thought. Ellie reminded herself Beri was asking her the same thing Wayne did, only in a different way. "You're causing me trouble with Vern," she said.

"So you're not getting along with Vern. Are you going to break up?" Beri clucked her tongue, like an old lady. "You're the sweet, soft type. You should be more exciting."

"What do you mean by that?"

"Then he wouldn't be so tempted to pick a fight," Beri said. "Affairs are essential, anyway. I can't understand how anyone could go to bed with the same person year after year, without variety. It would be too boring, wouldn't it?"

"I'd rather be in love," Ellie said.

"Always the same person?" Beri asked, incredulous.

"One at a time will do."

"Gawd, I can't even imagine having only one person."

"If you met the right one, you might feel different."

Beri had a vacant, scared expression on her face which Ellie read as worry about losing George because they weren't getting along. "What will happen if George moves out?" Ellie asked.

Beri's face focused into an angry scowl. "You're a hypocrite. First Moose, now George. What have you been telling George? He hasn't been speaking to me lately."

"When's the last time you saw me talking to George?" Ellie thought Beri was like everybody, so inconsistent in not knowing what she wanted, and so unsatisfied with what she had. The way she was made Ellie furious. "Why does everything fall on my head?" she yelled. "You've got a lot of nerve blaming me for your problems. I don't want to go to Stratford and help you pick up guys. You can go to Wayne for that."

"You don't have to get so uptight about it," Beri said serenely. "Maybe if you had a make-over, you would feel better. I'm going to get one."

Ellie thought Beri's remark was typical. She thought she must be stupid to be listening to Beri. Maybe that's why she was so depressed. Ellie inspected Beri as she talked. There was a great deal that could be pointed out, for example, how she hadn't shaved her moustache lately, how straw-like her hair was now it was bleached, how tough the expression was on her face with the cigarette hanging on her lip.

Ellie snickered so that coffee went up her nose. She choked, then she said with a tickle in her throat. "You could pay more attention to George instead of Moose and Vern and everybody else."

"That's not very nice." Beri's face was livid, but Ellie couldn't stop laughing.

"No, but why should I be nice? Why don't I just say what I think?" Ellie thought neither of them could afford to be superior, throwing a chink into the other's relationships, or get rid of their men. Ellie had to hang onto Vern, and Beri George, no matter what they actually said.

"Well, why don't you?" Beri sneered.

Ellie thought what would be the use? Beri never got the point, anyway, of the conversation. Ellie needed a friend and as a friend, Beri was lacking. Beri was always checking, cross-checking and interrogating Ellie as if she had to answer questions in court. And she was always mad at Ellie. And not listening. It was getting tiresome. There were more pleasant things to do in life.

"You would make a good chairman of a committee lobbying the government. It would put your nagging and fault-finding to good use."

Beri sucked her tongue. "Vern is a good man. You shouldn't be so mean to him. Don't you ever ask him what the trouble is?"

"I've asked him," Ellie said, thoughtfully. "But I never get a satisfactory answer."

"Then you should keep asking," Beri said. "Vern hardly needs any encouragement. He's a good listener. If you asked him what the trouble is, he would likely tell you."

Ellie resented Beri's smug remark. "What trouble? What do you mean?"

"Maybe you have been taking Vern for granted," Beri said.

"Who are you, a confidante? Has he been crying on your shoulder?"

"No, I just thought you could be more sympathetic."

"Really!"

"I just thought you wouldn't want to lose such a good man."

"Oh, really?" Ellie said, as pointed as she could be. "What's George doing these days? Working a lot of nights?"

"That was uncalled for. That was nasty." Beri's face looked pinched, disconsolate, and resentful.

"You asked for it. I can't see how my husband is any of your business. I think you can leave Vern alone," Ellie said. "If you don't, I'll tell George."

"You would, too," Beri nodded.

Ellie got up, and left some change for the coffee. Ellie thought she couldn't confide in Beri, and now that she'd delivered Beri an ultimatum, Ellie'd have to watch her back.

When Ellie went home, she got dinner ready. As she stirred the sauce, Vern handed Ellie a bag of notebooks that she hadn't been able to find. Maybe he had been hiding them because Vern thought her efforts were a waste of time.

When they made love that night, Vern seemed to like her more than usual. He held Ellie tight so that her breasts were squished against him. The way he was made Ellie glad she'd asked him for more affection.

"Soft," Vern said, as if the feel of her breasts was a great surprise. "I'm not very good at this after all these years." He fumbled with the hooks on her brassiere and slid his hands up under her shirt.

Moaning, sighing, and squeaking of the bed. Their efforts were more like they used to be. Familiar.

Vern was such a predictable, cranky fixture in her life Ellie hadn't considered losing him. Maybe Vern didn't like Beri that much after all, and maybe he liked Ellie better. At her worst, sophisticated sucking up, picking faults, and worming her way into people's marriages, Beri made Ellie feel used, trod over, as if her feelings were of no consequence. Beri used people when she tried to find a purpose in life and came up empty. Now Beri's actions were prompting Ellie to get back at her, something she would never have considered a few months ago.

Ellie was happy Vern was making a consistent effort to get along, but the next night, the way he was standing on the porch as she came home from work, waiting for her with an angry scowl on his face, made her wonder what had happened.

"Where have you been?" he asked, exasperated.

"I've been at work." Ellie walked right past him.

He repeated his question loudly into her ear.

"I said I was working." Ellie wanted to duck Vern.

He grabbed Ellie and swung her around. "You're lying. Answer me, you slut. You ugly, sleazy bitch. What were you doing down by the river? Someone saw your car at Moose's place."

"Who?"

"It doesn't matter who. Somebody told me you've been giving Moose rides home late at night. Are you two in love or what?"

"You're nuts. Can't we talk about this in a reasonable manner?" Ellie thought she was in trouble over nothing, just when things were starting to improve.

"Reasonable? You expect me to be reasonable?" He was spitting in Ellie's face. He wrenched her arm behind her back.

"Ouch, you're hurting me."

"Hurting you? I ought to kill you for making a fool of me." He slapped Ellie across the mouth so hard that she fell against the door and down the concrete steps.

Vern waited for Ellie to get up.

As she wiped the blood off her mouth with the back of her hand, her heart sank. She got up and tried to walk past Vern but he grabbed her arm.

"I thought you told me you were going shopping with a friend on the weekend," Vern yelled. "There's a lot of trust in this relationship, you know. It just blew out the window."

"It's true. I was in Toronto. I did go shopping."

"Well, how come Moose was there?"

"We went out for dinner."

"So, you did spend the night together."

"Nothing happened."

"I don't believe that for a minute." But Vern's voice had dropped to normal range.

"It's true. He slept on one bed and I slept on the other." It was a half-lie.

Vern laughed hysterically. "Hee, hee, hee," he said. "How did you get yourself in a sexless situation like that?"

Ellie felt her jaw for tender spots. Her hand was bloody from the cut on her mouth. "How do you think? Diane couldn't make it and I had to go myself."

"If I was going to spend a weekend with a woman, I would want something to come of it," he said.

"Like what?"

"Well, I would at least want some sex. Something that was more fun than you are. I can believe it, though. You would do something like that. You would go to Toronto with your boyfriend and not do anything, just to make a fool of me." Vern sounded incredulous.

Ellie carefully touched her teeth. She thought Vern might have really loosened them this time.

Vern snickered. "I had my teeth loosened. I know what it can be like," Vern said.

"So, it's pity now, is it?"

"No, it isn't. You make me so mad, I could just whack you," Vern said, holding up his fist. He followed Ellie into the house, but instead of whacking her again, he smashed his fist through the wall, leaving a large hole in the drywall. Ellie went stiff with fear. She stood against the wall, looking at the hole.

"Do you hear what I am saying?" Vern repeated, shaking his dusty fist.

"No, you aren't talking loud enough."

"I never felt like hitting you before, but now I could just drive you one."

"Why did you do it then, if you didn't feel like it?" Sometimes Vern liked her to provoke him, Ellie thought.

"You are one stupid bitch." He leveled his fist in front of her face. For the moment that his clenched hand aimed at her nose, she thought he was going to mash her face. Ellie looked him square in the eye and he dropped his arm. She didn't know what made her so bold. Or maybe he hurt his hand putting it through the wall.

Ellie started up the steps toward the bedroom where her children were sleeping.

"Where did you get that dress? It makes you look hippy."

"I like it or I wouldn't have bought it."

"You bought it for somebody else then?"

The pushy remarks made Ellie mad because no matter what she did, Vern would say she did the wrong thing.

"Are you having an affair with Beri?" she blurted. Ellie decided to create an issue because she had seen them come into the bar together just last week and the smug attitude on Beri's face had made her mad.

"Why do you ask such a stupid question?" Vern was immediately alarmed and angry.

Ellie burst into tears. "You're mean not to answer me."

"Oh dear, we're in a bad way, aren't we? What makes you so high-strung and suspicious over nothing?" Vern demanded.

"Well, are you or not?" Ellie asked. It wasn't a small matter to Ellie, but Vern acted as if it was a joke. He laughed in a queer manner, then he made a few disparaging remarks about Beri. Vern yelled at Ellie, "If the men aren't slobbering over you, you aren't happy are you? If you don't leave me alone, I'll get some pills to calm you down. Then, I'll prove you're crazy and take the children."

Ellie's nerves were like raw meat, with Vern picking at her in a negative way, peeling layer after layer. "Why don't you level with me?" Ellie said, wanting serious attention.

His face was ugly with a scowl which might as well be permanent. "I've always been a faithful husband to you. I just don't have the time to spend with you. Sex takes too long. It just isn't worth it to wait for you to be satisfied."

"I don't know what your problem is," Ellie cried. "But I can't stand it." She ran upstairs away from Vern and sobbed uncontrollably on her bed. She cried all night long. Vern spent the night on the couch.

Then, in the morning, Vern had one of his screaming rages lasting three hours. His eyes were wild, ringed with dark circles. Ellie could see Vern was upset but she was so numb she felt she had turned to mica or a lump of quartz, because Vern was an angry blast of air ready to blow her away. He was mad, too, that she didn't react.

Vern yelled in her face. "Your family is a bunch of crooks. You're sneaky just like they are. They've ignorant and so are you. I don't know why I give you the time of day. I should just belt you. I should just kill you and put you out of your misery." Vern spat his words, splashing her face. He shook her shoulders.

Ellie was desperate and scared. She had a terrible headache. How could she go to work in a shambles like this? She screamed at him. "I said I was sorry. I shouldn't have gone out with Moose. What else do you expect me to do?"

"You can walk off the face of the earth," Vern said.

"Fine. All right, then. I'll leave right now." Ellie was confused, wanting Vern to stop her, maybe, but she threw a few things into a box, walked out the door with Robert and Susan behind her and got into the truck.

As she started the truck, Vern appeared at the garage door. He had a hammer in his hand, and he ran toward the truck and threw the hammer against the windshield shattering the glass. The hammer bounced on the hood and slithered onto the ground.

Ellie stopped the truck and got out. She grabbed the hammer and threw it as far away as she could. Then, she ran at Vern and pounded his chest with both hands.

"What do you think you're trying to do? There's me and the kids in that truck." Ellie screamed with rage. "We could have been killed if the windshield exploded." Ellie ran back to the truck, jumped in and drove off even though she had to crane her neck to see through the myriad cracks.

Robert and Susan sat on their carseats, speechless, as Ellie drove to her parent's empty trailer, wondering how things had got so far out of control, where she went wrong.

As soon as they got in the door of the trailer, the kids were asking for their dad. Ellie was thinking of driving back home, but she hadn't figured why she would. She hadn't figured how she was going to go to work, so she phoned Beri to cover for her.

The next night, Friday night, August 26, when Ellie heard a knock at the door, she knew Vern would be there before she opened it. He was standing sheepishly on the doorstep. In spite of herself, she was glad to see him. She always liked Vern best when he decided to be extra nice to her.

"When are you going to give up this foolishness and come home?" Vern asked. His manner was gruff, but his face showed his heart was broken. He was contrite as anything.

Ellie said, "I'll consider it." She had thought she was never going back, but as soon as he asked she knew she would. But, she didn't want to give him the satisfaction of doing it immediately.

"What do you mean, you'll consider it? Yes or no?"

"I'll let you know." She shut the door in his face.

A few minutes later, Ellie went back home. When she got there, Vern put his arms lightly around her as if she was his grandmother. Ellie was disappointed in his lack of intensity, but they would get along fine because Ellie decided to try harder. But she felt the relationship was fragile, with the good sucked out of it. The pieces of the relationship were still there, but the love holding them together was lukewarm.

For some strange and unexplained reason, Ellie thought, Vern said he should make a special effort to get along. He said somebody told him he should pay more attention.

"Who?" Ellie asked.

"A friend," Vern said. He wouldn't say who when she pressed him, so Ellie thought that was an insult. He liked to keep secrets from her, which bothered her. Ellie was acting more thin-skinned than usual, and she thought Vern could always find reasons for saying or doing something.

Vern said their problems were no reflection on him, but were the result of her being a bit crazy, or having some hormonal imbalance in her body. "You're the problem, Ellie," he said.

Ellie thought they should both do something before they got themselves into a corner which they couldn't get out of. She mentioned marriage counselling, but he wouldn't hear of it. He didn't want to discuss private things with a stranger.

"We can spend more time talking," Vern suggested.

"I think I should get a medal for listening to you," Ellie said. She didn't like what he said and she knew things would only get better if he liked or respected her more.

"Maybe a pension, too?" he asked, joking.

Ellie laughed. Vern laughed, too.

"We're a crazy pair," he said. That was a poor excuse for a truce, Ellie thought, but she didn't say anything.

For dinner Saturday night, Ellie put a clean shirt on. Since Ellie had come home, Vern had said the odd complimentary thing. Ellie was suspicious as anything, wondering what he was up to. It wasn't like him to be nice. She caught him inspecting her out of the corner of his eye.

"What are you thinking?"

"I was just thinking about work."

Ellie couldn't help thinking the stuff he said was irrelevant, because during dinner, he didn't stop watching her. It wasn't a secret, happy look he gave her. It was a guarded, noncommittal expression as if he didn't know quite what to do with her. Or he would know what to do, and would do it immediately, if it was legal to bop her on the head.

Ellie waited, feeling nondescript, not pretty or desirable, not wanting to cause another fight so soon, for him to say something more. He hated it when she was quiet. He liked her to make the first move.

Vern patted her on the head.

"At least it was a better dinner than usual," Vern said. "It's an effort to keep my temper under control. It doesn't get me anywhere but into trouble. Don't you think I am doing a good job of it?"

Ellie kissed him on the cheek and put her arm around him, but to her surprise he held his body stiff and unyielding, as if he didn't want her and wasn't going to make an effort to be romantic.

* * *

CHAPTER TWENTY TWO

Although Vern was happy to see Ellie come back, he was mad she had to go into the Bedford. Much of the swelling on Ellie's face had disappeared. Ellie covered the bruise on her mouth with powder and lipstick and wore a new hairdo with a red bow to look different.

"What's your problem, Ellie?" Beri sneered in a caustic voice. "I just want you to answer a simple question." She tromped heavily around the bar. "How did your weekend go?"

Ellie could tell Beri was very angry.

"The weekend hasn't even started," Ellie said.

"I meant the one before!" Beri smacked ashtrays down.

"Super. It was super."

"Ellie," she pronounced icily, "you always say that after a weekend, even a normal weekend."

Seething with visible anger and jealousy, Beri clenched her teeth, making her jaw twist. "See anyone you knew?" she asked, finally, as if to ingratiate.

"Not really." Ellie could elaborate but the details would make Beri more angry.

"I don't believe it for one minute. You're a little liar." Her lips were thinly drawn over her teeth, in a furious grimace. There was no cut or swelling on those thin lips. When she turned, she knocked a beer glass over in her haste, splashing the contents everywhere.

Ellie wiped up the beer foam which had dripped over the leather on the bar. That irritated Beri, too.

"Oh, your personality is so exasperating," Beri said shortly. "Who gives a damn about the beer spilled? The whole place stinks anyway. I can't stand the way you're so particular."

"You'll get over it, maybe," Ellie said. Ellie figured Beri had heard she was away with Moose and had probably been the one to tell Vern. Ellie wondered why she felt so unconcerned when they were so mad at her.

Ruth rushed in. She sat down in front of Ellie, out of breath. "Know a good place to stay? I have to get out of here. I don't feel welcome." As Ruth slurped her beer, her sulky red mouth smeared the beer glass.

"I don't believe you. This town has alway been the same," Beri said.

"I used to be able to handle stuff." Ruth was almost in tears. Her painted red lips pursed. "Not any more. I lost my job. I'm too old, too slow, too ugly. Everybody seems to hate Ruth. They yell at her in the streets. They tell her to smile. They say nasty things such as, `Go fuck yourself.'"

"That's ignorant," Beri said. "Tell them it would be better than their wrinkled old dink."

Ruth laughed.

"Ask them how their ticker is," Beri said. "Ask for a second opinion if they say it works fine."

"I'd better not do that," Ruth said. "It's not the kind of thing any decent person would say, but they say it to me."

Ruth's voice was so dry and distant, she might have been talking about someone else. Ellie wished she hadn't taken her into her confidence. The way Ruth talked about her personal self like she was an object across the room made her seem a bit crazy.

The way Ruth talked made Ellie think of Wayne. Ellie wished everybody like Ruth and Wayne would leave her alone. Any of the times Ruth blatantly tried to recruit her, Beri would blithely ignore it and Ellie would be left to put her off politely.

"This is a nasty town. The other day, a car coming around the corner drove into an old lady. No one came for a long time even though I tried to wave them down. I may be next. Will you miss me?" Ruth continued.

"What about Mr. Blue?" Beri asked.

"I can't cope with men like Mr. Blue. If he doesn't get his own way, he harasses me. I'm getting older, you know. I'm not tempting any more." If so, why did he bother Ruth all the time, Ellie wondered? It didn't make sense.

Ellie sighed as she gathered up the empty bottles. She thought what a bad day this was, what a bad week it was. She had to listen to Ruth complain and Beri criticize.

"What happened to you? Your face looks sore," Ruth said to Ellie.

"I have a cut lip."

"The girls out front are talking about Ellie. She's changed, she's getting easy." Then Beri lowered her voice. "They think she's running around. Her love life's like a weigh station." Her face was smug and skeptical.

Ruth's eyes flickered with amusement.

"You can mind your own business," Ellie said. "My love life is not your concern."

Beri leaned across the counter and touched Ellie. But Ellie jumped back because of Beri's hostile attitude.

"Take it easy," Beri said.

"You could be in a better mood," Ellie said.

"Oh, I get crabby. Think nothing of it."

"I hadn't noticed," Ellie said angrily, as if Beri could say anything and nothing would happen.

Ruth continued in a monotone, about how she got started. "When I was a kid, a nasty old man and his nasty old friends said they would tell my parents if I didn't do what they wanted. They didn't bother my friend, just me."

"Where you scared?"

"I believed him because he was a prominent member of the community," Ruth said.

"What kind of a conversation are we having here?" Beri demanded. She was getting very drunk. "I've known men like that before. I can handle those kind of men. You can blackmail them. If he doesn't pay up, you can tell his wife."

"So you know what to do about Wayne," Ellie said quickly.

"If he was my husband, I would hit him over the head with a baseball bat." Ruth started to cry.

"You had better go home," Beri said.

"No," Ruth said. "I'll have another drink. It'll make me feel better."

"Go right ahead," Beri said. "Make the boss rich."

"Your boss is cool," Ruth said.

"No one else thinks he is cool," Beri snapped.

"He likes Ellie." Ruth ogled Ellie with her fish eyes.

Ellie almost choked.

"From what I see, he is real nice to you," Ruth continued.

Ellie didn't want to hear any more about Steve. It was all so disgusting.

"He likes Ellie almost as much as Moose does," Beri said.

"I just try to get along," Ellie said, feeling like smacking some sense into Beri. "How come you're making it so hard?"

"Are you trying to get back at me for something?" Beri's voice trailed off as both Ellie and Ruth stared at her.

"Now, why would I want to do something like that?" Ellie yelled so hard that Ruth jumped. Then she giggled.

"Do you want me to call you a taxi, Ruth?"

"Yes, but first, I want to have another drink. Do you think I am a baddie to have another drink?"

"No," Ellie said. "I just think you're interesting."

That pleased Ruth, but if she got any more relaxed she would fall under the bar.

Ellie couldn't have inert people lying about the bar.

"So the boss likes you, Ellie," Ruth shook her head. "The boss is nice but he talks dirty." Ellie wondered what she was referring to, as most of the time Steve watched Ruth very carefully.

"Everybody talks dirty," George Toogood said, as he came through the bar. "Except Beri. She asks questions. Questions you can't answer."

"Yeah, she likes to reveal private things connected to other people," Ellie said, relieved to see George.

George poked at Ellie's chest. "You're a stranger!"

"Doesn't look like it," Beri sneered.

"Are you jealous?" George asked Beri. Ellie loved his remark because it changed the subject and unbalanced Beri. George smiled and Beri scowled. Ellie laughed.

"Not a chance, you hotshot," Beri said. George left again after he gave Beri a triumphant squeeze.

"Want to know what I've been doing? Want to know about my love life?" Beri's voice went up a few notches.

Ellie cringed. When Beri had been with Vern, she was bursting to tell Ellie just to make her feel bad, but Ellie was determined to act the stoic. Lately, Beri wasn't succeeding. Ellie figured she must be getting tougher, more resilient, like a piece of gristle.

"Tell away. I'm listening," Ruth said.

"Take a taxi home, Ruth, before you fall off your stool," Beri said in a singsong voice.

"Yeah," Ellie said. "Go home, before we have to sweep you up with the broom and dustpan."

Ruth's face puckered as if she was about to sneeze, but she started to laugh. "What are you drinking?" Ruth asked. "You have one too. It's on me." She gave Ellie some money.

"Not now. Maybe later on," Ellie said. "But thanks." She put the money away. Ruth was always buying her drinks because Ruth still thought they were going to work together sometime and Ellie hadn't been able to discourage her.

Ruth and Beri giggled over nothing, their heads together, like the drunks they were.

Ellie said, "You had better straighten up because if the boss comes in here and finds you like this, you will lose your job."

Beri had just picked up her tray and taken another walk around the room, and Ruth had just stubbed out her cigarette and gone out the side door when Steve did indeed come in and order his draft for the evening.

He took a furtive look over his shoulder. He didn't see too many of his customers, so that his gaze landed on Ellie. Ellie didn't like it when the boss was looking at her.

"Where is everybody tonight, Ellie?"

"I don't know."

"I was wondering if you thought any more about our little business idea," Steve said softly. "You can't tell about people just looking at them, if they're good for business or not. It's called being nice to people."

Shit, Ellie thought, why do they all think if they say, "do or else," I will.

"They're probably watching the horse races," Ellie said.

"There are no horse races tonight," Steve said angrily. He glared at her.

"Oh." Ellie thought she was getting like everyone else, saying the first thing that came into her head.

"What's wrong with you and Beri? Can't you two get along?"

"I think she and George had a fight and she's taking it out on me." Ellie thought if Steve believed this, he'd believe anything.

"Oh," Steve said. After he finished his beer, he left.

"Want to see my new lipstick?" Beri dumped her purse on the counter. The contents went flying. Her tokes, which were in an embossed silver case, as if they were cigarettes, slid into the sink. Ellie caught them.

"Thank you," Beri snapped, grabbing them out of Ellie's hand. Beri had given Ellie tokes out of the silver case before.

"What's wrong?" Ellie asked, loudly, having had enough of her temper.

"You know damn well what's wrong," Beri said. "Do I have to spell it out for you, that nobody, but <u>nobody</u> likes you messing with Moose?"

"You win some. You lose some," Ellie said. "And besides, the boss is asking why we aren't getting along."

"Why we <u>aren't</u> getting along?" Beri snorted ferociously. "<u>You</u> aren't getting along with anybody! Do you see them around?" Her arms waved around the empty bar.

She meant the guys. Quantz and Moose had stayed away from the bar this week. It was just as well, since Ellie might throw something at them. But now Ellie expected them almost every night.

Beri glowered. She was so mad Ellie thought she would say she was sick and go home early. That's how she got back but Beri stayed until closing. Her foul mood hung about her like a smoker's ring.

Beri looked so lonely and grumpy sitting at the bar after closing waiting for George to come back and pick her up that Ellie almost put her arm around her. "George has to have it every night or he doesn't think he is a man. It's because he has only one testicle. I guess he has to prove himself," Beri said.

"Why would he feel that way?" Ellie asked.

"He's very jealous," she said gloomily, "if anyone so much as looks at me."

Ellie didn't believe it for a minute. She figured George would assert emotional control over Beri's behavior.

"Your infection cleared up?"

Beri's face registered complete lack of recall.

"It comes and goes," she said, shrugging after a moment's thought. "It's one of those monthly things."

"Oh." Ellie figured Beri lied about why they were going out to find a man, like she lied about everything else.

The cops came in and checked to see if everyone had left. Baker and Martin seemed to sniff the air the way they lifted their heads around. When Beri yelled at them, "Nobody in here," they walked back out.

Because she stayed after work to talk to Beri, Ellie was twenty minutes late getting home. Vern was counting the minutes.

"I don't know what your game is, but I'm sick of it."

Vern gave her such a tongue-lashing Ellie wept, got a pillow and blanket, and stayed on the couch.

After about an hour's sleep, Ellie awoke with a parched mouth. At first, she didn't know where she was. She was so startled she thought she had come to suddenly and was lying face down half-submerged in water.

Ellie recalled those nightmares in which she dreamt her mother was trying to smother her.

Ellie had a frightful headache. She wondered how she got herself into a situation where she was doing penance on the couch, while her husband snored upstairs. Everything was so dreadful. Unable to sleep, she went upstairs to bed whether Vern liked it or not. Vern slept on as Ellie slipped into bed.

* * *

CHAPTER TWENTY THREE

In the morning, Vern seemed to have forgotten the argument, as he put his arm around Ellie and gave her a kiss. The way he was so nice to her made Ellie think she was important after all.

Later that day, Tuesday, August 30, late in the afternoon, Ellie was working the Bedford Bar by herself.

Ellie noticed Tiny come in and peer at the men sitting in the lounge. Most of the men who hung around the bar looked as if they were still working, Ellie thought, with their T-shirts and patched jeans, in the grit under their fingernails, and the discouraged look about their eyes.

Ellie saw Tiny take his hat off. His dark matted hair stuck out at all angles. The logo on the cap had a skull and crossbones on it.

"Where's Moose?" he asked Ellie, who was waiting for him to sit down.

Ellie pointed where Moose had been sitting but the stool was empty.

Tiny leaned over the bar counter. He didn't look at Ellie and she couldn't hear what he was mumbling about.

His long hair brushed a customer's sleeve.

"Hey, watch it," the customer said sharply. When Tiny started to talk, the guy took his beer to a table. Tiny appeared disappointed.

Ellie noticed it happened all the time. People paid attention as long as Tiny listened to them, but when he started to talk, they got up and left the room. Ellie heard Tiny had been in court again over his daughter's fight at the bar. Maybe that's what he wanted to discuss.

Moose came back in. His blue shirt was so tight across his midsection the buttons were almost popped. Ellie decided it must be one of his old ones or he'd gained weight.

"Get lost," Moose said as Tiny followed him to his stool.

"I want to talk to you."

Moose waved the air. "You're wasting your breath."

"I mean it." Tiny looked at Ellie.

"Go kick some pop machines," Moose joked.

"What?" Ellie asked.

"Once, I got so mad trying to get one pop, I kicked the machine, and 30 bottles dropped out." Tiny grinned.

"Then he went around Champion and sold them for 10 cents each."

"That was a fluke."

"No, it wasn't. You regularly hit the machine with a mallet and sell the pop which falls out."

"Aw. I don't."

"Go." Moose flicked his hand. "Away. Far away."

Tiny must admire Moose for the risks he takes because he sat down beside him anyway, Ellie thought, to ingratiate himself for a favor or something.

"Why does it take five Newfoundlanders to change a lightbulb?" he asked Moose.

When Moose was silent, Tiny continued. "One to hold the lightbulb and four to turn the ladder around."

Moose said, "Listen. I'll buy you a beer if you'll go away after you drink it and leave me alone."

Ellie gave Tiny a draft. Ellie had heard these jokes before, which centered on the Newfoundlander who could usually find the hard way to do something.

"Did you hear the one about the French-Canadian swimming back to France with a Newfie under each arm?" Tiny asked.

Moose laughed in spite of himself. "Shut up," he chortled. "You have to be stupid to know stupid jokes."

George and Beri came in and sat down beside Moose and Tiny. "What do you know?" George asked.

"Know any French-Canadian jokes?" Tiny asked.

"Let's go to Montreal," Beri said to Ellie. "We'll have a good time. The guys there like us Ontario girls."

"When were you there?" Moose hooted.

"What concern is it of yours? I can go anytime," Beri said. "They are better than the guys you see around here."

"That's a low blow," George said.

"Why, what is the matter with us?" Tiny asked.

"Lots. You have got to give up your habit of staring at crotches, Tiny," Moose said. Tiny was gaping at a woman who just walked into the bar. "It's not civilized."

"I was looking at her ankles," Tiny said.

"Oh," Moose said, "Are they covered with varicose veins?"

"No, they are too thin."

Moose laughed and shook his head. "Better go on home to your wife before you do something stupid and get into even more trouble."

"You must be talking about yourself," Tiny said dryly.

"Jesus. Are you a mind reader?" Moose yawned as he stretched. A button popped off his strait-jacket shirt. "I guess I better go home, too, or Cathy won't be too cool." But he didn't make a move.

Ellie thought the men she knew had an image of themselves not related to reality. They were talkers rather than doers. Moose wanted to be bigger than life, but he was an out-of-work factory worker who sat around and talked too much.

"I like the old lady to be cool," Moose repeated, but Ellie could tell by the way he said it, that if he was plastered when he went home tonight, he would be asking for a fight and probably get one.

George, Beri, Tiny, and Moose all talked to Ellie at once. She thought it was like chinook season, the wind coming out their mouths was so hot.

"I could have a chick," Moose said, "nineteen or twenty years old, if the old lady isn't too cool." He wiggled his hands, watching for Ellie's reaction.

Ellie figured Cathy wasn't speaking to him right now.

"I could have ten chicks," George said.

"Well, why don't you?" Beri asked. "What's holding you back? Why are you hanging around here?"

"I want another drink." George drained his first one.

"There's your drink, Lover Boy." Beri pushed the beer to him as Ellie set it up.

"What's that supposed to mean?" George asked.

"It means you're doing things you're not supposed to," Beri said sharply. "Just like the rest of the guys around here."

George hung his head while Beri chewed him out. Maybe he was falling in love with Beri.

It was kind of funny to see them fight. Ellie could see Moose grin in a silly way.

Into the bar walked Steve and Wayne. Wayne was wearing a long white trench coat and a Spanish-type black hat. His bragging attitude meant to Ellie he'd just achieved something out of the ordinary.

"Look what the wind blew in," Moose said.

"I hope that means you're glad to see me," Wayne said.

"I'm not, because you mean trouble," Moose said. Ellie silently agreed with Moose.

Wayne towered over Ellie, his expression mean and condescending. He ordered doubles for all the guys. Wayne left the bar to sit down at a table, and the four men followed him. He took his hat off. After they drank that round, they ordered another.

"Let's go to Vegas and make a basket of money." Wayne waved his hat around as if he was a classy dude. From his swagger, Ellie figured he'd got a big promotion. His talk sounded like big-shot talk.

"We'll go for a week," Moose said.

"We'll go for five days."

"We'll go for four days."

"We'll go tonight and come back Monday."

"It would cost you about $1000."

"Ya know, five a week, but I've already been through all that." Wayne pushed his black hat across the table and back again. Ellie noticed he had a large bald spot on his head.

"You guys are all set to go to Vegas," Steve said. "But I can't. I have a business to run. Besides, the wife won't let me."

The plans were discussed for a few minutes. It sounded like no one could make it.

"Okay, I've had it with you yellow-necks, you spend all your time suck-holing the women. I'll go myself, then." Wayne planted the black hat on his head and adjusted it a few times. He left without letting anyone buy him a drink in return.

"He has piles of money," George said.

"I wish I had some of it," Moose said. "I know what I would do with his money."

"I wouldn't be sitting in Goderich trying to get somebody to go to Vegas with me, that's for sure," George said.

"I've started buying lottery tickets," Steve said.

"Win anything?"

"Not yet."

"See. You should go to Vegas," Moose said. "We should all go to Vegas."

Steve left and George followed.

"Wait, George. When are you going to pick me up?" Beri asked, turning all the way around on her stool.

George ignored her and left anyway.

"Jerk. How can you stand them when they get like this?" Beri asked Ellie.

"I don't hear any of it," Ellie said.

"I wish I could say the same," Beri said. "George is getting just like the rest of them." Beri watched Moose come back up to the bar.

"They're full of big ideas," Ellie said, "especially Wayne. I wish Wayne would keep his big ideas to himself."

"Hey, Ellie," Moose said as he sat down on his stool. "Come over here." In a low voice, Moose told Ellie he'd put in a good word for her with Wayne and Steve. "What's a friend for?" he said. "I could hug you," Ellie whispered. "How?"

"Don't ask," Moose said, "but you'll owe me one." Ellie was relieved Wayne was ignoring her, but maybe he was saving that trouble for later. She didn't trust Wayne.

"What are you talking about?" Tiny asked Moose.

Moose looked at Tiny and shrugged.

"Are you going to the union meeting?" Tiny asked. "Do you have a ticket?"

"Why don't you drink up your beer and go home?"

"Do you think you could get me in?"

"For Christ's sake! No!" Moose said.

Vern had told Ellie the men had to have special tickets to get into the union meetings and vote. It was for crowd control, because men who had nothing to do with Champion were coming to see and maybe cause the action.

"Maybe you shouldn't go to the union meeting either, Moose," Tiny said. "The men are looking for someone to blame. Give me your ticket."

"If they want anyone to blame, it should be you." Moose's eyes blazed with hatred. "You are a scuzzball, Tiny. You are the cheater. They should tar and feather you and run you out of town."

Ellie had heard all the men arguing over the union meeting, and what would be decided there. Vern had said which way the union would vote was a game of wits.

Ellie remembered they were angry about promises not carried out, and it wasn't until a walkout was threatened anything was done. At the meeting, they had to control the crowd or the men would riot. Nothing like a riot had happened in this town, Vern had said.

Ellie recalled Vern saying it was hard to keep a union meeting calm when six hundred men wondered vociferously if they would ever get another pay. They had heard the company was on the verge of bankruptcy and the bank was ready to call its loans.

"You're crazy, if you go to that meeting," Tiny said.

"Well, I can go if I like. I'm speaking," Moose said.

"What on?"

"I'm not telling you ahead of time," Moose said. Ellie thought his attitude was obstinate.

"It can't be that important."

"How would you know? You're only a bum."

"I'm not. I'm an employed man with a wife and children," Tiny said. "What right have you got to say that to me?"

Moose looked at Tiny in amazement.

"I've never seen you get so emotional," Moose said.

"You just think I'm a non-person," Tiny said. "I get tired of people like you shitting on me."

"You don't need to get so personal. I didn't mean anything by it."

"You can make it up." Tiny's lower lip trembled. "Get me a ticket to the meeting Thursday night!" Tiny raised his chin in a rally of confidence.

"If I did," Moose said, "you'd have to be in disguise because I know you sold your ticket. You're in a lot of trouble."

"You're the one who's in trouble, Moose," Tiny said angrily. "Take care." But he was talking to Moose's back.

Moose had slipped out of the bar, his jacket disappearing around the corner, quicker than Ellie had ever seen him go.

Tiny finished his draft and followed him. "Come back. I have something I want to tell you," he called through the door. "It's important."

Ellie could hear tires squeal in the alley.

"Damn," Tiny said as he went out of the bar.

* * *

CHAPTER TWENTY FOUR

Two days later, Ellie got time off work to attend the union meeting and count tickets, a job Vern had got for her. A couple other foremen's wives were there to help out, too.

The meeting was to begin at eight p.m. sharp and Ellie had taken her chair with the other two women. Vern stood with Quantz at the front waiting for the hall to fill.

At the double doors of the union hall Thursday night, Ellie could see Moose handing in his ticket for the meeting.

George took it from Moose, and looked it over, hardly acknowledging him. "Members only allowed, no onlookers or press," George said, after Moose had gone by him. "If you don't have a ticket you can't get in. There are absolutely no exceptions." Other big guys stood with George at the entrance, to keep the riffraff and everybody else out because they wanted the meeting to proceed in an orderly fashion.

Moose wended his way through the crowd toward the front.

"What do you know tonight?" Moose asked Vern, as he kept checking over his shoulder.

"The union is so hard-nosed they want continued layoffs if they don't settle. There'll be problems before the vote is even taken."

"I have a proposal too," Moose said.

"You're a union member. Union members can have the floor," Vern said in a patronizing voice.

"I can hardly wait," Moose said. To Ellie, Moose looked jumpy.

"Those supers are ass-holes. They say the fires and the fights are ruining Champion's reputation. They come to me. Put a stop to it. Find out who did it. Why me? What can I do?" Vern asked Moose.

"It would be like being in a slowly turning vice," Moose said.

Vern looked startled. "Yes, it would."

"How are they getting in to start the fires?"

Vern shrugged. "Break-ins through the roof vents and the long narrow windows just under the eaves. They're using rags, gas and explosives."

"What trouble are you scaring up tonight, Quantz?" Moose said as he saw Quantz approach. The meeting was about to begin. There was standing room only at the back, and an empty row at the front, which Ellie pointed to.

"Trouble just follows me around," Quantz said.

"I'm being followed too," Moose said uncertainly.

The three men sat down in the only seats remaining. The rest of the men coming in stood along the side and at the back.

"Who did you say was following you?" Vern asked Moose in alarmed tone of voice.

"Aren't you worried about what he might say?" Quantz said.

"Thanks for the vote of confidence," Moose said.

"No, I'm serious. Be careful what you say. There's a lot of enemies out there. They're desperate. A guy that gets all the overtime shouldn't counsel part-time. It causes hard feelings," Quantz said.

"This town will become a ghosttown, if this business closes down," Vern said. "We have to do something."

"Anybody that comes around me looking for trouble will get it in the neck," Moose declared.

"Keep your voice down," Quantz said.

"That's fine for you to say. You can live on your gambling. I could lose everything," Moose said. "Why should I be calm?"

"I agree. What's the point in working your ass off, doing overtime only to have it all eroded away," Vern said.

"There's Tiny at the back," Moose said. "He looks at me as if he could kill me." Moose laughed as if it was funny. "He thinks I'm a stoolie."

"I don't want to hear about it," Vern said. "Let's keep on topic."

At a few minutes after eight, the doors were shut and Ellie was able to start handing out the voting forms, a handful to the end of each row.

A short speech by management about the rollback was met by cold silence in the crowd. "If you have any better suggestions, let's hear them," the chairman said.

Speakers had three minutes each at the mike to express their point of view.

"It's what you've been waiting for," Vern said. "Go up there and get in line."

Moose pushed his way to the mike and bent it toward him. "What I have to say is no joke. Nobody likes less pay but we could work part-time and keep our jobs and our hourly rate. It would spread the work around until more orders come in."

There was an angry stir in the crowd. When Moose continued to explain his proposal of less pay, less benefits, he was heckled. Angry members with their arms folded across their chests booed so loudly that they drowned out his voice. When a show of hands was taken on Moose's proposal, it was thumb's down on the part-time work.

"If that's all the speakers for the main floor," the chairman said, "we can have a vote on the rollback."

When the tally of the vote for the rollback was in, they turned it down.

There were no choices left. Since they didn't agree to the rollback, the layoff would continue the following Friday. It was to be of three months duration with no pay. The one month's holiday they'd already had was paid as vacation pay.

"But the news isn't all bad," the chairman explained. The company had received news of a potentially large order from Saudi Arabia, and, if it came through, most of the six hundred men would be called back and the salesmen put on salary again.

The men voted to strike if no satisfactory contract settlement was reached once the original layoff ended next Friday. "They're treating us like we're saps. I won't go back until we get everything we ask for," Moose said.

"Don't lose your temper. What will that do?"

"It's just another sickening promise," Moose said. He sat angrily with his arms folded. Ellie noticed his reaction was mirrored in the angry sullen faces of the crowd in the union hall as they argued with each other.

"Don't make an enemy of me," Vern said. "Don't get in a fight here."

"I'll remember that." The sweat was running down Moose's face. The doors had to be kept closed for security reasons, so that, in the heat, the hall became stifling.

Ellie could see Tiny trying to make his way through the crowd. Maybe Tiny was wanting to talk to Moose. Tiny's face was frantic, but then he disappeared behind the huddle of guys.

Suddenly, the lights went out. The hall became even hotter and darker, unbearable and breathless like an underground cave.

Ellie heard a faceless murmur of alarm in the dark.

"Open the doors," she could hear Tiny yell. "I'm claustrophic."

A minute later, the lights were back on, momentarily blinding Ellie. The large double doors were flung open. With the sudden downpour and the cool breeze, the air felt cooler. Then, the meeting was adjourned with nothing positive accomplished as far as Ellie was concerned.

After the union meeting, Ellie went back to work and took over from Steve.

Moose and Quantz followed her in, and they seemed to be in good spirits.

As soon as they sat down, Tiny appeared.

"Are you afraid of the dark?" Moose sounded incredulous. "How did you get in?"

"Somebody gave me a ticket," Tiny replied. "You are a rat fink, not to give me a ticket."

"Why should I do that?"

"You're kind of a jerk. You did it for other people."

Moose grabbed him by the shirt. "Want to fight, eh? Deck me one. Go on, hit me." Moose rose off his stool, but Tiny remained sitting.

"Stop that!" Quantz held Moose back. "What's the matter with you? Calm down. Why do you want to cause a ruckus?"

Ellie noticed the tension among these men. Something was happening. Moose sat back down but he was very angry. His fists twitched.

Ellie saw Tiny's peaked hat was askew. His hair stuck out underneath it, making him appear at odds and ends, as usual.

When Moose regained his composure, he drained his draft. He had foam rim on his upper lip and red moustache. "You're just like a big brother to me," he said, so polite it was obvious to Ellie it was false. "I don't know what I would do without you." He smiled at Quantz so tightly his teeth were bared and his eyes were glassy.

"Lighten up. Hang loose," Quantz said.

Moose sighed. "If I only could."

"Everything is tits up for us now," Tiny said.

"What was the conversation we were just having here, or don't you pay any attention?" Moose asked Tiny angrily. "Why can't you leave us alone? You open your mouth and something stupid is sure to come out."

Tiny gulped his beer down. His eye was wild as he stared at Moose in silence for a moment. "You just don't understand, do you? You think everything is personal. Well, some day you will be sorry." Tiny choked with emotion, his face flushed. Then, he got up and left.

"Excuse me for living," Moose said after Tiny went through the door. He sounded disgusted.

"If you didn't live the way you do, on the edge all the time, if you didn't say so much, and start so many fights, things would be calmer," Quantz said.

"You're getting to be such an old woman. Who are you, my mother?"

Quantz laughed. "Somebody has to say something."

"I'm trying to get my mind on something else."

"How are those grammar classes coming?"

"Not bad. Maybe with no job, I'll git to univarsity." Moose exposed the accent his teacher was trying to eradicate.

"I don't think you'll pass," Quantz said.

"I will. I'm writing poetry again."

"Is it any good?"

"No damn good at all, but the teacher likes it."

"Is she a pretty young thing?"

"Yes."

"You'll have no problem passing then."

Moose took this was an insult to his intelligence. "I'm not a brown-noser. I am a better writer than she is." He pointed angrily at Ellie.

"I'll have to see it to believe it," Ellie said hotly.

"Okay, Ellie, you're on," Moose said. "We'll get teach to decide."

"The both of you are a pair of pot-lickers," Quantz said.

"We are garbage-pickers," Ellie corrected.

Moose threw up his hands. "For fuck's sakes." Moose got up and went out.

"Why didn't he laugh? I thought he would find that funny." Ellie was amazed.

"He is really touchy. About everything."

"Yeah, I'm really worried about him," Ellie said.

"I can see that," Quantz said. "It's happening quite a bit lately." His eyes were direct, as if he was searching for reasons or excuses.

"What do you mean by that remark?"

"Nothing," Quantz said. "It means whatever you take it to mean."

"You're playing with me."

"You deserve it."

"No, I don't. There's nothing wrong with us writing."

"That's not what I mean," Quantz said.

"Oh," Ellie said. "What do you mean?"

"You take me so literally," Quantz complained. He looked hurt, as if he had lost his best friend, because Ellie really wasn't listening to him as much as to Moose. Since she pretended she didn't know what he was talking about, Ellie was ashamed. "See yuh." He finished his beer in one gulp and followed Moose into the night.

Ellie was sad that he left her behind, to close up and have a drink on her own, but when she went home she felt a whole lot better.

Vern was in bed with the sheet over his head. The meeting hadn't gone well for him or he would have come to the Bedford with the other guys. The guys measured their self-esteem by their job. If a man lost his job, he might lose his house, and then maybe his wife would think about leaving him or she might take up with another man.

"You weren't celebrating," Ellie said to Vern's large back.

"What would I celebrate? No one believes the order will go through," Vern said gloomily.

"Everybody else was there."

"I suppose. When we're called back, Quantz will be in line for a super's job."

"Why?"

"He sucks ass. And Quantz doesn't seem to be the least bit worried about the layoff," Vern said. "Maybe he figures he could make a living gambling. He's one of those people who live in a dream world."

Since Ellie thought this remark might be directed at her, she didn't respond.

Vern went on and on about Quantz and Moose and the way they were and the way Ellie was and the way they never worry about anything important. Vern never missed a chance to pick a fight or criticize and that made matters worse.

"Vern, it's late."

"What the hell about it?"

Ellie didn't know if she was going to be able to keep their relationship together or not. They were ready to break up. For once, Vern was glad that Ellie had a job, any job, even a low-paying, unsatisfactory one. It was the only time she had heard him say anything good about the job.

* * *

CHAPTER TWENTY FIVE

Being out of work so long made it seem to Ellie they were on continual holiday. Vern and Ellie took their kids to the carnival during the last week of August. Goderich bustled with extra people from surrounding areas. There was a magic aroma of cooking onions and sizzling meat from the food tents, and frothy draft from the beer tents, making people line up.

Ellie wanted to look at the craft tents which she thought were both romantic and tawdry, so Vern took Robert and Susan to the musical rides. The booths had handmade earrings and bracelets for sale, in gold, silver, and semiprecious stones. There were handcrafted sweaters, rugs, and afghans, and local landscapes of shore, hill and river.

Robert and Susan soon had red marks from candied apple and spun sugar all over their faces. There were merry-go-rounds, and whirligig rides. While Vern watched the kids on the rides, Ellie squeezed his hand and left for a few moments.

Ellie saw Beri inspecting the bangles and necklaces.

"Are you going to buy some jewelry?" she asked Beri.

"Maybe." Beri leaned on Ellie because she wasn't standing beside a door jamb. Ellie moved aside, and Beri said, "You aren't pissed off with me, are you?"

"No." Ellie was a bit taciturn, remembering the arguments they'd had over Vern and Moose. "You should apologize," Beri said, still adamant.

"I never apologize," Ellie said.

"What?" Beri's face was skeptical.

"Why should I apologize for mistakes? I'm a human being; I make mistakes all the time."

"Oh, I see," Beri smirked. Ellie knew it was hard for Beri to back down from a stupid remark.

Beri paid for a row of six silver and bronze bracelets.

Ellie chose a necklace of ivory shells on a string.

"You should try these dangling silver earrings, Ellie. They'd look nice with your brown hair." Beri was looking down her nose at Ellie again, somewhere below her, so Ellie knew things were back to normal.

"I'd better not. Vern would think they were too big."

"Well, he might not mind these ones," Beri held out earrings as big as leaves fallen from a tree.

"Vern doesn't like anything ostentatious," Ellie said.

"Oh, pooh." Beri nudged Ellie's arm, and when Ellie glanced up, she saw Cathy watching them. Beri and Cathy grimaced at each other, moving their mouths, but not saying anything. For a moment, they made catlike faces at each other, Ellie noted.

"How are you and how are your wee ones?" Beri simpered as if she didn't mean the sentiment.

"Fine." Cathy seemed friendly enough, but guarded since Beri was around. Ellie thought they could probably tear each other's hair out if she let them.

Beri stood on one foot and then the other, as if she had to go to the bathroom, her face changeable and uncertain.

"Maybe we should have a barbecue next weekend, seeing as the summer is slipping away," Ellie said.

"Sounds like a good idea." Cathy smiled at last. She looked radiant, healthy, and burgeoning. Motherhood was becoming.

"What about you and George?" Ellie pressed Beri. Ellie thought it would be a good idea to get together and be decent, instead of always drawing battle lines and turning away from each other.

"I'll have to ask him," Beri said.

Moose and Quantz were in the beer tent. They yelled and waved. Moose came over and put his arm around Cathy.

"We're having a barbecue Saturday night," Cathy told Moose. "With Beri and Ellie."

"What will we eat?" Beri said, jiggling nervously, as Moose came near. "I'll bring some corn on the cob."

"Pork chops or steak?" Moose asked.

"All you think about is food!" Cathy said.

"What else is there?" Moose nuzzled Cathy's shoulder.

Cathy went away on Moose's arm. Her round face was turned up at Moose, and he gazed back, a loving silhouette.

"She's an optimist," Beri said, "thinking Moose means that show of love and tenderness."

"Yes," Ellie said. "Why be gloomy?"

"It means she's stupid to be thinking everything will always turn out well. It's just one screw-up after another." Beri's mouth turned down with bitterness.

Beri took off into the crowd and Ellie followed her.

"Everything will be okay, you'll see," Ellie said, gently touching her arm. "I've learned that much in thirty years. You have to be able to wait." Ellie thought of the love predicament she was in, the outcome which could turn one way or the other at any time. Maybe she was waiting for someone else to make a decision.

"I can't wait forever." Beri's mouth was hard and tight.

Ellie could see Beri wasn't convinced.

"I have to go," Beri said. "See you." After she disappeared into the crowd, Ellie sat down on a bench.

Quantz sauntered over and sat down.

"Let's have a drink?" He put his arm on the back of the bench. "I'm desperate."

Ellie hadn't seen Quantz for a few weeks, so she wasn't impressed. He was unshaven, his shirt was undone and behind dark sunglasses he looked as if he was falling to pieces.

"You look like a wreck," Ellie said, staring straight ahead. "What have you been doing?"

"Nothing." He touched her on the shoulder. "We have lots of time."

"What?" Ellie asked, shocked he'd be so forward.

"I mean right now," Quantz said. "Don't act so surprised. I'm desperate to make love with you."

Since he hadn't called her, Ellie figured he was mad at her like everybody else, when they heard the news that went around like wildfire, how Vern and Beri were seen together, when they found out she'd been away with Moose. "I couldn't," Ellie said. "I don't like to go with you, and then go into work and you know it." Ellie worried Vern might see them talking, and she gazed toward the rides.

"Forget it, then," Quantz said angrily.

"You're not mad are you?" Ellie blurted with alarm, afraid he might get up and leave, and she wouldn't see him again. As he leaned toward her, he smelled so familiar, so necessary because she hadn't had sex with him for weeks.

He hesitated and Ellie immediately changed her mind. "Okay!" Her voice was a squeak.

"Tuesday then," Quantz said, smiling.

"Okay." Ellie felt better.

Then he said, as if he wanted to pull a trick on her, "I just wanted to see if you would go with me on the spur of the moment."

Ellie thought what he said was a ploy, making her feel like a fool, but when she turned to him, Quantz had gotten up and walked away.

Ellie went toward the rides to find Vern and her kids and together they spent the rest of the afternoon at the carnival, until Ellie had to go into work at five o'clock.

On Tuesday, Ellie wore a dress and heels so that she would seem business-like and official. She intended to tell Quantz that she couldn't see him again, that she should lie low for awhile. But when Ellie got in the car, she knew she couldn't say what she had to say. All her resolve disappeared in the needs of the moment. When she had Quantz close to her, she realized how powerful her pent-up desires were. Her insides felt like they were in a turmoil. When Quantz turned his head toward her, when he touched her, she started to ache all over again. Everything familiar about him made her quiver with anticipated pleasure. He made her feel loved and tawdry, sexually necessary, all rolled into one.

"I see you're dressed up," he said. "Have you been somewhere?"

"Yes, I had lunch." Ellie was wondering why this was important.

"Did you have a good time?" Quantz continued after a moment.

"Yes." Ellie was feeling he was putting her off.

"Who with?" Quantz was insistent.

"Vern. Then he went back to work."

"Oh, he's starting to take notice now?" Quantz sounded surprised and a bit hurt.

"What?" For a minute, Ellie thought he might change his mind and leave, just when she needed him badly. Maybe he felt he wasn't needed, but he sure was. She could feel it in her belly. Ellie decided she couldn't tell him this would be the last time. What was she going to do? She needed him so and it was so obvious. Ellie realized the silence was getting long.

"I didn't mean that the other day, because I don't like to be with somebody unless I'm properly prepared, showered, and shaved," Quantz said.

It took Ellie a moment to realize he was still thinking of his spur-of-the-moment idea. Why would it still be bothering him? "I thought you were always ready."

"I don't like it on demand," he said, as if he was trying to pick a fight.

The things he told her on one day weren't the same as he told her on another. By now, Ellie counted on him as much or more than she did on Vern, because he kept showing up and asking and she kept saying yes. It was more than a habit. Ellie had just meant it as a joke, and he was justifying himself.

"You mean you would have been disappointed if we did go? I kind of regretted it," Ellie said. "After."

Quantz looked at her as if he didn't believe her. Maybe if he thought he could surprise her, he would catch her in a mistake, or a lie. If he did, then he could say the hell with her, she wasn't worth the trouble of having an affair with.

"Don't you believe me? Do you think I don't like you or something?" Ellie said, her voice straining.

"Sure I do." Quantz touched her hair.

This time, she needed to release her pent-up needs and her pleasure and satisfaction were quick. Quantz seemed to know what to do.

"I should be going." Ellie said it too soon and quick, What she intended to say about their future would be an afterthought now. So she kept her mouth shut. It made her feel absurd, wanting to say the exact opposite, that she wanted to stay and love him, instead of saying this is it forever, what she'd been planning since he asked her the other day. She was such an idiot.

Quantz looked bewildered. He put his hand to his head as if he didn't know what to do.

"I can't resist," he said. "You are all I think about. And I never do that. Maybe it means something. And I haven't been able to fix up things at home either."

"We've got that problem in common."

It's time we quit doing this, Ellie thought, but she didn't know how to make the break. She was sorry for the way he felt. She was miserable, too, but she couldn't say it because it would be the wrong thing. She put her arms around his neck and kissed him. If this wasn't the last time, Ellie thought, then next time would be the last time. There had to be an end to it, Ellie thought.

* * * * *

PART THREE

* * * * *

CHAPTER TWENTY SIX

Ellie had kissed Vern goodbye early Sunday morning. Vern was heading to Champion, the second day in a row. She noticed how happy he was to be back to work after all the dissension they'd had. Vern and some of the others were getting the machines ready for the callback Monday, when most of the workers would be returning to work. This weekend Champion was back in business after a month's layoff. To Ellie, back to work meant they were starting over.

Twenty minutes later, the phone rang. Ellie was surprised to hear Vern's voice when she picked it up. Vern was incoherent so it was a minute before Ellie realized what he was saying.

"I thought he was asleep but the steel was scattered in disarray around him. Then I noticed he was lying in a pool of blood spread out on the floor."

Ellie could hardly comprehend what had happened. "What did you say, Vern?" she asked. "Who?" Her heart skipped a beat as Vern repeated what he saw.

"Moose's dead for sure." Vern had found Moose under a fallen pile of steel pilings and his machine was still running. "I don't know when the steel crushed him, but he's cold now."

Ellie wondered how such a terrible thing could happen. In a moment, Vern had calmed down enough to explain.

"Whoever cut the bracing which are the chains securing the stockpile, and pushed it over didn't take the time to turn the machine off," Vern said. Then Vern suggested there was a possibility Moose had been murdered.

Ellie felt stunned. Then possibilities of who might have done it ran through her mind, and she wondered if somebody would leave the machine running so it would look like an accident.

"They'd have to be waiting there. But who? There were about twenty men in here yesterday calibrating the machines and setting up the work orders."

"I'll come right over," Ellie said. As Ellie recovered from the terrible shock of the news, tears ran down her cheeks.

"No, don't do that. There's nothing you can do."

Ellie started to feel really scared. It had bothered Ellie that Moose hadn't come to the barbecue when the others had, but then she thought he might be coming later, which he often did. She and Vern left early because Vern had to go into work the next morning.

"I've called the cops and I have to wait here. This place is spooky," Vern said.

Ellie could imagine Vern jumping at every noise. "I'll come over," she repeated.

"You won't be able to get past security," Vern said.

But Ellie felt Vern could be in danger too if the perpetrators hadn't been able to get out of the plant, so after she hung up the phone, she went over to Champion.

As Ellie arrived, Quantz pulled up in his Camaro. Quantz looked down at his boots, completely miserable, as he trudged across the lot. She went into the plant with him. "We're here before the cops," he said. "Where was security is what I'd like to know. I don't think you want to see this, Ellie, from what Vern was saying. You'd better wait out here."

"They might still be in there," Ellie said firmly as she followed Quantz through the security station as he showed his pass to the officer behind the counter.

They met Vern in the reception area coming out. Ellie saw Vern and Quantz put their arms around each other. Vern looked pale and discouraged, and seeing Quantz seemed to brighten him up. Ellie thought fleetingly that all the compassion she could muster wasn't going to make Moose's death right and solve their relationship problems.

"I was talking to him when I was here yesterday," Quantz told Vern. "He complained of the vicious remarks some of the men made. Some of them were jealous, Moose said, because most men weren't back to work and already he'd got overtime."

"About what time was that?" Vern asked.

"Just before I went to punch out. I asked him if he was coming to the barbecue and he said he was," Quantz said.

The plant was dim with only the natural light coming in the high windows and no artificial lighting on.

Vern took Ellie's arm. "There's nothing you can do. They're searching the building now. They're not too sure yet when the accident happened. But they are sure the ties were deliberately cut."

"Where are they parked? Who's searching if there are no cop cars outside," Ellie was immediately suspicious. She uneasily glanced into the shadows.

Vern paused for a moment and frowned. "Out back, I think."

"Was it yesterday or this morning?" Quantz asked.

"Probably yesterday, they think," Vern said.

"What clues could they possibly find in a huge, dark place of cement and steel?" Quantz said bitterly. "We'll probably never know what happened."

Ellie could hear doors slamming in the distance.

"Somebody has to go tell Cathy," Vern said. Ellie could tell from the way he wiped his brow that he was quite distraught.

"I will," Quantz said.

"Take Ellie out with you," Vern said. "I'm just going to put my work away and then I'll be home."

Ellie thought Moose's death was a climax of the violence that had been happening all summer, fires, fights, threats by the dozen. She was so upset, she was acting dazed, like a zombie the rest of the day, but Vern had no more information to tell her. Ellie wondered who else would be killed, if the people responsible, even outsiders, were still in the plant.

On Monday, Ellie was working at the Bedford, and she noticed details of the accident was on everybody's minds.

The air was full of smoke and the buzz of voices. The room was gloomy, dim and mournful. Vern and Quantz came in before five and sat down at the bar beside Steve.

"Moose was so incredibly unlucky," Steve said.

"It's not right something like this should happen," Vern said.

"No matter how it happened or why, we'll really miss him," Steve said.

Quantz hunched his shoulders in a guilty manner, Ellie thought. "I wasn't able to persuade him to quit working when I was there and leave with me."

Steve bought them a drink, and then they discussed all kinds of reasons why Moose had been killed, and Ellie had to listen, but she couldn't cry. Nothing came out of her mouth. Her eyes were like dry holes in her head. She felt dreadful. Ellie wondered if murder was suspected, who were Moose's enemies and who could have done it and for what reason. She thought it was fate for someone to kill Moose and have it look like an accident, and the authorities could call it that if they wanted.

"I didn't know you found him, Vern," Steve said. "That must have been a shocker. It must have been awful to see your best friend lying dead at your feet."

Vern said, "It was like a nightmare. I couldn't sleep last night."

"Since I was the last person to see Moose alive, according to the punch-clock, the police accused me of having something to do with it," Quantz said bitterly.

"They're trying to shake you loose," Steve said. "Trying to incriminate you."

"Yeah," Ellie agreed. She thought it was bad enough to lose your best friend without being accused of doing it.

"They could charge me," Quantz said. "I can't leave town. They suspect he was murdered. I don't know why they bothered me about it. I kept my head and I never told them anything. Like a politician, I gave answers that weren't answers." Quantz glanced at Ellie, as if to say what am I going to do now?

Ellie bit her lip to keep from crying.

"Sounds like you won't hear the end of it, soon that's for sure. They're crazy to try to pin it on you," Steve said.

"Late last night, the cops phoned Norma looking for me. He said he'd be at the station until four in the morning. Norma gave me hell. She said, `Who does he think we are, rattling about until four in the morning?'"

"Well, not her, maybe," Steve said.

"She doesn't think it's murder, either," Quantz said. "The cop asked about a previous assault charge that was laid on Moose, and if I knew anything about it; then he started in about Moose's death. I'll have to be more careful from now on. It's ironic that they bother me when I feel so guilty anyway."

"Well, I think I'll go upstairs," Steve said. His eyes had reddened. His took his glasses off and wiped them. Then, he put them back on and went upstairs to his wife.

"Isn't he nosy?" Quantz asked, after he left.

"I'm surprised you told him as much as you did," Vern said.

"He'd help me if I needed it and he might as well hear it from me as from somebody else. Pretty soon the whole town will know the cops think I killed him. I know what my lawyer will say--what is it this time, Quantz?"

"Most of the time those lawyers are at their desks trying to stay awake, and when something like this happens, they don't know what to do," Vern said.

"You're probably right."

"Let's have another quick drink before we go home," Vern said to Ellie. "You're off work now, aren't you?"

Ellie washed up quick and got them all a drink.

The next afternoon, Ellie and Vern arrived at Hodgin's Funeral Home just before the funeral was to start. Ellie wanted to say hello to Cathy so Vern found a seat with the rows of people who were sitting on the lawn, the chapel being full already, and Ellie went in.

Ellie found Cathy in the funeral parlor with her family and in-laws. They were standing beside Moose in the open casket.

Ellie could hear an older woman's impatient, bossy, acid voice speak to Cathy. "We're all having a difficult time."

"I'm weak in the knees. I don't know how I'm going to stand in front of everybody," Cathy confided to Ellie. It was obvious to Ellie she was grief-stricken.

"You'll be fine, somehow we'll get through the day." Her father-in-law gave Cathy's shoulders a squeeze.

Cathy whispered to Ellie, "It's been such a nightmare. I wish I could wake up in the morning and find John beside me. No matter what we've been through or all the other little things he did to me, I loved him so much." Even though she was in tears, Cathy seemed glad to see Ellie. Cathy was so hugely pregnant, in her navy dress and white collar.

The funeral director waved his arms and pointed at the door. "We're late. Time is running out." The funeral director took Cathy's arm, and they headed away from the casket toward the chapel.

Cathy immediately fainted and collapsed to the floor. During the commotion during which everyone else went out, Ellie learned from the funeral director there was another funeral service pending. "We'll get backed up," he said.

Ellie helped Cathy up, then she found the spot Vern saved for her outside. "Cathy should be outside. She just fainted in there," Ellie told Vern. Ellie could tell from Vern's bored expression he didn't want to be at the funeral, and had come only to keep up appearances.

Ellie and Vern went to the cemetery. Quantz joined them. "This is the biggest funeral I've ever seen," Quantz said. "Moose always said he wouldn't be caught dead at a funeral. And he's the big fish this time. Well, it was his joke and there's no point in being gloomy."

Every day the next week, Ellie worried when Vern left for work and when he returned. But no more accidents happened, except Vern drank every night. "I'm not the only one," he told Ellie. "Quantz had a binge lasting nearly all week, but you can't blame the guy. He would have been fired if I hadn't put in a good word for him."

When Ellie saw Quantz the following week, he said he'd quit drinking for now.

Ellie was glad to hear it, except she thought Quantz was jumpy and on edge more than usual and so serious he could have relaxed more. Ellie thought there wasn't much she could do, so she put her arms around him.

Quantz sniffed her shoulder gingerly, as if he was afraid of it. "You smell different. It's like a lake breeze. A new shampoo, maybe?"

Ellie was disappointed he thought she was new and different, and that he was treating her carefully.

"I was afraid that I had got lipstick over everything last time. Did I?" Ellie asked. She thought he might have been miffed about the lipstick, but from his face, he didn't know what she was talking about. He had forgotten when Ellie had been worrying for two weeks if he had been able to wipe it off or not. Ellie thought she worried far more than he did about the repercussions of this romance.

"What's with you? All this makeup stuff? What does it matter?" Quantz asked. To Ellie it was a letdown that he was so casual.

"It doesn't matter at all," Ellie lied. She had been frantic about being so careless. Maybe he didn't like her too much, she thought.

They made love as if it was a ritual. He was like a hammerhead until he came. When he was sober, Quantz had more to say: "I'm going to be sober for the rest of my life. I rather like it. Everything isn't so soft about the edges. Even you."

"I like that when you're not drinking." Ellie pointed at Quantz's still-hard penis, which made their love-making better.

Quantz laughed at her. "You need sex, to get filled up all the time. It's an addiction."

"Sometimes, I think I'm the one interested, and that you'd rather do something else," Ellie said. Mostly, she was after him, always making the moves. Maybe he was getting sick of her, and his feelings were getting dull when before he had been keen. It made her feel as if she had made a mistake, particularly when Vern was trying harder to be nice.

"Why do you think that?" Quantz kept looking out the rear window of his car.

"You keep looking over my shoulder. I don't like it."

Ellie didn't mean to be crabby and bitchy but that's how it came out.

"It's just I've got a lot on my mind right now."

"If you want to break up," she said angrily, "you can just tell me." Ellie felt like a fool because she didn't really mean it. What would she do without him?

"I won't be able to call you for a while," Quantz said. "I'm going away for a few days on an assignment. Then we're going to get a cottage and you won't be able to reach me."

Quantz held her chin in his hand and gave her a kiss goodbye. He didn't include her in his plans. Ellie thought it was a good example of how casual he was.

For several weeks, she didn't call him and he didn't call her. Ellie felt kind of empty to lose both her friends at once, but she thought that's the way life was. She could have used Quantz's arms around her. They could have been hanging on to each other, she thought, instead of being apart. They could have shared their grief longer.

Ellie had nowhere to turn, as Vern was sick at heart about Moose, too. Ellie wasn't ready to confide in Vern yet or even listen to him. His remarks and insights made her feel bad, which showed shortcomings in her own personality, more than it did Vern's. Vern was looking inward at his own grief and not noticing her feelings. He was talking about how Moose was this way and that way, and how Moose would have done this and that. Maybe that meant he was trying to recreate Moose again with his talk.

But Ellie was too hurt to listen. When he was living, Moose exasperated Ellie so much. When he was bugging Ellie all the time, she didn't take the time to tell him she loved him. Now that he was gone, there was empty space where he used to be, and there wasn't a thing she could do about it.

* * *

CHAPTER TWENTY SEVEN

Ellie didn't want to talk about Moose any more, but people wouldn't leave the subject alone. The next day, Tiny and his wife, Lou, came into the Bedford. Ellie thought it seemed strange for them to be drinking together.

"Quantz wasn't the only suspect," Tiny said. "I was, too. Most people thought I did it. Isn't that right, Lou?"

"They come right out and ask him," Lou said. "When he's up town, even." Lou talked with a lisp which made her hard to understand. "Tiny's unfortunate because someone seen him there Saturday when the accident happened."

"I wish they'd clear the matter up," Tiny said. "I'm tired of being questioned."

Ellie knew the cops had asked around about Tiny. It was felt that Moose picked on him, and Tiny was the victim. He was a victim maybe who went looking for his tormentor.

"They can't prove it," Lou said, sucking on her tooth like a chipmunk. "They had to let him go. They didn't have anything that would stick."

Tiny told Ellie he was released because his uncle said he and Tiny had spent the afternoon together drinking down at the river. "He's my drinking buddy," Tiny said.

"I'm here because he lost his driver's license and I'm driving him around," Lou said.

"The cops pull me over all the time. I have too many points off my license."

Lou said emphatically, "Since they've gone back to work, he just goes to work and comes home again."

Ellie thought since Tiny apparently knew who started the fires, maybe he also knew who killed Moose. He looked even more slovenly, if that was possible. He looked as if drunk was his current state of mind. "Did you do it? Do you know who did it?" She thought no one would believe her anyway, if he did tell her the truth about what he knew.

"Not me. I'm keeping out of sight until this matter is cleared up," Tiny said. "What do you think I should do?"

"I don't know," Ellie said. "All I know is you're not the only one who feels bad about Moose."

"See," Tiny said to Lou. "No one really cares."

Ellie didn't feel sorry for Tiny, because it sounded as if he wasn't really involved. Maybe he was questioned because of the gossip about him, or the poor way he organized his life. Maybe a cheater and a liar deserved the suspicion, but Ellie couldn't imagine he was involved and wouldn't say so.

"It would be hard to talk about," Ellie said.

"He was like a crazy person after Moose was killed. That's how I knowed he didn't do it. He went about laughing and crying. It was awful."

Then Tiny told Ellie how he hated Moose and he had wished he was dead, which made Ellie think Tiny was a little bit crazy. Apparently, Moose was the topic of an eerie drunken conversation between Tiny and his uncle in the gravel pit the day of his demise.

"Moose always seemed to be out to get me," Tiny said.

"Who else have you told all this?" Ellie knew of the gossip about Tiny. She thought it was curious people would talk about Tiny when he wasn't around, but they could hardly say hello when he was present. Ellie noticed the bar was losing business because if people came in and saw him there, they kept walking right out the door again. If Tiny came in and sat with people, they would drink up and leave.

"People are always watching me. It's not right," Tiny said to Ellie. Tiny had this wierd little moustache and wee pointed beard under his lower lip that resembled a smudge that should be wiped off with a rag.

He squinted at Ellie once in awhile to see if she was listening.

"Do you think there is something wrong with my voice? Do you think I act right? No one seems to like me," he whined.

He had Lou to listen to him, but her eyes were following Ellie too. It made Ellie wish she was somewhere else.

Ellie found them both scary, especially Tiny. It was his eyes that bothered her. He never made eye contact so that she thought he was shifty. She never liked him glancing at her when her back was turned.

When Tiny went to the washroom, Lou confided in her. Most of the time, she was afraid of Tiny. She said she was so depressed that she couldn't get her work done. She said her children were driving her crazy with their screaming all the time. "There are times when I think he's going to take it out on me. I don't know what's going to happen. Sometimes he looks at me like he hates me."

Tiny came back from the washroom and gave Lou a glare that made her jump. Her nerves were really bad, Ellie thought. Either that or the deadbolt scowl meant something.

Then he gaped at Ellie. Ellie wished he would quit gaping at her. He appeared to have a wild, mean, crazy expression as if he was waiting for Ellie to respond. She could think of no reason why she would, when he just talked about what other people said to him and did to him.

"People hiss at me when they make derogatory remarks." He ground his jaw in a menacing way.

"What am I supposed to do about it?" Ellie said, irritably.

"Oh, Tiny," Lou said. "Try to get your mind on something else and things will be better."

"Dry up, Lou." Tiny took his hat off and put it back on again, changing the position of the baseball cap on his head, flattening his hair. "Better him than me," he said to Ellie, "I could be dead, too, you know."

Ellie walked out of the bar even though she wasn't supposed to. She got change from the girl at the desk and went go to the john to use up time, hoping that they would be gone when she returned.

But, Tiny and Lou were still waiting. Tiny continued as she walked past. "At Champion, they're trying to make amends. The raw steel and parts on the shelves are rearranged so that the weight is distributed better, so that the piles aren't so high or apt to fall on anyone else. The safety measure is kind of after the fact, but then it makes them feel better to be doing something rather than nothing at all, to get the re-call started off on a better foot." Tiny's voice droned on in a monotone.

"I can't talk about it," Ellie said shortly. They were also suggesting Cathy would get some compensation, but what was the use of that now Moose was dead? Ellie felt discouraged.

When Tiny and Lou finally left, Steve came in.

"We have got to do something about Tiny," Ellie said.

"Why, he's not causing a fight is he? Isn't he acting like a customer?" Steve looked around.

Ellie shrugged. "We're losing business because if people came in and see him here, they walk out the other door again."

"I know that's discrimination," Steve said. "Not much I can do. It's a good thing Champion's back to work.

Two days later, Ellie heard from Vern that Tiny had disappeared. Maybe he had gone to the States, but Vern didn't know whether it was true or not.

Ellie thought her problems at the Bedford could be over and she was disappointed to see Mr. Blue Friday night. It was early yet so the bar was empty except for Mr. Blue.

"Are you sorry summer is almost over?" Beri asked Ellie.

"I'm sorry, period," Ellie said, "since it's the middle of September already." Ellie thought the weather was so changeable this time of year. Indian summer one day, a snow storm overnight.

"With Tiny gone, things will be back to normal," Mr. Blue said, "for everybody but me. My old lady doesn't love me any more." He bawled like a country singer.

"We don't want to hear that," Ellie said.

"Ruth went to some other town, Exeter, I think, for awhile," Beri said to Mr. Blue, "if you want to get hold of her."

"Don't do that," Ellie said to Beri in a hushed voice. "It's none of your business." Ellie was glad Ruth had moved on and couldn't hassle her any more.

"Why, what's wrong with telling him?" Beri asked.

"Look at Mr. Blue," Ellie said to Ellie.

Mr. Blue was drinking his second glass of port. His obscenities were almost audible. He asked himself questions, then he answered them.

"He's got it in another restaurant!" Beri went to grab his drink, but she didn't take it because he yelled at her in a loud voice. "What will we do?" she asked Ellie.

"He can't have any more."

When Mr. Blue asked for another glass of port, Ellie told him he couldn't have any. He gave Ellie an ugly look.

"All I ask is to be left alone," he said. His whining voice sounded like a whimper.

"Oh, mercy," Ellie said, exasperated.

He staggered out.

Ellie thought Mr. Blue had gone home for the night, but he came back into the bar from the hallway where the washrooms were, scratching the underside of his rather protuberant belly. The movement caught Ellie's attention. As he was doing up his trousers, she saw a mound of pink flesh which she would rather not have seen.

Then, he sat at the bar looking at Ellie like a hound-dog. He lamented his Ruth had taken his mother's pearls with her.

"You can only sit at this bar if you have pop or coffee," Ellie said.

Mr. Blue had an amorous gaze on his face. "How about it?" he asked Ellie. "I can pay you."

"Eh?" Ellie said, surprised, suddenly realizing why Ruth had been putting pressure on her.

"Are you frisky?" he repeated, scratching his belly.

Ellie almost choked right there and then. She'd have to be starving or threatened with jail to accommodate him in the way Ruth would, and probably even then she wouldn't.

"Excuse me!" Ellie went to the john. She took her time washing her face and putting lipstick on.

When she came back, Mr. Blue had gone.

"Why can't we do something about Mr. Blue?" Ellie asked Beri in a short tone of voice. "I shouldn't have to put up with that. It's not part of the job."

"Why, what did I do wrong?" Beri asked stupidly.

Beri sat at the bar, having a cigarette, since business was slow for a Friday night and the work was all done.

Steve came down for his evening draft. He sat beside Beri and bought her a drink. Then he sent Beri home.

"Mr. Blue is a scum-bum when he drinks," Ellie said to Steve. "It's getting worse. The losers chase away the business."

Steve shrugged and ordered another draft.

"Mr. Blue will never change, but he doesn't need to bother you, if you don't like him," Steve said. "By the way, the time you've had to think about what I said is almost up. Just men you like though, if they're nice to you. Have you thought about it?"

Ellie thought maybe asking all the time was all right with Steve, but it sure wasn't all right with her. Or maybe she hadn't expressed herself very well.

"I'm not going to be able to work here any more," Ellie said to Steve. She knew she should give Steve two weeks notice and stick it out until then, but she couldn't stand listening to the performance any more. She thought she should be tougher than this by now. When she walked out the door that night, she knew she wasn't coming back.

* * *

CHAPTER TWENTY EIGHT

When Ellie told Vern she quit her job, he said it was about time. She wondered what she would do for money, but she found another job, just part-time, as a receptionist for a dentist, so the hours were unpredictable.

Ellie hadn't seen Beri since she quit the Bedford almost two weeks ago, so that when she phoned, Ellie was surprised to hear her voice. Beri sounded so friendly. "You can't believe how things have changed at the Bedford since you've gone. How are things going with you?" Beri clearly didn't remember saying anything that upset Ellie, especially the personal remarks she'd made about Ellie and Moose.

After a moment of dead silence, Ellie said, "Fine, so far. But I'm still hoping to go out west. So many strange things have happened."

"I'm thinking of quitting, too. Why out west?"

"It's new and different." Ellie thought the west was a land of opportunity when jobs dried up here.

"Come over for a visit," Beri said.

"I don't know when I could come. I have this job."

"Are you working today?"

Since Beri sounded so genuinely reasonable and pleasant, Ellie agreed to go.

That afternoon, Ellie Menzies got in the Ford Explorer for the ten mile drive to Londesboro, an eyeblink of a village. It was a warm September day, at the fall equinox, and the leaves were tinged with color.

Beri lived in a small white frame house with a black roof and black shutters. As Ellie drove up, she noticed Cathy's blue jeep sitting in the drive. Beri held the door open.

When Ellie walked in, Cathy Chapman was sitting at the kitchen table with her newborn. Cathy had gone into labor right after the funeral and she had to go to London for a Caesarian section since she had so much trouble delivering. The baby girl, Johanna, was two weeks old.

Beri said proudly, "I'm godmother." The pleasant way Beri talked and smiled was different that it used to be, Ellie thought, more friendly. Ellie also noticed Cathy's red-faced baby looked exactly like John, neither cute nor ugly.

"What's with the tea?" Ellie asked.

"We have tea and fruit because everybody is on a diet," Beri said, then she smiled in a wan and peaked way. "The doctor's office just phoned. I'm two and a half months pregnant."

"Isn't that news?" Cathy said, rolling her eyes at Ellie.

"It's great," Ellie said, feeling she needed a stiff drink. Maybe this news meant a truce.

"You probably thought it would never happen," Cathy said, smirking knowingly at her own baby.

"I suspected it, but I don't know what George will say."

"You mean he didn't know you were trying? Maybe he'll move out," Cathy said.

"You won't get that lucky," Ellie said.

"I wonder if I've done the right thing," Beri said, hugging herself happily.

"I thought you wanted to be pregnant," Ellie reminded Beri, touching her on the shoulder.

"I'll have to quit my job. Won't that be awful? All I'll have to do is run my store, order stock, and do books." Beri grinned broadly.

"Store? Is this something else new?"

"George and I bought the variety store here in Londesboro and we'll move into the house behind it." Beri was happily talking about her acquisition. "We've borrowed the money from the bank to cover what we don't get from selling this house."

"What do you think of her?" Cathy said, laughing and gurgling with her baby. "She's knocked up and happy about it. She's ordering clothes, counting calories, and buying furniture, just since I came in the door."

"How are you doing?" Ellie asked Cathy pointedly.

"Don't look at me like that! I know my tummy is still out to here. I haven't been exercising or anything." Cathy sounded discouraged.

"You'll have to get started. Your life isn't over yet, you know," Beri said. "You'll be as good as new."

Beri was so understanding, saying the complete opposite of what she would normally have said to Cathy, a month ago or so. Ellie was surprised, but then she figured Cathy had received her insurance money and the compensation, and Beri would want to be extra polite to her.

"Maybe I'll catch some of your habits. Just the better one, not the vices," Cathy said. "You have quite a few of those, but maybe being a mother will change that."

"That's the fun part!" Beri laughed merrily. Ellie remembered that normally Beri would tear Cathy's hair out for her never ending store of barbed remarks, but today she loved it. Beri was absurd.

Ellie noticed Cathy was a smug bitch who laced into Beri every chance she got, maybe because she had an audience or a witness. Cathy never forgot a grudge. "When are you getting married? Or are you going to wait until after the baby comes?" Cathy asked and her smirk turned into a sneer.

Beri took a deep breath. "How I live my own life is up to me. Maybe I'll always stay common-law."

"Better get married," Cathy preached. "George is a little rough around the edges, but I think he'll do all right by you. The problem is you, isn't it? You're not ready to settle down. You're far too young."

Ellie thought Beri would laugh at herself, but she obviously couldn't. Beri's face twitched as she stubbed out her cigarette with a vengeance.

"What difference will it make what we do?" Beri yelled.

"It's better to have a husband than not to have one. I should know." Cathy started to weep. She bawled and her baby cried with her so it was a noisy situation all way around.

Ellie wondered if she should get up and leave. She thought they didn't want her there if they were fighting. The contorted expression on Beri's face looked as if she might start to weep. Eventually, Cathy's bawling was reduced to snivelling, and she fed her baby so it was quiet too.Cathy eventually said, "I can't be crying all the time, but it's hard." Ellie thought maybe attention, encouraging her to cry, wasn't helping matters.

Beri lit another cigarette. She was so nervous that her cigarette was wavering. Her body was hunched up in the chair as if she was trying to make herself smaller.

"I should call my mother, but she says I haven't given enough thought to the future, such as it is," Beri explained sarcastically, as if she didn't really care if her mother knew or not.

Cathy asked Beri all sorts of questions about how she felt. Then, Cathy said, "Oh, I was like that too," and discussed her experiences. Ellie was concerned Cathy shouldn't be opening up to Beri like she did, as Beri was likely to turn on her first chance she got.

Beri interrupted, "Gawd, you'd think you were the only person who was ever preggers, and the rest of us are know-nothings."

"You can get books on the subject," Cathy said, huffily. "You don't have to listen to me."

"Give it some time, Beri," Ellie said bossily, thinking she had to wait for Cathy to be understanding. "You're so impatient."

"How much more time? Actually I'm more than three months pregnant."

Ellie's mouth dropped open. Why would Beri lie about her pregnancy. She thought she could be endangering her health, then she thought she might be trying to cover up something. "Why?"

"I figured I knew what was wrong." Beri shrugged. "I thought I had ulcers again."

"You don't show much yet," Cathy said. "I was huge at three months. What are you going to name it? Or is George going to pick the name? Johanna's the only one I named."

"Maybe after my father. Paul or Paula. Or George or Georgina." Ellie thought Beri was poking fun at the way Cathy picked her baby's name.

Obviously, Cathy thought so too as she said angrily, "Very funny, criticizing the name Johanna. Excuse me while I go out to the jeep and get some more diapers." Cathy gave her baby to Beri and let the screen door bang hard behind her.

Beri cuddled the wee thing. "I hope mine is as good. She hasn't cried the whole time she's been here, except when Cathy started bawling."

"She is good," Ellie agreed.

Beri had a wistful look on her face and a tear in her eye. "I wouldn't want to bring a fatherless child into the world, like Cathy did."

"What?" Ellie said, thinking Beri was nostalgic and foolish. It had occurred to her that Beri might not know who the father of her baby was. If she wasn't leaning, elbows on the table, Ellie would have fallen on the floor with shock.

"Still, a baby would be something to remember Moose by."

"Why?" Ellie asked.

"I miss him."

Beri wiped her face with a napkin.

Ellie couldn't believe Beri was for real. She was so self-absorbed. Ellie wanted to say something positive instead of something sarcastic because Beri fought with Moose when he was alive and now was sentimental when he was dead. She was stupid. Ellie felt like choking her because of the way she used people, but she could hardly choke a mother-to-be on the verge of tears.

Beri took a slurp of her juice. She was drinking milk and grapefruit juice, and her face appeared rounder.

"You look younger. Not so thin," Ellie said.

The remark so pleased Beri that she even smiled and said, "There are times when I miss Moose, really miss him. I guess he will never grow old, like the rest of us."

Ellie hated it when Beri tried to be philosophical and rationalize things. "Did George know about Moose?" Ellie asked.

Beri shook her head. From the way she talked about George, Ellie thought that she didn't really love George that much. Beri was desperate or a bit out of focus, the way her emotions were playing tricks on her, obsessed with the man in the grave and knocking the one who was alive, just as she continually knocked Moose when he was alive.

"George is so casual, that's the thing, so laid-back. The complete opposite to John who was strung out," Beri said.

"What were you saying about John?" Cathy came in the door and this time she held it against the spring.

"About his nerves."

Cathy changed her baby girl's diaper. "That's not my fault, the way he felt about himself, the way he was raised."

"The way you are raised can really screw you up. When I was fourteen, my mother took me to the doctor to get birth control, just in case. Then, she watched me like a hawk," Beri said.

"Maybe she thought as soon as you reached puberty you were thinking of men and the pleasure that could be got from them," Ellie said.

Beri smirked. "I can't believe you said that. You've changed since I first met you, more fun-loving, easy-going. At the Bedford, the girls out front were asking me if you had a boyfriend on the side."

"I know what you told them." Ellie laughed as she recalled the remarks they'd made. Beri's face went red. "You asked too many personal questions. It was none of their business. I'm usually just joking," Ellie said.

"I know." Beri still had the amazing capacity to blush, but she wasn't laughing, she was serious. At least when she was pregnant she wasn't drunk.

Ellie thought Beri shit on her to make herself feel better. When Ellie wanted Beri to be supportive, Beri would say or do the opposite to add trouble.

"My mother is the cause of all my problems. Sometimes I get so mad when I think of all the things she's said and did. Sometimes, I just hate her because my past has ruined me."

"Your mother doesn't seem to have stopped you any," Ellie said, smirking at her self-pity.

"What do you mean?" Beri sounded instantly suspicious.

"Since when are you lonely?"

Beri sighed audibly. "She seems to have forgotten what it was like to be young."

"If you think she's bad, you should meet my mother-in-law," Cathy said. "She's a shrieking harpy, always bossing me around."

"She's probably just hard to talk to, like my mother," Ellie said.

"You mean she's hard to listen to. She never shuts it," Beri said. Ellie thought, if so, then Beri was just like her mother.

"You don't know what they think when they won't tell you things. We had terrible arguments, then I would get the silent treatment. Now, it doesn't bother me much. I made my own life," Ellie said.

"Me, too," Beri said. "Maybe she doesn't like it, but that's the way it is. In fact, I don't care what she thinks, especially about me and George."

"George is fine. He's a dink who needs a homing device," Ellie said.

"You're funny, but he acts like a dink from hell," Beri said. "He won't grow up and won't commit. I just wish he would get serious."

"Why, isn't George the father?" Ellie asked, since she'd been wondering since she heard the news who might be the father. Was it Vern or George or somebody else?

"Well yes, he is," Beri said after a moment's hesitation. Beri smiled ruefully. "It's just what will George think?"

"He might think it's good news," Ellie said. George made Beri stop messing around, so that her life was beginning to change, to be well-ordered and calm when she used to be crazy and have a tendency to freak out. She was almost normal.

To Ellie, George was an organized person, but he didn't look the sort. Maybe it was just the impression he gave when he was dressed in scruffy clothes. He was ordinary, regular, and worked hard. George calmed Beri down. When she was seeing Moose, she was angry and upset because he didn't spend too much time anywhere, especially with her. Most of the time, Moose wasn't where he should have been. George made Beri feel better.

Cathy was still nursing her baby which had fallen asleep with her head lolled to the side. Her boob stuck out of her shirt opening. Ellie wondered if Cathy had found Moose as upsetting as Beri had with all the stories he could dish out, or maybe she just took what life gave her.

Beri rifled through the catalogues flipping the pages for maternity clothes. She showed Ellie the large gap in her jeans, and the string holding the button and button-hole together. She had a rueful smile on her face.

"This is George's shirt. It covers up a lot."

Maybe Beri was just taking a breather from complaining and fighting all the time, the way she was getting ready for motherhood. Beri was no longer was the cool broad Ellie knew and rather liked, when she was sounding and acting exotic and cosmopolitan like a street in Montreal. She was getting to be a bit of a bore. Beri yawned as if trying to prove it.

"I need to go to bed too," Ellie said. She sure was boring, Ellie thought.

When Ellie went home for supper, she told Vern Beri had to quit work because she was pregnant.

"Well, how about that?" Vern said. "She had better drive a stake through George's pant leg. Or she'll be out in the cold."

"Why would you care that much about Beri?" Ellie asked, instantly angry. Vern had that stupid, knowing smirk on his face that she hated. Maybe he was the father, Ellie thought, despite what Beri had said.

* * *

CHAPTER TWENTY NINE

Ellie was pretty sure Vern wasn't the father of Beri's baby, but she watched the expression on his face very carefully.

"What did you think of the summer, now that it's over," Ellie said to Vern. It was frosty, definitely over.

"A lot's happened," Vern said thoughtfully, but his face was inscrutable. "We can't go back to what we were, can we?"

Monday night, Ellie was lying awake. She had awakened about one-thirty in the morning after having been asleep for several hours. Ellie was cold so she snuggled in behind Vern's back and she had got comfortable, almost asleep again.

The bed jerked. Vern sat up in a sweat.

"It's the police banging on the door," he said. He flung the covers back, exposing them to the cold, his arm striking Ellie's nose.

"Ouch." Ellie rubbed her nose."I didn't hear anything."

Vern leapt out of bed and went down to answer the door, while she listened.

"I must be going crazy, there's no one," he muttered when he came back upstairs. "I'm turning into a maniac. I dream people are listening and following me all the time. There are patterns of car lights and pacing of vehicles. They seem to be just waiting."

Ellie thought the extra stress of his job with the fire and Moose's death was causing him a problem. He didn't do it, she thought, but he was getting blamed. The headlights of traffic passing were making his nerves bad. The lights shone through the window and lingered on the wall. Why would there be so much traffic at this time of the night? Then, Ellie heard a banging noise. At first, she also thought it was someone at the door.

The wind made the door on the tool shed bang. Ellie went down, secured it with a piece of twine and knotted it twice.

When she came back upstairs, Vern was pacing the floor.

"It was just a bad dream. Go back to bed," Ellie said.

"It's not that simple," he said. "It was a dream about Moose dying. I woke up feeling I had something to do with it."

"Why would you be thinking about him?" Ellie thought it had been hard on him to find him.

"I got phoned today at work. The police asked me several questions about Moose. When I answered them, I wondered why they phoned as it was almost a month ago. It was so casual how they asked what I was doing that day and whether anyone could vouch for it."

"What did you say?"

"My mind was a blank. I said off the top of my head that I went fishing. I don't know why I said that because I don't even remember what I was doing that day, at the moment he died," Vern said uneasily.

"You said you were at the golf course. Don't you remember?" Ellie had a twinge of disbelief. What if they had to prove it? It might be true, people watching, asking questions.

"No. I'm in a quandary what to do."

Ellie was surprised to hear him say that, because up till this point she hadn't thought he was that much involved.

"How come you never told me before you can't remember," Ellie said, shocked there might be something to his lack of memory.

"When I woke up I thought, my God, they think I must be guilty. It was a horrid thing to awaken to."

"You didn't do anything."

"Yes, but I was convinced I was guilty. I dreamt I was on trial," Vern said. "I think I must be going crazy."

"Go to the doctor then, and get something to calm your nerves." Ellie tried to push the nagging guilty thoughts out of her mind.

"I get worked up. I think cars are following me and when I look back, they veer off."

"You're not a likely suspect. You're harder on yourself than anybody." Ellie tried to be supportive.

"That's fine for you to say!" Vern was all worked up.

Ellie decided that his dream was a guilt dream. "Is that the first time you've had that dream?"

"No, I wake up gagging."

"It's the first time you've yelled out."

He appeared to be in a streak of misery in a lifetime of mostly optimism, sitting on the bed holding his head. Maybe, he believed his bad dreams.

"Why would you be feeling guilty, Vern?" He lied, a bad sign, and for sure, they'd keep digging. Unless Ellie or he could think of some way to solve it.

"You keep asking that? We all feel responsible," he said loudly, angrily. "I can't help it if it affects me. My life is hell. How can you be so blind? I'm warning you about doing things to make me angry!"

All Ellie wanted to do was go back to sleep if possible, but it didn't look as if Vern would let her. He always ended his arguments warning her if she wasn't careful something would happen.

"No, I just want you to feel better. Why don't you tell me what to do?"

"I'm not hungry, if that's what you mean," Vern said curtly.

"It might help you sleep. It always does," Ellie said.

"I'll be awake the rest of the night!" Vern sat up in bed with his arms folded across his chest.

"Go right ahead." Ellie rolled over. She didn't like Vern to be stubborn. The light was suddenly switched on. It blinded her. She put her arm over her eyes and groaned. "I'm trying to sleep."

Vern decided to read. He flipped the pages.

Ellie turned to face Vern and raised herself on her elbow. Her nightgown strap fell off her shoulder and one boob fell out of her nightgown.

Ellie noticed Vern looking her over. She was trying to be titillating but it wasn't working.

Then, Vern said in a quiet, prodding voice, "Do you have anything you want to tell me?"

"Such as?" Ellie teased, lifting her leg.

"Why now? The night must be half over." Vern sounded irritable.

Ellie wondered what could be bothering him. Lately, he was very inquisitive about her whereabouts. He was timing how long it took her to do anything or go anywhere and asking for an itinerary.

"Where did you get that nightgown?" he asked.

"Up town." The gown wasn't new, but it was the first time she'd worn it.

"Did you buy it for someone else?"

Ellie denied it, but he looked as if he didn't believe her. Vern was hard to answer, hard to figure out what was bothering him, Ellie thought.

"What are you reading, Vern? I'm trying to sleep."

"And you're interrupting me." He watched her, stroking his chin. Then, he reached under his bed and flipped through his assortment of skin magazines in an impatient manner, probably to find the largest spread.

"Do you need my light to see better?"

"No." Ellie switched it on anyway. Seeing the skin magazines made Ellie mad after she'd tried to be enticing.

"Overhead light, too?" She got up and switched it on. The bedroom was extremely well lit.

Vern gestured with impatience. His discarded book fell from the to the floor with a thump. Ellie leaned over the bed to see the Guide to Insurance Policies, with a dark cover. Who had he taken a policy out on and who was the beneficiary, she wondered.

"Something the matter, Vern?" she asked angrily.

He snorted, squinting at her sideways.

"Your nightgown is kind of a dowdy color," he said.

"I thought you liked it."

"But, it's grey, so blah, not very exciting," Vern pronounced.

Ellie studied her front. It was true the nightgown was grey, but it also had a wide band of lace across the bust and neat pleats which Ellie thought were very romantic.

Ellie didn't think this color problem was any big deal, as it was his thing to pick a fight before sex. She just thought, if it wasn't one thing he was complaining about, then it was something else.

"It's too ordinary, is that what you're trying to say?"

Vern put his magazines away.

"Why don't you take it off? Or do I have to beg?"

Ellie had to have a think about this. "Why sex at this hour of the night? It's almost morning."

Vern got up and searched for X-rated tapes for his video-recording equipment. Maybe he thought if she saw the images she would remember how to do it.

Sometimes, Ellie thought Vern was perverse, especially after an argument. She was romantic, and he acted as if he had warts on his penis.

Ellie noticed he was ready, hard as a rock as he walked nude around the room, searching in the drawers. Ellie took off her gown and hung it on his peg, as he approached the bed.

She sat on the side of the bed with her nose at about the level of his member, it's hole looking at her like an eye. It's ripe, bitter smell was overpowering.

"Give me a suck," he said.

This way was his favorite, or one of them, so Ellie went at it with her head bobbing back and forth, like a piston in a motor. After awhile, she had a sore jaw waiting for him to be through or to try something else.

"Get on the bed," Ellie said.

He lay on his back on the bed, hanging onto the headboard.

Ellie bent over him and it seemed her mouth was his favorite hole today.

When Ellie had it stuck in her throat, he said, "Say something."

After he repeated himself several times, Ellie lifted her head off him and blurted, exasperated, "What do you expect me to say when I have your cock in my mouth? Do you think words will come out my ears?"

The rude language meant something to Vern. He loved it. He sighed audibly and relaxed completely. His eyes rolled up into his head so she could only see the whites of his eyeballs. Ellie thought he was going to sink right through the bed. She was so surprised at his reaction, she drew away from him to watch. He said, "Don't stop now."

He was ready, so Ellie soon got a mouthful that make her choke. When she leaned over to kiss him, he turned his head away.

"It must be my dinky breath," she said.

He made a face, like he was sucking lemon, and she laughed at him. She sat on the bed and crossed her legs.

He asked, "Do you love me?"

"Do you love me?" she answered back. Ellie couldn't think of anything else to say. They never got this issue resolved, even after eight years of marriage so there must be something between them. "Sometimes I think you don't."

"I'm here, aren't I?" he said shortly.

Ellie thought this was a typical male response, and it was typical of a female either to be insecure about the male or tired of him. Ellie thought she vacillated between these poles.

Right now, Ellie would have said Vern was tiresome. She felt sorry for him. Vern wasn't himself unless he was complaining or upset. He would have been insulted if he thought Ellie felt sorry for him, as if she was promising to get to him later. Vern didn't like pity.

"What would you say if I had an affair?" he asked.

This floored Ellie. She knew that he would do it, but talking about it was something else again, especially after going to bed. She wondered if he was just causing a fight, or if he was already having a new affair, and wanting to make an issue out of it.

"An affair?" Ellie asked, innocently, as if she was a know-nothing. She was already pretty sure that he had been seeing Beri. Beri was asking what the matter was with them, besides other personal remarks. But Ellie hadn't wanted to do anything about it.

"That china-doll face will crack some day," Vern said, hostile.

Ellie ignored that remark. Then she considered it could be true. "I thought I had asked you about Beri and you denied it," Ellie said. "Maybe you have somebody else in mind."

"Who would that be?" he asked smugly.

Ellie didn't know, but she said, "You can do what you want, but I don't have to stay here."

Vern scratched his head. "What are we going to do now? Are you having an affair?" he asked suddenly.

Ellie covered her head with the sheets. "It's awfully bright in here," she said, discouraged, not knowing what to say. Quantz hadn't called but she knew she wouldn't say no.

"You could show a little more interest. If it's over, I don't want to hear about it," Vern said.

Vern turned off the lights and went to sleep, but Ellie lay awake. She thought Vern took everything she said the wrong way. It sounded like things weren't satisfactory for him, as they sure weren't for her. Any time she mentioned something romantic, like taking a bottle of wine and a blanket to the woods, Vern would scoff at the idea, saying he didn't have time to wait around.

Ellie tossed and turned. She felt bad. She wasn't getting anywhere thinking, other than wearing herself out. She and Vern pretended they were both faithful lovers who kept careful check on what the other was doing. He would start an argument every night and morning, screaming at the top of his lungs. Ellie thought he was more temperamental than usual. If he continued the way he was, threatening her not to make him angry, criticizing her, trying to put her at a distance by cutting her off from his affection, Ellie wondered what would happen to them. She was confused about what to do. Maybe he was trying to cover up something like his own misdoings.

Ellie woke up later angry and scared. She had dreamt she was on a rickety staircase. The landing had gigantic holes in it. The flimsy railing moved in an alarming way if she leaned against it. The staircase behind her seemed to fade away and she couldn't climb down. Just as she was about to take risks, to step out, she woke up with a gasp. It was then she realized she was in an old hotel, condemned because it was in a run-down condition, the customers skeletons or corpses half-disintegrated. Ellie couldn't believe how anxious and upset she was over such a scary, unlikely dream.

Ellie thought these dreams meant they should change their lifestyle by getting a house in the country, and she should change her image of herself by being more wifely, obliging, loving. They were heading for a breakup. That was why she was having these anxiety dreams. The bad dreams keeping her awake at night was starting to show on her face. Her eyes were so puffy and dark powder couldn't cover it up.

* * *

CHAPTER THIRTY

Ellie surmised Vern hadn't heard any more questions from the cops over Moose's death. He hadn't mentioned any more guilty feelings, but Ellie didn't feel any better.

Tuesday afternoon, Quantz came to visit Ellie at her home. Ellie's kids were playing in the kitchen while she made some brownies.

"You shouldn't be here," Ellie told Quantz.

"I don't care any more. I've missed you." Quantz wrapped his arms around her and kissed her.

Ellie didn't want to tell Quantz to leave, as she missed him so much. "Don't you worry about appearances? The neighbors will talk."

"You'll think of something to say."

Quantz sat at Ellie's antique oak table and drank the beer out of her fridge.

In half an hour, when Vern came home and saw Quantz sitting at the table, he scowled. Vern's face appeared as if he expected trouble. Ellie thought Quantz must be wanting to talk to Vern about something.

"It's been awhile since I've seen you so I thought I'd come around," Quantz said.

Vern got the second last beer out of the fridge. "Generous of you to leave me any beer at all," he said sarcastically. Vern's scowl had relaxed into a frown, but Ellie thought Vern was furious, even though he was trying not to show it. Ellie figured Vern was real mad, because he wouldn't look at her. Quantz was trying to smooth things over. If Quantz will do it to Vern, he will do it to you, Ellie thought; he'll try to score without your knowledge. It was the cold voice of reason. She didn't trust him anyway.

"You don't have much beer. I could get my beer out of the trunk," Quantz said, to be annoying, Ellie thought. Quantz's voice was a bit slurred. He burped. "I've been drinking all day."

"Looks like it," Vern said. Ellie thought Vern was pissed-off. "You're moving in on my territory," he said. Vern hit Quantz a cuff which Quantz returned in a lazy, neighborly way. Vern hit Quantz again, a resounding, attention-getting thump on the arm.

"Ow," Quantz said.

"That's for saying what you said about me." Vern punched Quantz in the mouth. A tiny river of blood flowed down his chin. When Quantz spit the blood on the floor, a gold and white tooth went with it.

"One of my prize possessions," he said. "You heard wrong, I didn't set you up at all."

"I could put a bullet between your eyes," Vern said to Quantz.

"That makes me pretty safe. You can't hit the side of a barn door," Quantz laughed. Vern yelled with rage and went at Quantz, punching him in the stomach.

"You don't listen to reason, you stupid son-of-a-bitch." Quantz swore and hit back. Vern was the smaller man, but he was wiry. Vern pushed and Quantz tried to hold him off. The harder Vern pushed, the angrier he got. "You know you're out of line by being here and by spreading false rumors about me. There's no excuse for you."

They were two grown men fighting as if they were boys with a grudge, pounding each other's head against the floor.

Quantz didn't back down for a minute. He was grunting and groaning with stress and excitement. Vern was tough and mean when he was angry, and he soon flipped Quantz on his back. They rolled about the floor.

Ellie was alarmed. They were fighting for real. They were fighting over work, too, not just her, and perhaps a difference of opinion from the sounds of their argument. Ellie was filled with trepidation. Vern had to beat up on somebody, to get rid of his frustrations. She hadn't expected to see that he was such a good fighter.

"Quit right now, or I'll call the cops," Ellie said. Were they going to do some damage or were they just venting rage?

Vern stopped to glare at Ellie. "Go right ahead," Vern said, "and see where that'll get you."

"You would too, wouldn't you?" Quantz said. "Why don't you mind your own business?" His nose was bloody. He wiped it with his hand and got it on his shirt.

Vern was huffing and puffing. Ellie could see he was under strain.

"Here, let me wipe the blood off your face. You look silly," Ellie said. Vern's face was bloody.

Vern looked at Quantz sprawled on the floor. "Your nose will be a cauliflower, soon."

Ellie dabbed at Vern's face, but it was mostly blood from Quantz's nose. Vern pushed her out of the way. Maybe she wasn't the cause of this fight. It was over something else and she was uncertain what to do. She sat down to wait.

"You're not a crazy person. You just act crazy. What will I do with you?" Quantz said. He was holding his head in his hands. "Better quit while you're ahead."

Vern laughed, a tired, hollow laugh sounding from somewhere between his ribs. He got up and stood with his hands on his hips. He still looked angry.

"Look, old man, I didn't mean to get you upset. Friends?" Quantz asked. He held out his hand to be helped up.

"Sure," Vern said. "It's just me. I freak out all the time."

"Oh?" Quantz grunted as he got to his feet.

"It's because of my trouble with Ellie, here."

"Oh? How?" Quantz smirked.

"Ellie is the one who belongs in the hospital," Vern continued. "Believe me, I know, for the things she says and does. She's got emotional problems."

Ellie's mouth dropped open in protest. She wondered if she had heard Vern right, or maybe he thought that was an ordinary acceptable remark. She was angry that Vern was not showing responsibility for his actions and telling intimate stories about her personality.

"It's hard to keep her under control. She's moody." Vern was looking for a confidante. Ellie wished he'd shut his mouth. Vern was unpredictable in his arguments, issuing ultimatums and punctuating them with his fists. Yesterday, he was crazy. Today, it was her. Ellie understood Vern was under pressure and was taking it out on her.

"He's always saying that," Ellie said to Quantz, by way of apology. "I'm so moody." Ellie thought she was as evenly calm as possible considering the circumstances.

"I think she has emotional problems," Vern repeated.

"I don't think you're so hot either," she said.

Vern started to laugh. "Ditto," he said.

Quantz looked sheepish, as if he didn't want to be in on this argument. If he didn't want to be in on this marriage, why didn't he leave, Ellie thought.

"He's always finding fault!" Ellie got up from the table. Ellie didn't think discussing things would help. Vern being so critical had been a problem all along.

"Well, if that's the way you feel," Vern said, throwing up his hands in a smug way.

"How would you know about the way I feel?" Ellie's voice rose. She felt like screaming. She couldn't win no matter what she did.

"There she goes again," Vern said. His voice cracked.

Ellie thought their insecure feelings had got the best of them.

"Come here, you obstinate son-of-a-bitch." Quantz put his arm around Vern.

Ellie got them a cup of coffee since they were both feeling pain. They drank their coffee slowly.

"You can leave now, Elaine," Vern said, as if it was a flat statement and she was actually going to do it. "I lost my temper once. It was over Elaine, there. What do you think I should do with her? Do you think I should kill her?"

"I wouldn't do that," Quantz said. "You could go to jail for that."

Ellie was stunned. Maybe Vern meant it as he was saying it ahead of time, something different. There was silence for a few moments while she waited to hear Quantz reply. They were making plans and Quantz was going to be in on it. If so, Ellie thought she would go crazy.

"She makes a good mother," Vern said.

"I was in jail once, but that was before we lived here. I was just a kid," Quantz said.

"What did you do?"

"I stole a car," Quantz said. "I tried to run away from home, but they always brought me back, so I thought I could raise some cash by stealing a car and trying to sell it."

Maybe he was trying to make Vern feel better or something, Ellie didn't know. Ellie realized uneasily the subject was off her and she didn't know whether she felt afraid or not.

"I was taken advantage of when I was young," Vern said, "because I was smaller than the others."

This was nothing Ellie hadn't heard before. Every now and then he would be in a rage about what happened at work and things Ellie did or didn't do and blame it on his youthful experiences.

Vern took a deep breath before he continued. "I count to put in time before I made a decision. Try it," he told Quantz. "It works."

"I just try to keep cool," Quantz said. "I don't like surprises. The cops watch to see if I'm nervous. They look for any sign of unease. I don't like to be caught off-guard."

"I've had lots of things happen to me," Vern said. "You probably wouldn't believe me if I told you."

Ellie observed that Vern and Quantz were friends now, talking with a weary drawl, as if the fighting made them feel better. Vern was more offensive than she anticipated in a fight, and Quantz didn't acquiesce to his temper, either. Their fighting made her so upset.

Ellie put out the trash so she could get away from them. When she was outside, she heard Vern's voice. "You probably don't believe this either, but I love my wife."

"I know," Quantz said agreeably.

Ellie felt pulled apart, as if she was the one who was the problem, causing the trouble, not recognizing love when she had it, not being satisfied and looking for more. Maybe Vern did love her. Vern was the kind who didn't show love, even if he meant it. Maybe their trouble was trying to keep married, and always fighting rather than making love. Ellie wondered when was she going to decide if fighting was love she didn't need, rather than feel bad all the time.

They sipped their coffee. They nursed their cut lips. Why should she feel sorry for them? Quantz would probably tell Norma that he got in a scuffle in a bar and Vern would spend the rest of the day ignoring her.

"You guys are just like animals the way you fight," Ellie said as she got the dinner ready.

"You shut your mouth," Vern said.

"Why, don't you like to be criticized?" Ellie asked bitterly.

"I have never felt like belting you before, but now I sure could give you one." Vern smacked Ellie across the face with his open hand, hard enough to make it red. The smack stunned her. It hurt Ellie's feelings deeply because he did it in front of

Quantz. "It's okay, Vern, leave her alone," Quantz said.

Vern scowled at Quantz as if he should mind his own business. "You look like hell, Ellie. Have you been crying or what?" Vern said.

Ellie didn't know what to say.

"I better go home," Quantz said, "and let you two be alone." Quantz gave Vern a friendly slap on the shoulder.

Ellie felt totally isolated. She knew her smile must be somewhat tremulous. She knew she must be at their latest whim whether she liked it or not.

"Stop blubbering," Vern snarled at Ellie. "What are you looking at, you stupid bitch. Look at all the trouble you cause. You're nothing but a no-good slut."

Ellie's kids came from the front room where they had been watching TV. They looked at the adults.

Quantz ducked out the door. He waved goodbye to Vern, got in his brown Camaro and drove away. Ellie waved to Quantz, but he had turned his head to back out the lane. Ellie had thought Quantz had come to talk to her and she was quite upset with the way things turned out. She hadn't wanted him to see the way Vern treated her. If Vern had wanted to make Quantz back off, Ellie figured he was successful. Ellie wanted to tell Vern how upset she felt about him hitting her in front of Quantz, but he turned his back on her.

Vern got in his truck and drove away to goodness knows where. Ellie didn't watch to see which direction he turned, but she just went back into the house, letting the screen door bang. September was almost over, and it was too cool in the evening to stand outside.

Ellie and her kids ate their supper.

When he got home again, it was really late. He pulled into the drive and sat in the truck using the steering wheel for a pillow. He had puked all over the side of the truck door, and he was too plastered to get out of the truck and walk into the house.

"I should leave you here," Ellie said, as she looked at the mess on the side of the green Ford Explorer. Then she gingerly opened the truck door and took Vern's arm.

"You would too," Vern said.

"I'll have to clean that truck tonight," Ellie said unhappily. "I wouldn't want anybody to see that." Ellie was ashamed things were so bad, especially as she wanted to believe she was trying, but it was getting harder and harder.

Vern wobbled into the house and up the steps.

"Oh dear, I'm so drunk." Vern sighed as he sat on the edge of the bed. She helped him off with his boots. He lay on his back, opened his mouth and started snoring immediately.

Ellie felt pulled to pieces. She couldn't help wondering why Vern came home drunk like this. Maybe he still wanted to come home, but she found it harder and harder to be happy to see him.

* * *

CHAPTER THIRTY ONE

Ellie hosed down the truck before the vomit dried, so Vern could go to work early in the morning. She figured her life was a continuous effort to keep up appearances.

Ellie tried to reconcile her feelings about Vern, what it meant when Vern slapped her, that maybe she didn't love him any more. She thought the slap was a rebuke she'd been ignoring although the signs were there. She had thought she could love Vern like she should, and everything would be okay.

After Vern and Quantz had their big fight, Quantz didn't come around her. Ellie thought it was just as well.

But, in her second week of work as a dental receptionist, Ellie thought about Quantz as she filled out forms and answered the telephone. When she picked up the phone, she thought she might as well be dead, she couldn't see him or touch him or phone him.

"Why is everyone so gloomy?" Dr. Beasley, the dentist asked. "I mean you, Ellie, not the patients."

Ellie thought her face must be sulky as she looked down at the papers or maybe he was just trying to be friendly. Ellie hoped he hadn't had to ask her twice for anything, her mind was so far away.

Dr. Beasley, the dentist, smiled at Ellie and put his hand on her shoulder. He had a face like a road map, with ridges, creases, and dead ends. Since he had recovered from a serious heart attack, he said he was happy to be alive, so he should start over again.

"How are things at home?" The dentist asked as he leaned toward her.

"What do you mean?"

It sounded like the way she and Vern got along was common knowledge. Ellie felt very vulnerable that her new boss found her personal life a source of interest.

"I mean you're too serious. You should enjoy yourself more. You're a pretty little filly that needs livening up," he said. "I don't know what the matter is with you two. But then maybe it's the open arrangement you people have or something that causes insecurity. I can't see anything on your face, not even calmness. It's obvious on his."

"Maybe it's the strain of being polite," Ellie said tightly. She wondered who had told him. The way he talked meant people couldn't mind their own business. She found their cynicism and smugness hurtful.

The dentist snickered. "You just need to relax, to calm down, to enjoy yourself more."

Ellie thought his familiar attitude would make it hard for her to work there. He wanted to discuss what he already knew, wanting to get personal. He knew Vern fairly well, so she figured she had got the job because of that. Right now Vern was more of a friend than a husband, concerned but distant.

"I'm trying to concentrate on my job, get things sorted out," Ellie reminded him.

"That's true. Things were in kind of a mess."

"I'll see yuh tomorrow." Ellie grabbed her jacket, put it on over her shell-pink uniform, and went out of the clinic. She was glad to be through for the day.

As she walked down the street, a horn beeped at her. She turned and saw Quantz was waiting in a new car, an ice-blue Chevy. It was such a surprise that she almost didn't recognize him. He waved impatiently.

"I thought you were going to walk right on by." He glowered as she got in beside him. "But then you were always like that, in a world of your own."

Ellie wanted to talk to Quantz so she suppressed the impulse to ask him what his problem was. "These wheels fit your new image?" She wasn't impressed with the fact he hadn't called her.

"Didn't I tell you I was getting it?"

The ice-blue Chevy was much more sedate than his brown Camaro, fitting his new salesman image as business at Champion had dramatically improved.

"How come you're here? Somebody might see us."

"This will only take a minute."

"Oh, I didn't know where I stood with you." Ellie wasn't impressed with Quantz the night of the fight, because he wasn't even a friend. He acted like he didn't know her from a doorknob. Men were like that. They valued their status over your feelings; then they wondered why it bothered you.

"I thought I'd caused enough trouble," Quantz said. Ellie thought both of them caused trouble, and it bothered her, but not so much she wouldn't go. She figured Quantz cared about her.

They went down to their regular spot and he stopped the car. Quantz acted as if he just swallowed a raw egg and didn't know how to begin.

Ellie immediately put her arms around Quantz and covered him with kisses. To her surprise and dismay, he pushed her away. She felt she had been too eager.

"Is that what you're like? You just pick up where you left off?" His voice was brusque.

Ellie's mouth dropped open. "No, I just thought that's what you wanted."

"For old time's sake? Is this significant?"

"I guess so."

He was so skeptical and standoffish. He wanted to stare out the window and not look at her. Why did he stop her after work in such an indiscrete fashion?

"Is that what you wanted to see me for, to pick a fight? I don't have time for it. You sound just like Vern. I don't like it."

Quantz glared at Ellie. She could see his face had reddened. His bright blue eyes were focused hard on some pinpoint behind her head.

Ellie blinked and angrily kept talking. "If you're thinking of giving me more of what I've already got, you better give your head a shake."

"It doesn't take much to get you going." Quantz looked as if she had damaged him in some way, and Ellie was so mad she was glad to see it. He continued, "I want to know where I stand. Are we going to break up or what? Or are we just going to keep playing head games every now and again?"

"You're going away, aren't you?" Ellie demanded. She thought he must be wanting to tell her something important.

She felt hurt to be second-guessed, to be asked suddenly for it to be over, as if their love affair was a mistake or something. "Well, this is kind of a surprise, isn't it? You can't just blow through now and again. I don't like it."

"I don't know why I haven't phoned you before this," Quantz apologized.

"Well, what am I supposed to do?" Ellie felt hurt.

"I guess I want it to be more than just sex."

"What else would it be for? Conversation?" Ellie was surprised at how much she missed his arms around her.

"It means more than that." Quantz was trying to be friendly.

"You're just saying that. What am I now? A closet person, somebody you won't take out in public. I don't think I can measure up. I don't know where my head is. I know my feet are on the ground." In spite of herself, Ellie sounded bitter. She wanted to sound coping, optimistic.

"You want too much sex. It's disgusting."

"It's not. It's for hugs and kisses. It's for dreams."

"Well, you could handle ten men."

"You must be joking. I couldn't." Ellie thought he was insulting her.

"You could so."

Ellie reached for the door of the ice-blue Chevy, but Quantz grabbed her wrists and held onto them so she couldn't get out. "Ouch! You're hurting me." Ellie felt she over-reacted as she could easily wrench away from him.

"Don't look at me with such a square jaw," Quantz said. "Why do I have to beg you to stay?" Quantz was getting like Vern, insulting her all the time.

Ellie quit squirming. "You can let go any time. Finish saying whatever it was you were going to say."

Quantz released her hands and gripped the steering wheel instead. He was smirking in the way men do when they know they have all the cards.

"I'm not going to be around town that much from now on," Quantz said.

Ellie tried to keep her emotions in check, so she shrugged. "I'll try not to let it affect me."

His smile grew broader and his face grew florid. She knew he wasn't bluffing as he tried to cover up his feelings. "It's going to be hard not seeing you every week or so."

"Do you think I don't love you or something?" Ellie blurted.

"I'm in love with you, too, but not so much I would ask you to leave your husband," Quantz said. He kissed Ellie on the cheek. "We both need a new direction."

Ellie thought she managed a smile, but for sure she didn't mean it. She felt unimportant. "You sure don't need to crowd me all the time." She folded her arms across her chest and stared straight ahead. She felt numb to hear about his new job.

"If you're mad, I'm sorry," Quantz said.

"Well, I'm not. I've got things to do," Ellie snapped.

"Sure." Quantz drove Ellie back to her truck and kept the motor going.

"You're right, we both needed a new direction. You're not staying and I'm not going to Brazil or wherever," she said angrily. She almost said, "I could, you know," but she stopped short.

Ellie got out of his brand-new car and slammed the door.

"I'll call sometime," he called through the window.

"Why bother?" Ellie shrugged. It was obvious to her he was going to keep stringing her along. Why did she let him?

"Jesus, you're mad."

When he drove away, Ellie felt a deep ache of loneliness. She thought her body and her need for Quantz ran her life. She hated it and she needed it. She felt used. The fact Quantz had to earn a living didn't make her feel better. Her needs overwhelmed her, but she had to learn to constrict them. It was the only thing that would work, she thought.

Ellie got in her truck and put the keys in the ignition. She felt so out-of-control, not knowing which way to turn. She was squeezed in a groove or stuck on a pin. In the equivocal, two-faced relationships she had, she sorted out what part of her life belonged to whom. Quantz was at one corner and Vern was at the other and she swung between the two. She felt guilty because they might feel cheated when it was her doing the cheating.

Ellie thought her affair was worth it, though. When her needs were met, she was intoxicated on love, transported, ethereal. She had glorious sex, with no argument until lately when she was with Quantz.

When she had Quantz, she could cope with practically anything that was thrown her way. She was calm, doing fine. She thought it was love.

She thought Quantz realized how she felt or why would he keep calling and explaining. He accepted her love without question, saying he was happy, saying when he was with Ellie he felt so smooth that nothing bothered him. What will happen to that when they both go different directions?

Goodbye for good was left unsaid, as if he was going to think about it some more. Ellie was pissed off, so she never even waved or looked. If he dropped dead, she wouldn't have to worry about him any more. She felt a muscle spasm, a grip in her belly, but it was just physical and it would disappear, given time.

Ellie stopped her truck at a tavern, "Freddie's," where they had a country and western band.

In the late afternoon, a cool thick layer of mist hovered over the roof of the tavern and skimmed the ground along the edge of the lot. The white mist hid the half-naked maples beside it. The surreal neon sign on Freddie's lit the parking lot.

When she heard some men talking at the far end of the lot, she realized she'd made a mistake. As far as she was concerned they were the wrong guys, so she continued on home.

For a week, after Quantz left for Brazil, Ellie sat around dazed, wondering what to do. She wasn't able to do anything, except she threw away the mood-elevating pills Moose had given her months ago. She hadn't taken them and she likely never would.

Whenever she noticed Quantz around town, he sometimes waved and stopped and sometimes he wouldn't. He kept on going. Ellie never let on it bothered her. It didn't help to realize how much he meant to her.

Ellie felt her life wasn't as important, not as joyful, any more. She had thought love would solve everything, but it hadn't. She thought Quantz didn't care that much about anything, especially her. He didn't like to commit. Quantz was a person who lived in the present and didn't want to remember how things were between them, like she did.

When Quantz was selling graders in places like Brazil and Tunisia, he probably never thought of her. His absence made her feel discarded. His second thoughts made her think she had to find some way to improve her life. When he had told her he sort-of, kind-of loved her, he probably didn't mean it at all. His love was just for the time being, an interlude.

* * *

CHAPTER THIRTY TWO

Since Ellie had asked Vern not to slap her around in public, she noticed he watched her very carefully as if he was wondering what else does the silly bitch want?

They had gone outside to rake leaves, and out of the corner of her eye she could see Vern squinting at her.

The leaves had decidedly turned, and most of them had fallen so there was no going back to summer.

Ellie, Vern, Robert, and Susan raked the leaves into piles.

"What's with you, going around with a cloud over your head?" Vern asked loudly as if he demanded a report.

"Nothing," Ellie said sulkily.

"When the nothing is over, let me know. I'm here, you know, most of the time," Vern said sardonically. Ellie thought Vern was undemonstrative now, no kissing or hugging.

"For all I care, you can stick it somewhere."

"You don't really mean that, you would be mad if I did."

"Whatever you say!" Ellie clenched her teeth.

"You know you don't pay that much attention to me any more," Vern said. He was acting like a know-it-all, smirking as if he had power over her emotions, making her squirm one day by ignoring her and demanding why hadn't he got it the next. She hated it when he did that. "Look at the way you filled the bag. Most of the leaves fell out."

Ellie dumped the plastic bag entirely and wrenched it open for Vern to fill it properly. She thought it was typical of the way they got along, when everything she did was a cause for comment. She adjusted the bag at the wrong time, and Vern missed the opening and the leaves went everywhere.

"Your temper just gets the better of you. Here, I'll hold it," Vern said, "And you fill it. Can you?"

Ellie said, "I don't know if it's possible for me to do anything right for you."

"All I want to do is finish this job, not make a marital catastrophe out of it," Vern pointed out.

Ellie thought he acted like he wanted to pick a fight. Seeing his face get stubborn like that made Ellie feel bad.

When Ellie was crazy for Quantz, she sort of forgot about Vern. She ignored him, then she felt guilty about it, because she thought her affair was hard on Vern. Ellie thought Vern was uneasy and unsure of himself. Ellie always thought he knew what was what.

He wasn't always the reservoir of mockery and solitude that Ellie thought he was. She was so surprised when he was vulnerable that she was ashamed of herself. Vern had regular things he criticized her for: appearance, job, work habits. Criticism became the only attention she got. His customary harangue became a rigmarole, something that he perfected with practice.

First he was an enemy, then she felt sorry for him, and it was Ellie's turn to be wanting, when Quantz was gone and Vern was hard on her. Ellie wondered how she would get back at Vern.

Maybe her affair was why they weren't getting along rather than the result of it. Affairs were supposed to be a sign of trouble, or they made life more interesting, or you were beneath the others, dirt under their feet. An affair was a secret, private matter, not anything Ellie wanted anybody making a judgment about, as if she was lacking in good sense, or whatever.

After Vern and the kids had gone into the house, Ellie put the rakes and bags away. They put their heavier coats on and went up town. Vern had gone into the hardware store and Ellie was waiting.

Ellie saw Beri was round as a pumpkin, or a wagonload of pumpkins.

"How's Vern?" Beri said.

"Wait and you can ask him yourself," Ellie said, "if he's speaking. He's in such a bad mood."

"Why?" Beri's face showed amusement at Ellie's discomfort.

"Vern is giving me a hard time. I can't do anything but he walks over me about it. Can you see the tread marks on my face?" Ellie was joking because Vern had stopped slapping her when she asked. "I can't even finish a sentence."

Beri snorted and immediately corrected her. "He just does that to get you to do things for him. He believes you and trusts you, so he doesn't know why you act wounded all the time, the way you do. It's just a test, to get you to admit you love him." Beri had her eyes shut as she talked to Ellie so she couldn't see any objection Ellie might have had.

She didn't have to be so pious. It was a side to Beri that Ellie disliked. She was similar to Vern that way. They were so hypocritical. What was okay for them was not okay for her, like their sneaky ways they hoped she didn't notice. She didn't think they were still seeing each other anyway.

"Maybe you know him better than I do!" Ellie raised her voice in anger. "I bet you don't have to listen to him unload the way I have to. Maybe you just see the good stuff."

Ellie figured Beri knew what Vern could be like, as she'd seen and heard him often enough. Beri must think Ellie was an awful dunce not to notice what had been happening between her and Vern.

Ellie laughed at Beri's reaction and the shocked way she looked. Her protruding belly made her dress fall like the sheets over a rounded corner of a bed.

Vern came out of the hardware store with some antifreeze.

"Here's the man himself!" Beri smiled brightly.

"You look like you got caught bending over once too often," Vern said. It was an ignorant thing to say, but it made her laugh, skittishly, like a mare's neigh, in the same toothy fashion. He patted her tummy gingerly. She'd gained sixteen pounds, she said, in one month. Even her feet were chubby, flesh pinched in her shoes. "Ellie, here, won't stay put long enough." His thumb poked the air over his shoulder at Ellie.

Beri flushed and glanced at Ellie. "She's getting so skinny."

Vern rubbed Ellie's arms. He fingered her cheeks the way he used to touch Beri. "It keeps her from getting seized up, stiff with age."

Beri got fire-red with humiliation which pleased Ellie to no end. Did she get took for a dummy by Vern or what? Ellie thought.

Vern, of course, just followed where the grease was thickest, where regard, money, sex, was the most of everything. That's what Ellie thought, anyway. When he was ignorant like that, thinking he was so clever with his trust fund of rude jokes, Ellie wondered why she would feel sorry.

Ellie didn't try to make her feel better like she usually did, inviting her to come around, and Beri didn't mention when Ellie could come to her house.

"Who's the father? Or did you draw straws?" Vern joked.

Beri laughed rather lamely.

"It looks like it's going to be twins. Two fathers."

"Vern!" Ellie was shocked he'd made an issue out of something so personal.

Beri shifted about uncomfortably. Finally, Vern pushed Ellie along the street. He hadn't mentioned Beri in a long time. He had an enormous opinion of himself, so image-conscious, and Ellie or whoever had to measure up.

The dentist, Dr. Beasley, came out of his clinic. Vern stopped to talk. Ellie saw him watching her through the window of the clinic when they were up town.

"Been on the golf course, lately?" the dentist looked at the gallon of antifreeze in Vern's hand. "How does Saturday sound?"

"I guess I should. It'll soon be under snow drifts."

The dentist smiled at Ellie as he waved goodbye to Vern.

Ellie whispered to Vern, "Watch what you tell him, because I have to explain it at work." Ellie dreaded explaining her personal life to her boss.

"Does he pick on you?"

"No, but he's curious. He's like an old woman the way he likes to gossip."

"Okay," Vern said. "By the way, I saw Quantz today and he asked how you were."

"How am I?" Ellie said rudely. "How nice of you to wonder!"

"He's off to Morocco tomorrow." Vern shrugged happily. "Anyway, he's missing all the fun."

"Fun?" Ellie was surprised.

"I'm enjoying myself. Why not? Why worry about things? Golf, you name it. Everybody's inviting me."

Vern could be wonderful when he wanted to be. He could visit for hours, jovial as hell, and people laughed at his jokes, Ellie thought in amazement.

Ellie was waiting for him to rub it in about Quantz asking so she could get him about Beri, but he didn't.

Vern and Ellie got in the truck and drove home. When Ellie got in the door, the phone rang.

When she picked it up, there was silence then it went dead. She got a lot of bang-ups when she answered the phone. Every day. She felt they got the wrong person, rather than the wrong number. Ellie thought it was somebody new calling for Vern and getting her by mistake so it made her jealous and suspicious. "Who phones for you all the time?"

"Who was that?" Vern asked.

Ellie shrugged.

"Well then, how do you expect me to know?"

It was a typical response for Vern to make.

Vern and Ellie want to bed. Vern sighed with pleasure. He felt great now, at least he acted like it, but Ellie felt terrible. The contrast made her low mood more obvious, but Vern never noticed it, and that made Ellie mad. He was like a newlywed with his eyes shut and only one thing on his mind; that he wanted to go to bed all the time. He was overwhelming. Ellie couldn't believe it. She wondered why things were going good for a change. She watched Vern relaxing, wondering what he was thinking about, because she was keyed up and he hadn't seemed to notice.

Ellie thought her face didn't register emotion so that maybe Vern started to think she didn't have any. She may have looked the same as usual, but a knot of tension at the back of her neck made her feel dreadful. Ellie couldn't see how she felt in the mirror, either. Her face had the same round, smooth countenance. What was new with Vern? He acted like everything was great, snoring peacefully, and Ellie thought Vern couldn't know how bad she felt. It was hard to keep cool.

The next morning the weather was perfect: Indian summer, red sumacs, and fallen fruit. Ellie should have felt good, but someone might have hit her over the head with a hammer. Her head was over the toilet. She was retching. Any more and she would turn inside out.

"What is the matter with you?" Vern asked.

"What does it look like?"

Vern started to laugh. Only a dummy could have missed how sick she was. Right at that moment, she felt a killer rage rising, but she was in no position to do anything. She had to grip the sides of the toilet bowl to keep from collapsing.

"I think I'm pregnant again. Will I get an abortion, or shoot the doctor, or what?" Ellie tried to joke. At first, Ellie was angry as it wasn't supposed to happen when she was on the pill. But, she heard it happened to lots of people and in the most inconvenient of circumstances.

"How did that happen?" Vern asked, apparently as happy and serene as could be, but his eyes flickered.

"I don't know," Ellie said. "Isn't it a problem?"

"When?" he asked, looking at the calendar. "Did you just find out?" Vern looked worried. "I think it's quite a surprise," he said drily.

"Well, it wasn't supposed to happen, was it?"

"You would know," Vern said. "I guess you'd also know whose it was."

"I guess so," Ellie said. She was sure it was Vern's baby, so she put her arms around him and gave him a kiss.

Vern was in a good mood about it. He was smiling, hugging, and kissing. When he was telling everybody, Ellie's queasy stomach sank to her heels. Eventually, she got used to the idea. She started to think this baby would be good for them. After six weeks, she started to feel better.

Vern had a happy expression in his eyes for the longest extended period of time that Ellie could remember. She began to think they were worth saving, that they had love after all, and that it wasn't so bad being married when a few weeks ago it was a daily hassle. It looked as if Vern was going to accept this baby. Ellie thought since Vern's reaction was positive and accepting that she could save her marriage.

Ellie was convinced they would stick it out for good, even if they weren't back to square one. Was it just a truce or what? Maybe it was true love. Since they'd been together eight years, they'd stay together another eight. Ellie figured that, without love, she was nothing. She decided she needed her husband, and she would forget about Quantz.

In her more romantic moments, Ellie wanted her and Vern to be more like lovers, but in reality their getting along was just an eye or a clear patch or a rainbow. It only lasted a short while.

* * *

CHAPTER THIRTY THREE

Once Ellie started to feel better, she took long walks. In late October, she noticed the beach sand underneath her feet had a kind of crust on it from the leavings of the lake water and the lack of footprints ahead of her. The skies were gray and gloomy and it looked to Ellie as if it could snow overnight. People who had been there for the summer months were long gone.

Geese weren't waiting either. They headed south in groups, and Ellie could hear their honk as she stood on the pier.

Ellie went down to the harbor. She saw rigs lined up at the elevators, a procession to carry away the grain. Trailers full, they headed up the hill.

Ellie walked beside two freighters secured alongside the dock, and when both were filled to capacity with grain, the hatches clanged shut. Then, the freighters left the harbor, ponderous and slow, their masters not worrying yet about the late fall storms. Ellie watched one move out and wait for the other to leave harbor. Then, it too waited at the breakwall for the first one to go over the horizon. Ellie thought there would be another month or two of runs and then they would head for waters that stay open or go into a shipyard or dock for winter lay-up.

Down at the harbor, the Megamyth Two, Turnbull's yacht, was being hauled out of the water. Turnbull had arranged a sale of his business, Champion, to a foreign buyer. The sale was accomplished in a week during the summer time, and Vern didn't hear about it until after. Maybe if they had known Champion was for sale, the guys wouldn't have gone back to work as easy as they did, Vern said.

While Ellie was waiting for Vern to be through for the day at Champion, she watched the crane hoist the yacht out of the water to get it ready for their round-the-world cruise.

Ellie thought it was just coincidence to see Turnbull at the harbor and to hear their voices carry on the wind.

She trudged up the hill even though she still had time to put in. The wind was so brisk that it blew through her sweater making her shiver. Summer was over, for sure. There was sadness in the smell of smoke from the burning piles of leaves drifting across the sidewalk into Ellie's face as she went past. The smoke smarts in her eyes made them water.

As Ellie walked up the street, Quantz came out of a restaurant near the corner. At first, Ellie thought he didn't want to recognize her. But he turned, swivelling unsteadily on one foot, and waved at her. He waited and his face got very red as she went up to him.

"Hi," she said brightly, surprised and pleased at this unexpected meeting. She thought he wanted to see her.

He patted his head where the hair was thin, and he cleared his throat. "I went home one day and found my wife and children gone, my bank account cleaned out. Everything was gone but the tears. Norma and her lawyer are giving me a hard time. But you won't want to hear about that."

"No, really. It's okay. I'm sorry about the way things are for you," Ellie said. She had heard they broke up, so it wasn't news. What could she say to commiserate?

He put his arm around Ellie, giving her shoulders a squeeze. Ellie could smell booze, raincoat, and aftershave, in order of strength. "I've really missed you, Ellie." He gave her another squeeze. On the street, too.

Ellie thought maybe Quantz was waiting for her to say something romantic. It wouldn't have been too cool.

He looked healthy, happy, and almost edible. He looked as if he might have wanted it. It made Ellie want it.

"I'm home alone when I'm not overseas. I don't know why I haven't called you before this," he said.

"You usually just come around, don't you? Well, don't you?" Ellie stared at him. She didn't know if she was wistful or slightly provoked, wishing he would make a date as it had been so long. She could see he had his car keys in his hand, but he wasn't so rude that he jangled them.

"We aren't the same people we used to be," he said, almost apologizing that she hadn't been a priority and that he hadn't called. "Maybe we can never go back. Isn't that what they say? What do you think?"

"I feel like a needle stuck in a flaw or a scratch! Don't you think life is a broken record?" Ellie was suddenly discouraged. By comparison, Ellie was motionless in her life and her job.

"Is it better than being jerked around like a ping-pong ball?" Quantz laughed uneasily.

Ellie resisted the temptation to ask whose fault that was. She thought maybe she wanted to see him for awhile.

They blinked at each other. Ellie considered a few seconds of indecision seemed forever, before she decided she should say something or not. She hadn't before. He was either nonchalant or frustrated. Ellie didn't know the difference like she used to. He wasn't quick to react so he was like somebody she didn't know too well. It put her on her guard.

Quantz didn't say anything about her appearance, about her tummy, which normally would be the first thing he would have noticed. He didn't say anything at all about the way she was looking, her hair, nothing. Ellie was confused and put off by his lack of reaction.

"I have to go to a meeting," Quantz said.

"Is it an important one?"

"Yes, very." He yacked for several minutes about what would be going on. "But, I'll give you a call sometime." He was friendly and exuberant, keen from talking about his work.

"I'm kind of busy right now," Ellie said quietly. She didn't know why she said it. Maybe she didn't want to be the kind he could pick up with right where he left off.

"See yuh, Ellie." His eyes were like bullet holes looking right through her. He got in his ice-blue Chevy, and drove away without a backward glance or a wave.

Ellie wished she had reacted quicker. She couldn't believe that she let Quantz leave in a huff like that without doing anything about it. Usually, she would be right after him, hanging onto him.

Quantz drove down the street and around the corner and out of sight, as if he was leaving her behind forever. Ellie wished he hadn't come out of the restaurant like that, making him impossible to avoid, making her feel she did without now, remembering how good things used to be with him. Ellie still wanted to be with Quantz. He made her feel good, and he made her feel special.

She never thought it would hurt so much to see Quantz drive away. It was like opening old wounds, a healed injury that was suddenly starting to ache. Quantz was somebody she knew she would never take up with for keeps, but she still kind of hankered for. He was either nothing or he was everything. Then, she thought that she lived in a dream world, a place of hopes so fragile it would shatter.

It was much too depressing to go into the restaurant now for a cup of coffee so Ellie walked the rest of the way to Champion. She got in the truck and waited for Vern.

When Vern came out of Champion and got in the truck, Ellie was crying.

"What the matter, now?" Vern asked, exasperated.

"Nothing."

"You're like this all the time," Vern said. "I sure will be glad when the baby comes."

"So will I," Ellie said.

After they got home, Ellie took Robert and Susan for a walk. They gathered chestnuts and bit them with their teeth. A squirrel chittered at them and scampered up the tree.

"We could save some chestnuts for it," Robert said. "Can we, Mom?"

"Sure," Ellie said, happy they were thinking ahead.

"It's not going to be an it," Susan said wisely and bossily. "It's going to be a boy or a girl."

This fall Robert had started preschool classes and he saw a cloud in a circle and a smokestack in a pencil. His teacher was amazed. Ellie thought school just kept him out of a lot of a lot of trouble, such as falling off his tricycle and scraping his knee.

Susan had afternoons at day care while Ellie worked for the dentist. Her fat little legs had stretched this summer, so Ellie thought her kids were practically grown up. She could hardly wait until she had another wee squeak to look after.

It wasn't long until the gloomy skies turned into snow. As they walked back home, the swamp at the end of the street was a fantasy. The multicolored foliage, bird's nests, and cattails were covered with wet snow.

* * *

CHAPTER THIRTY FOUR

Meanwhile, over the winter, Ellie had a miscarriage. Ellie fell down the basement steps in her duplex when Vern wasn't home, and there wasn't anything they could do to save their baby. She felt a sense of loss after the pain she went through, and immediately she thought maybe if she got pregnant again, another baby would make up for it.

Ellie had started taking music lessons again, the first since she was a teenager, and she thought the keyboard lessons were an attempt to replace the love lost in her life.

In February, Ellie and Cathy were getting ready for a Valentine's Dance. On Thursday night, they were having a practice at the Bedford. The bar wasn't the best place for a dance as the dance floor was small. Ellie was to fill in at the electric keyboard because their regular player was sick. Cathy said she would do fine after a practice and besides, it would help Ellie get her mind off painful things.

"What things?" Ellie asked Cathy.

"Your miscarriage. It's hard on a person."

"I'm over it," Ellie said, wondering what facet of the pain Cathy was referring to.

"Still, it must be hard." Cathy grimaced, as if she was the one feeling the pain. "I'm glad it never happened to me."

Ellie, who remembered the fights Cathy used to pick, said, "I think you're doing awfully well on your own."

"John said I was like a little football player, so he didn't worry about me too much," Cathy said. "I wish I had been more understanding. Then, maybe John would have liked me more, and then he wouldn't have been so uptight all the time, and then he wouldn't be dead." Cathy dissolved into tears.

Cathy had changed, Ellie thought. She had lost about fifteen pounds and looked like the kid she was. She wore jeans, boots, and leather belts around her waist. Her thinness made her double chin disappear.

"You have lost a lot of weight," Ellie said. Ellie too had gotten so thin her boobs almost disappeared.

"Look at the wrinkles around my eyes," Cathy said, " And I hate my heavy copper hair." Cathy flipped her hair, much redder than Moose's had been.

Ellie could see Albert, the drummer, rubbernecking as they talked. Cathy had met Albert in a bar, and he was the reason she had this job in a band.

"Have you gone over Cathy's song?" Albert asked. Albert had written it down for Ellie to memorize the chords.

Cathy wrote a song about Moose, how his death and losing him affected her.

She sang it with Albert's arrangements.

"Her voice needs to be louder. You need to sing with her," Albert suggested to Ellie.

"He wants me to shriek it out." Cathy smiled, and Albert put his arm around her. Albert was so ugly, so unlikely for Cathy that Ellie asked her about him when Albert went back to his drums.

"Why do you like a guy like that?"

Cathy shrugged. "He doesn't mean anything by it. Besides, he helps me."

But Albert's friendliness bothered Ellie. He was too old, and he was too ugly for Cathy. His attentions would lead to trouble and Cathy didn't need trouble.

The practice wasn't going well. Cathy flubbed her song and Ellie stood at the keyboard waiting for Cathy to start over. There was an awkward silence.

"You could put a little more life into it," Albert said. "Show that you care."

"Give me a break." Cathy grabbed her purse and stomped off the stage, pushing Albert out of the way.

"Watch it," he said. "You could be replaced, you know."

Cathy's face was shocked and hurt.

"Thanks a lot," Cathy snapped. She threw a guitar case at Albert and it glanced off his shoulder, clattering to the floor.

"Hey, cool off," he said. "We have lots of work to do before we can get out of here."

Cathy started to cry. "Jesus, what is happening to me?"

"You're tired, you're emotional," Albert said. "You need help." He put his arm around her. "Go home. Take a break."

"That's big of you, but I think I'll stay," Cathy said.

"No, go ahead. Really, we don't mind," Albert said.

"Okay, fine. You don't need me anyway." Cathy was in tears. Albert just shrugged and walked away.

Ellie was standing at the keyboard waiting for Cathy to start her song over.

"What is the matter with me?" Cathy asked Ellie in tears. Ellie thought they were temperamental idiots, and she wondered how she got herself into this.

Albert smiled in an toothless way at Cathy.

In a moment, they did Cathy's song and it went without a hitch. Then they attempted to finish the set, practising "Stand By Your Man," Ellie's favorite.

When Albert flubbed the beat of this song, Cathy screamed at him. "You're a dummy. Can't you even keep a steady beat? You're screwing up the song."

"It's because you're singing so fast that I can't keep up," Albert said.

"I'm not," Cathy shrieked.

"I wish you were that loud when you were singing!" Albert shrugged and rolled his eyes at the ceiling.

Albert grinned at Ellie as if this was some sort of joke. He was one of ugliest men Ellie had ever seen, with a large gap in his teeth that showed up when he smiled and eyebrows that went right across his forehead.

"Maybe it's me getting you worked up, Cathy," Albert suggested.

"Don't flatter yourself," Cathy said. "If you can't pay attention to your music, perhaps we should get someone else." She swung her long hair around and belted out the next song as loud as she could.

At the end, the drummer smiled in a dreamy, relaxed way and he said to Cathy, "I'm ready any night you are."

"Do us both a favor and drop dead," she said huffily.

Ellie wondered why they weren't getting ready for the next song. She had never seen Cathy have such a temper tantrum. Cathy was partly right because the drummer tended to accelerate rather than stay at a steady tempo.

"Maybe you're ready," Albert said. "You're a nice girl."

Ellie saw the red, constrained look on the drummer's face, and she realized maybe he was trying to keep his lascivious feelings under control. Ellie disliked this guy because she thought he didn't like Cathy enough.

"Gawd. I can't do anything right. It's not a good song," Cathy said. "The words are all wrong. They aren't up to the subject matter." Although people listened to her respectfully, she was not enthused about going to Nashville.

Cathy had used some of her insurance money to rent a local soundproof studio to cut their own record. Some of the local radio stations played the song and it got some airtime out west.

"Write another song," Albert said. "All it takes is one song that's a hit to be famous. She has to keep writing songs. Tell her to write songs." Albert pointed from Ellie to Cathy.

"I'm not a songwriter," Cathy said. "I think it's wrong of you to expect me to come up with another. I can't help it if it was just a one-time thing."

"Well, you can try harder, can't you?" the drummer said.

"You try!"

"I can't keep my mind on it long enough to write a song."

"Well, neither can I," Cathy said shortly.

"I know what you are thinking about. I know what you need. You are wanting it," Albert said dreamily.

"I can't believe you said that. It's none of your business."

"You can't avoid it, you know. Think about it."

Cathy turned her back on him. The drummer fawned and grovelled like a tomcat. The way they argued made Ellie on edge, waiting for them to solve the tension between them.

"What else is there besides sex. Fame?" Albert was middle-aged, but he still dreamed of stardom. He hoped it meant he wouldn't have to work on his pig farm any more, but play two gigs a week, Friday and Saturday, and spend Sunday resting up, and practicing the following week. He told Ellie, "I think Cathy is silly to look opportunity in the nose. What does she have besides her song?"

"I'm not a songwriter. I'm just a mother," Cathy said.

Ellie could see from her exasperated expression that Cathy had become irritated with Albert's remarks. "All I get is a hassle," Cathy said. "I just turned twenty-six and my nineteen-year-old brother called me an older woman."

Ellie said, "I can see how that wouldn't make you feel any better at all." Ellie thought it was really rather funny, but she had better not laugh at Cathy. She knew Cathy had had a different man in her bed every weekend for awhile. It was the local gossip. Everyone had heard it and everyone asked about it, but no one could believe it. It looked to Ellie that Albert was trying to be next.

When they called the practice over, Albert left.

"Albert bothers my mother, because he is as old as she is. She thinks I'll just come to grief with him," Cathy said.

Ellie thought Cathy's mother was probably right, if the way they presently got along was any indication.

"Do you think we'll be ready for tomorrow night?"

"We'll be fine. You did fine. We don't always fight like that," Cathy insisted.

"That's good," Ellie said, with relief.

The dance tomorrow night would be like old home week, Ellie thought, as everyone they knew was coming.

Vern came. Beri and George had a slow dance together, clinging as if they were romance discovered all over again.

The band played one more slow one, then they quit for ten minutes. Ellie noticed the young people really enjoyed the music, especially Sally and Betty Lou, who were sitting quietly with Lou Grosste.

"What's the big occasion?" Vern asked George and Beri.

"We got married today."

"That's the way to do things," Vern said. "Didn't you just have a baby?"

Beri grinned like a cat. "Last week. A boy."

Vern opened his mouth and shut it again.

Beri tittered. She was drinking after a long dry spell.

"What do you think of the band?" George asked.

"I wouldn't have missed this for the world," Vern said.

"Look at Cathy," Beri said disapproving. "Look at her top. Sleazy."

Cathy had on a low-cut top that showed the top part of her breasts when she bent over.

After their break, during which Ellie had a drink, the band sounded better to her, or maybe it was just the influence of the crowd.

By the end of the night, it was obvious to Ellie that Cathy was pissed to the eyeballs. Cathy was zipping around visiting everybody she knew, until she plopped in a chair between Beri and Ellie.

"Don't you care about your children?" Beri laced into Cathy.

"What?" Cathy said breathlessly.

Ellie, too, couldn't believe Cathy was like this, as Moose had always let on she didn't understand his needs.

"Do you think it's right to carry on the way you do?" Beri continued.

"What way? Don't you have George?" Cathy, puffing, pushed her bangs off her steamy face.

"Yes, but I think you should hold back a bit before you get yourself into trouble. Those men's eyes were popping out of their heads," Beri said.

"Don't you think I need one?" Cathy pointed out.

"You're still young. It never hurts to wait. Use your head," Beri said, in an increasingly pleading tone of voice.

"For God's sake, you sound like my mother!" Cathy got up in a huff. "When did you stop wanting it?"

"Well, excuse me. I'm just trying to help," Beri said. "Cathy thinks I'm out of it," she whispered to Ellie.

"Yes, isn't it funny," Ellie said. "She used to be the uptight one. And now you are."

Beri gave Ellie a dirty look. "It seems a long time ago. Do you ever think of Moose?"

"Once in a while," Ellie said.

"What would Moose think of her now?" Beri whined. "She looks so foolish prancing around."

Ellie thought Beri was awfully straitlaced all of a sudden. Both George and Beri looked stuffy with their coats on sitting in their chairs waiting to leave.

Ellie thought Beri looked wan and peaked. Maybe it bothered her if Cathy got lucky, because she was embarrassing. Beri forgot that she used to be embarrassing. It wasn't funny then, either, the way Beri was high all the time, and the way Cathy was upset.

Beri yawned and George said it was time they left, and they got up, did up their coats, and left. Like they were one person. It was funny, Ellie thought, the way they acted like dutiful relatives.

Vern sat at the bar with Steve and Wayne. Vern looked tuckered out, Steve was in deep discussion and Wayne glowered directly at Ellie, but she turned away from him, even though she thought Vern might think she meant him.

Ellie and Cathy had a late night drink after they had got packed up. Ellie noticed Albert was ignoring Cathy. He left right at one o'clock with his equipment.

"Have you been seeing the drummer quite awhile?" Ellie asked Cathy.

Cathy nodded sadly, as if she was a forgotten waif.

"It's none of my business, but you're miserable, aren't you?" She said that because Cathy acted like she was missing out on something, like good sex, or a pretense at love.

"I'm beginning to think older men aren't the answer," Cathy said.

"No, they're irascible," Ellie said. Ellie wondered what Cathy would do if they didn't keep together, then maybe she would quit the band altogether. In that way it wasn't fair. Albert would keep playing and Cathy wouldn't.

Ellie was getting drunk. "When you're fighting all the time," Ellie said to Cathy, "maybe you should look for the reason why."

Cathy nodded. "We're fighting more than we're screwing."

Ellie laughed. "We can get drunk," she said.

"We sure can," Cathy said.

After the dance, Cathy sold a few records.

Ellie thought because the circumstances surrounding Moose's death hadn't been satisfactorily explained, they were still discussing it. Cathy said the success of her song was because of the notoriety, because of John and the way he died.

"I better get going," Cathy said, "or I'll be late for work in the morning at Schaefer Pen and the supervisor will give me hell. There are times when I hate John for being dead, in spite of the fact that I wanted him so much. I want him and hate him, just like when he was alive. I can't figure out why life has played such a nasty trick on me."

Ellie could empathize as she had begun to wish for someone special, too. Ellie thought lovers she didn't care about were surrogates, and easy to explain, but when she began to wish for someone special Ellie wanted to see Quantz again.

Ellie thought that even though she could still see Vern patiently sitting at the bar. Ellie didn't know if Vern was waiting for her to take him home, or if he was waiting for Wayne to be on his way. Either way, Ellie went over and she and Vern went home together. "Not a bad band," Vern said, "but it needs more work."

* * *

CHAPTER THIRTY FIVE

Since the dance in February, Ellie had got beat up by Wayne. She put in a complaint to the cops, but nothing was done. Ellie went to bed for three days telling the dentist she had the flu. She told Vern the same thing, but she could tell from his face he didn't believe her. Vern was different now, instead of yelling at her and criticizing her all the time, he was silent and distant.

She was so stiff it hurt to walk, and Ellie did her best to try not to draw attention to it.

When Quantz called, Ellie still had bruises.

Ellie wondered why he called her. It was such a surprise to hear his voice on the phone, as usually he relied on chance or hung around after work until she showed up. She thought it must be something more important than just not seeing her in awhile. She'd heard he wasn't living with his wife, so maybe this meeting was something special.

Since it was almost spring, she didn't know whether to wear a light coat or a heavy one, so she chose a bright red melton one with gold buttons. The coats she wore were a reflection of how she felt. She was standing in front of the mirror, trying to look as good as she possibly could. Ellie had lesions and wounds of a varying sort, some of them visible and some of them not. A new outfit, a new coat, a new hairdo and some makeup, and she would be as perfect as possible, she thought.

The weather was getting ahead of her, as it felt almost spring, but it was still winter in March. There was a fresh layer of snow on the ground, enough to make the grass, roads, and fields slick. The wet snow stuck to the cedars, fences, and branches. The air was calm. It was postcard beautiful.

Quantz drove a short distance out of town and parked his ice-blue Chevy. They had a good place to park, because they were on a road without farm buildings, that no one was likely to use. The car was running, but the window was open.

"I don't have much time," he said. Ellie thought he had gotten bigger, put on weight. There was a larger roll at his waistline, his face had fleshed out and his blue eyes were embedded in pockets of skin.

"I have the rest of my life," Ellie said, joking. Maybe she did want to spend the rest of her life with him.

He laughed. "I should take you up on that!" She thought this was another promise for the future. His eyes were expressionless, but his smile was the same as it used to be.

Ellie had gotten quite thin, angles where she used to be round. She hadn't mentioned how fat he'd gotten, and she thought maybe that was why he didn't mention her thinness.

Ellie figured he was home for a break, he was in a hurry and he wanted a quick one. He was pushy and ravenous and Ellie felt the same after not seeing him for five months. That was the thing about lovers, their tensions, and their continual need to get it released. Ellie thought it could get tiresome, if she was lucky enough to love Quantz that long. She was wondering if he really liked her, or if it was just because he wasn't back with his wife.

"Are you trying to get Norma to come back?" At first, Ellie felt tense, almost wanting to pick a fight to clear the air. Quantz had told her he didn't think she was worth leaving his wife for, but now that he had, had his opinion changed? Ellie knew it was better to try and get along with your spouse if it was possible and when there was children involved.

"I don't think she will, but I'm working on it. Who have you been seeing?"

"Nobody." Ellie knew this was true but what would Quantz think? She and Vern were already looking seriously for a house in the country, but nothing else had changed.

"It's not like you to be sitting on ice like that!" Quantz squinted at her suspiciously making her think he didn't believe her after five months.

Their relationship was like a broken record. He wanted her and he didn't want her, she thought. Did they have a future or didn't they? Until now, she thought they really didn't.

Ellie thought Quantz was jealous of her, and she was jealous of him, too. Passion was their main problem. Always at first, they were tense and then when it was time to go, they would have another fight. It was always because there was the threat of somebody else, maybe more than one for Quantz. He'd never really say.

Ellie thought she was still crazy about him like she was before, so maybe she was not too worried if he thought about somebody else once in awhile.

Ellie's eyes were all over the place, except on Quantz, as if she were gingerly eyeing something that might disappear if she stared at it too directly.

"I guess you won't find it too exciting here now," she said, comparing her dull life to his exciting one of travel.

He had a painful expression on his face, as if it was all too true.

Ellie had just meant to break the ice. "I'm always saying the wrong thing. I just meant I feel boring, compared to all the people you've met."

"Give me a break," he said, turning his face away. "There's no one but you. You can't say the same."

She thought he meant the others didn't mean a thing when he was face to face with her, in the expediency of the situation. She thought he said things to get nicely through a situation.

"Yes, I can," she said. Quantz was still talking like he wanted to be with her. How serious was he? she thought. He called her, didn't he?

"And I'm next on the list?" Quantz said. Maybe he was trying to get her to feel sorry for him.

"I don't have a list," Ellie said. "It's not like you to be so critical."

"I guess I'm feeling a bit on edge."

"Why?"

He sighed. "I no sooner get home than I get questioned. I had to get out. Because I'm travelling a lot, they think I'm a go-between for Wayne, that I carry drugs and other goods," he said drily.

So that was it. Ellie figured he had extra problems associated with his job, and she wondered how Wayne figured in. She'd also noticed how uptight and tense he got when Wayne came around.

Ellie wondered where she stood. She felt no different than before, strung-out, feeling turned on and off, wanting to and thinking she shouldn't like him as much as she did, so if she did love him and meant it, what would happen?

He was so eager when they made love that it was over quick, like firecrackers, smoldering and then exploding. Then, he zipped up.

Ellie knew why she never really turned him down, and she thought she was in love because their tensions immediately disappeared once they made love. She thought their tenuous affair lasting one meeting at a time could become something stronger.

"It's an hour before dark," he said. "Do you want to stay for awhile?"

"Sure," she said. Vern would wonder where she was if she stayed too long, but she would stop at the grocery store on the way home.

She was wedged between Quantz and the steering wheel, facing him. They were hanging onto each other, and over his shoulder, Ellie saw a black and white cop car drive by on the side road behind them. But the driver didn't turn his head. She noticed the movement of the intruding car carry onto the next section. Then, they were alone again.

Ellie put her arms around his neck, convinced they were made for each other. She hung on even though it was more dangerous than ever when they were observed like this.

"You're so beautiful," Quantz said. "I'd like us to stay this way forever."

Ellie noticed the new snow, out of place as it had fallen so late in the season, still coated the laden branches. Even a bluejay perched motionless, as if it was watching them, its eye careful. When Ellie moved away from Quantz, the jay screamed, "thief, thief, thief."

All of a sudden Ellie felt scared. There was only a certain length of time she could wait before unease propelled her into action, before there wouldn't be an answer to Vern's questions. Was Quantz wanting her to move in with him, or was he just expressing his hopeful thoughts for the future?

"Let's go," she said, anxious what her reception would be with Vern if she was late.

"Soon." He squeezed her tight. All of a sudden, Quantz seemed to have all day. Ellie thought they were lucky, not having met anyone else on the road. If someone saw them together, they would tell everyone they knew.

Ellie was anxious to go, but he was stalling. She didn't see him often enough she thought. "When will you call again? Or will I just have to wait in line?" she asked testily. She thought it had been way too long since the last time, since then she'd lost a baby, been threatened, and it seemed a lifetime away to her. She'd changed, she thought, maybe she was tougher than she used to be, but the fact he was leaving and their relationship was still in an uncertain state bothered her more than it should have.

"The last time was three guys ago," he said, immediately trying to put her at a distance.

Ellie slid further away and he didn't stop her. "You sure say a lot, don't you?" she asked angrily, upset he was still jealous over nothing.

"I don't like you asking me questions all the time," Quantz defended himself.

"Maybe it's because you don't like to answer," Ellie said fiercely.

"I just like to agree with you. I just like to please you. We're having a good time. No hassle," he said, "till now."

"It's been a long time since we've had a hassle," she said bitterly.

"I know," he said. "Is it my fault I'm not around?"

"No." Ellie poked the floor with her foot.

Ellie hadn't intended to start a fight. Maybe a fight gave her a reason to forget about their relationship until the next time. She thought the only way they were going to stop fighting was if they either stopped seeing each other or got married.

"Here's something I've been meaning to give you." Quantz pulled a gold chain out of his inside pocket and gave it to Ellie.

"Oh, it's nice." Ellie happily took the fine filigree chain.

"I want to know where I stand," Quantz said, "if it's all right to call you or not."

"I just wish it wasn't such a surprise." Ellie put the necklace on and did it up. She thought it wasn't helping to be a landing mechanism a few times a year. Their love affair was better when it was regular. The romantic image has flaws. Ellie wanted to know where she stood, too, maybe because reality was setting in, and the constant parting was becoming more than she can handle.

"I guess I want it to be oftener," Ellie continued. Ellie thought she wasn't too good at being a casual lover. She had to be in an up mood and in control all the time. She thought the necklace meant he would try to keep his promises.

"Well, it would be if I could manage it," Quantz said, "Maybe you can even fly to meet me some time."

"Maybe." Ellie kissed him, but she thought that likely would never happen. She didn't have anything more than a part-time job. She thought it was stupid to fall in love. It was useless to argue with Quantz, whether he was faithful or not, whether the relationship would last, or whether it would end in a small pile of cold used ashes.

"We'd better go." Quantz started his car.

On the road, Ellie saw blood on the snow as they drove past, where a dog had caught a rabbit. Tracks of the chase led through the underbrush. Ellie saw movement in the brush, a grouse startled.

Ellie rolled her window down. The breeze felt warmer. Any minute, it might rain, a cleansing rain, a harbinger of spring. Where there had been snow, there was now mud.

On the way back to town, they met a cop car coming back out. Ellie was sure it was the same one who had passed them a half hour before. The cop car pulled over, and he appeared to be pulling out a notebook.

"Looking for somebody. Me, probably. I'm getting sick of being questioned, but there doesn't seem to be a thing I can do about it. I'm always involved in something. Trouble follows me around, but at least I'm still alive and kicking. Why me, is all I ask?" Quantz threw up his hands.

Ellie wondered if she should mention it was the same cop as passed them earlier, but she decided not to say anything to Quantz. It was a public road. Anybody could use it, even the cops. But their incessant presence bothered Ellie. It was none of the cop's business what Ellie and Quantz did.

Almost every time Ellie went out, she always saw a cop, parked or cruising. There wasn't anything a cop in a small town didn't know, if they kept their eyes open. But she wondered why they were always so curious about her.

It made her think she was on thin ice, when Quantz was gone and Vern didn't give a darn. She felt she was in kind of a fishbowl with so much happening she didn't have control over. She wondered what was going to happen to her. She thought being in love must be a crime, the way she was being shadowed by the law all the time. They never really did anything; they're always getting ready to do something.

Quantz kissed her goodbye and promised to see her a couple more times before he left for Venezuela.

Ellie figured the necklace Quantz gave her was something to remember him by since he was away most of the time, and because it meant Quantz was going to live up to his promises, maybe some of them. Maybe something would come of their relationship if Norma didn't go back with him.

Her affair with Quantz was becoming a more or less permanant affair, and she would be available when he came into town. Seeing him once in a while would give her something to look forward to. With Quantz, she could be escapist from real life if she wanted to. Was that what she had in mind at first? More she thought, because she didn't think their affair would last this long.

Ellie thought she loved Vern enough to stick it out with him, even though things weren't always good. With her marriage the way it was, she had to set aside her personal feelings to stay married and keep her kids.

Ellie thought if she was tougher, not so sensitive and thin-skinned, the things Vern said wouldn't bother her so much. There were things Vern couldn't do, otherwise she'd leave; for example, she'd delivered an ultimatum about the smacking she'd got, if it was in front of people. But she knew it was just an uneasy truce. Vern kept careful track of her and when she went to the grocery store after seeing Quantz she knew she would have to answer questions about where she was. She must love Vern, or what he said or did wouldn't hurt her so much. She removed Quantz's necklace and put it in her pocket before she went home.

She'd told Vern about Wayne bothering her, and that was the main reason they decided to move.

Right now, Ellie thought about herself more as taking one day at a time, otherwise she figured she was a loser if she looked at the long range of things.

When she went up the steps of her duplex carrying the two bags of groceries, she could see Vern was waiting for her. He didn't speak to her. Out of the corner of her eye, she thought she could see he had his belt wrapped around his right hand.